Praise for the

SEDUCTIVE AS
Flame

SUSAN JOHNSON

BERKLEY SENSATION, NEW YORK

THE BERKLEY PUBLISHING GROUP
Published by the Penguin Group
Penguin Group (USA) Inc.
375 Hudson Street, New York, New York 10014, USA
Penguin Group (Canada), 90 Eglinton Avenue East, Suite 700, Toronto, Ontario M4P 2Y3, Canada
(a division of Pearson Penguin Canada Inc.)
Penguin Books Ltd., 80 Strand, London WC2R 0RL, England
Penguin Group Ireland, 25 St. Stephen's Green, Dublin 2, Ireland (a division of Penguin Books Ltd.)
Penguin Group (Australia), 250 Camberwell Road, Camberwell, Victoria 3124, Australia
(a division of Pearson Australia Group Pty. Ltd.)
Penguin Books India Pvt. Ltd., 11 Community Centre, Panchsheel Park, New Delhi—110 017, India
Penguin Group (NZ), 67 Apollo Drive, Rosedale, Auckland 0632, New Zealand
(a division of Pearson New Zealand Ltd.)
Penguin Books (South Africa) (Pty.) Ltd., 24 Sturdee Avenue, Rosebank, Johannesburg 2196,
South Africa

Penguin Books Ltd., Registered Offices: 80 Strand, London WC2R 0RL, England

This is a work of fiction. Names, characters, places, and incidents either are the product of the author's imagination or are used fictitiously, and any resemblance to actual persons, living or dead, business establishments, events, or locales is entirely coincidental. The publisher does not have any control over and does not assume any responsibility for author or third-party websites or their content.

SEDUCTIVE AS FLAME

A Berkley Sensation Book / published by arrangement with the author

PRINTING HISTORY
Berkley Sensation mass-market edition / December 2011

ISBN: 978-0-425-24490-6

BERKLEY SENSATION®
Berkley Sensation Books are published by The Berkley Publishing Group,
a division of Penguin Group (USA) Inc.,
375 Hudson Street, New York, New York 10014.
BERKLEY SENSATION® is a registered trademark of Penguin Group (USA) Inc.
The "B" design is a trademark of Penguin Group (USA) Inc.

PRINTED IN THE UNITED STATES OF AMERICA

10   9   8   7   6   5   4   3   2   1

SEDUCTIVE AS
Flame

CHAPTER 1

Groveland Chase, November 1894

THE DUKE AND Duchess of Groveland were entertaining at their hunting lodge in the West Riding. The original party had been small, although more guests had arrived yesterday, and tomorrow the local squires and farmers would come out for the day's hunt. As was often the case with country house parties, those invited arrived with unexpected companions. Charlie Bonner, for instance, had come with his wife, who neither rode to hounds nor liked the country. *"Sorry Fitz,"* Charlie had murmured with a grin for his host. *"I couldn't shake off Bella."* And surprisingly, Lord Dalgliesh had brought *his* wife. They barely spoke. But her young son had wanted to see a hunt, someone said, and Lord Dalgliesh doted on the boy.

Not that all aristocratic marriages were as ill conceived and regrettable, although love matches *were* a rarity in the haute monde. Long-held custom in the fashionable world had always viewed matrimony as a business transaction and marriage settlements as a means of enhancing family wealth, prestige, or bloodlines. Should anyone be looking for love, that was available elsewhere.

Naturally, there were exceptions to prevailing custom. Three of those exceptions were currently having coffee and brandy in a sitting room off the terrace. The Duke of Groveland and his friends, Lords Lennox and Blackwood, were having an early morning eye-opener while waiting for their beloved wives to come down for breakfast.

"To family." With a smile, the duke raised his cup. "May our tribes increase."

"A pleasant endeavor," Oz Lennox murmured. "I'll drink to that."

Jamie Blackwood lifted his cup. "We're fortunate, all of us."

"Indeed. To kind fate," Oz said softly and drained his drink.

A small silence fell, each man fully conscious that life was uncertain, a gamble at best. They all understood how impossibly long the odds had been against meeting the women they loved in the great vastness of the world. How bereft their lives would have been had they not.

Into this contemplative moment a striding figure intruded, sweeping past the long span of French doors. The woman was tall, with magnificent flame-red hair, the spectacular lynx coat she wore equally resplendent.

Fitz smiled as she disappeared from sight. "Rumor has it she's a witch."

"In more ways than one," Oz drawled, pushing himself upright in his chair in sudden interest. "What?" He shot his friends a grin. "I love my wife, but I'm not dead. Did you see those flashy spurs? I'll bet she's a wildcat in bed."

"And you should know," Fitz waggishly noted.

Oz cast a sardonic glance at his friend. "Please—as if either of you were Puritans before you married. Hell, Fitz, you had Willery's bountiful daughter sizing you up under Rosalind's eye last night at dinner. I thought she might lean over just a little more and let her plump, quivering breasts spill over on your plate. And Bella practically ate Jamie alive while we were having drinks in the drawing room." He shot a look at James Blackwood, who'd spent years standing stud to not only Bella but a great many other ladies.

"Did you have to make amends to Sofie afterward? She didn't look happy."

"Bella's always been difficult," Jamie coolly replied. "Sofie understands."

"I beg to differ," Oz drolly said. "I know Sofie. She doesn't understand at all."

"Let's just say I was able to atone for Bella's sins. Satisfied? And the enticing Zelda happens to be my cousin, so mind your manners."

Oz grinned. "You're kidding. Zelda? What a perfect name for a bodacious lady witch."

"Her name's Griselda, so relax," Jamie muttered. "And the gossip about witches arose because she's recently returned from the jungles of Brazil with some native artifacts she chooses to wear. She's no more a witch than you or I."

"She raised all her younger siblings when her mother died, didn't she?" Fitz commented.

Jamie nodded. "All five of them."

"So witch and earth mother," Oz waggishly noted. "Every male fantasy."

Jamie gave his friend a warning glance. "Fucking behave."

"Or?" Oz's grin was brilliant.

"Or I'll tell Isolde you're lusting after my cousin," Jamie silkily returned.

"And I'll tell her I'm not."

"Screw you," Jamie muttered.

"I'm afraid I'm no longer available," Oz sweetly replied. "My wife doesn't approve."

The stunning apparition suddenly hove back into view, arresting the raillery. Coming to a stop at one of the doors, the flame-haired woman opened it and stood for a moment on the threshold, her tall form limned in golden sunshine.

The extravagant lynx coat fell to her ankles, her flamboyant hair was untamed and wind tossed, her long, slender legs buckskin clad, her booted and spurred feet firmly planted. While a faint smile graced her lovely mouth, mild query arched her dark brows. "Am I intruding?"

"No, not at all. Do come in, Zelda," Jamie quickly offered, rising from his chair along with the other men. "You're up early."

"It's not that early. Hullo, everyone." The rowels on her spurs jingled quietly as she walked in and shut the door. "Father and I've been out riding since dawn," she said, turning to the men and stripping off her gloves. "Although I seem to have lost him somewhere between here and the stables."

"No doubt he stopped to talk to someone." Sir Gavin was everyone's friend. "You know Fitz," Jamie observed. "And this is Lord Lennox. Oz, my cousin, Zelda MacKenzie."

"A pleasure," Oz said, moving forward and putting out his hand. "You must tell my wife where you found your coat. It's magnificent."

"Thank you." He had a very lucky wife, Zelda thought, shaking his hand, and he must care for her or he wouldn't have mentioned her in his first breath. "A wonderful tailor in Edinburgh made this for me. I can give you his name if you like."

"I would." Oz's smile was boyishly warm. "You weren't here last night."

"We came in very late."

"Would you like a drink?" Fitz interjected, because Oz charmed without even trying and Jamie had warned him off. "We're drinking our breakfast."

"Fitz has smuggled brandy so it tastes much better," Oz said, shifting slightly to include his friends in the conversation. "I recommend it."

"Perfect. Just what I need. And may I compliment you on your jumps, Lord Groveland," she added, turning to her host. "They're wicked. I'm looking forward to the chase."

"I can't take credit for the hedges. They were planted long ago. But I've added an obstacle or two over the years to make the run more interesting. Please, have a chair. I'll get your drink."

Zelda was shoving her gloves into her coat pocket and Fitz had turned to the drinks tray when the door to the hallway suddenly opened and a large, dark-haired man walked in. "Morning, gentleman." The Earl of Dalgliesh advanced into the room. "It's a perfect day for hunting—frost, crisp, cold. You couldn't have ordered any better weath—" His cool blue gaze suddenly fell on Zelda and a warmth entered his eyes. "Good morning, ma'am." A connoisseur of beautiful women, he automatically surveyed her as he strode toward her—taking in her glorious face and form, the exotic garb, particularly the tight buckskins that left nothing to the imagination. He'd never seen a woman dress like that in public. "I don't believe we've met," he said, bowing slightly as he reached her, looking down at her with a beguiling smile. "Dalgliesh at your service."

"Alec, allow me to introduce my cousin." Jamie moved closer to Zelda, Dalgliesh's interest apparent and his reputation such that female relatives required protection. "Alec Munro, may I present, Griselda MacKenzie, Sir Gavin's daughter."

"A pleasure, sir." Zelda smiled and put out her hand.

Grasping her fingers lightly, Alec brought them to his mouth and brushed her knuckles with his lips. For a lingering moment, he held her fingers in his warm, cupped palm before releasing her hand. "I haven't seen you before." His voice was velvet soft, lazy with provocation.

But his gaze wasn't lazy; it was predatory, like an animal on the scent. "My father and I are down from Scotland," Zelda replied, half breathless under the unmistakable lust in his eyes, the warmth of his hand still tingling on her skin; her heart was suddenly pounding.

Their eyes held for a moment—pale blue and amethyst—and a flurry of ripe, unguarded expectation shimmered in the air. Hotspur and graphic.

Alec recovered first because he wasn't given to blind impetuosity. "You've been out riding, I see," he smoothly said.

"Yes, I was just telling Lord Groveland what lovely acres he has." Zelda, too, had regained her composure. "Have you hunted here before?"

"He has several times," Fitz said, stepping in to diffuse what was clearly a volatile encounter. "Alec has a hunting lodge in the neighborhood. Come, both of you, please have a seat. I'll see to the brandies and coffee."

"*There* you are, Alec!" a female voice vexatiously exclaimed, the high, sharp cry shattering the faint hush of carnal ambivalence. "I've been searching for you everywhere!"

Five pairs of eyes swivelled toward the open doorway.

A fashionably gowned, diminutive blond woman dressed in crimson cashmere stood dwarfed by the lofty doorframe, her frown marked. "Christopher was wondering when you were coming back."

"I'll be up in ten minutes."

"Would you like coffee, Violetta?" Fitz politely inquired. He couldn't very well not ask. Although her husband offered her no welcome.

"No, thank you. I have to go back and calm dear Christopher." Lady Dalgliesh's smile held a hint of melancholy. "He's such a high-strung little boy. You won't make him wait long, will you, Alec?"

"No." Soft and dismissive.

"You shouldn't have run off like that," she scolded, either not noticing her husband's dismissal or not caring. "Chris was upset to find you'd gone off. But I'll do my best to console him until you return."

The earl's jaw clenched. "Mrs. Creighton's more than capable of consoling him."

"Really, Alec," Lady Dalgliesh said with a sniff of disapproval. "I don't know why you insist on that woman. She's so common."

"Chris likes her. Now, if you'll excuse me," the earl said, a dangerous edge to his voice.

The small woman hesitated fractionally, then with a toss of her blond curls, she crisply said, "Very well, don't be late," and flounced off.

Dalgliesh exhaled quietly before turning to the others. "Please forgive the drama. Violetta always enjoys making a scene. A large brandy for me, Fitz. No coffee."

"There's nothing to forgive," Fitz calmly said. "Please,

everyone, sit. One large brandy coming up. How about you, Zelda?"

"Just two fingers of brandy please with coffee." She took the chair Jamie offered her.

Once everyone was seated and their drinks were in hand, the talk turned to hunting, the discussion focused initially on Fitz's hunting pack. Ten generations of Moncktons had succeeded in breeding the fastest pack of hounds in England with the nose, voice, and stamina to handle the coverts and bogs natural to the area. Yorkshire was the most sporting part of Her Majesty's dominions, the county where fox hunting had been first established.

The subject of thrusters came up next—riders ready to jump anything in sight with no care for the hounds. It was agreed that the men would all do what they could to restrain the louts. Riders of that ilk could raise havoc with the dogs by throwing them off the scent, or worse: A pack worth thousands of pounds could be seriously damaged if ridden over.

Everyone in the room was experienced in the field. Oz had first hunted in India with leopards as coursers, Jamie had ridden to hounds in Hungary and on the Continent, particularly with the Empress Elizabeth, who liked to surround herself with handsome, world-class horsemen. Fitz and Zelda had hunted since childhood here and abroad.

Consumed with her own thoughts, Zelda only half listened to the conversation. Comfortably ensconced in a large, down-cushioned chair, she sipped her drink and tried not to stare at Dalgliesh. But he was murderously handsome, dark as a gypsy, with sleepy, bedroom eyes, his hunter's gaze shuttered now that he was lounging relaxed in his chair, his brandy glass resting on his chest. His legs were stretched out before him, his hard, muscled body of unusual height— that height particularly attractive to a woman as tall as she. He didn't wear correct hunting dress—nor did anyone in the room; she was among men who shared her disdain for conformity. Or perhaps like she, they rode for pleasure, not to parade their pretensions or wealth.

Dalgliesh's coat was black not red, his riding pants buff not white, his boots devoid of the pink or brown tops of the fashion-conscious hunter. But his broad expanse of shoulder was shown to advantage under his elegant tailoring, and his green foulard waistcoat was buttoned over a hard, flat stomach. The powerful thighs of a superb horseman were evident under his tight buckskins as was his virility, impressive even in repose.

A sudden suffusion of heat she didn't in the least wish to feel stirred deep inside her. Wrenching her gaze from his crotch, she upbraided herself for such recklessness. Good Lord . . . Dalgliesh was married, with a child—and a difficult wife. Nor did she usually respond with such madcap indiscretion to a man. In fact, never. Not that she was some virginal miss. She lived her life with considerable freedom, her independence nurtured, she supposed, by the casualness of her upbringing.

Although no question—Dalgliesh had been offering her more than cultivated pleasantries a few minutes ago. He'd been offering her an invitation to unbridled sex.

She'd couldn't accept, of course. It would be the greatest foolishness to antagonize a spiteful woman like Lady Dalgliesh. Particularly in the midst of a country house party with so many people in attendance.

Good God! Meaning what?

If there weren't so many people about . . . might she *consider* being foolish? *Of course not,* a little voice inside her head sternly asserted. Her father was here, for heaven's sake, and while Papa probably wouldn't notice with his mind rather narrowly on sport and drinking, this was hardly the venue for such rash behavior.

Get a grip, she told herself. And with that pragmatic injunction, she turned her attention to the men's conversation.

She was unaware her scrutiny hadn't gone unnoticed by the object of her attention. More practiced, however, Alec's surveillance of the splendid Miss MacKenzie was well disguised. But he was having second thoughts about a carnal flirtation. Apparently the lady's father was here for the hunt.

He'd met Sir Gavin before, the hard-drinking Scottish baronet typical of his class: bluff and friendly, physically large in the hardy Norse tradition, his life entirely devoted to sport and drink.

And at base, Dalgliesh reflected, he *had* come for the sport. Fitz's gamekeepers were superb, his lands extensive, his hunt master the best in England.

As for amorous amusement, there was plenty enough of that in London, he reminded himself. And had not the sudden, unexpected vision of the exotic Miss Mackenzie captivated every libertine nerve in his body, he might have more sensibly controlled his initial reaction to her.

Furthermore, both Violetta and Chris were in residence; surely that was reason enough for restraint. *Starting now*, Alec decided after a glance at the clock. His ten minutes were up. Draining his glass and setting it aside, he came to his feet. "If you'll excuse me," he said. "We'll see you all outside. Chris is looking forward to his first hunt." He turned to Zelda, his smile urbane. "A pleasure to meet you, Miss MacKenzie." There, that wasn't so hard. It was just a matter of self-discipline.

"Indeed, a pleasure," Zelda replied, smiling back, ignoring the inconvenient little flutter coiling in the pit of her stomach.

After the door closed on the earl, Fitz gruffly said, "I've never understood why he doesn't divorce her."

"Rumors are rife in that regard." Oz had heard the stories from Marguerite when he was spending a great deal of time in her luxurious brothel and bed. "Margo says it's something more than the boy that keeps Dalgliesh fettered." Oz shrugged. "I'd divorce the bitch, pardon my language, Zelda, scandal be damned."

"Perhaps he doesn't wish to hurt the boy," Jamie remarked. "The lad's still quite young, isn't he?"

"About six I think," Fitz answered. "He was two when they married." The duke had a son who was two and was fully aware of the attachment between a parent and child. "I suspect the boy has come to depend on Alec. They're very close."

Zelda looked up, her brows lifted. "The boy's not his then?"

"No, Violetta was a widow when they met. Or rather I should say when they became reacquainted. She'd grown up near Alec and returned after her husband died. They married rather quickly soon after Alec came back from South Africa to visit his ailing mother."

"Marry in haste, repent at leisure," Oz murmured. "Although not in my case," he added with a grin. Oz had married Isolde after having known her only a few hours. "I'm happy to say, I'm the exception."

"None of us had a long courtship," Jamie pointed out with a smile for his cousin.

Zelda shrugged. "Hardly a requirement if you find some-one compatible."

"You didn't meet anyone in the Brazilian jungle, I gather," Jamie teased.

"They were all rather short. The native tribes," she added. "And while the local landowners were charming enough, I'm afraid I towered over most of them as well. Not that I was actually interested in a permanent stay in Brazil. I'd miss the children."

"Zelda was on an orchid-hunting expedition in Brazil," Jamie recounted to his friends. "You came back with some precious specimens I hear."

"Yes." Zelda smiled. "I won't bore you with the catalogue, but suffice it to say, the conservatory will soon be awash with colorful blooms." Then she said for no good reason or per-haps for entirely reprehensible reasons, "Why South Africa?"

None of the men so much as blinked an eyelash; they'd all spent considerable time in dalliance prior to marriage. In fact, the three men together held the distinction of having serviced a record number of women here and abroad.

Jamie glanced at Fitz. "You know more about Dalgliesh than we do. Explain South Africa."

"It was an accident, as I understand," Fitz began. "Hav-ing left after a pitched battle with his father—they had a long history of strife—Alec was on his way to India and decided to stop in Cape Town. The new Transvaal diamond discoveries were coming to light, and he invested in a small mining venture that made everyone a fortune. He returned to England when his mother took ill. Happily, she recovered, although his father died soon after. Alec and his father were in a heated argument apparently when the old earl collapsed. He lingered on for a few days, unable to speak or move." Fitz shrugged. "Alec's father was a brute. No one mourned his loss."

"Is Dalgliesh's mother alive?"

"Yes, although she's in uncertain health. Alec remains in England because of her, I suspect, and, of course, for Chris. He and the dowager countess both adore the boy."

"Why did he marry?" Zelda asked, her gaze searching. "He and his wife seem incompatible—although many aristocratic couples are, I suppose."

"No one knows why they married," Fitz replied. "There were rumors of a stillbirth, but he's never spoken of it, nor has she. A word of advice, dear, and I mean it most kindly. I saw how he looked at you. He has a reputation for profligacy."

Zelda smiled. "I'm warned. And coming from profligate men such as yourselves"—she scanned the handsome group—"I'll take your advice to heart."

"Formerly profligate," Oz corrected with a flashing grin.

"Just take care, my dear," Jamie gently said. "Dalgliesh is known to break hearts."

"I was mostly curious about him, that's all," Zelda casually replied. "Thank you for the abridged biography, Fitz. His wife was so bloody unpleasant, I just wondered what sort of man would marry a woman like her."

"The entire world wonders," Oz drawled.

"Should you find out why," Jamie pointedly said, knowing Zelda for a purposeful woman, "you might wish you didn't know." His cynical view of the world had been tempered by a loving wife, but not entirely suppressed. He knew better than most that men were imperfect at best and occasionally reprehensible.

"I don't expect to find out. I'm generally more sensible

than impulsive. Had I not been," she said with a flash of a smile, "I would have married Johnnie Armstrong when I was fifteen and let Da raise the children himself."

"I'm sure your father appreciates what you did."

"I'm sure he doesn't. He didn't even notice."

A fact impossible to refute. "Is this where I say you'll get your reward in heaven?" Jamie facetiously noted.

"I'll be getting it long before that," Zelda sportively replied as she came to her feet in a ripple of glossy fur. "I've enjoyed this chat, gentlemen. I'll see you all in the field."

After she was gone, Oz raised his glass in homage. "There goes a dazzling and engagingly candid woman. If I didn't adore my wife, I'd envy Dalgliesh."

"Perhaps there won't be anything to envy," Jamie retorted with exacting precision.

Oz looked at him from under his lashes, his dark gaze amused. "Such cousinly anxiety. If she wasn't related to you, I'd bet a thousand Dalgliesh doesn't last the weekend."

"I agree," Fitz said. "Which means we'll have to shield Zelda from Violetta's sharp claws. We'll take turns holding the bitch at bay."

"Ah, what delightful entertainment's in store," Oz murmured. "A quixotic seduction, a snarling wife, a possible pursuit and retreat." He looked up. "Will Dalgliesh actually refuse her?"

"I doubt it," Fitz said.

"Hell no, he won't," Jamie muttered. "Who would with a wife like that?"

CHAPTER 2

ZELDA WAS ALREADY mounted and waiting in the drive with a score of other hunters when the earl and his stepson rode around from the stables. The young boy was flushed with excitement, his glance darting back and forth from his pony to the earl riding at his side. He was a slender child, fair of face and hair—like his mother, Zelda thought. And as the pair brought their mounts to a halt on the verge of the gathered horsemen, Dalgliesh leaned down, gently touched the boy's shoulder, and spoke to him quietly.

It was a charming picture, the large powerful man, dark as sin, treating the boy with such open affection. A rarity with men, more rare in public with curious gazes at the ready and gossip the lifeblood of society—with the state of the earl's marriage well-known. Then the boy said something in return that made the earl laugh, and she felt a little unwonted tug at her heart.

Having raised five children, she understood those small sweet moments in a child's life that were neither sensational nor dramatic but were magical nonetheless. She abruptly looked away. She refused to cry over some sentimental nonsense that had nothing to do with her. Or if it did, she wouldn't allow herself to wallow in self-pity, if that's what this sudden fit of distemper represented.

She'd sacrificed her youth for her siblings, but she'd never regretted it. Her brothers and sister were all grown, healthy, and happy, Francesca recently married to a boy she loved. And while her father was a kind, loving man in his fashion, he would have been utterly incapable of fathering his brood—other than in the hunting field. That he knew, and when it came to sport, he'd raised a family of distinguished horsemen and first-rate hunters who loved the outdoors. Furthermore, Scots to the bone, he'd instilled in his children a taste for fine whiskey and French wines.

Everyone had their particular areas of expertise, she understood, nor was Papa any different than most country gentlemen she knew who drank hard and spent every waking hour in the saddle.

She looked across the assembled riders to where her father sat his mount, surrounded by a group of his friends. The men were partaking of the stirrup cups servants were passing around and guffawing over some drollery. Sir Gavin looked up, caught her eye, and waved, his smile warm and affectionate. Then a companion drew his attention and he turned back to the company of his friends.

Moments later, the hunt master led the riders down the drive and out into the fields, the whippers-in set to work, the pack was soon in full cry, and the chase began. Any little incidental regrets Zelda harbored instantly gave way to a more familiar and transcendent exhilaration. She loved the high hedges and fast turf, the excitement of a bruising ride and soaring jumps, the feel of a good, sound, high-couraged hunter under her running smooth as silk. She felt invincible, happy, in her element—irrepressibly free.

Some people rode to hunt; she hunted to ride. She adored the thundering pace, the clean, fresh air, the ecstasy of flying leaps and perfect landings. There wasn't an obstacle she and her mount couldn't soar over with room to spare. The thrilling sensation of being tested physically and mentally, of tempting fate at every jump, of riding full-out was wondrous and indescribable and quite effectively banished Dalgliesh and his son from her thoughts.

The same couldn't be said for the earl, who couldn't help but admire Miss MacKenzie's brilliant, nervy riding. She rode like a Tartar, with short leathers, loose reins, and a forward seat. A bold rider over the jumps no matter their height, her balance was superb, her hands impressive, her center of gravity matching the forward thrust of the jump. And her flame-red hair was impossible to miss in the field, as was the color of her flying coattails.

But she very quickly rode out of sight.

Since Chris couldn't manage the jumps, they were reduced to going through the gates instead of over them, nor could his pony match the swift pace of the field. But regardless Miss MacKenzie was no longer visible, Alec couldn't so easily dismiss the bewitching lady from his thoughts.

Bloody hell.

Bloody, bloody hell.

In an effort to dissuade himself from behaving impulsively, he punctiliously reminded himself of all the reasons Miss MacKenzie was currently beyond the pale; the word *currently* unfortunately both inadvisable and opportunistic. Bloody hell again. But seriously, she was unmarried and with her father—either of which should have warned him off; together they were formidable impediments.

It wasn't as though there weren't other women here, safely married women, who would welcome him into their beds. Country house parties were famously rife with conjugal infidelity. He suspected Violetta had insisted on coming along because Lord Mytton was on the guest list. Not that he cared so long as she conformed to the rules established before their unnatural marriage. Which reminder of unadulterated misery always served to blacken his mood— the last four years ones of blighted hope and disillusion. Save for the fact that his mother thrived because of young Chris. The boy had brought joy into both their lives.

His groom had accompanied them in the event Chris

tired before the fox was brought to ground. It was impossible to gauge the length of the chase or how long the wily fox would last; a run on occasion went on 'til dark.

As they came to a stop on the top of a windy hill, the field of riders barely visible in the distance, like any six-year-old after an hour in the cold and wind, Chris said in a reedy little voice, "Papa, I'm tired."

"Should we rest for a time and then go on?" the earl asked, perfectly willing to accommodate the boy. "Or would you like John to take you back to the house?" A question mildly put but pregnant with possibility.

"I don't want to hunt anymore. I'd rather see the new puppies in the stables. May I, Papa?" the little boy asked, his expression hopeful.

"Of course." The earl glanced at the groom. "If you'd be so kind, John, the puppies first." He turned to Chris. "Afterward, I expect the cook can find you some of that cake you liked at tea yesterday."

A wide smile appeared. "May I have two pieces?"

"I'm sure you may," Alec replied with an answering smile. "John knows the cook, don't you, John?"

"She's my cousin, Master Chris. We'll both have two pieces of cake."

"Yahoo!"

How simple life was at six, Alec thought.

"I want to stay in the kitchen until you come back. Please, may I?" The boy's brow was suddenly creased with worry.

"Certainly," Alec gently said, reminded that Chris's life wasn't so simple after all with a mother like his. "We'll have John send for Creiggy. She'll play cards with you."

Chris's cheeks flushed with excitement. "For money?"

Alec smiled. "Only a very little. Get some extra change from the butler, John."

"Yes, sir. We'll make sure to wait for you in the kitchen." The groom spoke in an undertone at the last.

Alec nodded. "I don't foresee a problem with the other guests arriving today. I expect *everyone*," he said with significant emphasis, aware that Violetta had risen much earlier than usual, "will be busy with their own amusements."

"Very good, sir." John took the pony's reins. "Come, Master Chris, we'll go find the puppies."

"I had a very nice time on the hunt, Papa," the little boy said, remembering his manners.

"I'm glad you did. Perhaps next time it won't be so cold. Now, if you get sleepy before I return, have Creiggy find you somewhere to nap."

"I'm too old to nap," the little boy protested, drawing himself up very straight in the saddle. "I'm six and a quarter."

"I forgot," Alec kindly said. "Of course, you're entirely too old to nap."

"Look, Papa, I can turn my pony myself." Chris tugged the reins from the groom's hand. "See? I'm getting better."

"Indeed you are," the earl agreed.

"Soon, you'll need a larger horse," the groom generously suggested.

"Papa said I can have a stallion, didn't you, Papa?" the little boy called out over his shoulder as the pony turned.

"As soon as you learn how to jump Petunia."

"I know, Papa, I know." The little boy thumped his heels into his pony's flanks. "Look, look how fast Petunia runs!"

Alec watched the two ride away, his gloved hands resting on the saddle pommel, his mind preoccupied. Only when his hunter shifted his feet and snorted did Dalgliesh bestir himself and rouse from his reverie. Drawing in a deep, measured breath, he struggled to subdue his indefensible cravings. What the hell was he doing letting Chris and John go back without him? More to the point, why was he thinking what he'd been thinking. It was like looking for trouble to give in to impulse. No, not *like*: It *was* looking for trouble. And he knew better.

He sat his mount for another indecisive moment, his gaze unfocused, knowing what he *should* do, contemplating instead the road to hell.

Then with a slight shift of his weight, he smoothly turned

his hunter and lightly touched his spurs to the horse's flanks. He'd been wanting to ride with Miss MacKenzie ever since he saw her take that first fence with over a foot to spare. She was a magnificent, fearless rider—audacious and bold. The next thought was predictable, of course. Unwanted, but predictable.

Would she ride his cock with equal boldness?

CHAPTER 3

WHEN DALGLIESH CAUGHT up with the hunters, however, Miss MacKenzie wasn't with the company. He'd heard the huntsman blow "Gone to Ground" while he was still some distance off, and as he'd arrived on the scene, the master was trying to decide whether to leave the fox in peace, signal for the terriers to be brought up to dig out their prey, or move on to another covert to flush out another fox.

He couldn't ask anyone where Miss MacKenzie had gone—or when—without revealing his interest in her. Well aware of his reputation, he didn't care to subject her to the inevitable gossip. She didn't deserve it. Although if he had half a brain and a more benevolent nature, he'd leave her in peace.

It was a casual observation only.

He had no intention of doing so.

He wondered briefly if she'd escaped the crowd with another gentleman? His sudden sense of umbrage was both unwarranted and unwanted, and he quickly brushed aside the lunatic feelings. How could it possibly matter if she was with someone else? Exclusivity had never been of interest to him—for which a great number of ladies were grateful.

He didn't *have* to concern himself about her whereabouts, he acknowledged. Now that he was alone, he *could* simply accept her absence and join the hunt. Had she not jolted every sexual nerve in his body, had not that sledgehammer blow occurred, he might have more easily allowed her to go off with some other man. As it was, the thought offended him. He chose not to question why, he simply intended to find her, and if she wasn't alone, he'd run the other man off.

He should have challenged his extraordinary determination.

Had he been capable of objectivity, he might have.

Instead, he rode the perimeter of the milling group of riders, idly socializing with his friends and covertly surveying the ground for fresh hoofprints.

If she'd left the chase some time ago, his chances of finding her were minimal. If, however, she'd only recently ridden away, he'd likely track her down. *Likely*, the operative word considering the vast acres. But then logic and carnal desire were mutually exclusive, and the lady was a veritable enchantress—tall, shapely, dazzlingly lovely, with a nervy bravado that took her over the highest jumps with aplomb. That fearlessness was rare among women; or at least the women he knew. And God knows, he knew enough.

The ground was still covered with a light frost, the sun not yet strong enough to have entirely melted it away. His scrutiny revealed three separate instances of riders having separated from the group. Which one first?

Mentally tossing a coin, he settled on the middle track.

A false trail as it turned out, for ten minutes later he almost ran into a couple who apparently couldn't wait for the comforts of a bed. Fortunately, his horse had pricked up his ears in time, and the earl came to a stop well away from two of Fitz's guests who were busily fornicating on the cold ground.

The risqué vision should have been a lesson to him. There was nothing so ridiculous as a man with his breeches down and his bum pumping like a steam piston. What was worse,

Alec recognized the pair. Who would have thought that Fitz's parson had a letch for Lady Lambton; she was fifty if she was a day.

The service at Groveland Chase this Sunday definitely would be of more interest than usual.

Quietly reversing course, he rode back to the clearing where the fox had gone to ground and found the hunters had ridden off. Apparently, the hounds had picked up another scent.

A troublesome little voice surfaced, chiding him for having lost his wits over some unknown woman. Although one of the stable lads had mentioned in a tone of unmistakable fascination that Miss MacKenzie was a witch—a concept he was tempted to give credence to because he was trying to decide which of the two remaining tracks to follow when he shouldn't. When he'd never chased after a woman before.

Not that handsome men of wealth and title ever had to exert themselves in that regard. Rather the opposite was the case. As was the world's fawning servility to great wealth like his.

Although he doubted Miss MacKenzie would prove obsequious.

Part of her temptation he speculated.

He was tired of fawning women.

Alas, route two proved equally unsuccessful, ending in a farmyard where the tracks stopped at a hitching post to which a rather ordinary hack was tied.

On his second return to the clearing, he more seriously questioned his dogged compulsion. He should return to the house rather than pursue this reckless path. Or so said his rational intellect. His less rational emotions however sensed something indefinable and novel in Miss MacKenzie. Something beyond her wild beauty and wilder horsemanship.

Impossible, of course. A woman was a woman was a woman no matter how novel or splendid. Long a cynic of the human condition, he considered amour no more than a self-indulgent distraction—as it was for the ladies who shared his libertine pursuits.

All of which caused him to view his sudden departure from habit with distrust and a mild bemusement.

On the other hand, he'd not felt such naked craving in years.

Why the hell was he even questioning his motives?

TWENTY MINUTES LATER, he rode into a pristine little hamlet. Fitz was a generous landlord who afforded his tenants not only a good living, but exemplary housing and subsidized tradesmen. The main thoroughfare sported a public house with a small stable adjacent, a blacksmith shop, a school, a mill by the river, a small dress shop, a greengrocers, a tobacco shop, and a bookstore. And as fortune would have it, Miss Mackenzie's magnificent hunter was being brushed down outside the stable.

Riding up to the livery stable, he swung down from the saddle and gave his reins to a young boy who ran up. Handing him a coin, he said, "Zeus could use some oats and water and a wipe down. Here's another," he added, dropping another coin into the boy's hand, "if you tell me where the lady is who rode in on that horse." He nodded at Zelda's blue roan.

"She went for a cup o' tea." The lad jerked his thumb at the pub.

Struck with a rare sense of exhilaration, Alec shoved his hand in his pants' pocket, pulled out a gold sovereign, tossed it to the boy, and strolled off.

His eyes like saucers, the boy cried, "Thankee, sir!" to the earl's back.

Alec lifted his quirt in acknowledgment as he walked toward the picturesque Tudor-style pub of timber and wattle. A few moments later, he dipped his head as he entered the low doorway, stood upright, and scanned the sunlit room. The publican stood behind the bar, his expression curious but friendly, several patrons who were enjoying their breakfast ale openly stared, and a pretty barmaid came bustling up with an admiring glance for the very large, very handsome lord.

"I'm looking for a lady," Dalgliesh remarked with a polite smile as he stripped off his gloves. "I saw her horse outside."

"Aye, the lady what wears men's pants." But the servant girl's eyes were twinkling, her voice lighthearted. "The highborn do be a bit eccentric." She jabbed her finger at a closed door to Dalgliesh's right. "In the parlor, she be. Who should I say is callin'?"

"She's a friend. You needn't announce me." He shoved his gloves into his coat pocket. "Bring me a brandy and coffee, if you will though."

"She said exactly so. Are ye out on the hunt, too?"

"Yes." *You might say that.* After another polite smile, he turned and moved toward the closed door, conscious that every eye in the room was following him.

Uncertain of his welcome, he didn't knock, but pressed down on the wrought iron latch, pushed open the door, bent to clear the lintel, and entered the small sunny parlor. His head almost brushed the low rafters so he took care as he bowed faintly. "May I join you?" he asked, shutting the door behind him.

Zelda frowned. "How did you find me?"

No fawning there, nor—as expected—any obsequiousness. "It wasn't easy," he said in vast understatement. How cool she was sitting there, brusque and unaccommodating—and bloody alluring, her long, shapely legs crossed at the ankle as she lounged in a chair by the window, her notable breasts visible for the first time with her coat discarded, the supple leather of a form-fitting deerskin waistcoat drawing attention to her ripe curves. "But I had good reason to be persistent," he said with a small smile.

"I know your reason. I should send you on your way." He hadn't moved, but there was nothing of the penitent in his posture. Rather a kind of patient assurance characterized his careless stance.

"Why? We're both of age." A hint of amusement underscored his words.

"You're blunt, Dalgliesh."

He smiled. "I only meant we needn't concern ourselves

with propriety in this private parlor since neither of us are adolescents."

"Allow me to doubt your explanation," she sardonically murmured. "Issues of propriety aside though, you have a reputation." She wasn't sure she wished to be amused by a man whose name was a byword for casual debauch. "I've been warned off by my cousin."

"I thought you were the one with the reputation," he said as if she'd not rebuked him. "Aren't you supposed to be a witch?"

"I thought that's what they called your wife."

He threw back his head and laughed uproariously. "Christ," he murmured some moments later, a smile still lingering in his eyes. "You're a brazen little piece."

"I'm not little. As for brazen, I could say the same of you. Tell me why you're here?" His wife apparently wasn't a problem, nor was his confidence. She was curious how or whether he'd ask.

"The truth?"

"I prefer it."

"You entice me."

"From what I hear, all women entice you."

"Not like this." He blew out a small breath, unnerved by his sudden truthfulness. "Although by and large," he said, restlessly tapping his quirt against his boot, feeling the need to nullify his unwitting disclosure, "honesty is rare in these situations."

"Speak for yourself. I prefer the unromantic truth. Isn't that what we're talking about? Sex not romance?"

His brows rose. "Are you always so frank?"

"Generally. It saves my time and patience. I deplore prevarication. And you of all people even suggesting a private parlor might be of concern is laughable. The upstairs maids at Groveland Chase are all hoping you'll give them a tumble this weekend. The girl who helped me dress this morning was quite explicit in her enthusiasm."

He stood very still for a moment, then flicked his quirt in a rudimentary gesture. "May I sit?"

She smiled for the first time. "Have I thrown you off your pace?"

"Perhaps a little," he said.

"What if I said you may not sit?"

He took note of her small equivocation, took pleasure in it. "Naturally, I'd remain standing."

"For how long?" But she was smiling, too.

"For as long as you wished, of course," he said. "A gentleman always gives a lady what she wants," he softly added and was gratified to see her cheeks flush. "And consider, Miss MacKenzie, I've been looking for you for over an hour, so you might at least offer me a chair. We could talk about horses rather than sex, if you like. That flashy hunter of yours for starters."

"He is rather lovely, isn't he?"

"Rare, I'd say. You don't see that color often."

"Oh very well," she said with a sigh. "Please join me, Dalgliesh. We'll compare horses."

But he took notice of her quick intake of breath as he approached and knew she was responding to him, knew she was feeling what he was feeling—had known it from the moment they'd met.

As he took a seat in a chair next to hers and dropped his quirt on the floor, the door opened and a servant girl entered with his coffee and brandy. "Would you like breakfast?" he casually asked, relaxing in his chair, back on familiar ground with a woman wanting him. "I didn't eat much this morning."

"I can always eat," Zelda replied, immediately blushing a deeper pink at the inadvertent sexual innuendo.

"I'm happy to hear it." Her blush was alluring to a man who couldn't remember when last he'd seen a woman blush. Most of the women he knew were long past such innocence. He turned to the servant girl who was placing his cup on a table beside his chair. "What can the kitchen offer us this morning?"

"Porridge, eggs, bacon, fresh scones and apple tart, and some rare fine apple cider, if you like. The apple harvest was right good this year."

Dalgliesh glanced at Zelda and said with punctilious politesse now that they were no longer private, "How does that sound, Miss MacKenzie?"

"Very fine, Lord Dalgliesh." She, too, was capable of good manners in public. "And another cup of this." She pointed at her cup.

"I'll try the apple cider," Alec said. "And all the rest as soon as may be. I'm starved." Sliding down in his chair as the girl left the room, he looked at Zelda from under his impossibly long lashes and, accomplished at putting women at ease, urbanely said, "I didn't have time to eat. I had to help get Chris ready. He was so excited at the prospect of his first hunt he couldn't stand still. Have you ever tried putting a pair of riding boots on a child's limp foot?"

"Yes, as a matter of fact. Many times."

"You have children?" His urbanity yielded to a soft tone of avid interest.

"Would it make a difference if I did?"

"Of course not."

His smile was fatally attractive. She felt its warmth clear down to her toes and in other less innocuous places. "Sorry to disappoint you," she dulcetly said, knowing what he'd been thinking. "I raised my five younger siblings when my mother died. I'm not promiscuous like you. As for one little boy's limp foot, that's paltry stuff. Try five pairs of feet and a father outside bawling for us to hurry before the dogs go wild."

He laughed. "I'm suitably chastened. Are any of them here with you?"

She shook her head. "They're all grown. My only sister is married and the boys are now men, with the exception of Duncan, who's at school in Edinburgh."

"You look too young to have done all that."

"You mean I don't look haggard after raising five children?"

"I mean you look eighteen," he said with gallantry and charm.

"No, I don't, but thank you." She inclined her head. "*You* look as though you've done this once or twice before."

He smiled. "How does one look after that?"

"A certain jaundice in your eyes, an insolence, too. Do women ever refuse you?"

He hesitated. They didn't, of course.

"Ah—there's my answer."

"Does it make a difference?"

"Not as much as your wife does."

His expression changed, the nonchalance stripped away. "Are you looking for a husband then?"

"Not particularly. I meant she looks dangerous. I'm not sure I wish to take on a woman like that for nothing more than an amorous romp."

"She won't know."

Zelda's smile was sardonic. "Care to make a wager?"

"Then let me say she won't care."

"You don't know women as well as you think, my lord."

"Unfortunately I know her," he said, icy and cool.

"Perhaps we could do this some other time instead." Zelda accepted her outrageous attraction to him, and wanted, also, strangely, to comfort him from the misery of his marriage. "I don't mean to be coquettish. It's just that the circumstances aren't convenient. My father's here. Not that he has jurisdiction over my life at my age, but still, he's here. And seriously, your wife is a real stumbling block."

"We could go to my hunting box." He watched her with a skeptical neutrality, wondering if she wanted something more or what she wanted, because women always did.

"We'd be missed if we left Groveland Chase."

"I don't care if we are."

"Yes, you do. I saw you with your stepson this morning. He'd notice if you went missing."

"Jesus," he softly muttered, sliding lower on his spine. "Are you my bloody conscience?"

She smiled faintly. "He's important to you. I could tell. In fact, I had a small sentimental lapse looking at you two together this morning on the drive. I expect I was missing my siblings."

"I saw you, too." A gruff, reluctant admission. "It was all I could do not to ride over and talk to you."

It shouldn't have mattered, but it warmed her heart. "I'm trying to be sensible about this. You interest me. There, I said it. But I'm not interested in making a spectacle of myself this weekend."

"When then?"

"For someone notable for his amorous skills, that was rather crude."

"Forgive me, I didn't mean to be uncivil," he said, his smile a little lopsided and wholly disarming. "I feel like a grass-green youth, eager, impatient, bungling. In fact, I was seriously considering the possibility that you were a sorceress during my search for you because I don't normally do things like this. Follow women. Pursue women. Sound like some gauche boy on his first assignation. So," he softly said, "let me rephrase my question. Might I have another opportunity to spend some time with you? Private time. Very private time," he said, sliding upright and reaching across the small distance between the chairs and taking her hand. "You fascinate me and I mean that most sincerely." He smiled again in that boyish way that warmed his eyes. "Unlike you who prefers honesty, I'm seldom truthful at times like this. I am now. I have no idea why, but there it is." With a gentle squeeze of her fingers, he released her hand and, shocked at his sincerity with this woman he barely knew, he sat back in his chair, mildly shaken.

"That was very sweet."

He softly exhaled. "Don't tell anyone."

"You don't wish to put your prodigal reputation at risk?"

"Christ, I don't know. I don't even know why I'm here."

"They must all be the same."

He looked up and fully met her gaze. "They are. You aren't, of course, which is the reason for my discontent."

"If it's any consolation, you rather stand out from the pack as well."

"Pack?" he said, a distinct coolness in his voice.

"Surely you of all people aren't going to take issue with experience."

He frowned. "How experienced?"

"You'll have to wait to find out." His smile was instant and quite beautiful. It erased the coolness from his eyes, she noticed, and replaced it with that hot desire she'd seen when first they met.

"You *are* a witch," he whispered, "because I'm thinking about moving heaven and earth so I don't have to wait. Name the time and place and I'll be there."

"After your wife's gone and your boy. If that's possible," she gently added. "I can see how you feel about your stepson. You don't leave him often, do you?"

He shook his head. "He's afraid if I do."

She didn't have to ask who frightened the boy after seeing Lady Dalgliesh in action. "Your wife doesn't hunt, does she? Why did she come?"

He should tell her it's none of her business. With anyone else he would. "We have an arrangement," he said, soft and deliberate. "Not much different from many noble marriages. You know how these country house parties can be carnal frolics once the lights go out. There's someone here she favors."

"How do you live like that?"

"I'd prefer not to, but"—he shrugged—"that's the way it is."

"I'm so sorry."

"You needn't be. I'm relatively inured."

"But constantly in need of distractions."

"Do you mind?" he gruffly said. "I'm not in the habit of discussing my marriage."

"Forgive me. I've spent the last ten years listening to children's confidences. I'm afraid it's a natural reaction—asking questions. Tell me, did they manage to unearth the fox?"

"Not so far as I could see. I think the dogs found another scent." How tactful she was. Unlike Violetta, he reflected when he shouldn't. "I was off looking for you so I'm unsure of what happened. Did you know Parson Tollefson is fucking Lady Lambton? I almost rode over them."

"I thought everyone knew."

"I see I must pay more attention to gossip," he said with a flicker of a smile. And then, obsessed or infatuated or maybe just curious for the first time in his life about something other than a woman's willingness to fuck, he asked, "How old are you? It doesn't matter. I just want to know."

"Twenty-six. How old are you? It doesn't matter," she mimicked. "I just want to know."

"Twenty-eight."

"You were young when you went to South Africa. I asked Fitz about you. You see, I'm equally captivated. You're very handsome, but I expect you know that."

"And you're every man's fantasy, but I expect you know that, too."

Her eyes flicked to the door and she gave him a warning look.

He wanted to say, *Eat fast. I have plans*, as a servant came in with their food, but he chose to be circumspect instead. And over the course of an excellent breakfast, he spoke of mundane things.

Zelda was more than willing to enjoy her breakfast and chat about nothing.

But it was much harder once the bland topics had been discussed and they had finished eating. When Alec had coaxed her into drinking some of the superb cider, and they were both warmed by the potent liquor, it was much harder to ignore the heated desire that had become a palpable presence in the room and, more disastrously—in their bodies.

"Let me get a room," he said, his voice barely audible across the debris of breakfast. "I don't want to wait," he said, suddenly impatient with pretense. "I'm not sure I can. There must be a room to let upstairs."

"I'm more selfish than that." She glanced at the clock. "There's very little time. We'll be missed soon."

"Time enough. You've put me in full rut."

She smiled. "Perhaps the servant girl would accommodate you."

"I'm sure she would."

"Well then." She held his insolent gaze. "Everything's settled. I'll see you back at the house."

"I could make you stay," he whispered.

"Not after saying what you said."

He exhaled softly. "Need I apologize?"

"Not in the least," she crisply said. "You may fuck whom you please."

"Except you."

"Let's just say I want more than twenty inconsequential minutes of your time."

"Why?" He wanted her to tell him why this was happening; he wanted the words for his feelings, some explanation for this insanity.

"Like you, I don't know. In fact, I don't know why I came here."

His heated gaze met hers. "You were waiting for me."

She shook her head. "I'm not sure. I often avoid the kill. Only the riding appeals to me, not the slaughter."

"*Maybe* you were waiting for me." He was surprised how important her answer was.

"Yes, maybe. Are you happy now?"

"Strangely, yes. Thank you. Although, since we're going to postpone our—er—friendship and you've aroused the hell out of me, I suppose you'd be angry if I used the servant girl just to get rid of my hard-on," he whimsically said, a half smile on his face.

"I suppose I would. Although, what you choose to do has nothing to do with me. We only met a few hours ago."

"Terrifying thought," he grumbled, feeling suddenly as if his back was to the wall.

"The height of stupidity," Zelda said in a voice no less afflicted. Dalgliesh was nothing but trouble.

"I'm not sure I like feeling the way I do—unbalanced, hindered—all for a fuck."

"I *know* I don't—particularly with a wife like yours."

He softly groaned. "I should get the hell up and walk away."

"Good idea," she muttered.

"Why is this happening to us?" he grumbled.

"I have no idea. I'm normally very pragmatic. Someone in the family had to be. Papa is completely without sense unless he's gauging the height of a—"

"Monday," he roughly said, interrupting her, his voice hard, his gaze scorching her across the table. "I can't wait longer than that. We'll go to my hunting box. I'll think of something to tell your father. Mrs. Creighton and Chris will have to come along, but that won't be a problem. Violetta never comes to the hunting lodge, thank God. And you're not allowed to say no or equivocate or look at me like you're surprised at what I'm saying. Either we'll be together on Monday or I'll be fucking dead."

"I can see why you're in such demand with your velvet-tongued gallantry," Zelda said, smiling widely. "I hardly know how to respond."

He grinned. "Sorry. I'm quite demented. But happy. A rare feeling of late."

"Then I'm happy, too."

His smile was wickedly roguish. "Happy enough to let me use that servant girl for five minutes—two minutes?"

She hit him squarely in the face with the remnants of a scone. "Behave or I'll go home on Monday."

"No, you won't. I won't let you."

"Oh, ho, is that a challenge?"

"No, just fact. I'll truss you up, if necessary, and carry you away."

"My God, Alec," she whispered, a flood of longing melting through her body in a hot, lustful wave. "I'll die before Monday."

He liked that she called him by name. He liked that she was as frantic as he. He liked that he felt happy after so long. He discovered, too, that he possessed a chivalry hitherto unknown, that he was willing to disregard his throbbing cock to please her. "Let's go riding. It'll take our minds off this oppressive need for restraint." She was right, too, about waiting; he wanted more than twenty minutes with her.

"We'll see if you and your showy roan can keep up with Zeus and me."

"Keep up?" She flashed him a defiant look, her cravings blunted by the tossed gauntlet; racing was in her blood. "A hundred says I beat you back to the stables. Make that two hundred."

"Five hundred says you don't."

She abruptly came to her feet. "Anytime," she briskly said.

With a father like his, he'd always protected his mother. He saw to Chris's care now, too, and his business interests and the many people who worked for him, but he'd never felt such edifying virtue before as he did in rescuing Miss MacKenzie from her avaricious desires. He hadn't known he was capable of such sexual benevolence. Realistically he still might deviate from the path of virtue, although fortunately he was slightly less aroused with his mind on horses. "May I call you Zelda?" he asked, rising from his chair. "Considering."

She was reaching for her coat and turned. "Considering what?" she lightly inquired.

"Considering I'll be making love to you soon. Although if you prefer Miss MacKenzie, I'm more than willing to oblige you in that regard."

"As long as I oblige you, you mean," she said with a grin.

"We'll oblige each other," he softly said, walking over to help her with her coat. Taking the light fur, he stood behind her and held it as she slipped her arms into the sleeves. Settling it on her shoulders, he drew her tumbled hair away from her neck with a sweeping fingertip and, bending, kissed her nape. "Now, go," he brusquely said, giving her a shove toward the door. "Or I'll fuck you on this table."

She came to a stop.

"Don't you dare," he muttered and, taking her hand, dragged her to the door, opened it, and pushed her through. "One of us has to be mature about this," he said, giving her a sidelong glance. "And I see it's going to have to be me."

She watched him flirt with the barmaid as he paid their

tick and felt a strange warm glow standing next to him, as though his mere presence brought her joy.

She wasn't so silly as to read anything more into their rapport than that he was charming and she was willing to be charmed. She understood why he had a reputation for the ladies. He was impossible to resist. And if not for the evil eye and vicious tongue of his wife, she wouldn't even think about waiting until Monday.

CHAPTER 4

ZELDA'S HUNTER WON by a nose, the ride back a wild, close-run race, the horses flying over the ground with their ears flat back on their heads as though they understood the competitive nature of their riders. Both horses were tiring at the end, but Zelda's blue roan took the last fence with gutsy courage and brought her into the drive a half second before Zeus.

They were laughing as they reined in their horses, intoxicated by the breakneck speed, the risky jumps, their well-matched equestrian skills.

Zelda glanced at Alec as they rode toward the stables. "You didn't *let* me win, did you?"

"Hell no. You almost *didn't* win."

"You needn't pay the wager." She shot him a grin. "It was such a glorious ride, I should pay you."

"And have it said I reneged on a bet? Not likely. Why don't I bring your winnings to your room," he suggested only half in jest.

"Don't you dare."

He grimaced. "Are you really going to make me wait until Monday?"

"Send your wife home and I won't." Zelda laughed. "You should see your face. Are you never thwarted?"

"You forget, my dear, I'm thwarted every day of my married life," he drily said.

"I'm sorry. I didn't mean that."

"I know what you meant. And there, no, I'm never thwarted. Now I've made you angry again. Could we talk about horses? It's the only subject we can safely discuss."

"Until Monday."

"Thank you. I needed that. Don't be alarmed if you see me drink myself into oblivion tonight. I'm in a vile mood."

"I understand."

"I'm sure you don't. But that, too, would be a useless discussion."

They'd ridden into the stable yard and two lads came up to take their horses. Dismounting, Alec walked over to Zelda and held up his arms.

"People might see," she whispered.

"Fuck 'em." He was feeling the burden of his marriage more intensely than usual. "I'm waiting," he brusquely said at her continued hesitation.

There was bitter challenge in his words she dared not oppose; he was perfectly willing to make a scene. Quickly throwing her leg over the pommel, she slid from the saddle into his waiting arms.

He held her hard against his body for such a long time the stable lads turned red-faced and averted their eyes. His gloved hands were firmly clamped at the base of her spine, his rigid erection was pressed into her stomach and, blushing with embarrassment as well as from her body's arousal— his rampant cock a spectacular invitation to pleasure—Zelda finally hissed, "Alec, for God's sake, stop!"

He looked up, startled, then dropped his hands. "Sorry." He took a step back. "We need our quirts, don't we?" he said in a normal tone of voice. "And your coat." She'd decided to tie her coat behind her saddle before their race.

"I'll get it," Zelda quickly said.

"The lady needs her coat and quirt," the earl ordered, indicating the garment with a flick of his finger. He turned back to Zelda. "I'll leave you here." He took his riding crop from one of the lads. "Chris is waiting for me in the kitchen." He needed to get away. Brute lust was fueling his senses, and he had no experience with sexual restraint or female resistance.

"Do you mind if I come with you to see Chris?"

Fuck yes, I mind.

His expression was hard as nails. "I'm sorry," Zelda apologized, her heart beating against her ribs with his caustic gaze on her. "That was overly intrusive, wasn't it?"

She looked very young with her cheeks flushed, her hair in disarray, her violet gaze mortified. Although everything else looked ostentatiously adult—her lush body in her tight riding pants and leather vest, her open-necked blouse that made him want to slip his hands inside and feel the warmth of her skin and the ripe softness of her breasts. "You're not intruding in the least," he said, when she was disrupting his entire life and he was powerless to resist. But his voice was a courtier's voice, smooth and affable, adjusting to circumstances without pause. "I'm sure Chris would like to see you. He's horse mad, too."

"Thank you." Less capable of silken politesse, her voice was quietly earnest.

"You're entirely welcome," he replied, polished and suave. He glanced at the stable lad holding out Zelda's fur coat. "Send it up to the house." Then his gaze swung back to Zelda and he dipped his head. "Shall we?"

As they walked away, Zelda said, half under her breath, "I didn't want to leave you. I'm sorry. How tiring this must be for you."

"Not in the least. We should be safe enough in the kitchen," he mildly said, preferring less unnerving earnestness. He was already in deeper than he'd like, racked with indecision, struggling against a disturbingly violent lust.

"I envy you your calm. I'm impulsive by nature and also not as practiced as you." She smiled. "Perhaps I can learn."

"No, don't learn," he muttered, chafing memory prompting his tone. "Practiced women I know by the score."

"And you're looking for something different."

"I'm not looking for anything." The naked, unsimple truth.

"But I just fell into your lap."

"Not yet." His instant smile was a triumph of audacity over good judgment. "But I'm hopeful. So screw it all," he added apropos nothing and everything. Then he reached out and took Zelda's hand because he couldn't stop himself, because his craving for her wasn't completely sexual, because he felt an incomprehensible joy. "Seventy hours to go." He gave her a sidelong glance. "Can we do it?"

"We have to," she said like she did in her frank way. "It won't be forever."

"It'll just seem like forever," he gruffly said. "But since *have to* isn't in my vocabulary, I'd recommend you lock your door tonight."

"Consider me warned."

"Do you play cards? Chris is learning."

He was deliberately changing the subject. "Of course," she said with equal tact, glad in a way to be distracted from her outrageous feelings. "What else is there to do on cold winter nights with five bored children? They didn't like to read, not even Francesca."

"Your sister who's married?"

She nodded. "She was young but insistent, and it was either that or Papa having to go over to the Elliots next door with a shotgun. Not that Ian was against marriage. Everyone just thought they were too young."

"How young is young?"

"Seventeen."

His brows rose into his hairline. "I wish them luck."

"And good health. She's having a baby next spring."

"Was the marriage in time?"

"Absolutely. They've been married almost a year."

"What do you do now that everyone's gone?" He was surprised at his question. He didn't, as a rule, inquire into the lives of the women he bedded other than to ask them their preferences in jewelry.

"I've been traveling the past year. I just returned from Brazil. Before that I was in Constantinople, Venice; Florence is lovely in the spring."

"Do you travel alone or with a companion?"

"Generally alone, sometimes with a maid, but I dislike having to accommodate someone else."

He didn't realize he'd been holding his breath. With a woman of her splendor, he'd anticipated a male companion. Although the elation he felt was disturbing. "Chris likes to win at cards. Just a warning," he said, deliberately altering the direction of his thoughts.

"Don't all children?"

"I suppose they do."

"Didn't you?"

Winning wasn't an issue in his childhood so much as surviving. His father's drinking and explosive temper had been a constant danger. "I don't remember," he said, not about to discuss his troubled childhood. "And you?"

She grinned. "Need you ask. I *love* to win."

He laughed. "Silly question."

"I'll be winning on Monday, too," she said, knowing her heart was in her eyes and not caring.

"We'll both win, darling," he smoothly replied, refusing to acknowledge her look or the pleasure it gave him. He reminded himself that this was just a country house flirtation—soon over and no different from all the rest. "Here we are," he went on in the same insouciant tone, having escorted her through the kitchen garden to the kitchen door. "Now Chris can be demanding. Let me know when you get tired of playing cards."

They found Chris with Mrs. Creighton and John at a table in a corner of the huge kitchen, busily playing cards. Chris looked up. "Papa! Look how much I won!" He pointed to a small pile of coins.

"You're getting much too good," Alec said, affectionately

ruffling the boy's flaxen curls. "Soon I won't be able to win against you."

"You already can't!" the little boy said with a broad smile.

Alec winked. "Maybe I've gotten better." Turning to the nanny and groom, the earl politely said, "Thank you, you've done your duty. We'll take over now." Sliding his arm around Zelda's waist, he drew her close. "Mrs. Creighton, John, allow me to introduce Miss Griselda MacKenzie. She and her fleet roan just beat Zeus and me in a race. She's a magnificent rider."

The retainers both paid their respects, although afterward Creiggy regarded Zelda with a fixed gaze. Alec had never introduced one of his paramours to her. "I see you have the MacKenzie hair." A tall, grey-haired Scots woman, stern of countenance and slightly forbidding, Mrs. Creighton met Zelda eye to eye. "That distinctive color breeds true, doesn't it?"

Zelda expected Lady Dalgliesh had trouble with Chris's nanny. She wasn't the retiring type. It helped to have Alec's arm around her waist in the way of security. "You must be familiar with the Highlands," Zelda said.

"I have a second cousin who married a MacKenzie. I've been up that way on occasion. Alec came there with me once." Creiggy shot him a look. "Do you remember?"

"Of course I do. I was eight, not two. I remember perfectly." He grinned. "You fell into the pond."

"I believe you pushed me," Creiggy said with a sudden warm twinkle in her eye. Her bright-eyed gaze swung to Zelda. "Now, don't take any guff from the impudent lad, Miss MacKenzie."

"I won't."

"He likes to have his way too much."

"I've noticed," Zelda said with a small smile.

Alec rolled his eyes. "Do you mind, Creiggy?"

"I expect you to behave, that's all." His old nanny's gaze slid down to his hand gently stroking Zelda's hip.

"I always do," he blandly said, not moving his hand.

"Don't forget I can still rap your knuckles."

"You'd have to catch me first," Alec drawled. "And I don't believe that's happened since—"

"Humph, impertinent scamp. Now you enjoy yourself, Master Christopher," the nanny said, turning to her current charge. "Your Papa will send for me when you're ready to go back to the nursery."

"I'm too old for the nursery. *Papa,*" Chris vehemently exhorted, "there's babies up there!"

"And also some children your age, Master Christopher, don't forget," Mrs. Creighton said in a soothing tone. "In fact, Billy Cannadine was asking for you this morning."

Chris's gaze swung up to his father. "Billy has his own knife! He let me hold it! May I have a big knife like that— pleeease?"

Alec glanced at the nanny with raised brows.

"I was there," she succinctly said.

"Perhaps someday you may have a big knife," Alec kindly noted. "Now how about another game of cards?"

As the trio in the kitchen began their play, Mrs. Creighton and John walked through the kitchen door and out into the downstairs corridor. "I've never seen anything like it," Mrs. Creighton murmured. "Did he speak to you about Miss MacKenzie?"

"Not a word." John had been Alec's groom since he was young. He and Creiggy had followed the countess and Alec when they'd escaped the main house years ago and went to live in the Dower House. They knew all there was to know about the family, and their loyalty to the earl was complete. "She's a first-rate horsewoman though. Maybe that's her appeal."

"A whole lot more than that, I'd say. Although, did you see how she was dressed? Mannish—not his usual style."

"A beauty though. That's his style." A small, slim man, he had to look up slightly to Mrs. Creighton's greater height.

"Still—it's very strange. He's never introduced one of his lady loves to us. I don't know if I should wish him well or wonder what kind of scheming woman she might be?"

"It makes no never mind what she is. He looks happy and he could use a bit o' happiness."

"What about his wife?" Creiggy muttered. "*She* doesn't want him happy."

"Herself has her eye on Mytton. She might not even notice. And his lordship don't care anyways what she thinks."

Mrs. Creighton gave the ex-jockey a narrow-eyed look. "If Violetta's in a pet though, she'll take it out on Chris."

"Then tell his lordship. He won't abide it."

"The old villainous earl has much to answer for," Creiggy muttered.

"And his son's payin' the price every day, more's the pity," John said with a frown. "If'n the countess rode, I'd see that her saddle cinch was cut a wee notch. With luck, the bitch would break her neck and be off in hell with the old earl."

"A matched pair of walking evil, those two," Creiggy snapped.

"His lordships seems right happy now. Maybe it's a sign o' better times."

"Pray God," Alec's old nanny said with a sigh.

MEANWHILE, CHRIS WAS delighted with his new playmates. He adored his father, and a warm friendship was instantly established between Zelda and Chris when she asked him whether his pony was fast. His eyes lit up and he proceeded to explain in great detail how very fast Petunia could gallop and how just as soon as he could teach his pony to jump, his Papa would buy him his *very own* stallion.

Then Zelda showed him how to play a new card game for money, he kept winning and winning, and life couldn't have been any better for an exuberant little six-year-old.

In the course of their play, after Chris's winnings had piled up markedly, the cook took apple pies from the oven and brought them all a serving. They ate pie with Chantilly cream along with a sarsaparilla drink from the still room while Chris talked like a magpie between bites: about his favorite book about guns, his bestest friend, Thad, who could run faster than anyone, about his Papa's big desk that he could sit at in his own chair, and any number of subjects that Zelda responded to with interest, diplomacy, and the occasional informative commentary that inevitably brought a wide-eyed look to the young boy's eyes and the exclamation, "How do you know that when you're a girl?"

"I have four brothers," she'd answered the first time and in variations on the theme the other times he'd been astonished at her knowledge of manly things.

Having finished eating first, Alec lounged in his chair and contemplated the homey scene before him with warm satisfaction. The rapport between his son and Zelda was gratifying to see. Chris was happy as a clam, talking animatedly, his cheeks flushed with excitement, and Zelda was marvelous with the boy, engaging him in the intricacies of a new children's card game—apparently one of several in her repertoire. She was patient in her instructions, quick to praise when Chris grasped a new concept, and openly affectionate—touching his arm or hand, ruffling his curls when he made her laugh.

Yet she never overstepped the casual role of friend, nor asked him prying questions. Alec found that particularly appealing. So many ladies he knew wanted to insinuate themselves into his life; they would have used the boy to cultivate a closer intimacy with him.

"There now," Zelda said, her explanation complete. "Try counting what you have in your hand and I'll finish my pie. Remember, the ace is worth twice as much as all the rest— here, start with these on the end." With a quick smile for Chris, she turned to her dessert.

And an even more satisfying scene ensued.

One of a highly libidinous nature.

The earl watched with rapt attention as Zelda began to eat her dessert, the simple act taking on a decidedly erotic cast. Or perhaps whatever Miss MacKenzie did was sexually arousing for him—her mere presence putting a strain on his self-control. But the sight of each spoonful of syrupy pie with Chantilly cream sliding into her mouth served as a kind of delectable foreplay. Was it unconscious or deliberate? Was she playing to an audience of one? Or was Miss Mac-Kenzie unaware of the picture she presented?

Not that it mattered; the result was the same.

Shifting slightly in his chair to accommodate his rising erection, Alec briefly debated carrying her away on some flimsy pretext. Or no pretext. And if Chris hadn't been inches away, he would have.

As it was, he was reduced to a frustrating voyeurism and a burgeoning horniness—each ensuing transfer of the confection from plate to mouth further ratcheting up his lust. His gaze was riveted on the languid sweep of the spoon, on Zelda's every movement, each subsequent bite ingested adding dimension to his cock. Her obvious enjoyment of the sweet pastry was a lewd tour de force: The way she slowly opened her full lips as the spoon approached, the charming way the tip of her pink tongue would suddenly appear to delicately lap up the lush concoction, the manner in which she chewed, savoring the flavors, relishing the taste, and the way she swallowed particularly engaged his interest.

The titillating display suggested a more salacious activity to a man of Dalgliesh's libertine propensities; he could almost feel her mouth on his hard prick. Fortunately, the table hid the huge bulge in his buckskins from public view, although the fierce, insistent ache in his cock was destroying his concentration.

Jesus, how the hell was he going to last until Monday?

Opportunely or perhaps inopportunely, Zelda looked up and smiled. "Isn't the pie wonderful?"

"Among other things," he murmured, his voice tight with constraint, the lascivious image on the other side of the table provocative as hell. "You have a dab of cream on your bottom lip."

She licked her bottom lip. "Did I get it all?"

You'll get it all on Monday. "Almost," he said, and reaching across the small table, he slid the pad of his index finger over her full bottom lip and scooped up the remnant of cream. "There, that's better." His deep voice resonated with a subtle authority, as if he had the right to monitor her appearance. Sitting back in his chair, he slipped his fingertip into his mouth, held her gaze, and gently sucked.

"Oh God." A spiking rush of flame-hot desire shook her to the core, and too late she realized she'd softly moaned the words.

"Careful, darling," Alec whispered, and quickly leaning forward, he took the spoon from her trembling hand. "Relax." A soft breath of warning.

Shakily inhaling, she tried to ignore the frenzied carnal urgency electrifying her senses, confounding her good judgment. There were countless people in the kitchen as well as a young boy in close proximity. This was hardly the time to succumb to overwrought passion.

He gently touched her fingertips. "Would you like something more? A cup of tea perhaps?"

"Thank you, no," Zelda replied, marveling at his self-discipline, trying to govern her voice to an equal mildness. "Everything was delicious." There, that was a suitably decorous tone. "Not that I needed any of it, but who could resist. And I don't mean *that*, so kindly stop smiling."

"I'm just smiling in general," he said, looking amused. "I like the cozy kitchen, the company, the lack of an audience, the domesticity. It's all very nice. Don't you agree?"

"I do. It's charming—a comfortable interlude in a busy day." It helped her composure that he spoke so casually, lounged in his chair so casually, dealt with women in his life so casually; a warning there. "And thank you as well for the opportunity to meet your son." Her gaze fell on Chris's bent head as he was busily counting his cards. "It reminds me of—" Unexpectedly, tears welled in her eyes. "Forgive me." She sucked in a quick breath and blinked away the wetness, blaming her restive nerves for her vulnerability. "It's just a bit of nostalgia," she said, able to speak with a degree of tranquility once again. "I'd forgotten what a pleasure it is to be with a youngster. I do so enjoy children."

"I could give you one," he said, a teasing note in his voice.

She smiled faintly. "Wouldn't that be nice."

In that small, hushed moment, with the cooks cooking and the heat and smells of the kitchen wafting around them, with busy servants everywhere and the small boy between them counting his cards, an impromptu exchange of two short audacious phrases cataclysmically altered their well-defined lives.

It was as if a key turned in a lock and suddenly a door opened and they stood on the threshold of a bright new world of staggering possibility.

Then, taking a small breath to rid herself of irrational hope, Zelda calmly said, "Nice but impractical, my dear Dalgliesh."

"But not impossible." He was a man of great wealth and with it great power, and suddenly, without reason, he wanted this. He sat very still, his large hands resting lightly on the table, and then he slowly turned them over palms up in silent offering. "You decide," he said, this man who'd never thought about a child of his own before, nor asked a woman for anything. "Just think about it," he whispered, rash and reckless, ignoring the world, the entire universe.

"Papa, Papa, look! I have the right number! I won again!"

A small, sticky hand holding a fan of cards was shoved in Dalgliesh's face, reality intruded, and with it the clashing discord of his life.

"If you men will excuse me," Zelda lightly said, refusing to let her voice quiver, refusing to break down over something so foolish. "I remembered a matter I must see to." She abruptly came to her feet, escape utterly essential before she lost control.

"Can't it wait?" Chris exclaimed. "Tell her, Papa, tell her it can wait!"

"Miss MacKenzie has family here, Chris. She can't spend all afternoon playing with us." He'd been saved from the very edge of the precipice.

"Why not? Can't they take care of themselves?"

"I'd love to stay, Chris," Zelda said. "Perhaps tomorrow."

Chris's lower lip projected in a pout. "For certain?"

What was certain was that she'd indeed like to play with

his father until the end of time. What was less certain was whether the profligate Earl of Dalgliesh, who amused himself with a great many women, would agree. "Why don't I try. How would that be?"

"She must try, mustn't she, Papa! Tell her, tell her!"

"If you'd like, Chris, we could go riding tomorrow without the hunters. Perhaps Miss MacKenzie would agree to join us?" Alec said, as if he'd not just stepped back from the brink, as if he wasn't completely crazed. "She's a very good rider. She could teach you a thing or two about jumping. And we could all have lunch somewhere."

Chris's eyes swung up to Zelda. "Please, please come! I want to learn how to jump. I'll be ever so good, I promise!"

"We'd both like you to come," Alec said, a wicked gleam in his eyes as he uttered the word *come*. "Say you will." He could no more relinquish her company than he could stop breathing—or fucking—which saner thought mitigated his disquiet. "Why don't we say eight. Is that too early for you, Miss Mackenzie?" He'd have her all day.

How could she refuse when she was being offered unalloyed bliss? "I'd love to," she said, relegating reason and logic to the black void, her happiness tied to this man who'd been a stranger mere hours ago.

"Well, then, that's settled," he blandly said. "We'll meet you at the stables at eight. We could walk you upstairs if you like."

"No, no, please don't—that is . . . I'm quite capable of finding my way. Don't get up!" she cried as Dalgliesh made to rise. He'd proclaim their friendship before everyone, damn his recklessness.

"It's easy to find your way, Papa," Chris artlessly said, immune to the emotional tumult. "The stairs go right up into the dining room. Come, Papa, show me how to count the picture cards."

"I'll leave you to count cards, Dalgliesh. Until tomorrow."

"I'll see you at dinner." It was an ultimatum no matter how softly spoken.

Both alarmed and filled with joy, she nodded. "Until dinner then."

CHAPTER 5

PLEADING FATIGUE, ZELDA avoided teatime. The hunters hadn't returned yet, so the company would be largely female. She wasn't quite up to displaying the necessary indifference to Dalgliesh's wife. Which in itself was disturbing. How should it matter? It wasn't as though the marriage was a love match and she was trespassing on hallowed ground. Although she *had* crossed an unprecedented boundary by replying so impulsively to Dalgliesh's unbelievable offer.

When she shouldn't have.

Currently removed from temptation, however, logic more readily held sway, and the impossible and impractical were more easily jettisoned. Zelda took the time before dinner to put aside foolish things; she revived her more discerning sensibilities, reclaimed her equilibrium, and primarily reminded herself that she mustn't make too much of Dalgliesh's attentions. He was notable for amusing himself in lady's boudoirs; this was no more than another flirtation for him. And as everyone knew, country house parties were notorious for amorous games.

Not that she was necessarily averse to the game, nor had she entirely eschewed such playful sport in the past. On occasion she'd enjoyed the company of some lovely man for one of those lovely long weekends. Other times she'd preferred her own company. She wasn't a slave to temptation.

Or hadn't been.

Dalgliesh was different.

Bewilderingly so.

But a good talking to, a short nap, a leisurely bath, a gossipy maid who helped her dress and put up her hair went far to temper her mad, heady feelings and return her to a more sober reality. She'd simply accept Dalgliesh's company for a brief dalliance, thoroughly enjoy herself on Monday, and bid him adieu with the casualness she was sure he'd prefer. A man of his sexual repute only played at love, his shocking offer in the kitchen notwithstanding. She was sure he was as relieved as she that Chris had interrupted that astonishing exchange.

On the contrary . . .

Try as he might, Dalgliesh hadn't been able to dislodge the startling concept from his mind despite deliberately staying with Chris in the nursery until it was almost too late to dress for dinner. In an effort to avoid facing the disturbing Miss MacKenzie, he'd ignored the first bell signaling that it was time to dress; he'd also ignored the second bell indicating drinks were being served. But once Chris had finished his nursery supper and was assembling an intricate puzzle, Creiggy gave Alec a searching look across the small table. "No dinner for you tonight?" she murmured.

He was forced to at least answer, if not make a decision. "What do you think?" he said like he might have twenty years ago.

"You must make up your own mind," she answered like she would have then.

"That's the problem."

"She seems very nice," his old nanny blandly said. "I like

that MacKenzie hair. It's magnificent—like a blaze of glory."

"As if I care about that," he muttered.

"She won your race. Is she really that good?"

He smiled. "She's good, but not that good."

"I thought so. That horse of yours likes to win."

"Zeus can afford to be polite on occasion."

"When you're being polite."

"I had reason to be," he gently said.

"Speaking of those reasons, are you worried about—" She rolled her eyes.

He didn't have to ask whom the eye roll denoted. "It could be a problem."

"It never has been before."

"I never gave a damn before."

She hid her shock. "I see," she calmly said.

"Which is why I can't decide if I want to go down to dinner."

She looked at him for a contemplative moment. "I didn't raise a coward, my boy."

"It's not me. I'm not sure I care to hurt her."

"Maybe you won't."

"Of course I will. I have nothing to offer a woman."

Mercy me, there is a God. But Mrs. Creighton only said, "Your mother isn't as fragile as you think."

"What if you're wrong? Then what?" This wasn't a new discussion.

"Very well. But I don't think Miss MacKenzie is breakable. She looks like a strong woman to me. She's Scots for one thing."

Dalgliesh chuckled. "The woman of Achruach, you mean." It was Creiggy's favorite story.

"'The day I cannot keep my countenance and hold men in their place and work my will on them, that is a day you will never see,'" Creiggy softly quoted, a half smile on her lined face. "Now go and see if your MacKenzie lass can put you in your place." She glanced at Chris. "I'll have him ready at eight tomorrow morning. Go."

* * *

Stern talking to or not, Zelda had been equally reluctant to face Dalgliesh, and she came down late for the drinks hour. Alec must have changed his mind, she decided; he wasn't in the drawing room. Standing in the doorway, she saw her father near the fireplace in the midst of his cronies. She was still debating whether to walk in and if so what to drink, when Oz Lennox, splendidly handsome in evening rig, walked up, smiled, and asked, "Whiskey or champagne?"

"It depends what kind of whiskey," she replied with an answering smile.

"Follow me, my dear, and I'll dazzle you with the array." He offered her his arm. "Come, she won't bite."

"How perceptive."

"I had a lot of practice before my marriage. I know who bites and who doesn't—figuratively speaking, of course," he added with a grin. Taking her hand, he placed it on his arm. "Come, this'll be easy. And after a drink or two, I guarantee you, nothing much matters."

She glanced at him, amused. "More of your practice?"

He laughed. "An ongoing process in my case. But I have a darling wife who allows me to be troublesome at times. As I do her," he said with a quirked smile. "I'll introduce you later. She's still with the children in the nursery."

"How many children do you have?"

"Two—both the most beautiful children on the face of the earth, of course. Ah, here we are." A servant stood behind a drinks table. "I'd suggest the whiskey from Locaber; it's clear as glass, smooth and strong, and full of wonder."

After collecting their drinks, they moved to a quiet corner, drank the fine whiskey, and talked about the hunt, the weather, Fitz's hounds.

Oz was facing the door, so he saw Dalgliesh walk into the drawing room looking like he'd just come out of his bath. He was slicking his wet hair back behind his ears with a quick brushing gesture as he scanned the room. It was clear that he'd seen them, but he didn't come over; instead, the earl grabbed a glass of whiskey from a servant passing by with a tray of drinks and kept his distance.

Several moments later, having covered all the conventional topics, curious about Lennox's distinctive features, and perhaps less restrained with the whiskey warming her blood, Zelda asked, "Where do you live?"

"Cambridgeshire mostly."

"Then where do you come from with this?" She brushed her finger up his bronzed cheek.

He smiled. "India—Hyderabad."

"Ah—I should have known. You're incredibly handsome, although I'm sure you know that. Why are you here charming me?" she pleasantly inquired. He was affable and urbane but not flirtatious.

"I'm on duty—very pleasant duty, I might add. I'm saving you from Violetta," he said with a flick of his eyes in Alec's wife's direction. "In case she forgets her manners."

"Oh Lord," Zelda murmured. "Was it that obvious this morning?"

"The look that passed between you two could have powered London for a week. Also your absence at the hunt was noticed." He shrugged. "Violetta may have heard."

"But does she care?"

His smile was droll. "Seriously? With someone as beautiful as you? Even if she didn't care, she'd make sure to mark her territory just for the hell of it."

"I probably can deal with her if necessary."

"But why should you have to when I'm more than willing to be boorish in your stead?" he cheerfully said. "By the way, I've never met a witch."

She smiled. "Nor have I."

"What about this?" He ran a finger over the rough-cut emeralds circling her neck, clearly an artifact of some ancient culture with the beaten-gold pendants dangling from each jewel.

"It was a gift from one of the Amazon headmen."

His brows rose. "He thought you were a witch, too."

"I think my height impressed everyone—and perhaps my hair."

"You should touch my little Ceci and Raj for good luck."

"I'd be happy to, although I'm not sure it would do much good."

"Perhaps you don't know your powers, my dear. Ah, here's your real protection," he murmured. Dalgliesh had abruptly left the group of women surrounding him right after Oz had touched the emeralds at Zelda's throat. He was shouldering his way through the crowd now, looking grim.

Zelda turned to look and, against all prudence and reason, felt breathless with delight.

"I was guarding Miss MacKenzie, in case you were wondering," Oz said as Alec reached them, full of affront.

The earl's frown vanished. "Thank you. I appreciate your kindness."

Oz grinned. "Miss MacKenzie thought she'd do well enough on her own."

"Did she now?"

"I'm sure you'd know best in that regard. Au revoir, my dears." And Lennox strolled away.

"You shouldn't be talking to me," Zelda said.

"You shouldn't be blushing."

"It would be much easier for you not to talk to me."

One dark brow rose very slightly. "If only that were easy. I almost didn't come down. I tried not to."

"I debated coming down to dinner as well. So many people," she murmured. "All interested in scandal."

He glanced around as if in assent, when in fact, he was marking Violetta's location; good, she was in conversation with Mytton. "You're safe enough for a minute. Don't move," he brusquely said. "I'll be right back."

But perhaps his wife had her eye on him as well, because the moment he walked away from Zelda, Violetta excused herself and began moving toward her newest rival. She *had* heard of her husband's absence from the hunt with this woman.

Jamie smoothly stepped into Violetta's path, intercepting

her progress. "Are you enjoying your weekend?" he politely inquired.

"Well enough. And you?" Her eyes were hostile. "I see Bella's here." Jamie had been Bella's favorite lover before his marriage.

"Is she? I didn't notice."

Violetta sniffed. "Men—you're all alike." She began moving around him.

"I don't believe you've met my wife," Jamie smoothly murmured, moving a half step to obstruct her advance. "Come, let me introduce you." A bodyguard to a prince prior to his retirement to Scotland, Jamie Blackwood was more capable than most of protecting people. Taking Violetta by the hand, he ignored her stiff-backed reluctance and, asking her a question about Mytton's new yacht, drew her away.

His wife had been apprised of the situation, and after she and Violetta had been introduced, Sofia immediately mentioned their many common acquaintances. She further engaged Violetta's interest by confining her comments to several men about town both women knew. Ignoring Jamie's faint scowl since she was comparing notes on young bucks only as a conversational gambit and specifically as a service to his cousin, Sofia lightly said, "Don't you agree, darling. Lord Cosgrave is one of the better polo players in England." She turned to Violetta with a smile. "Did you know Jamie played polo all over the world? Such lovely strong muscles one develops playing that game. But you know that, don't you, since you and Cosgrove are such good friends. Jamie, dear, why don't you get us both a little drink," Sofia murmured. "I'm sure Violetta would adore that nice cherry eau-de-vie."

Left à deux with such an intriguing subject, the ladies' conversation continued apace, Violetta was calmed, her assault diverted, and Zelda was spared.

In the meantime, Alec pulled Fitz away from a group of his guests who were discussing the day's hunt. "Sorry," he said once they were away from the other men. "But dinner's about to be served and I need a place card changed. I want to be seated next to Zelda."

"Do you think it's wise?" Fitz had seen Jamie stop Violetta before she reached Zelda.

"I don't care if it is or not."

One look at Alec's face and Fitz said, "I'll have Neville take care of it."

"I appreciate it."

"You know what you're doing, I presume."

Alec grinned. "Fuck no, but it feels good." And turning, he strode away.

The duke caught his butler's eye, called him over with a nod, and a moment later Neville was detailing the duke's instructions to an underling.

Returning to Zelda, Alec smiled. "That went well. Now I can entertain you at dinner."

"You're mad!"

"Probably."

"You shouldn't have!" She bit her bottom lip in dismay and consternation and outright alarm. He was being entirely too rash. "Promise me at least you'll be discreet," she said even as her pulse rate accelerated.

"I can't promise that."

"You *must*!"

He shot her an incredulous look; women didn't give him orders.

"Let me rephrase that," she swiftly amended, knowing she had no authority over his actions. "I dearly *wish* you'd be discreet."

"As do I, but Christ, it's been a fucking long day of incredible self-restraint. Oh hell, I'll try," he quickly said at the sudden alarm in her eyes. "How would that be? Really, I'll try," he added, his voice soft and low.

"Thank you," she whispered. "I so dislike everyone staring."

"They're only looking because you're gorgeous tonight in that green velvet gown," he lied, knowing full well why they were staring. "Like a lovely Christmas package, I thought when I first walked in and saw you. *My* present," he said in a husky rasp. "If I can last sixty-four hours more."

"If I can last," she said on a small caught breath.

His smile was instant and sweet. "Let me know if you change your mind," he softly said. "I'm always available."

Her fingers closed over her fan struts so hard her knuckles went white. "You're not being helpful," she whispered.

"Oh, yes, I am. Believe me I'm accommodating as hell. I would have fucked you this morning after breakfast if I'd not been charitable."

"Alec, stop!" she hissed, her cheeks pinked with fear and arousal.

"Yes, dear." His smile was pure sunshine, his world suddenly rich with promise. He may not have to wait until Monday after all.

But dinner was an ordeal even for Dalgliesh. He'd never had to curb his libido under so many watchful gazes. If it wasn't so grueling, he would have found it amusing.

"Don't these people have any other interests?" he whispered.

"Apparently not," Zelda said under her breath. "Including your wife. She's watching you."

He'd noticed. Violetta rarely watched him. It wasn't a good sign. Would he have to protect Zelda from her spleen? Good God, this fuck was getting complicated. Signaling a footman, he quietly said, "Keep my whiskey glass full," and proceeded to drink his dinner.

Which in itself was alarming to Zelda, who lived in a household of four brothers and a father who enjoyed their whiskey. There was no accounting for a man's behavior when he chose to drink instead of eat.

But Dalgliesh soon turned his attention to his dinner companion on his right and devoted the remainder of the meal to Lady Ponsonby.

He stayed with the other men when the table was cleared and the port was brought out, merely nodding to Zelda as a footman pulled back her chair and she rose to follow the ladies into the drawing room for tea and sherry. And when he came in with the other men afterward, he didn't approach her, spending the next hour instead in the midst of one group of men or another. Not that women didn't come up to him several times and attempt to engage his interest, but he politely declined all their advances.

A fact that didn't go unnoticed.

Zelda marveled at his finesse. None of the ladies left angry. He must have left them hopeful, she pettishly thought when she shouldn't. When she had absolutely no right to take issue with other women in his life. When Monday was appearing increasingly distant and unmanageable.

How in the world was she going to last 'til then? Could she?

She'd found a chair in the corner of the room in order to avoid conversation, but her solitary position actually left her more open to male overtures—all of which she courteously rebuffed. Until she finally said for the last time to an importuning man, "Thank you, but morning comes early. I want to be ready for the hunt," and rising to her feet, she walked over to take her leave of her hostess. With a polite smile, she thanked Rosalind for a lovely evening and quickly escaped.

Or almost escaped.

She found Violetta waiting for her outside her room, her gown of black lace festooned with crystal beads shimmering in the half light, the diamonds at her throat and ears glittering.

Her eyes were glittering, too—with malice.

"I don't want you talking to my son," Violetta said in a deadly whisper. "I don't want you anywhere near him. Not this weekend or ever!"

"Do I know you?" Zelda calmly said, not intimidated by a woman half her size, unmoved as well by threats from anyone—large or small.

"I'm Lady Dalgliesh, you bitch!"

"Ah—I've met your husband then."

"Stay away from him, too," Violetta snapped. Dalgliesh never flaunted his inamoratas; he kept his private life private. This woman was a disagreeable change in the status quo.

"You should probably talk to your husband about that," Zelda casually said. "I'm not sure he takes orders from you. I know he doesn't from me. Now, if you'll excuse me, it's been a long, tiring day."

As Zelda reached for the doorknob, Violetta slapped her wrist with her fan. "I'm not finished with you yet," she acidly said.

Zelda glanced at her wrist, then at Violetta. "I wouldn't do that again if I were you." She'd grown up with four very large brothers she'd had to wrestle to the ground on occasion in their youth. This woman was inconsequential in size and in every other way.

"You don't frighten me, you slut," Violetta said with venom in her voice and gaze. "Stay away from my husband and son or you'll be sorry."

"*I'm* sorry this conversation is even taking place," Zelda softly said, tempted to slap the stupid bitch silly. Lady Dalgliesh was the last person to expect fidelity from a husband with her intemperate life. "Now get out of my way or I'll make you get out of my way."

"If you touch me, I'll scream," Violetta hissed.

"Good Lord," Zelda muttered. "Are you drunk?" Then she heard running footsteps behind her, saw Violetta's gaze narrow, and resentfully thought, *Just what I need. To be caught in the middle of a domestic spat.*

"That's enough, Violetta." Coming up to his wife, Dalgliesh grabbed her arm and, rapidly altering the coarse, explicit words racing through his brain, growled, "Haven't you something better to do? Mytton must be waiting for you somewhere. Go and find him." He swung her around and gave her a push. "Stay out of my life."

His voice was so harsh and cold, Zelda wondered that their marriage endured. Divorce wasn't out of the question if one had money.

The earl watched his wife flounce off, waited until she was out of sight, then turned to Zelda. "I can't tell you how sorry I am," he said. "I saw her leave the room with Mytton. I thought you were safe."

A moment of shock. "Safe?"

Alec lifted his shoulder in the faintest shrug. "She's a spiteful woman, ruthless, coldhearted . . ." His voice trailed off. "I'm sorry," he quietly said. "About her, about this, about every fucking thing."

Zelda chose her words carefully. "The possibility of any further relationship between us appears more difficult than I anticipated."

"I understand." His voice held a certain flatness.

"Your wife's obviously upset. I was under the impression your marriage was an informal arrangement."

"It is. I have no idea why she confronted you." Unfamiliar with the role of supplicant, he couldn't bring himself to explain his marriage with any specificity—nor could he for other reasons as well. As for Violetta—no explanation would suffice for her rudeness. "Are you all right? She didn't—"

"No, I'm fine. She surprised me, that's all." In any number of ways, but she wasn't about to detail them to the woman's husband. "But under the circumstances, perhaps we shouldn't continue our friendship."

"I don't blame you." He'd half expected it. "You shouldn't have to deal with Violetta's abuse." He paused, opened his mouth to speak, and changing his mind, said instead, "If you'll excuse me, I have to check on Chris. Violetta may have upset him. I apologize again. I should have been more vigilant." He bowed faintly. "She shouldn't be back. Sleep well."

Zelda watched him until the shadows in the dimly lit corridor swallowed him up. For a moment more, she stood in the hallway—indecisive and bewildered, feeling a profound sense of loss.

Then she turned, opened the door, and entered her room.

"I'll undress myself," she said to the waiting maid. "I won't be needing you tonight. And I'll take breakfast downstairs in the morning." She just wanted to be alone, now and later—without servants to intrude on her solitude. She was deeply unhappy. When she shouldn't be. When she hadn't even known Dalgliesh existed this time yesterday.

How very strange life could be.

Convoluted and inexplicable.

Wretched for no good reason.

Dropping into a chair by the fire, she stretched out her legs and studied the toes of her green silk slippers as though the answer to her emotional quandary lay in the gleaming silk. Or in the glowing fire, she mused as her gaze lifted to the small blaze on the hearth.

But no answer arose in the dancing flames, nor in her heart or mind.

Only the wanting remained, keen and avaricious, rash, desperate.

And stubborn.

CHAPTER 6

"PAPA, IS THAT you?" A frightened little voice.

"Yes. I'll be right there." Alec had been talking softly to
Mrs. Creighton outside Chris's bedroom door. He further
lowered his voice. "John will drive you in the morning. I'll
be over to the hunting lodge as soon as I make my excuses
to Fitz. And thank you again for fending off Violetta."

"The lad heard her though. He was shaking when I went
in afterward. You really have to do something about that
woman," the nanny murmured, a stubborn jut to her jaw.

"I know. Not tonight, though." Turning away, Alec
pushed open the door to Chris's room. "Can't sleep?" the
earl sympathetically inquired. "Would you like a story?"

Chris soon dozed off as he always did when Alec sat with
him and told him a tale about knights or pirates or animals
that talked. But after the young boy fell asleep, Alec
remained seated on the bed, his eyes half closed, his mind
racing, every muscle in his body taut with restraint.

He knew what he wanted to do, what he shouldn't do.

And he was leaving in the morning.

When Mrs. Creighton opened the door and motioned for

him, he carefully rose from the bed in order not to wake Chris. Quietly walking out, and as quietly closing the door, he leaned back against the old oak panels and shut his eyes, overcome by an overwhelming weariness. Violetta seemed more of an encumbrance tonight—burdensome, obtrusive, unnecessarily hurtful to her son. And what had always appeared manageable was suddenly unmanageable. What had once been a marriage of expediency was now stifling and oppressive.

All because he couldn't ignore an ill-advised compulsion for a woman who, through no fault of her own, tempted him beyond bearing.

His old nanny came up and touched his arm. "Go and get some sleep, laddie."

Opening his eyes, he came out of his musing with a good-natured smile for the woman who'd taught him his manners along with the strength of will to face the world. "You, too, Creiggy. I should be at the lodge by noon."

"We'll be fine." She patted his arm. "Take your time. John and I can entertain Chris"—she smiled—"almost as well as you."

Dalgliesh bent and kissed her cheek. "I'm in your debt once again."

"Nonsense. You've made me a rich old lady. But take some advice, laddie, and talk to your mother when you return home. You've more than done your duty by her."

"Please, don't start," Dalgliesh murmured. "I'm in a foul mood."

"As if you don't have reason to be. You're too dutiful, laddie, that's your problem. I wouldn't have put up with your wife so long, but that's neither here nor there, nor my business in the end. Just don't wait so long that she ruins the boy."

"You're right. He shouldn't grow up in fear."

"You should know about that."

"I had you, Creiggy." Alec smiled faintly. "He didn't dare touch me."

"Still, laddie, it leaves its mark. But enough o' that. Your father's long dead. Now go, get some sleep."

"Yes, ma'am," he cheekily replied.

"Humph," she said in that sharp, quiet voice that had made her the authority not only in the nursery, but in the household. "Don't forget who changed your nappies."

Dalgliesh laughed and, with a wave, departed.

Before he returned to his room, however, he made a brief detour.

As was the custom at country house parties, cards were slipped into brackets on bedroom doors, identifying the occupant. It ensured that a guest didn't accidently enter the wrong room—although there were times when an inebriated guest did, the most celebrated instance when Charlie Berensford jumped into the Archbishop of Canterbury's bed by mistake. But there was no mistaking Alec's destination. He'd made a point of knowing which room was Violetta's, as he did with everything concerning his wife. He had good reason not to trust her.

Stopping outside the proper room, he warned himself not to lose his temper. Although the sudden light trill of Violetta's giggles provoked a grimace. The confrontation was unavoidable, however, so drawing in a breath of restraint, he grasped the doorknob and, knowing the doors were left unlocked for the servants, he shoved it open.

"Please, there's no cause for alarm," he casually said as he entered his wife's bedroom and observed the couple in the bed scrambling to cover their nudity. "I won't be long."

"How dare you, Alec!" Violetta cried, pushing into a seated position and clutching the bedclothes to her breast. "Get out or I'll scream!"

"Spare me the theatrics, Violetta." The earl's voice was softly contemptuous. "I just came to tell you I'll be gone in the morning, so you'll have to make your own way back to London. I'm taking Chris with me."

Her indignation turned to affront, temper flared in her eyes. "Where are you going? You can't just take my son away! He needs his mother!"

"Christ, Violetta, keep in mind who you're talking to when you play the maternal card. But we'll be at my hunting box if you require anything, although it looks as though Mytton is satisfying you well enough. Don't let her work you too hard tonight, Freddy. She likes it first thing in the morning, too, although you probably know that." Dalgliesh lifted one eyebrow. "Now, if you have any message for your son, I'd be happy to convey it to him."

"Of course I don't. That's not the point," Violetta testily said, letting the sheet slip downward slightly to show off her fine bosom.

"I know what the point is," Alec curtly replied, wondering if she really thought he gave a damn about her breasts. "And I won't have the boy used as a pawn. Is that clear?"

His voice was so cold, his gaze like ice that even Violetta, who knew just how far she could force the issue of her son, opted for prudence. "I'll miss the dear boy, but if you insist," she pettishly said.

He ground his teeth at her damned playacting. "I do insist." The words were blunt as a hammer blow. "Just a last warning, Violetta," the earl said with less passion, his temper curbed. "Do what you will, but you know the rules. The risk is yours to assess." He'd told her the day they were married that she could go her own way, but if she were to become pregnant again, he'd see that she had an abortion. The marriage may have been forced on him, but he wouldn't have a by-blow as his heir.

"See here, Dalgliesh," Lord Mytton sputtered, feeling he should come to his lover's defense. "Don't want you threatening the lady. Not the thing, damn it."

"I could threaten you, if you prefer," Alec softly said, the menace in his voice smooth as silk. "Name your weapons if you think she's worth it."

Freddy Chambers was shocked, then alarmed. "Good God! No one duels anymore, Dalgliesh! Are you mad?"

"Resentful is the word, Mytton. But that's where you come in to take my wife off my hands. I wish you a night of agreeable fucking. I won't say superlative fucking because I know better, but then life isn't perfect, as we all know." Obliged to marry for money, Mytton had been able to barter his title and handsome face for a fortune. As was often the case, however, an antidote of a wife and her parvenu family had come with the fortune. "If no one has any further questions," Alec said with a curt nod for the couple in bed, "I'll take my leave."

For a moment, he stood motionless and indifferent as his wife stared at him with murder in her eyes and Mytton looked stunned.

Then he walked out and closed the door behind him.

As he traversed the quiet corridor, he gave himself the required lecture about doing the right thing, about not being reckless, about not being bloody-minded enough to take advantage of a woman who didn't deserve it.

Go to your room and get some sleep.
Be sensible.

CHAPTER 7

IT WAS CLOSE to midnight when Zelda heard the door open.

She was still sitting in the chair by the fire, still baffled by the trackless tangle of her thoughts, still discontent. "Go away," she muttered.

"I would if I could." Shutting the door, Alec advanced into the room. "At least I didn't have to break down the door."

"I'm sure Fitz will be pleased. I forgot to lock it." Along with forgetting to move for a very long time; the fire had burned low.

He didn't ask if he could sit for fear she might say no. He dropped into the chair on the other side of the fireplace. "I'm sorry for disturbing you. I tried to stay away."

She finally looked at him. "Where's your wife?"

"I have no idea," he lied. "Violetta went up to the nursery and frightened Chris. I sat with him until he fell back to sleep." He stretched out his legs and exhaled softly. "She uses the boy against me—or tries to. It's an ongoing battle." He was tired, the grinding hostility exhausting. He looked away for a moment, his nostrils gently flaring. "I feel like

I'm under siege at times. Tonight particularly. And Chris is getting to an age where—" He abruptly stopped. Personal confession was rare in his life, unprecedented in these circumstances. "Forgive me. It has nothing to do with you. It's been a long day."

"It *is* late." Zelda tried to speak in a neutral tone. "Everything will look better in the morning, I'm sure." Although he looked so unhappy she felt an almost overwhelming urge to take him in her arms and comfort him.

"If only platitudes would bring resolution to my life," he sardonically replied.

"I'm sorry. Hackneyed phrases are rather useless, aren't they?"

"In my case, yes. My life is an ungodly mess, and I'd apologize for involving you in it if it would do any good." He shut his eyes briefly before he quietly said, "I shouldn't be here. I really shouldn't."

"I don't care about her." Zelda held his gaze, her eyes half shadowed in the light from the fading fire. "I've been sitting here telling myself to be prudent." She shrugged. "To no avail."

"Tell me about it," he muttered. "I'm not in the habit of calling attention to my—"

"Amorous affaires?"

"Diversions," he brusquely corrected. "This isn't though." He slid lower in his chair. "I didn't care tonight if everyone knew. It's madness."

"Speaking of madness."

"Don't, please." He knew what she was going to say, had thought of little else since afternoon.

"It's been on my mind," she said, ignoring him because she was the least likely woman in the world to respond to authority. "What you said in the kitchen was—"

"Stupid. Don't give it another thought."

She studied him for a moment, brooding discontent in every aspect of his face and lean, lounging form. "But I have thought about it—don't look at me like that. You were the one who said it. Why?"

He looked across the fire-lit space and met her gaze, his heavy-lidded eyes clouded with doubt. "I don't know," he guardedly said. "If I knew the answer to that, I could—" He exhaled softly.

"Forget it?"

"Exactly." He turned and stared into the dying fire. "Having a child has never mattered to me," he softly began, trying to arrange the tumult in his brain into a reasonable narrative as he contemplated the flickering flames. "I don't need an heir. I have a cousin I'm fond of who has a large and growing family. And I've already seen to it that Chris is financially secure." He chose not to say: *With a father like mine, the notion of fatherhood lost its luster.* "So whatever bizarre impulse prompted me to make that offer to you is best forgotten." His voice was crisp at the last, as though putting period to his monologue. Turning back to her, his smile was replete with well-practiced charm. "Now, tell me, was I discreet enough at dinner? I hope you noticed that I gave equal time to old Lady Ponsonby."

He'd politely ended any further discussion of children. "I noticed. Lady Ponsonby was quite enamored." Zelda understood the topic was absurd. Dalgliesh's reputed sexual skills would be more than enough tonight.

"That was because we discussed the outrageous affront to society of the suffrage movement. She called it a mad, wicked folly. And all the misguided females who so forget every sense of womanly feeling and propriety should get a good whipping."

"Witless cow," Zelda muttered.

Alec grinned. "Apparently she's not alone in her opinion. I was told the queen herself agrees. God created men and women differently and so they should remain each in their own position. The argument is irrefutable, Lady Ponsonby insisted. Would you like me to show you your position," he sportively said, back in form, the game familiar. "I'm quite willing."

"Or I could show you yours," Zelda lightly replied, suddenly feeling breathless and young, as if she were fifteen again. Although Dalgliesh wasn't her adoring Johnnie Armstrong, but a confident libertine sure of his appeal.

On the other hand, she was a confident woman.

And he *did* appeal.

"Since we're neither adolescents as you pointed out this morning," she murmured, offering him a captivating smile, "this won't be a seduction so much as a lustful meeting of minds."

"Minds? I hope not," he drolly replied, beginning to unbutton his waistcoat as though having been given leave to proceed.

"Well, my mind at least will be involved. As for you, I'll soon find out what's involved, won't I?" She lazily stretched, watching him begin to undress with delicious anticipation. "I must say, Dalgliesh," she murmured, her voice a soft contralto, "I've been thinking about you, about this—a great deal."

He paused an infinitesimal moment in his unbuttoning, she noticed, before he continued the downward progress of his fingers. She smiled. "Does that make you nervous?"

"What?"

"You heard me. Am I not allowed to think about you?"

"It depends what you're thinking."

She softly laughed. "We've agreed to dismiss your strange offer. But that aside, how many traps have there been to make you so wary?"

"None I couldn't manage." He sat up, shrugged out of his coat and waistcoat, and dropped them on the floor.

A gleam of amusement twinkled in her eyes. "I'm warned then." She opened her arms wide. "Rest easy. I only want a bit of your time and your very splendid cock."

His smile was instant and unguarded. "Those I gladly give. You're most unusual," he said, half musing. "No flattery or coquetry. It's very appealing."

"You're too handsome and too rich, Dalgliesh, and I expect news of your enormous cock has preceded you. Why wouldn't they all want a piece of you?"

"They want more," he drily said.

"I don't, I assure you." And in the rational part of her

brain, she meant it. As for the irrational part, she'd long ago learned self-discipline and self-sacrifice. Who wouldn't with five children to raise?

He kicked off his evening shoes. "Come here." He indicated the space between his spread thighs.

"You have to say it nicely."

"*Please*, come here," he dulcetly murmured, reaching down to take off his socks.

"Or you could come here," she said as sweetly.

He looked up, amused. "Do you think I'll say no?"

"I'm not sure."

"I'd never be so foolish." Barefoot now, he rose from his chair with an effortless grace. "He's been waiting for you since morning," he said, glancing downward to his erection lifting the soft wool of his trousers. "And he's quite willing to oblige you in just about anything."

"*Just* about anything?" She was feeling ravenous and greedy, the ostentatious display eliciting a soft suppressed gasp as he drew near.

His smile was knowing and assured; the woman before him was ripe for mounting. "Correction—*anything*. Anything at all."

She shut her eyes against the hot rush of desire rippling up her vagina, and when she opened them again, he was still smiling.

"Tell me what you want first."

"Arrogant man. I should say no to you."

"It wouldn't matter if you did." Blunt and unequivocal. "You're here, I'm here"—his gaze flicked downward—"he's here, and at least two of us are obsessed." Jerking open the bow on his white tie, he pulled it free, dropped it, and unbuttoned the collar of his shirt. "So let me show you what obsession feels like. Come, darling," he said in a softer tone, leaning down, taking her hands, and pulling her to her feet. "You can have as many orgasms as you want. You first. How would that be?"

Her shoulders and arms were bare, her mounded breasts partially visible above the low décolletage of her gown, the flickering firelight tinting her pale flesh peach and rose and grenadine. Her brilliant hair was gilded with amber, her eyes were dark with passion, and he thought as he had that morning that she was the most stunning woman he'd ever seen.

She looked up, wide-eyed and breathless. "Tell me it's perfectly normal to feel this way—ravaged by desire, swallowed up by unquenchable lust—shaking." She gripped his hands harder to steady herself.

He drew her close, so their bodies lightly touched, so his rampant cock spoke for him as well, and he answered her quietly. "It's normal for us."

She drew in a shuddering breath. "I'm not sure that helps."

"I know what will help." Smoothly turning her, he began unhooking the closures at the back of her gown. "Decide what you want me to do first while I take off your gown."

How could he speak so casually when she was already trembling on the brink and he'd barely touched her? How could he calmly unfasten the long line of concealed hooks down her back with such complacency when she didn't know if her knees would give way under the violence of her need, if she could find breath enough to breathe. If she could resist the urge to shamelessly beg him to stop unhooking so she could feel him inside her—*now*, this instant.

"Please," she said in a ragged whisper a moment later because she couldn't help herself; she was sick with desire, her craving insatiable. "I don't care about the dress."

"A minute more, darling." His voice was husky and low, his libido equally uninterested in delay. But he was capable of restraint—one of his great charms as a lover. Along with his stamina.

"Stop, stop!" Swinging around, trembling, flushed with arousal, her cheeks pinked from more than the fire, Zelda hissed, "Stop right now!"

"Yes, ma'am." Reaching around her, he ripped the last few hooks free and shoved the gown down her arms, her hips, the shimmering velvet descending to the carpet in a soft whisper of sound.

He masked his surprise.

She was nude—lush, shapely, resplendent, and *naked*.

Not that he wasn't familiar with the lined and boned evening gowns that required less lingerie. But generally a lady wore petticoats, at least, and silk stockings. He should have noticed her bare feet. Had he not been distracted by everything that made this evening both difficult and exceptional, he might have.

He liked that she'd been waiting for him. Or perhaps she was waiting for anyone to satisfy her desires, he more cynically reflected. Although with the current state of their mutual arousal, it didn't matter because he happened to be *anyone*.

Lifting her in his arms, he quickly carried her to the bed, pulled away the embroidered coverlet, and deposited her on the cool sheets. "Is that too cold?" An automatic politesse only; he was already unbuttoning his trousers.

She shook her head, incapable of comment with her gaze on Dalgliesh's fingers rapidly moving down his trouser placket, the buttons on his underwear. And a moment later, his erection freed, the mattress dipped under his weight, and he settled smoothly between her legs.

She fleetingly noted the vivid width of his muscled shoulders beneath the fine cambric of his evening shirt, grateful for the fact that he'd barely undressed to accommodate her. "I'm sorry—to be so—desperate," she whispered, breathless and trembling, sliding her hands down his back to help draw him in.

"God, no, don't be sorry." His voice was rough and half breathless, too, as he positioned the head of his cock so it was nuzzling her cleft and invaded her sleek passage the merest distance. "You needn't wait." And he gave her what she wanted, penetrating slowly at first, cautious about hurting her, watching her face from under his lashes. Then as her sleek flesh yielded to the forceful pressure of his turgid cock, he drove in deeper and deeper yet until he was buried to the hilt in her hot, melting flesh.

She shivered. He was so big—the pressure extreme.

He knew why she shivered, liked that she did, her vulnerability triggering a dangerous excitement. Like a rutting animal, he growled deep in his throat and forced her thighs wider for better access, apologizing softly as he pressed deeper, not meaning it. But he waited a fraction of a second before he slid his hands under her bottom, alert to any indication of distress in her erratic whimpers.

But the small breathy sound was familiar; frenzied, feverish, asking for more.

Appreciative, not particularly surprised, he lifted her to better feel the plunging depth of his strokes, and he thrust into her hard, hard, hard, slowly, then not so slowly—to the sweet extremity of ravishment, to the soul-shattering point where excess and tolerance recklessly merged. Then rash and unthinking, he pressed home an unforgivable distance more.

She gasped, overwrought, gorged.

He whispered, "Jesus," in mystification and wonder.

But a heartbeat later, he took a deep breath and shook off his momentary delirium because he wasn't a romantic, this wasn't about anything but physical sensation, and he was long past mystical wonder. Resuming the smooth ebb and flow of his lower body, he did what he'd come here to do, expertly, methodically, with unimpeachable finesse.

Wrapping her arms around his neck, Zelda met his provocative rhythm, and as Alec drove in and slid out with deft, glossy ease, her world increasingly narrowed to raw feeling and prurient craving.

Very soon, he was only half aware of her, absorbed instead in the flesh-on-flesh physicality, in his driving, hotspur lust, in the shocking degree of pleasure bombarding his senses. Surprised and astonished, dazzled by the fierceness of his carnal response, he wondered if she was *indeed* a witch because none of this extravagant sensation fell within the normal range of his amorous adventures.

Simultaneously, Zelda was wondering if one could actually die of bliss. She was quivering, engulfed in a sea of indescribable sexual desire, adrift in a storm of longing, powerless against the violent, insistent, rising desperation that throbbed and swelled inside her. Hot, frenzied, blissfully glutted at the extremity of each plunging downstroke, she was frantically approaching orgasmic fever pitch.

He instinctively recognized her breathy little whimpers, the sudden tension in her body, and forced himself to concentrate on the mundane practicalities rather than the possibility of sorcery at play. And a moment later as her whimpers turned into explosive little cries, he politely suspended the rhythm of thrust and withdrawal, held his rigid cock hard against her womb, and felt her first small tremors begin.

He smiled faintly as her screams rose unchecked and she clung to him as she climaxed as if he were her lifeline in a storm, her orgasmic cries escalating to a charmingly dynamic pitch. Sorceress or not, he found her untrammeled sexual enthusiasm enchanting. Furthermore, the lady had climaxed in what was, even to his profligate history, record time. How delightful in terms of the remainder of the night.

But then she rode that way, too—hell-for-leather.

For a fleeting moment he debated climaxing with her. But ever practical and experienced, he curbed his libido and, tightly lodged in her succulent body, politely waited for the lady's orgasm to wane.

He glanced at the clock only once as he waited, and when Zelda finally opened her eyes, he smiled. "You're fast."

Reaching up, she trailed a light, brushing caress down his cheek. "And you're very good. Thank you. That was lovely."

"But not quite enough, I'd guess," he softly said.

Her eyes were a deep heliotrope in the dimness and suddenly wide with surprise. "I didn't think you meant it. About having as many orgasms as I want."

"I wouldn't have said it unless I meant it."

A faint smile lifted the corners of her mouth. "So *that's* why all the ladies are in hot pursuit. I thought it was for less unusual reasons."

"It's not unusual for me."

Her smile widened. "I'm awestruck, Dalgliesh."

"Alec."

"Alec," she said half under her breath, starting to tremble again, the thought of such largesse as tantalizing as his hard prick moving and swelling inside her. "If you don't mind then," she said with a small catch in her breath as he shifted his hips. "It's been quite a while."

He wanted to ask, *How long?* but he didn't because it shouldn't matter. That it did, he chose to ignore. "I don't mind at all. Tell me when you've had enough"—he grinned—"and I'll probably stop."

An amused delight animated her gaze. "You're every woman's dream. As for the stopping"—she smiled faintly—"I'm not sure I'm in the mood."

"Lucky me," he murmured. And he set out to please her and, ultimately, himself. No emotional involvement was required—only an expertise he'd first acquired as a youth from the duchess on a neighboring estate whose husband was much too old for his twenty-five-year-old wife. In subsequent years, he'd perfected his sexual talents to a fine art, which accounted in part for his popularity with the ladies.

Since Miss MacKenzie wanted orgasms, it wasn't a question of acrobatics at this stage but instead a matter of positioning his rock-hard cock in exactly the right place enough times to hear that little fierce gasp so familiar to a man of his experience. With a well-honed, meticulous precision and extreme courtesy, with sweet kisses and, more importantly, an indefatigable erection, he brought the lady to climax multiple times in an amazingly short interval. She was prodigiously orgasmic—a fact he'd suspected from the moment they'd met. Having pleasantly confirmed his opinion, he now only awaited her satisfaction and, after that, his.

Her hands were strong, her grip unyielding on his back, her legs wrapped around his waist at times or pulled up to her hips other times to allow him deeper penetration. For perhaps fifteen minutes, she assuaged her lust like some goddess with a hardworking acolyte at her command. And like an imperious deity, she unabashedly made use of her virile attendant and his sturdy cock.

Until finally, she threw her arms wide, uncurled her legs

from his hips, lay sprawled beneath him, lithesome, graceful, breathing hard, and smiling. "You're released . . . from
your duties . . . my darling Dalgliesh," she panted.

She'd apparently reached her limit.

But he didn't move.

He wasn't that unselfish.

He did ask though, polite and gracious, "You're sure now?"

After a protracted moment, she languidly lifted her gaze.
"I'm very sure. And thank you again."

He found her simple frankness charming. Different from
the usual flattery that always smacked of pretense. "You're
welcome," he said with well-bred grace, as if he were
exchanging courtesies after a game of croquet, as if his
massive erection wasn't stretching her sleek tissue taut.

She smiled. "Your endurance is impressive, but please
be my guest. You've been more than patient."

"In that case," he replied with an answering smile, "I've
been thinking about this since morning." With masterful
strength and smooth dexterity, he rolled on his back without
dislodging his cock and helped her sit up. Adjusting her
position on his thighs, his huge penis solidly embedded in
her slick warmth, he ran his hands over her hips in a light,
proprietary gesture. "I've been wondering if you could ride
my cock as well as you ride your blue roan." Raising his
hips along with her weight, he slid off his trousers and
underwear and kicked them aside. "There, that's better." He
grinned. "I didn't dare disturb your concentration before."

"How considerate." Bending, she kissed his smiling
mouth. "You're really quite exceptional, you know," she
murmured, sitting up again. "I must return the favor."

He flexed his hips lightly and felt her body softly yield.
"It shouldn't be a problem. I'm already feeling immensely
favored."

His pearl studs on his shirtfront gleamed with his movement and she lifted her brows. "No diamond studs?" She
hadn't noticed before, intent on other things. "You of all
people. I'm surprised."

"Do you like diamonds?" A sudden coolness had entered his voice.

She laughed. "So cynical, Dalgliesh. I don't want your diamonds. You know what I want."

He grinned. "Where have you been all my life?"

"Waiting for this." She touched him where their bodies met.

"Perfect." Thinking the gods were definitely looking on him with favor tonight, he lightly gripped the outside flare of her thighs, and thrust upward, forcing her wider, filling her completely, utterly, to the limit.

Then—with consummate grace—a modicum past the limit.

She shut her eyes—the sensations excruciatingly fine, the pressure compelling, ravishing, the sense of powerlessness she felt with his hands holding her firmly, perversely satisfying.

"There, there, relax . . ."

His voice reached her through a hot haze of desire, and it took a moment before she opened her eyes, before she'd recovered enough to whisper, "I may not survive the night."

"Of course you will." He spoke softly, gently stroked her legs, soothing her, calming her. "We'll take our time."

"Such assurance. I won't ask you how you know."

And he had no intention of telling her. "Trust me, you'll be fine."

She smiled. "What I don't know, you can teach me."

"That's not necessary. Believe me, you can do no wrong."

"At least I know how to ride." And with that smiling statement, she gracefully rose to her knees, hovered for a fraction of a second on the very crest of his erection before lowering herself again in a warm, silken flow that added a new dimension to his memory of lascivious sensation. He dragged in air through his teeth as she repeated the exercise, his nerves jolted by ravishing, agonizing shock waves. When she came to rest a second later, fully impaled on his cock, he shut his eyes and gave himself up to her slow, languorous rhythm, each gliding, tantalizing skin-on-skin ascent and descent blazing a new fiery trail to Nirvana.

Her exquisitely accommodating rise and fall was facile and fluid, her thighs strong, her sleek vaginal muscles toned, resilient, forceful, and before long, Alec found himself resentfully wondering what it had taken to develop those muscles. This from a man who liked supple women who knew how to use their bodies. This from a man who'd always preferred sexually proficient females.

"You're not paying attention." He'd missed a beat.

"The part that matters is paying attention," he said, his eyes half shut. "Don't stop."

"You're not in a position to give orders right now," she playfully murmured.

He opened his eyes fully. "What if I wanted to be?" His voice was suddenly softly speculative, his gaze less so, brute temptation rising unchecked. "Take charge, as it were. Of you."

She smiled. "By all means—do."

His engorged penis surged higher as if already given leave to take what liberties he wished. Her soft groan in response was gratifying and familiar. "You like hard cock, don't you?" But his voice was taut, sullen. How many men had heard that soft, sensual groan, had stood stud for her, had been offered carte blanche?

She moved her hips in a faint rotation, measuring the towering grandeur inside her. "Shouldn't I?" She smiled. "Surely, you of all people shouldn't be questioning female arousal."

"I'm not." A blatant mendacity. Raising his hands, he cupped the plump weight of her resplendent breasts and struggled against a rash need to exert his authority, to mark her somehow as his. Fighting the urge to ruthlessly crush the soft flesh in his hands out of some inexcusable anger over something that shouldn't matter, he gruffly said, "Show me what else you like. Entertain me."

It was impossible to overlook the umbrage in his voice. "I'm sure your repertoire is more extensive than mine," she said, not sure she dared smile, although she found his sulkiness appealing. "But I'd be happy to try entertaining you because I'm very pleased you're here." Rising smoothly to her knees, she slid her finger down his slippery cock. "And mostly here," she added, plunging downward again, shuddering as her bottom met his thighs and their bodies were irresistibly joined.

It only took a moment to erase the unwanted images of other men enjoying her largesse. He was a sensible man. "Yes, definitely there." But still troubled by his mad, unconscionable passion for this woman, by his outrageous cravings, his voice held a hint of curtness. "Now a little more speed, my pet, or I might decide to leave."

She knew he wouldn't. She knew he could no more leave than she could. But he'd given her so much already tonight, given her countless orgasms with exquisite artistry and skill and courtesy she could do no less for him.

He didn't last very long after that.

And she wondered if he was so expert that he could come at will. Whatever the reason, he said, "Thank you," through gritted teeth a few moments later, lifted her off him, and climaxed in his shirttails with a kind of efficiency she found strangely annoying. When it shouldn't matter in the least. When they were both here for casual sex. When neither wanted anything more.

Correction. The Earl of Dalgliesh inexplicably wanted to possess her body and soul, own her completely, not let another man touch her. He wanted her with a blind rage and with an undemanding tenderness, and he could never have her that way or any way.

He was married.

He had responsibilities.

It was impossible.

CHAPTER 8

DALGLIESH HAD ROLLED off the bed so quickly after he'd climaxed Zelda was tempted to teasingly say, *Was I that bad?* But clearly he wasn't in a playful mood; he was obviously determined to resist further dalliance. And while she sympathized with his wish to avoid entanglements, self-ishly, she preferred he wait a few more hours before he reverted to type. "Don't leave just yet," she said, her voice deliberately mild, well mannered. "Please."

Dalgliesh was stripping off his soiled shirt, and once his head emerged from the garment, he said without looking at her, "I shouldn't have come."

"But now that you're here, why not—"

"No." Dropping his shirt, he reached for his trousers.

Zelda's lounging pose altered at the sight of his tautly muscled body on full display. She'd not seen him completely naked before. He was magnificent—like a gladiator from ancient times, she thought, coming up on her elbows to better take in the bonny sight. His tall, broad-shouldered form was honed to the inch, a hard, tensile energy and brute force conspicuous beneath the perfect conditioning.

His dark skin was even darker in the checkered light, his rough-hewn strength enhanced by the gloom, the raw, primal image stark—as if a barbarian had entered her bedchamber, or perhaps the devil in disguise or maybe only an archetypical libertine with an indefatigable cock.

Not that conjecture or cerebral concerns mattered in the least with lust flaring through her senses, ungovernable desire beating at her brain, Dalgliesh's magnificent erection, splendid in profile, tantalizing her gaze. "Please, I'm without pride," she whispered. "Don't go. I *need* you."

He turned, his dark brows drawn together in a slash of discontent. "Sorry, I can't help you."

"Why not? I only want a few more hours of your time."

"My time?" Mocking and truculent, he slid one leg into his trousers.

"You know what I mean." Sitting up, she slipped off the bed and moved toward him because she couldn't bear to let him go without at least trying to dissuade him.

"Look, this was a mistake." He thrust his other leg into his trousers and jerked them up at her approach, as if shielding himself from temptation.

"Do I frighten you that much?" She gazed up at him from very close range.

"Yes." He took a step back.

"What can I say to change your mind?"

He surveyed her lush, shapely form—a swift, expressionless glance. "Nothing. You're too tempting, that's all." He finished buttoning his trousers.

"It's only sex," she softly said.

"That's the problem. It isn't." He wanted to fuck her until he couldn't fuck anymore, and then he wanted to fuck her some more.

"It *could* be only sex."

"I'm leaving in the morning." He reached for his coat. "Did I mention that?"

"No." Her heart began beating wildly. "Why?"

"Violetta. Why else?" he said, sliding his arms into the coat sleeves. "I'm taking Chris with me."

"If we won't be seeing each other again, surely you can stay a little longer." She marveled that she could speak so calmly when she felt as though she were falling off the ends of the earth.

"Jesus, will you stop?" But his erection was throbbing with every beat of his heart, and he saw her glance at the obvious bulge in his trousers.

"Perhaps he wouldn't mind staying."

"I'm years past such juvenile impulses," he growled.

"May I touch him then?"

"No." He took another step back.

She followed him that time, reached up to lightly run her fingertips down his throat, and when he sucked in his breath, she slid her hand lower, over the crisp, dark hair on his chest, the hard, ridged contours of his stomach, the dip of his navel, stopping for a moment on the trouser button at his waist before beginning to slide it free.

"Don't." He brushed her hand away. "I'm not looking for any more problems in my life," he said, his voice softly caustic. "And you're a problem."

"I won't be I promise. It's only sex, *only* that. In the morning you're free of me. Please stay."

He still hadn't moved.

She was encouraged enough to slide her hands inside his open coat, twine her arms around his waist, lean into his tense body, and glancing up past his rigid jaw, offer him a small smile. "I'm without artifice, if that helps. I only want . . . him," she said, moving her hips faintly to underscore her statement.

For a lengthy interval he didn't breathe, every muscle and sinew in his body taut with restraint, self-denial contesting gut-wrenching desire. When his lungs were beginning to hurt from the strain, he finally exhaled. Then without legitimate excuse or justification, without so much as a modicum of logic or reason, he said, "You win." His gaze narrowed. "But I leave at first light."

"Yes, yes, whatever you say." Her smile was bright with

joy, and pulling his head down, she kissed him in exultation. "You won't be sorry," she whispered, releasing him, beginning to slide his coat from his shoulders. "You may order me about at will."

"Christ, don't say that." He lifted his hand in a small wordless gesture of futility. "I'm already out of control."

"We both are. If you hadn't come, I would have found you, so don't talk to me about control. And I never prowl the hallways looking for a bed partner—a particular bed partner," she amended at his sudden frown. "But I would have tonight, so do me a favor and stop thinking so much." She held out her hand. "Come, I want to feel you inside me for however long you can stay."

A faint smile appeared. "Is that all you want—a five-hour erection? Why didn't you say so?" But he took her hand and brought it to his lips, his gaze amused. "So then," he murmured, his breath warm on her fingertips. "It seems I have my work cut out for me. How would you like it, Miss MacKenzie? Standing, sitting, or lying down?"

"All three."

Sometime later, after being dazzled by Dalgliesh's intemperate inventory of voluptuary sensation, after a particularly intense orgasm that left her light-headed and faint, Zelda lifted her head from his shoulder, slowly raised her eyelids, and expressed amazement in the high arch of her brows. "That was a professional performance."

I know. "You're easy to please," he said instead. "Can you stand or should I carry you to the bed?"

"I consider myself"—she drew in a ragged breath—"very fortunate to have met you. I can stand."

Unwrapping her legs from around his waist, he carefully set her on her feet. "We're both fortunate," he said, dropping a kiss on the bridge of her nose. "Would you like to rest a moment?"

But toward dawn, even two wild, insatiable lovers needed some rest, and lying side by side, they momentarily paused in their exploration of prodigal sensation.

Zelda may have dozed briefly. But he must have sensed her coming awake, even though it was dark, even though she hadn't moved. She'd only opened her eyes.

"Please," he said into the silence. "I dislike pillow talk."

"As do I. I was about to frighten you instead." She felt him stiffen and wondered how many women there had been to so prejudice his response. But a woman who'd braved the jungles of Brazil wasn't easily intimidated. "I just wanted to tell you I think I'm in love. You needn't reply. You're only indirectly involved. Did you sleep?" she asked, as if she'd not uttered the word *love*.

Crisis averted, he softly exhaled. "No, I didn't sleep."

"Do you lie awake often?"

"No, never."

She giggled. "Dare I hope that—"

"No, you may not. And I don't want to talk about that either."

"What if I want to?" She'd never been in love before; the sense of wonder was difficult to ignore.

"Later," he said, and rolling over her, he stopped her from talking in the way he knew best.

But it was different in the end, like it always was with her, the sunny landscape beyond the threshold of that open door luring him on, offering him not only sensual delight but a mystifying happiness. He wouldn't call it love; he was less impetuous or perhaps more cynical. But whatever it was, the concept of a future suddenly held promise when the word had been obliterated from his vocabulary in the last few years, when he'd been living day to day, minute to minute. Without hope.

Head over heels, heedless of logic, Zelda was blissfully steeped in love, the impossibilities muzzled, the world brushed aside, only the presence of the captivating man who dispensed pleasure so effortlessly of any significance. "Tell me we're completely alone in this enchanted universe," she whispered.

He smiled. "Of course. The universe is ours alone."

"Do you believe in fate?"

"I do." Another lie, but the truth wouldn't serve.

She softly laughed. "How glib you are."

"With you, I'm not sure what I am," he said, scrupulously honest in that, at least. Not that nuances of truth mattered with dawn fast approaching. Taking note of the faint light beginning to extinguish the shadows in the room, he said with a novel feeling of regret, "We still have a little time, darling. Kiss me."

CHAPTER 9

HE SHOULD HAVE left long ago. He actually did
once—or nearly did, but Zelda pulled him back. Not that
he needed any persuasion with her warm, welcoming body
the ultimate Nirvana and his libido operating within the
very narrow range of sex, sex, and more sex. When the
meaning of Keats's phrase, "O for a life of sensations rather
than of thoughts!" had been gloriously revealed in all its
sensual manifestations, and he'd not quite had his fill.

"Stay, stay, stay," she'd whisper when he'd contemplate
leaving.

"Give me reason to stay," he'd softly say.

She always did.

She had a fertile imagination.

To which he'd add a refinement or two, his entire nervous
system slave to sensation.

But even hot-blooded lust was ultimately susceptible to
besieging reason, and the increasing sounds of activity in
the hallway gave warning that the household was stirring.
Servants would be knocking on the door shortly, wanting

to light fires and draw baths. Soon the entire house party would be awake.

While Dalgliesh was indifferent to respectability, he knew Zelda was vulnerable to scandal. "I really *have* to go," he finally said, coming up on his elbows, resting his weight on his forearms. "Unless you relish being the titillating topic of conversation at breakfast," he dryly added.

"I'm not sure I care, but yes, yes, go." Zelda reached up to lightly brush the dark stubble on Alec's jaw. "And thank you again, my dear Dalgliesh, for your many and spectacular"— she smiled—"kindnesses."

"My pleasure." But her smile gave rise to an odd rush of unwanted affection and, swiftly withdrawing from her body, he rolled off the bed, putting distance between himself and temptation. Although the sight of Zelda all rosy and pink from lovemaking lying within reach was damned enticing. He drew in a hard breath and spoke with the civility the occasion demanded. "In terms of kindness, darling, you were perfection. I've never enjoyed myself more."

Exquisitely indulged, the sweet, lush afterglow still pulsing through her body, Zelda smiled. "Such a tame word— enjoy . . ."

"Ring the word in diamonds and pearls and trumpet it in the square for all to hear," he said with a grin. "Is that better?"

She laughed. "I didn't know you had a poet's soul."

"And I didn't know you were Circe's sister. You kept me here *much* too long."

"In that case, this must be where I politely say—if you're ever in the Highlands . . ."

"I'll stop by and visit," he smoothly replied, and bending, he kissed her lightly as he would any woman who'd entertained him for the night. But rather than feel the need to escape as was his wont, he found himself reluctant to leave. A circumstance both terrifying and—tantalizing. Although it was pure lunacy to want her still after so many hours of fucking—a total breach of custom and realistically *unac-*

ceptable. Which thought firmly coerced his insubordinate feelings into compliance. "Perhaps I'll come up for salmon fishing next summer," he pleasantly said.

"You'll have excellent fishing." She didn't believe him for a minute.

"I'll bring Chris." Another lie.

"I'd like that." They should have been on stage.

"You should try and get some sleep."

"I couldn't possibly sleep. I'm still blissfully aglow, thanks to you." Zelda languidly stretched, feeling infinitely content, sated, replete. Check off another satisfied conquest for the talented Earl of Dalgliesh, she reflected without malice, relaxing against the pillows as he began gathering his clothes. He was truly talented, with a subtle finesse unusual in a man his size. No wonder he was in demand. "So how did I do?" she playfully queried.

He looked up, his waistcoat dangling from his fingers. "Do?"

She grinned. "Did I meet your expectations?"

His smile was charming and boyish and quite genuine. "You far exceeded my expectations in *every* way."

He didn't ask her whether he'd met her expectations, she noticed. But then he no doubt knew from considerable experience that he had. "Will you stay at your hunting lodge long?" His smile vanished so swiftly, she was tempted to say something outlandish. "I was only making conversation," she remarked, deciding to behave. "You needn't take alarm."

"Then, no, I won't be staying long." But his voice held a palpable reserve, as if he'd learned to be wary of women asking questions.

"I'm off to France next week for more hunting." That should calm his fears.

"Where?" His clothes gathered, he was swiftly dressing.

"Fontainebleau."

"Excellent coursing ground. You should have some good riding." At which point, adept at morning-after small talk, Dalgliesh turned the conversation to safe topics like horses and hunting.

Zelda understood the protocol; she carried her part with

equal politesse. But she couldn't deny the fact that Dalgliesh intrigued her. A shame he was unavailable.

Although, he *had* sought her out last night, when, by his own admission, he would have preferred remaining aloof. He'd also stayed much longer than he'd wished. Was it possible she'd engaged his interest beyond the ordinary?

Might she enjoy his incredible talents again?

Alas—his reputation suggested otherwise.

"Lost in thought?"

She looked up to find the earl standing at the bedside, dressed, or more aptly, semidressed, with his shirt unusable, his waistcoat stuffed in his pants' pocket, his shoes in hand, and a polite smile on his handsome face. She grinned. "Yes, and you don't want to know."

Her reply set off warning bells. "Then I'll thank you again for a lovely evening and take my leave."

"It *was* rather splendid, wasn't it? My compliments, Dalgliesh, on your competence."

He grinned. "Pleased to be of service." With a dip of his head, he turned and strode away.

Damn, damn, damn. An overwhelming sense of loss washed over her. She felt bereft, as if some sweet magic had eluded her, when plainly no magic was involved, only the Earl of Dalgliesh's glorious cock, unrivaled skill, and stamina. *For heaven's sake, get a grip,* she charged her errant emotions. *It's only sex.*

But her heart leaped as he paused at the door.

He'd already turned the knob, releasing the bolt from the strike plate—a slight tug was all that was required. *Do it!* the voice inside his head commanded. A second passed. *Don't be a fool! Open the door!* But he didn't and another second elapsed, a third . . .

As the silence lengthened, a servant's giggle in the hallway outside was magnified in the hushed room. A mounting tension filled the air.

Zelda opened her mouth to speak, thought better of it. Dalgliesh was unlikely to respond to a woman's plea.

Restless, his nerves raw, Alec fought against an unspeakable lust that had taken up occupation in his brain and wouldn't be evicted. Wouldn't respond to reason or sanity, or calls to conscience and duty.

He swung around, patent repulsion on his face. "You *must* be a witch, damn you!" His gaze was fierce, sullen. "I always look *forward* to leaving after—"

"A night of fucking?" She could be rude, too.

He scowled. "Call it what you like."

"You know what I'd like to call it, but you wouldn't approve." Although perhaps she wasn't alone in her obsession, she thought—Dalgliesh's black look aside. "Look," she said, trying to mitigate what could only be an embarrassing revelation for a man like Dalgliesh, "I'm as mystified as you about this—us—this curious predicament."

"Predicament?" His expression was contemptuous. "You're fucking up my life!"

"I could say the same of you," she tartly retorted. "I'm not in the habit of dissolving into a puddle of love just because I've had incredible sex. I'm not that scatterbrained. As a matter of fact, I'm not scatterbrained at all."

"You've had incredible sex before?" he growled.

"Are you even listening?"

"Have you?" Edgy and querulous.

She came up on her elbows, her scowl matching his. "Not this good. You're the best. Satisfied?"

Restive and disturbed, his mind in tumult, he didn't answer. "I've never had anything like this happen to me." His voice was harsh with disgust. "Never."

"Feeling something beyond lust, you mean."

He couldn't pretend not to know what she meant. "Yes," he muttered. "That."

"You're not alone, if it's any consolation."

He stared at her, moody and obstinate. "I'm not looking for consolation. I'm looking for a way out."

"Then you should go."

"Damn right I should."

She sat up in a surge of temper. "I have no intention of begging you to stay, if that's what you want," she snapped.

"A pity," he drawled.

"Life is full of disappointments."

"Spiteful bitch." Amusement suddenly glittered in his eyes and his mouth twitched. "Christ Almighty—what am I going to do with you?"

"You seemed to know what to do last night. So many times I lost count."

He didn't speak for so long she thought she'd been too flippant.

Breathing quietly, his feelings locked away, he stared at her.

She stared back, never self-effacing or timid, too long a woman of independence to give way to a man. Also, the view was particularly fine, if truth be told.

Dalgliesh was leaning against the door, barefoot, bare chested, sleepy eyed, his dark hair disheveled, his state of undress testament to a night of excess.

A powerful, unmistakable sensuality marking the man.

A quiet authority as well.

As if he knew he had but to beckon and she'd come.

He adjusted his shoulders slightly against the solid door, a small compensatory gesture perhaps to offset his irresolution. Then, deaf to reason and intellect, he gave voice to his capricious will. "So . . . what are we going to do?"

Tamping down her wild jubilation, Zelda forced herself to speak calmly. "We?"

He looked startled, as if she'd coined a new word, as if he'd not uttered the pronoun seconds before. "Did I say that?"

She smiled. "I'm afraid so."

"Christ, I'm losing my mind." Dropping his shoes, he pushed away from the door, crossed the room with his long, easy stride and, reaching the bed, stood motionless for a moment, thoughtfully regarding her.

Unnerved by his scrutiny, she felt a sudden compulsion to clarify her position. "I'm not asking for anything beyond simple sex."

He smiled. "Or not so simple. But yes, I know."

"Stay or go. It's up to you."

"I know that, too."

She gazed up at him, her violet eyes guileless. "I shouldn't have mentioned the word *love*. It was stupid, like your—"

"*That's* not up for discussion."

"Well, neither is love from now on. How's that? Better?"

"Fuck if I know," he said when his idea of *better* had to do with Zelda locked away in his bedroom at Crosstrees until he fucked himself to death. Deprived of that option, shackled in a vicious marriage, frustrated and resentful, tantalized beyond sanity, he abruptly leaned over and, gripping her shoulders, revolted against circumstance. His kiss was vastly different this time—not casual, but fierce, deep, his hands on her shoulders leaving bruises, a kind of desperation fueling his ardor. Abruptly shoving her onto her back, he followed her down, forcing her thighs wider, settling between her outstretched legs, his erection insistent and hard, his mouth ungentle, his brute urgency redress for the anarchy savaging his brain. "Can you feel this?" he growled against her mouth, grinding his trousered cock against her sex. "Tell me."

"Yes, yes . . ." Sliding her fingers through his thick hair, she whispered, "It's heavenly." Zelda welcomed his wildness, her own passions unrestrained and explosive, all the insuperable difficulties momentarily effaced by flame-hot lust and forbidden love. By the feel of him in her arms, the sweet taste of him on her lips, his desperate wanting heady and provocative—like a powerful drug coursing through her veins.

And as always, swift and predictable, as if he was her aphrodisiac of choice, soon—headlong and impatient—nothing mattered but orgasmic fulfillment.

Her familiar small whimper was a stark clarion call to sanity, the sound jolting Alec back to harsh reality, reminding him of what she wanted, of what he mustn't do. Of the price he'd eventually pay for ruining her life—and his. Jerking upright, he leaped from the bed.

"Damn you!" Zelda shrieked, lunging for him, missing as he sprang away. "Don't you dare leave me like this!"

"Jesus, hush!" He shot a glance at the door, half expecting someone to come running.

"I'll scream if I want," she hissed.

"I shouldn't have—" *Spoken to you yesterday, followed you at the hunt, come anywhere near you.*

"But you did, you did, you *did*, damn you! Oh God, oh God . . ." Falling back in a sprawl, flushed, nude, shuddering, she shut her eyes briefly against the violent, throbbing ache pulsing between her legs.

"I'm sorry." His voice was low, tormented. "But the servants are everywhere," he said, trying to sound reasonable. Making excuses.

"Lock the door."

"Lady Melville may have heard you." He wasn't sure Zelda cared; he'd have to care for both of them. "She thrives on scandal."

"Screw Lady Melville."

"I don't believe that's possible," he drawled. "I have my standards."

Zelda giggled. "Oh hell," she muttered, pushing herself up against the pillows. "You've talked me out of it now."

"I have others to consider or I wouldn't have to talk you out of anything," Alec gently said, relieved and not relieved, his brain in chaos. "Unfortunately my life is—" At a loss for words, he half lifted his hand.

"What it is. I understand." Her smile was properly agreeable; she had no claim on his time or person. "Although you've seriously disrupted my life, too." Her smile widened. "Perhaps witchcraft is involved after all."

"Or fairy dust," he said with a faint grin.

"Better yet," she lightly replied, conscious of the obligatory civilities, of men wanting to leave and women left behind. Of the inherent inequities in amorous liaisons. Particularly with a man like Dalgliesh.

"Perhaps we'll meet at another hunt," Alec said, not inclined to prolong the misery.

"I'm sure we will." She felt as though someone else was mouthing the lie—someone more gullible.

"Then I'll say au revoir rather than good-bye."

"Yes, au revoir." She was as capable of good manners as he.

It was over, she thought, watching him walk away.

Another brief flirtation for an unprincipled, wildly adept lover of women.

It was a form of sport for him.

While she wasn't sure she'd ever be the same, if such absurdities actually existed beyond the perimeters of poetic license.

He abruptly stopped midway to the door, and her breath caught in her throat. She watched him slowly turn. She watched his nostrils flare as he drew in a deep breath. She watched him slowly exhale, her heart beating like a drum.

"Come with me to Crosstrees."

His voice was so low she had to strain to hear it. "Are you sure?" *Good Lord, since when was she a martyr?*

"No, does it matter?"

"Not to me," she quickly replied, feeling very unmartyr-like, feeling as though the world was suddenly bathed in eternal sunshine. "I might have come anyway."

She saw the flickering surprise, then the shuttered look, and knew she'd made a mistake.

"On second thought, it's probably not a good idea," he coolly said.

"Am I allowed to disagree?" He didn't answer for so long, she almost blurted out, *Please, please, please let me come!*

A protracted silence ensued while Dalgliesh debated the pressures of his domestic affairs against the rash impulse prompting him to invite a woman he barely knew to his hunting box. Crosstrees had always been his refuge from the world, far from pursuing females and contentiousness. On the other hand, he told himself, rather than admit to anything more, sex with the fascinating Miss MacKenzie— pursuing or not—was powerful incentive. "Oh, hell," he finally said, "I'd like you to come."

She couldn't say, *I know.* "I was hoping you'd change your mind," she mildly replied, not wishing to alarm him again.

He laughed. "You would have come with or without an invitation, wouldn't you?"

"I'm not sure. Probably not. Although"—she smiled—"you're much too accomplished to willingly relinquish after one night."

His teeth flashed white in a smile. "So I'm to serve as stud until you're sated."

"If it wouldn't be too much of an imposition."

He hesitated, habits of a lifetime difficult to ignore. "No," he said somberly, "you're no imposition. But"—his gaze clouded over again—"Chris comes first."

"Of course. I'll stay out of sight if you prefer."

"God no. He likes you. I heard nothing but boyish adulation after you left the kitchen."

"Well then, I'll be on my best behavior."

"And I'll be on my best behavior in bed."

She smiled. "There's no need for you to behave."

"I didn't mean *that*."

"Oh good, because I'm quite looking forward to whatever *that* entails."

"Christ, stop or I won't leave, and we'll scandalize everyone by not coming downstairs for a week. Consider, darling," he warned, "I'm long past redemption. You might prefer less notoriety."

"I may not care."

"Your father might," he drily said. "Now then"—his voice took on a crispness—"why don't I have John stay behind to escort you to Crosstrees." He smiled, affable and at ease, the vexing issues having been cavalierly set aside. "I look forward to showing you my stables."

She had what she wanted. She was more than willing to accommodate Dalgliesh's change of subject. "Are you leaving soon?"

"As soon as I change clothes and thank Fitz for his hospitality. Don't worry, I won't mention you."

"I'm not worried. Say what you like. Or would you rather be discreet?"

"It might be wise, not for my sake but for yours. Violetta can be vindictive."

"In that case, I'll concoct some story for public consumption. As for Papa, I'll tell him the truth. He understands my life's my own."

"Would you like me to speak to your father?" Good God, what was he thinking?

"How sweet," she murmured. "But unnecessary."

"Because you do this often?"

His scowl was back in place; she found it quite charming. "No, because I never do this. Papa'll be pleased I'm enjoying myself."

"Forgive me. That was uncalled for."

"I like your jealousy."

The word shocked him, but before he could think of a reasonable reply, the redoubtable Miss MacKenzie rose from the bed like Venus rising from the sea and sent shock waves through his nerve endings.

"I suggest you leave, darling," she said with a flicker of a smile. "Or I might be tempted to make you stay."

Fuck if she couldn't, he thought, surveying her voluptuous form that he'd tasted, caressed, screwed every imaginable way. He shot a glance at the clock on the mantle.

She noticed and opening her arms, playfully winked. "Staying or going?"

"Why don't you breakfast at Crosstrees instead?" he silkily replied. "We won't be interrupted."

"Is that what you'd like?" A honeyed tone, a gentle sway of her hips.

Her plump breasts quivered with the movement, his randy cock swelled higher, and lust took on a powerful life of its own. "Don't play the tease," he said, raspy and low. "Or I'll carry you out of the house like that."

"You wouldn't," she nervously said.

"In a minute."

Her sportive intent gave way before Dalgliesh's cool gaze, and a second later he heard the key turn in the bathroom lock.

Good idea, he thought.

He stood motionless for a few moments, allowing his erection to subside enough to traverse the halls without calling attention to himself. Or calling undue attention. His state of undress was likely to attract notice.

As luck would have it, he reached his room without meeting anyone save a few servants who knew better than to stare. After bathing and dressing, he went in search of his host.

Dalgliesh found Fitz alone in the breakfast room reading the morning paper, a cup of coffee at his elbow.

Fitz looked up as the earl walked in; he set aside his paper. "You're up early. Or knowing you, you probably haven't slept."

"As a matter of fact, I haven't." Alec moved toward the buffet. "Thanks to kind fate."

"Fate?" Disbelief colored the duke's tone.

"Why so amazed?" Alec said over his shoulder.

"Because I've known you a long time," Fitz bluntly retorted. "You don't believe in fate."

"People change." The earl turned from the buffet with a cup in one hand and a coffeepot in the other. "Myself included."

"Indeed," Fitz murmured. "Does this fate of yours have a name?"

Alec grinned. "So cynical, my friend." Reaching the table, he set down the coffeepot.

"Realistic," Fitz drawled. "If you recall, I changed your seat for dinner. You also disappeared rather early. Claremont was hoping for a high-stakes game."

"Then I saved him some money," Alec blandly remarked, dropping into a chair. "I'm sure his father's grateful."

Fitz watched the earl fill a cup, quickly drain it like a man requiring sustenance, refill it, and repeat the process. "Why don't I have a servant bring you some food?" The duke waved to summon one of the many footmen lining the walls.

Alec put up a hand to forestall him. "I'm having breakfast at Crosstrees."

"You're leaving?"

"Yes. Change of plans."

"Will your wife take issue?"

"She already has."

The duke's brows rose. "Violetta jealous? I'm surprised."

"Not as surprised as I." Dalgliesh pushed his empty cup aside in a small, restless gesture. "Since Violetta enjoys scenes and I don't, I'm leaving to avoid any public spectacles."

Fitz looked amused. "You're not leaving alone, I presume."

"No, Chris will join me."

"Not Zelda?"

Dalgliesh shot him a startled look.

"Your pursuit of her last night was rather blatant," Fitz pointed out. "Why don't I make some excuse to the others for you two?"

"For my part I'd say yes, but I'm not sure what Zelda wants said. She's rather cavalier about this." Alec frowned. "Is she always so . . . well—independent?"

"Jamie knows her much better than I, but to my knowledge, her independence, as you put it, doesn't generally extend to licentiousness. Is that what you wanted to know?"

"Christ," the earl grunted, sliding lower in his chair. "Am I that transparent?"

"Out of character, I'd say. But then Zelda's an amazing woman."

Dalgliesh's gaze took on a sudden belligerence. "How the hell would you know?"

"Relax. Jamie's her cousin. He's talked about her." If Fitz didn't know better, he might have thought Dalgliesh was actually emotionally involved with the lovely Zelda. But past history rather put that notion to rest.

"Forgive me for taking offense, but I'm obsessed at the moment. Don't look at me like that. I find it incomprehensible, too. With luck, the feeling will quickly pass."

"It generally does," Fitz urbanely said. "But I wish you joy in the interim. There's pleasure in that kind of madness.

As for your and Zelda's departure, I believe I'll plead ignorance."

Alec grinned. "Always a safe choice." Sitting upright, he pushed his chair away from the table. "I'm off," he said, coming to his feet. "Zelda will follow with John. She's promised to help teach Chris how to jump his pony."

"There's no one better. She's a spectacular rider."

"Yes," Dalgliesh softly said. "She is indeed. Quite spectacular." His brief reverie gave way to the matters at hand, and his voice took on a brisk cadence. "Thank you again. Stop by and see us, if you like. You, Oz, Jamie, your families. I've ponies for the children and my kitchen knows how to accommodate a child's palate. Anytime after tomorrow." He grinned. "For completely selfish reasons, of course." Then, with a farewell wave, he turned and walked away.

Dalgliesh's good cheer was conspicuous, Fitz thought, watching him with a contemplative gaze, intrigued by the astonishing reversal in the earl's behavior. He'd used the word *us*. This from a man who generally viewed women with casual indifference, the world with qualified reserve, and relationships with abhorrence. And he wasn't averse to entertaining with his newest inamorata at his side. Children included. Interesting. Amazing really.

It might be wise to avoid Violetta this morning.

CHAPTER 10

ZELDA FOUND HER father in the stable yard where his favorite hunter was being saddled. Sir Gavin was chatting with the duke's stud manager, himself a Scots, a brilliant trainer, and long a friend of the family.

Greetings were exchanged, the weather and the merits of Sir Gavin's mount were briefly discussed, and just as Zelda was about to ask her father for a moment alone, Smythson was called away. Taking her father by the arm, Zelda nodded to the stable lad saddling Golden Turk. "We'll be right back," she said and drew her father away.

As they exited the bustling yard where the work of readying the score or more horses needed for the hunt was in full swing, Sir Gavin shot his daughter a sidelong glance. "You're not hunting today, I gather." Zelda wore a black riding habit, a homburg over her fiery hair that was bound at her nape, and low boots without spurs.

"No, not today."

"But you're going riding." His brows rose. "Surely not in that?" A riding habit required a sidesaddle.

Zelda twitched the hem of her skirt aside enough to show

her deerskin breeches. "I've not lost all reason," she said with a smile. "I'm just choosing to be a little less conspicuous."

Sir Gavin scrutinized his daughter's face, wondering why she was suddenly concerned with drawing attention, wondering as well why she was forgoing a hunt when she rarely did. "Come, my dear, what's this all about?" he quietly said. "Are you avoiding Dalgliesh this morning? Is that why you're not hunting? If he did something to displease you, I'll—"

"No, Papa." Zelda came to a stop. "On the contrary. I've been invited to Crosstrees."

"Ah." Sir Gavin frowned faintly. "You might want to think twice before involving yourself with a man like Dalgliesh. Rumor has it he's left a number of broken hearts in his wake—if not more significant problems," he cryptically added.

Did that mean Dalgliesh's comment about giving her a baby was commonplace? Did it matter? "I can take care of myself, Papa. Dalgliesh, no matter his disreputable ways, is less dangerous than trekking into the wilds of the world. And I'm going eyes wide open," she added for good measure, her father's voiced concern unusual. "It's a lark, no more."

His expression lightened. "I suppose you know what you're doing. You've always been an adventuresome lass with courage to spare. Ye might need it with yon earl," he added in a muted tone, lapsing into a brogue as he often did when in doubt.

"No, I won't."

"That may be, but dinna forget—should ye need my help, ye have but to ask."

"He's not an ogre, Papa."

"Nor is he saintlike and heaven born, lass."

She softly sighed. "Please, I'm not fifteen. Nor even twenty."

"I'm done, lass." Sir Gavin smiled. "Ye're like your mother. She always knew what she wanted, too. I was lucky she wanted me," he softly added. "But remember"—a sudden briskness entered his tone—"your brothers and I are always there for ye."

"I don't need protection, Papa. Really, I don't."

"Ah, weel, ye niver know. Dalgliesh's wife came up to me after dinner last night. Unpleasant woman," he murmured. "She mentioned something about her son." Sir Gavin held Zelda's gaze for a moment. "I wouldna let her get too near, lass. She's a might unreliable," he added in casual understatement. "Now then, do ye want me to make your excuses? Easy enough for me to do."

"I already spoke to Fitz and thanked him." She'd stopped in the breakfast room before coming out to the stables.

"Ah, then ye have yourself a nice time, lass. Dalgliesh is a damn sight better than most Anglo-Scots, I'll give him that. And he handles a horse with the best o' them."

The ultimate praise from her father. "I agree. And it's just a short holiday. I won't be gone long."

Sir Gavin acknowledged his daughter's rejoinder with an indulgent smile. "Ye always were a sensible lass."

Zelda grinned. "Someone had to be."

Lightly grasping Zelda's shoulder, he opened his mouth to speak, then shut it, and awkwardly patted her shoulder instead. "Mind you don't take any high fences now, lass." Which was as close to expressing affection as Sir Gavin was capable.

"I won't."

"Ye'll stay in touch."

"Of course. You should have good hunting today. The weather's pleasant at least." Zelda glanced at his waiting mount. "Golden Turk looks ready to run."

"Ay, he's fit and fine drawn. But we'll miss ye, lass."

"I won't think of you—not once," Zelda teasingly replied.

Sir Gavin laughed. "And so it should be, lass. You're young and bonny and full of life."

JOHN HAD BEEN waiting across the stable yard, watching the pair. When Zelda walked away from her father, he followed at a discreet distance, coming up behind her only as she approached the house. "Miss MacKenzie?"

Zelda turned and smiled. "You must be John."

"Yes, miss. I just wanted to let you know that your roan is saddled and waiting."

"Thank you. I'll have my luggage brought down."

"A trap's ready at the side entrance. One of the stable lads will drive it over. Would you like me to wait for you at the house or the stables?"

"The stables, I think." She preferred not attracting Violetta's notice. Although she suspected Dalgliesh's wife was a late riser.

"Very good, miss. If you like, I could wait behind the yard and we could ride cross-country to the lodge."

"Excellent. Give me ten minutes or so." She was hoping Rosalind had come downstairs. She'd like to thank her as well.

"Take your time, miss. It's a short ride."

The breakfast room was astir, those guests planning to hunt having their morning repast. Standing for a moment at the entrance to the room, Zelda perused the crowd, searching for Rosalind. Fitz saw her and waved. She returned his smile and wave, but with no glimpse of Rosalind, she turned to leave.

And almost walked into Oz.

He caught her by the shoulders, steadying her. "I was expecting you to go the other way." He dropped his hands and took a step back.

"I'm afraid I was lost in thought. It's too early." She smiled. "Or at least that's my excuse."

"Always a good one," Oz blandly remarked, rather than comment on her sleepless night; he'd briefly spoken to Fitz earlier and heard of Dalgliesh's radical transformation. "Have you breakfasted? Would you like company if you haven't? Or do you prefer solitude in the morning?"

"I don't. But I'm breakfasting later."

"Ah—I see." He shot a glance at her spurless boots. "And you're not hunting with us. Our loss is Alec's gain I hear."

"From whom?" A touch of unease colored her query.

"Dalgliesh spoke to Fitz before he left. It's not common gossip. Nor will it be."

"Thank you."

"Although don't be surprised if you see us again. Fitz said Alec invited us to Crosstrees."

Her eyes flared wide. "He did?"

"He did. Fitz was equally shocked. Dalgliesh is normally a recluse at his hunting lodge. You have a gift, my dear," he gently said. "I told you that last night."

"If only I did," she pleasantly replied. "Alec is just more susceptible to kindness with a wife like his."

Oz's brows arched faintly. "A multitude of women have tried to engage his interest by various means—kindness included. To no avail." His sleek black hair fell forward slightly as he dipped his head. "I repeat, you have a gift." He wasn't so crude as to say beyond her obvious flamboyant sexuality, clearly something more than sex had prompted Dalgliesh to invite her into his private lair.

"Then I consider myself fortunate. Alec is extremely charming."

"As are you, my dear. Although as a couple, you present rather more of a pagan image to my mind, a certain untamed wildness defines you both." He smiled sweetly. "Not that I'm discounting the merits of charm."

Zelda laughed. "Nor am I discounting the merits of wildness. Very perceptive of you, by the way. Do bring your wife when you come. I'd like to meet her." Oz Lennox was powerfully charismatic. She'd like to see what kind of woman had captivated him.

"I will. In fact, Dalgliesh invited our children, too, so expect us to descend on you en masse. But not until after tomorrow Fitz was warned." His dark brows flickered in sportive comment. "Realistically though, you're safe from callers until after the house party breaks up on Monday."

Zelda smiled. "I'll tell Alec he's safe for two days at least."

"I'm sure he'll be pleased." He'd bet his banks on that. "Oh, hell, Bolton's coming our way," he murmured, his gaze on the rotund dandy mincing toward them. "I'll let you escape. He's a bore."

"You're too kind," Zelda whispered.

"I have my moments," Oz roguishly observed, and stepping around Zelda, he entered the breakfast room to intercept the viscount. "Did you win or lose yesterday, Bolton?" Oz pleasantly inquired as he met the young viscount with a penchant for vivid waistcoats, pink-topped boots, muchringed fingers, and pungent cologne.

"Both. Care to give me odds on who misses the first fence today?"

"Hell no. That's too easy. Crawford, of course. Unless you want to bet on when he falls." Bolton's conversation was limited to horses and gambling. But Oz bet on most anything, so a few minutes with the viscount wasn't a hardship.

"Two hundred says ten minutes out."

"Five hundred and five minutes," Oz countered.

"Ummm."

"Make it a thousand." Oz owned the largest bank in India and several around the world.

"Damn you, too rich for my blood," Bolton muttered.

Which was the point. "Come, Percy," Oz said, putting his arm around the young viscount's shoulder. "Let's have a drink instead. Have you had Fitz's smuggled brandy? It's smooth as a young maid's bum."

Before long, young Bolton was cheerfully drinking Fitz's brandy, his mind distracted from betting on a losing proposition. Excusing himself after the first drink, Oz strolled over to Fitz.

"I just saved the Earl of Norbury a thousand pounds," Oz drawled, dropping into a chair beside his friend.

"Damn puppy's going to beggar his father," Fitz drily said.

"At least not this morning. Did you see his waistcoat? It's blinding."

"Fortunately I didn't. Better yet, I haven't seen Violetta."

Oz slid into a lazy sprawl and smiled. "Let me do the honors if she appears. There's something about women like Violetta that bring out the devil in me."

"No scene."

Oz's eyes widened, his gaze unblemished innocence. "I'll be the soul of discretion."

Fitz snorted.

"Ah, ye of little faith. Women like me." Oz gave his friend a wicked grin. "I might have to turn down an invitation into Violetta's busy bed, for all you know."

"Whose bed?" Jamie came up behind Oz and ruffled his hair.

"Dear Violetta's, of course," Oz said breezily. "I'm thinking about letting her seduce me."

"Isolde might take a dim view of that." Jamie pulled out a chair at the table, sat, and nodded at the brandy bottle near Fitz.

"And well she should if I were in earnest."

Taking the bottle Fitz shoved across the table, Jamie uncorked it. "What the hell's going on?"

"Oz wants to have some sport with Violetta. Personally, I'd steer clear of the bitch. Why look for trouble?"

Since Jamie had spent most of his adult life in dangerous situations, having relinquished his former occupation, he was averse to looking for trouble. "Isn't she relatively inconsequential?" he said, pouring brandy into a cup.

Oz laughed. "Violetta would castrate you for such a slur."

"She could try," Jamie drily said over the rim of his cup. He'd left a good number of dead bodies in his wake. "Really, how can she matter?" He tipped the brandy down his throat.

Oz shrugged. "Good question."

"With Zelda and Dalgliesh both gone, perhaps you're right," Fitz said.

Jamie looked up from refilling his cup. "Gone?"

"Dalgliesh is and—"

"Zelda's following shortly." Oz nodded toward the doorway. "I just met her in the hall."

Jamie pursed his lips. "I hope she knows what she's doing."

Oz arrested his hand, holding his cup of brandy midway to his mouth. "She's happy. Visibly so. Tell him Fitz about Dalgliesh's novel and startling attachment," he directed, carrying the cup to his mouth.

"The man's smitten, at least," Fitz recounted. "Zelda seems pleased as well. Whether Alec's passion transcends the purely sexual, however," he added with a jaundiced gaze, "is highly uncertain."

"Uncertain?" Jamie said with asperity. "To whom is it uncertain with *his* record? I'll give him three days at the most."

"I'll say a week. The showy Miss MacKenzie could bring a corpse to life." Oz shot a glance at Fitz. "What do you think? You talked to him."

"I'll split the difference. Five. He's not a man interested in permanence."

"The state of his marriage a case in point," Oz said with a grin. "Shall we say, a thousand on our estimates?"

After which the conversation quickly turned to other wagers won and lost. The three men of wealth enjoyed all the vices common to affluent aristocrats—save one. They loved their wives and families, were in fact, devoted to them.

In that regard, they most felicitously broke with precedent.

CHAPTER 11

GRATEFUL FOR OZ'S intercession, Zelda was making her way through the maze of corridors toward her room. Since Rosalind would visit soon, she needn't track her down this morning.

With freedom beckoning, or more to the point, Dalgliesh in all his glory, she only nodded or smiled at those she met, not wishing to stop and exchange pleasantries with paradise awaiting her at Crosstrees. She was actually giddy with excitement, a tingling anticipation agitating her senses, her feelings so rare she refused to even consider Dalgliesh's faithlessness and profligacy, nor the tenuous nature of his liaisons. This was a carpe diem weekend—no more—and heedless and unapologetic, she intended to revel in it.

She'd packed earlier; a simple process for one who often traveled alone. But she needed a footman to transport her luggage downstairs. As she passed down the last corridor to her room, she met a sturdy young man balancing a breakfast tray on his shoulder and asked him to come for her luggage once he'd discharged his task.

Now then—one last survey of her room to check that

she'd left nothing behind, and she was off for a weekend of wanton frolic with a man who gave new meaning to the phrase *sexual gratification*. At the moment she didn't even begrudge him the practice required to school his body to such virtuosity. Especially with the heat of passion already beginning to warm her blood.

The bawdy words of the folk ballad "The Wanton Trooper" came to mind in playful affinity with her impassioned mood, and Zelda was humming under her breath as she opened her bedroom door.

"I was beginning to think you'd already left," a familiar voice unpleasantly said.

The melody stuck in Zelda's throat. Coming to a halt, she decided that at least one reason for Dalgliesh's marriage was now blatantly clear.

Violetta—shockingly voluptuous—was lounging on Zelda's bed, her artful pose reminiscent of Goya's *The Naked Maja*. Goya's lover had been painted unclothed, but Violetta was nearly nude, her curvaceous form clearly visible beneath the sheer lace of her white peignoir. Her heavy breasts were almost completely exposed save for small scraps of lace cupping the fleshy weight. There was no question either that the color of Violetta's pubic hair matched her golden coiffeur.

Zelda was surprised she'd walked through the house in such a state of undress. Was Lady Dalgliesh an exhibitionist? Had she expected to find her husband here? Did such unblushing dishabille appeal to Alec? Or was Violetta simply making her assets known to a rival? At which thought, Zelda silently groaned. There was no rivalry, no need for this confrontation.

"You might want to shut the door." A soft, dispassionate directive.

You don't have to speak to her, Zelda thought. *Go, leave, walk away.* Whatever the cold-eyed woman had to say, she didn't want to hear.

"If you leave, I'll simply tell everyone here what you did last night with my husband. I can give them details. I know him. And I have no compunction. None at all."

Zelda briefly considered whether what Violetta said to others mattered. She also *reconsidered* involving herself with Dalgliesh. The first issue was easily dismissed. As for Dalgliesh . . . he was less easy to dismiss or, in fact, resist.

Regretfully, deplorably, he was impossible to resist.

So she stepped fully into the room, shut the door, and coolly surveyed the woman who was wife to a man who deserved better. Or maybe not, with Dalgliesh's reputation such as it was. He and his wife might be exquisitely well suited. Not that any of it quashed her runaway longing. She wanted him still, and the fact that his wife was staring at her with palpable hostility was disagreeable but not prohibitive. "Very well," Zelda said. "Speak while you may. A footman will come for my luggage soon."

Violetta shrugged. "It makes no difference to me if he hears."

"It does to me. I'm not interested in theatrics or an audience or actually in anything you have to say."

"But you *are* interested in my husband," Violetta said in a poisonous murmur.

"I'm not alone in that regard," Zelda calmly remarked. "As I understand, he's in great demand."

"With sluts like you."

"A novel assertion from someone like *you*. Did you enjoy sex with Mytton last night?"

"Of course. Would I bother otherwise? Now then." A steely edge entered her voice, knife sharp and biting. "I hear you're going to Crosstrees. Don't look at me like that. What are personal maids for if not to keep one apprised of the latest news." Violetta spread her arms across the pillows piled behind her, deliberately showcasing the ripe plumpness of her breasts. "So taciturn, Miss MacKenzie. Apparently Alec's not interested in you for your conversation."

"You'll have to ask him where his interests lie." Surely that pose was better put to a man.

"I already know where they lie. Although you're just one in a long line of females ready to spread their legs for him." A wicked amusement flickered in her eyes. "Alec *is* quite sensational though. Physically, of course, he's magnificent. But he has a certain genius as well, don't you think, when it comes to, shall we say—technical flair?"

"Why are you telling me this?" *Does she think I wish to share intimate specifics with her?*

"In the event you thought you were the first. I didn't know how unenlightened you were, coming from the remoteness of the Highlands."

"Not that unenlightened," Zelda drily said. "Unfaithful husbands are hardly rare."

"Ah, perfect. Then I'm sure you can find someone else to warm your bed. I suggest you stay away from my husband and, more importantly, my son. For your own safety, of course."

"You can't be serious," Zelda said, mildly surprised as before by Violetta's threats.

"But I am."

"You must be deranged or supremely foolish. Or just plain silly." Zelda softly sighed. "This is too melodramatic for my taste."

"As if I care what you think," Violetta replied, oversweet and smiling. "As for my sanity, I'm quite sane. More pertinently—I'm dangerous. Disregard my warning and you'll discover just *how* dangerous."

Good God. The woman was clearly irrational or perhaps—hopefully—only angry and lashing out. "You should take up these issues with your husband." Zelda's voice was deliberately neutral. "I have nothing to do with the state of your marriage."

"Oh, but you do."

"You're mistaken. And that, too, you should discuss with your husband. As you said, I'm only one in a long line of women he's entertained."

"But never flaunted." The last word gritty and hard and exasperated.

"I'm sure you're wrong. About that and everything else having to do with me." But the words *never flaunted* echoed Alec's admission last night and warmed her heart when she should know better. When Alec Munro was the least likely man to consider a woman more than a passing fancy.

"This isn't a debate." Each word was tart with temper, inflexible. "I'm not here to debate you. I'm here to tell you to stay away from my husband and my son!"

The sudden knock on the door was relief and deliverance. "The servant's here for my luggage." Another sane person, thank God. "I suggest you leave or *I* might embarrass *you*."

An unpleasant trill of laughter issued from Violetta's cherry-red lips. "You embarrass me? Impossible. But you're unwise to ignore me," she added, sliding off the bed and stepping into her white satin slippers.

"As you are to think you can frighten me." Zelda turned to open the door. With a smile for the footman, she waved in the direction of the armoire. "My luggage is over there."

As the liveried servant entered the room and moved toward her luggage, Violetta sauntered past Zelda in a whisper of silk and a fragrant whiff of perfume, indifferent to the presence of a male servant viewing her barely clothed.

"Oh, by the way," she said over her shoulder as she strolled away. "I took your scissors to your clothes."

Stunned, Zelda momentarily stopped breathing. Then a second later rage flooded her brain, and only enormous self-control stopped her from throttling Violetta, who was still within range. One second more and her temper had cooled enough to reconsider making a scene in the hallway. Let her go. She had more pleasant prospects before her—a holiday with a delightful man, for instance. A man of marked sexual versatility and seeming indefatigability.

After which pleasing reflection Zelda's composure was restored enough to address the footman gathering her luggage. "A carriage is waiting at the side entrance," she said. "A small trap, I believe. And may I say, I appreciate you arriving so promptly."

"You're welcome, ma'am. Sorry about your clothes," he added, wheeling her trunk toward the door. "Everyone steers clear of Lady Dalgliesh, ma'am. In case you didn't know."

"Thank you for the warning." Unfortunately, he was two encounters too late.

"Everyone feels right sorry for his lordship."

"Indeed. I can see why."

"Give him my best, ma'am," the footman quietly said, walking out the door. "Tell him Ned sends his regards."

"I shall." Zelda was amazed how quickly rumor spread through the staff. Not that she was unaware of the below stairs conduit in every household, but still—she'd not even known Dalgliesh at this time yesterday.

It was remarkable.

She smiled. But not as remarkable as the bonny earl.

Nor as remarkable as her reckless, headstrong, utterly thoughtless, covetous, and avaricious passion for the licentious Earl of Dalgliesh, who could have given Don Juan and Casanova a run for their money.

It was totally mad, of course, for someone who'd always been sensible.

Mad, bad, dangerous, and God knows—irresistible.

TEN MINUTES LATER, Zelda and John were riding at full gallop over the colorful, autumnal downs, the air fresh in their lungs, the sun brilliant in a cloudless, blue sky, their mounts running powerfully and smoothly beneath them.

"It's just over that yon hill, my lady!" John shouted, waving his whip westward.

"I'll race you!" Zelda shouted back. She gave Blue his head, and the huge roan leaped forward as if he'd been standing still. "Good boy, sweet, sweet boy," Zelda crooned as he picked up speed. She experienced the rush of pleasure she always did riding full-out, but today, with the prospect of seeing the man who made her heart sing, she felt rapturously happy as well, flushed with joy—on top of the world.

He was waiting for her.

CHAPTER 12

DALGLIESH WAS INDEED waiting for Zelda.

With a rare impatience.

A novel impatience.

A frightening impatience, if he'd allow such introspection.

But he waited with a sense of joy as well. And for a man who'd viewed the world of late as devoid of jubilation, the feeling was immensely satisfying.

As for the captivating Miss MacKenzie having wrought such a revolutionary transformation in so brief a time, Alec suspected life would return to normal once the lady left for France. In the meantime, he decided with a grin, the prospect of her company was bloody enticing.

A servant came running out of the house as he paced in the drive.

"They're ridin' over the last hill, my lord. Comin' fast, Maxwell says." Alec had a man on watch in the east tower.

"Thank you. Will you see that Mrs. Creighton and Master Chris are informed? Tell them Miss MacKenzie is in sight." Creiggy had suggested she keep her charge in the schoolroom until Zelda's arrival was imminent, and thus avoid the constantly asked question: *Is she here yet?* "And see that Rowan alerts the kitchen. We'll be in the breakfast room shortly."

"Yes, sir."

"That will be all." He hoped to have a few minutes alone with Zelda. They'd have little privacy the rest of the day. Chris was excited about Zelda's visit; he'd talked of little else. The earl smiled. Not that he wasn't pleased that Chris liked Zelda; he was.

The sound of riders approaching from the east and riding hard was faintly heard at first and distant. They'd have to come up the drive or chance jumping the wide, deep ha-ha, and John had more sense than to put Zelda at risk. Or more aptly, he knew Alec would disapprove.

As the drumming rhythm of galloping horses grew louder, Dalgliesh waited, his gaze trained on the point where the drive disappeared into the shadowed forest planted by long-dead Munros. After running a fingertip over the loose tie of his cravat, he snapped his shirt cuffs into place, then raked his fingers through his hair—as if it mattered that he be well turned out for his visitor, as if he were sixteen and waiting for his first female guest.

He shook away the adolescent memories and momentary unease. Zelda was a wild, impetuous woman. They were both long past juvenile games. And the reason he'd invited her and she'd accepted was unequivocally adult.

There. Sanity restored. His head came up, the thundering hoof beats closer now. They were very near. Very.

A second later, the horses and riders exploded out into the open where Capability Brown had manicured nature into acres of exquisite vistas, the thoroughbreds racing neck and neck, the horsemen careening headlong around the final curve of the drive, both whipping their mounts to more speed.

Zelda was laughing, even John was smiling—a rarity.

But Miss MacKenzie wore conventional female riding garb today, black, severe, tailored. Nor did any flame-red hair blow in the wind, her unruly hair tied back and barely visible beneath her black homburg. Although she rode astride as usual, rode full tilt as usual, with her customary madcap recklessness. In fact, she almost came out of the saddle as she leaned forward to press her cheek against her roan's neck and urge him on. The brim of her hat caught on the bridle, tilted askew, flew off, and sailed away. Then her hair came loose, unfurled in a silken blaze, and as Blue took the lead and rocketed toward the house, she whooped in delight.

Alec smiled. Ah—now there was the woman who'd matched him in wildness last night. No conventional female in conventional riding garb, but an untamed, headstrong beauty with prodigal, insatiable desires and a body, as he well knew, made for pleasure.

And she was *his* for the next few days.

If he lived, he whimsically reflected.

She was riding straight at him.

Unmoving, his booted feet fixed on the raked gravel of the drive, he watched the distance between them swiftly narrow.

He trusted her horsemanship. Or *maybe* he trusted her horsemanship, he corrected with no more than a dozen yards separating him from a half ton of racing horseflesh.

At the last second, with uncanny intuition, Zelda hauled Blue to a brilliant, rearing, plunging, back-on-his-haunches stop. Gravel flew, flailing hoofs churned the air, tore up the drive, and horse spittle from heaving lungs sprayed far and wide in a warm, wet trajectory.

Smiling faintly, Dalgliesh wiped the spittle from his face with a swipe of his hand and watched Zelda leap to the ground while Blue was still curveting and chopping the air. Landing lightly, she flew toward him, her long skirts leaving a trail in the gravel.

He smothered a grunt as she hurtled into his body. Then he closed his arms around her and felt like he had almost from the first with her . . . joyful. "You're damned good, darling." His smile was teasing. "I live to see another day."

"I was in . . . a hurry," she breathlessly said, returning his smile. "I haven't seen you—it seemed like . . . *forever!*"

"It *was* forever." He raised his wrist enough to see his

watch over her shoulder. "Almost two hours. What took so long?"

"This and that." She dragged air into her lungs. "Packing—the usual."

Something in her voice, perhaps the sudden tension in her body contradicted the casualness of her words. "Jesus," he said, half under his breath. "What did Violetta do now?"

"It doesn't matter." She lightly brushed the graceful curve of his bottom lip with the pad of her index finger. "Don't give it a thought. I'm here now."

"God, I'm sorry." His nostrils flared. "Again," he added on a soft exhalation. He glanced up. "Thank you, John." The groom was leading away the horses. As his gaze returned to Zelda, he grimaced, wondering how many more times he'd have to apologize for his damned wife. "She ordinarily never gets up before noon. Still, I should have waited for you. Protected you."

"I'm fine—really," Zelda replied. "She doesn't frighten me. And we have more pleasant things to consider," she added, her smile sunshine bright. "You"—she tapped his chest—"and me alone for an *entire* weekend."

My God, she was understanding. "In terms of full disclosure, darling—no, no," he quickly interjected as her eyes flared wide. "Don't be alarmed. I have no skeletons in my closet." *Or none to concern you.* "It's only that we don't have the weekend *completely* to ourselves. In fact," he noted with a nod in the direction of the house, "I believe the small impediment to our privacy has arrived."

Chris had broken away from Creiggy and was running toward them, screaming and waving his arms.

Dipping his head, Alec put his mouth to her ear. "I have to share you today," he murmured. "But tonight you're mine."

His warm breath on her skin triggered hot, graphic memory, and she shivered as vaulting desire streaked through her senses. "I may not last that long," she whispered.

He groaned. "Don't say that. You have to, *we* have to. Chris will be underfoot all day."

"I know. I knew that. It's just that you in close proximity

compromises my good intentions. Does he take a nap?" Her gaze was playfully beseeching. "Give me hope."

"He doesn't, but perhaps I could bribe him." With Zelda close, his restraint was questionable.

"Or perhaps Creiggy could be bribed."

Sooner expect virtue be corrupted. "I'll think of something," he said with a reassuring smile.

"You're incredibly sweet." Rising on tiptoe, she kissed his cheek.

His libido took note of the upward ascent of her soft, shapely body, of the scent and feel of her, of the interminable hours before nightfall. "I don't know about sweet, but I should be able to outsmart a six-year-old. Fingers crossed," he added with a grin. "He argues about everything."

"Creiggy might be easier to persuade."

"True. She likes that I'm happy. "

Zelda fluttered her eyelashes in coquettish play. "I could make you happier."

He laughed. "Now there's potent spur to improvisation. Consider a nap time in the offing. Ours. My word on it."

"You're so-o-o loveable," she purred. "And I mean it in the most benign way, so you needn't panic."

"I'm not panicking." But his shuttered gaze cleared, his sudden smile dazzled. "You're extremely loveable as well—in the same benign way," he said with exquisite grace and charm. "Now brace yourself. Here comes your smallest admirer."

But Dalgliesh scooped up Chris before he barreled into them, and holding him, gently directed, "Now mind your manners and greet Miss MacKenzie properly."

"Good morning, Miss MacKenzie," the little boy dutifully pronounced in his high, piping voice. "I'm pleased you could come for a visit." He glanced at his father, who gave him an approving smile and set him on his feet.

"Now you may ask what you're dying to ask," the earl kindly said.

"Might we, I mean if you don't mind," Chris exuberantly exclaimed, "would you and Papa show me how to jump

Petunia"—another quick glance up at his father, who nodded—"after breakfast?"

"Of course, I'd be happy to help. And I'm a very fast eater," Zelda added with a wink.

"Yahoo! I mean, thank you so much, Miss MacKenzie," he amended under the watchful eye of Creiggy, who'd arrived after a more sedate progress down the drive.

"Welcome to Crosstrees, Miss MacKenzie," Creiggy said, with a lilt in her voice. "I just won five shillings from the footman. He didn't think you'd stop that brute of a horse in time."

Zelda smiled. "Blue minds well. I trained him myself."

Creiggy shot an amused glance at her employer. "There's a warning, my boy. Not that most men couldn't use a bit of training. Some more than others," she added with a lift of her brows.

"You mean to say there were deficiencies in your tutelage?" Dalgliesh drawled.

"Let's just say some pupils are more mule headed than others."

"I'm sure Miss MacKenzie can correct whatever faults I may have."

Zelda smiled. "Naturally, I'd be delighted to try."

"And I'd be delighted to let you try," the earl replied, all suave grace and roguish charm.

"Now, now," Creiggy drily said with a glance at her youngest charge and a warning glance for his father. "We have a busy day before us."

"As you see, Miss MacKenzie," Alec sardonically said, "I pay to have my conscience constantly on duty."

"If you had a conscience of your own, my lord," Creiggy said with equal sarcasm, "my diligence would be unnecessary."

"You're an idealist, Creiggy. I'm a nobleman. I don't need a conscience."

"Humph. Do unto others, my boy."

"Don't tempt me, Creiggy," he softly said.

She only lifted her brows. Understanding. He put up with

a great deal from his wife. Even took care of—she never knew what to call the poor wee thing.

"Papa, Papa!" Chris tugged on his father's hand. Clearly the adult conversation had nothing to do with his jumping lessons. "Let's go in for breakfast! We don't want to keep Petunia waiting."

"Ah—of course," Alec said with feigned gravity. "We mustn't keep your pony waiting. May I interest you in breakfast, Miss MacKenzie?" Without waiting for a reply, he took Zelda's hand and said to his impatient son, "Run ahead and tell Rowan we're on our way."

As Chris raced off, the Earl of Dalgliesh turned to Creiggy, his thoughts focused once again on more pleasant things. "I might be willing to send that favorite nephew of yours to Eaton if you'd entertain Chris for an hour or so this afternoon."

"You're sending Ian there anyway."

"Ah—that's right." He smiled. "Do you have other nephews perhaps who could use my patronage?"

"Several, all of whom you're already supporting. But Master Chris will be ready enough to take a walk to the village and see what's new at the toy shop, if that suits your lordship." Her voice was without inflection, her expression bland, only a hint of good humor in her eyes as she met the earl's gaze evidence of her fondness for the man she'd raised from infancy.

"Understanding as ever, Creiggy," Alec murmured. "Would you like an increase in your wages?"

"If I needed one, I might."

"A Scot who turns down money. Let me mark the day."

"It's a right fine day if you ask me, money or not," Creiggy crisply said. "Now I don't know about you, but I'm famished."

"I believe we're all famished one way or the other," Alec murmured. And as Zelda blushed, Alec politely extended his elbow to Creiggy, tightened his grip on Zelda's hand, and escorted the two ladies toward the imposing entrance of his hunting lodge.

CHAPTER 13

CROSSTREES PAVILION HAD been built as a hunting box for the tenth Earl of Dalgliesh in the reign of George III. The Palladian structure had been much enlarged over the years and recently refurbished. The size was impressive, the luxury impressive, the furnishings a combination of old and new—all costly. The earls of Dalgliesh had always been men of wealth, apparently, Zelda decided, taking in the tasteful opulence as they made their way through a number of rooms and corridors to a sunny breakfast room with enough servants on hand for a royal levee.

Dalgliesh seemed not to notice the oversupply of servants or the opulence, nor did his son or Creiggy, for that matter. While Zelda's family had considerable land and bankable assets and a good deal of money on the exchange, this was clearly the household of a very rich man.

She didn't wonder that Dalgliesh, his handsome looks aside, had scores of women in pursuit. Not only had he inherited the family fortune, but he'd augmented it with a new fortune in diamonds. And as everyone knew, rich, handsome peers with ready access to diamonds were viewed with favor by the ladies.

However, in contrast to the plutocratic magnificence of Dalgliesh's establishment, breakfast was en famille and cozy—the staff very much part of the warm intimacy. Gossip and banter were unrestrained, as were the various discussions concerning events in the neighborhood, and it was some time before Alec turned to Zelda. "Forgive me. I haven't been to Crosstrees for several weeks. Everyone's filling me in on the local gossip. Are you getting enough to eat?"

"More than enough, thank you."

"Have you tried Chris's favorite—caviar and mashed bananas?"

Zelda nodded. "I liked it."

"Creiggy's sister is governess to the Tsar's children. She sends us more caviar than we need. The staff has taken a liking to it as well." He glanced at his majordomo presiding over the table service. "Haven't they, Rowan?"

"They have indeed, my lord." Alec's elderly butler, conscious of his position, was slightly more constrained than the rest of the staff, but his smile was genuine, his affection for the earl obvious. "Including the mashed bananas, sir."

"The Tsar's children like caviar and mashed bananas for breakfast," Alec explained. "So we've become equally cultivated," he added with a grin. "Although I'm more than content with a good steak and a mug of ale as well."

Which he'd been consuming with obvious enjoyment, Zelda noted, his appetite for food similar to his other appetites. The thought didn't bear contemplation, however, with hours yet to go before her sexual desires would be fulfilled.

As if reading her mind, the earl reached out, gently touched her hand, and quietly said, "We'll have lunch early. That should help."

Zelda forced a smile. "I'm sure you're right."

"Right about what?" Chris piped up from his seat on his father's other side. "About going? Are we *finally* going?"

"Hush, Master Chris," Creiggy admonished. Seated across the table, she'd witnessed the hushed exchange between Alec and Zelda and recognized it hadn't been about jumping lessons. "Let your father and Miss MacKenzie enjoy their breakfast."

"But *I'm* done. I was finished a *long, long* time ago!"

Alec gave his son a stern look. "Then you may go and wait at the stables if you prefer, but let Miss MacKenzie finish her meal in peace."

"I'd rather wait *here*," the young boy countered with a wide smile, unabashed by his father's censure.

Dalgliesh must be a lenient parent, Zelda thought and obliged her restless student by catching his eye and saying, "I'll be ready as soon as I finish my coffee."

"Yipee!"

The boy's high-pitched cry startled the maid pouring more ale for Alec, the liquid slopped over the rim of the glass, and a puddle began spreading over the tablecloth.

The earl tossed his napkin on the spill and shot a critical look at his son, then at Creiggy. "We need some better table manners."

Creiggy shrugged. "He's just like you were at six."

"Is that explanation or defense?" Alec sardonically inquired, helping the maid sop up the mess.

"Neither. It's simple fact. And as far as I can see," Creiggy said, reaching for a piece of toast, "a little screaming here and there didn't adversely affect you. As to what may have adversely affected you, I'd say—"

"No you may not," Alec softly interposed. "I prefer a pleasant breakfast."

The old nanny said, "Aye," and began buttering her toast.

Not just a lenient parent but an indulgent employer, Zelda thought, liking Dalgliesh for it. Too many men unnecessarily exerted their authority. Not that she was personally vulnerable, but she'd seen women enough who were. "There, I'm done." She set down her empty cup. "Everything was delicious."

Alec waved away the maid. "Don't let Chris hurry you."

"No, really, I've eaten a great deal. Although I wouldn't mind a quick washup before we begin the lessons." She wished to discard the long, trailing skirt of her riding habit, the yards of black serge unwieldy.

Chris groaned; Alec ignored him and nodded at his butler. "Rowan will have someone show you to your room." He didn't dare escort her himself. The temptation to lock the bedroom door behind them and stay there until he couldn't fuck anymore was too great. "We'll meet you in the stable yard."

Zelda was shown to a large bedchamber by a nervous maidservant who immediately disappeared. It must be Alec's room, she decided, surveying the masculine decor. Clearly he was defiant of propriety to so openly house her in his suite. Which meant he either trusted his servants or cared nothing for gossip. Not that his degree of wealth couldn't buy privacy.

And a good deal more, she reflected, like the legions of women in his life. Although she happened to be the current female of choice—lucky her. And as soon as she changed, she'd be once again in the company of the disarmingly seductive man who thoroughly bewitched her.

As she moved to her trunk set next to an open armoire, she realized why the maid had left so swiftly. Apparently, someone had begun unpacking her trunk but stopped when they'd seen the ravaged clothing within. Only her butchered lynx coat and one tattered evening gown had been hung in the armoire.

Damn vicious bitch, Zelda testily thought. That coat was a favorite of hers, and it wasn't as though she could have another tailored to size with dispatch. The Russian furs had been rare, one-of-a-kind skins, handpicked by George Campbell at an auction in Novgorod.

Moving to the armoire, she examined the damage to her coat in the hopes it was repairable. On the contrary. Violetta had slashed through the skins with amazing thoroughness. Bloody lunatic.

On the other hand, she reminded herself, no one had been hurt, her clothing could be replaced, and if she required redress, the prospect of unparalleled sexual gratification at the hands of the very accomplished Alec Munro would go far in the way of compensation.

At which point a lascivious tremor fluttered up her vagina and spread outward in skittish little messages of carnal hope. Oh God—how long must she wait? She glanced at the clock on the bedside table.

Two, three hours, four at the most before she'd experience the full hospitality of the sexually gifted earl. Lord, please not four. Especially when the beautiful, hard-bodied Dalgliesh would be more or less continuously within sight and sound and touch.

She restlessly smoothed her skirt, cautioned herself to observe the proprieties in public, and focus instead on the activity at hand—Chris's jumping lessons. But it took a moment to curb sensibilities that had become addicted to the pleasure Dalgliesh dispensed. And another moment to refocus her thoughts.

That done, restively, but done, she set about discarding her skirt. The black serge slid to the floor and, stepping over the crumpled fabric, she picked it up. Since she'd be wearing it for the interim, she hung it in the armoire.

Now there was a sight—the ugly next to the demolished. Eventually she'd have to explain her limited wardrobe. But for now—she turned and surveyed her image in the cheval glass. Her deerskin breeches and black jacket were adequate for the stable yard.

Adequate wasn't the word that came to mind when Alec caught sight of Zelda approaching the riding ring. Stimulating, titillating, provocative as hell more aptly described her attire. His nostrils flared as he tamped down his lust. There were hours yet before they'd have any privacy. Although, no question, luncheon would be set well forward today.

He wrenched his gaze from the short row of buttons securing her form-fitting breeches and, summoning every ounce of willpower he possessed, he greeted her with well-mannered civility. "You make a fetching figure," he pleasantly said. "I wish I'd had a riding instructor like you."

"I'd be happy to give you some lessons later," she murmured. "If you promise to stop looking at me like that." She lifted her brows. "Please."

"Of course. Forgive me."

She marveled at the instant change in him. His gaze, his expression, his very stance—he'd put a small distance between them—bespoke a bland, sexless neutrality. "Such versatility. You should have been on the stage."

"Sometimes I am—in a manner of speaking."

"Are you now?"

"In a manner of speaking," he repeated with a small smile. "Since I can't do what I wish to do."

She blushed.

"Papa, Papa, hurry!" Chris was perched on his pony in the center of the riding ring. "Petunia doesn't like to wait!"

"We'll be right there," Alec replied before turning to Zelda. "Now then," he went on, temperate and composed, "whenever you tire of this exercise, feel free to stop. Chris can try one's patience at times."

"I expect he'll become bored soon enough." Zelda used the same polite tone. "Children and lessons aren't exactly compatible. Although," she added in a slightly less impersonal inflection, "I need something to take my mind off *other* things, so I welcome the distraction."

"Indeed. Unfortunately your breeches are *hellishly* distracting for me."

"I'm sorry. If I had—" She paused, felt her face flush. She'd spoken out of turn.

"Had what?"

Conscious of Dalgliesh's sudden piercing gaze, she softly exhaled. "I was going to wait to tell you, but"—she shrugged—"as it turns out I have nothing else to wear. Your wife cut up my clothes."

"She did *what*?" he rapped out.

"She was waiting in my room at Groveland Chase when I came back from speaking to Father this morning. Apparently she'd been busy with my scissors while I was gone."

"Jesus God," he said with disgust. A tick appeared over his cheekbone and his voice was terse when he spoke. "I'll remedy that. Your wardrobe. As for Violetta, I'll take care of her . . . later," he added in icy accents.

"Please don't retaliate on my account. The clothes don't matter, nor does she, if you must know. She has no impact on my life."

He wished he could say the same. "I'll replace your clothes at least. Don't say no. I insist. Do you shop in Edinburgh or London?"

"Papa! Papa!" A fidgety six-year-old's strident wail. "I'm *tired* of waiting!"

Zelda smiled. "Should I take the first round?"

"Please do. He'd prefer you." Dalgliesh held her gaze for a potent moment. "We'll talk about this other matter later."

As Zelda walked away, he beckoned to John, who was chatting with the stable master across the yard.

When John came within earshot, he took one look at his employer's face and raised his brows. "Trouble?"

"Nothing that can't be resolved." Dalgliesh delivered several brief, pointed instructions to his groom. "Have Mrs. Drewe waiting as well," he added at the last. "Find someone to take care of her children."

And so the jumping lessons commenced, the matter of Violetta's wickedness left unresolved, the two lovers under duress but determined to master their desires, both directing their attention to a young boy's entertainment.

Zelda was a superb teacher, patient, kind, never disapproving, and Chris blossomed under her teaching. Before long, he'd mastered the three-point position—standing in the stirrups, leaning forward, and moving his hands up the crest of the pony's neck on the approach to the jump. He learned when to settle back into the saddle, how to give his pony *more leg* to make him lengthen his stride; he began to understand the concept of riders and horses who have *feel*.

After a time Alec took over, both adults consummate equestrians, their tutelage both a pleasant and successful learning experience for the youngster. Until such a time as Petunia expressed her discontent with further lessons by stubbornly refusing to move.

"You did really well today," Zelda lauded, helping Chris dismount. "Ponies can be temperamental, but Petunia will be ready to work again by tomorrow. Now, I'll bet you have some favorite toys." A diversion to occupy the time was essential. "Maybe you could show them to me. If that's all right with your father." She glanced at Dalgliesh.

"I'm at your disposal, Miss MacKenzie." His voice was placid, his gaze was not. It was covetous, intense.

And instantly triggered a flame-hot response in its recipient.

But before prurient desire had completely overwhelmed Zelda's sensibilities, Chris grabbed her hand. "I have a big, big, *big* train set! I bet you've never seen one so big!" Beaming with delight, he tugged on her hand. "I'll show you."

A little boy's sweaty hand and hurly-burly ebullience effectively curtailed even rash and reckless craving. "I'd like . . . that," Zelda said, half breathless. "I don't have a train set . . . at home."

"Well, you're a girl, that's why." Little boys didn't notice subtle nuances in breathing.

Big boys did and took pleasure in it. "Girls like lots of things boys do," Alec volunteered as he guided the pair from the training ring, smiling at Zelda over his son's head.

"Don't either," Chris contradicted.

"Riding for one," Alec said with a wink for Zelda.

"And hunting," Zelda offered, having heroically mastered her excitable passions. She shot a playful glance at the earl. "Women are good at hunting."

"No, they're not," Chris rebuffed with childish certainty. "It's mostly men in the hunting field."

"Well, what about fishing?" Zelda suggested. "I love to fish."

"You're different," Chris quickly retorted. "You're not like all the other women. You're fun."

Alec resisted the impulse to second his son's comments in an altogether inappropriate way. Instead, he said, "Don't forget, Miss MacKenzie was raised with four brothers. She knows what men like—don't you, Miss MacKenzie?" he gently added, enjoying the blush pinking Zelda's face.

"I suppose I do. Practice makes perfect, I've found," she sweetly replied with a sportive wink for the earl. "Just like practice will give you confidence to take on any jump before long, Chris," she mildly added.

While the earl quietly seethed at the thought of *practice makes perfect* in regard to Zelda's past, Zelda cautioned herself against becoming too enamored with a man who viewed all women as available.

The fact that Crosstrees was less a hunting box than a palace was a potent reminder of the full magnitude of Dalgliesh's allure. The reigning beauties, bored wives, and young misses playing at seduction all willingly acquiesced, she suspected.

A cautionary tale best heeded.

But a woman who'd braved jungles, climbed the pyramids, traveled the Silk Route by camel caravan wasn't faint-hearted. So fie to all the other women, she decided, and fiddledeedee to caution. This weekend was very selfishly about pleasure—pure and simple. She intended to take delight in every hedonistic second of her visit until such a time as one or both of them brought their little idyll to an end.

Life was to be lived, after all—a lesson learned long ago when her mother had died in her prime.

Chris had run ahead of them, impatient with the adults' strolling gait, and as Zelda observed him racing up the rise toward the house, she experienced a poignant sense of déjà vu. It felt as though she'd been at Crosstrees before, in these exact circumstances—walking beside Alec in companionable silence, the autumn sun warm, the sky blue and cloudless, her feelings of content beyond measure.

Reaching out, she took Dalgliesh's hand, as if it were a perfectly natural gesture. Glancing up, she smiled. "Happy? I am."

"Very." He smiled back, neither questioning his reply nor the ease with which he made it.

She waved her free hand toward Chris, who was nearing the crest of the rise. "He seems to be enjoying himself, too."

"You're good for him. He's having fun."

"As am I. It's nice to have a young child around again." She grinned. "A general comment only. Nothing personal."

Alec smiled faintly. "I'm damned tempted to make it personal."

"But not entirely foolish enough to do so."

"Unfortunately."

"We shall live for the moment instead." Her voice was blithe, full of cheer. "We shall taste all the diverse, beguiling pleasures of the flesh."

He laughed. "All of them? Now there's a challenge."

"But a perfectly delightful one."

He looked at her sharply. "You know that for a fact?"

"Don't use that tone with me." She jerked her hand away. "I'm not your wife."

"Then don't act like her," he snapped, the thought of Zelda with other men maddening. When it shouldn't be, when it *couldn't* be. "Forgive me," he hastily amended, having regained his senses. "I shouldn't have said that. Your life is your own, of course."

She shot him a heated look. "Damn right it is."

He should agree, her statement was perfectly valid. With any other woman, he wouldn't even consider an alternative. But the world was less doctrinaire than it was two days ago, less certain, and what had always been unequivocal about the position of fuckable women in his life was suddenly in doubt. He softly exhaled, debating how to proceed, whether he wished to, in fact, whether it would be more prudent to remain silent. Or reply with some practiced flattery or mea culpa.

"We need some ground rules."

Her cool voice interrupted his musing. "I don't like rules," he said with equal coolness.

"Perhaps you can't always do as you please," she tartly said. "Everyone isn't impressed by your wealth."

"Everyone meaning you?"

"Yes," she said, clipped and narrow eyed, quickening her pace as though to give vent to her spleen.

"I don't know what money has to do with fucking."

She snorted. "Surely you're not that naive."

"Is this going to cost me then?"

Rude and silken, the query hung in the air for a fraction of a second.

"*This* is over, so *this* won't cost you a farthing, you insolent prick!" She never should have come. She knew what he was like from the first. A shameless libertine, a brazen adulterer, a man with way too much money!

Bold-faced bitch, he fumed. Pretending she had scruples. Why the hell had he invited her? He must have been deranged. Then he suddenly heard himself say, "Wait," as if some mysterious inner voice had nullified rational thought, and grabbing her wrist, he pulled her to a stop.

Bristling, she shook off his hand.

He released her when he wouldn't have had to. When he could have locked her away if he wished. When a century ago he might have without a qualm.

She glared at him. "I dislike belligerence with my sex. This was a bad idea—my coming here."

Her acrid voice broke into his intemperate thoughts, and his temper flared higher because he knew what she liked with her sex, knew a good deal of what she liked. "What if *I* think it's a good idea?" he silkily murmured.

"I don't give a damn what you think." Her voice was peevish. "Arrogant men like you offend me."

Not all the time. "Perhaps I could change your mind." Wanting what he wanted, he reined in his temper for more satisfying pursuits. For sex with the incomparable Miss MacKenzie. For several days of sex with the incomparable Miss MacKenzie.

"Don't bother." A petulant sniff for good measure. "I'm not in the mood to be charmed."

"Then I won't try. But I'd like you to stay."

Her initial surprise was replaced by a cool scrutiny. "Why?"

"Christ, I don't know. I wish I did. You entice me. I told you that already." Each word was crabbed and gruff.

But heartwarming and, she suspected, rare, and at base, charmingly effective. "If you're trying to woo me, you should get rid of that frown." She brushed her fingertips across his furrowed brow.

It was amazing how light a touch could give rise to such pleasure. He smiled. "How's that? Now tell me what else I must do."

"As if you take instruction," she neatly said.

"For some reason I'm very much inclined to at the moment. So tell me. What do you want?"

She grinned. "Is this where they usually say diamonds?"

"If I were disposed to ask them what they want, they might."

"Brute."

"Temptress."

"Oh hell." She grimaced. "We both know why I'm here."

His smile was angelic. "I thought the question was whether you were staying or not."

"Humph," she said in quibbling chagrin. "For your information, I'm not sure I'm interested in a filthy-rich autocrat who can buy anything or anyone. Even with the incredible sex."

"If we're being blunt," he said, "I dislike wanting you so much." He paused for a transient moment, gauging her expression, the set of her mouth, the lingering challenge in her gaze. But he'd never been fearful, when even as a boy he should have been, although his voice dropped slightly as he spoke and took on a contemplative tone. "Everything's different with you," he quietly said. "The world, me, the wanting, the not wanting, the raging need, the satisfaction and content—everything. I'm not sure what's real. How something like this can happen so quickly. Whether the outrageous happiness I feel is even allowed."

If Chris hadn't almost reached the house, Zelda would have thrown her arms around him and declared her undying love. But little boys didn't take kindly to waiting, and at base, she was chary of a man with an amorous reputation of such enormity. "Why not say it's allowed for a weekend, at least," she said with a smile.

"Or a week or a month." He smiled back, feeling an inexpressible relief, feeling strangely victorious. "How long can you stay?"

She sighed. "Not too long."

"Why? You don't *have* to go to France. Go on the next hunt or the one after that. The season's just begun." An autocrat in full operating mode.

"We'll see."

He frowned. "What does that mean?"

"It means I don't know."

His frown disappeared. He'd convince her to stay. He was a confident man, pleasing women a well-honed skill. "You can decide later," he offered, conciliatory and affable, his own plans crystal clear. "After Chris shows off his train, after lunch"—his heavy-lidded gaze was lush with promise—"I'll see what I can do to help you make up your mind."

"That's not fair."

"I'm not interested in being fair."

She made a playful moue. "Despot."

He grinned. "Hell no—I'm thoroughly besotted. I'm also damned near out of my mind for want of you," he murmured, his gaze flame hot.

"Lord, Alec, don't look at me like that. It's hours yet before—"

"Lunch will be served soon," he said, a small impatience in his tone. "I sent instructions with John."

"But what if Chris won't—"

"Creiggy will see that he does."

"You're sure?"

"I'm sure."

The unmistakable voice of authority. "How nice," Zelda said.

"I'll see that it's more than nice," he murmured.

She smiled. "I know you will. That's why I came."

CHAPTER 14

THEY SPENT THE next hour in Chris's playroom, where he demonstrated all the intricacies of his train set to Zelda. The large, tabletop display resembled the area surrounding Crosstrees: The little hamlet where Alec had tracked down Zelda was reproduced in miniature; Crosstrees was replicated to size, as was Groveland Chase and the downs and woodlands between. It was an extravagant assemblage, the toy trains exact copies of contemporary railroad lines, the rural landscape faithfully duplicated, a vast number of little figures from farmers to brakemen to a field of hunters adding detail and character to the scene.

Familiar with the tableau, Alec lounged in a comfortable chair while Chris explained all the particulars to Zelda. She appeared genuinely interested, asked pertinent questions, listened attentively, and when offered an opportunity to operate one of the trains, managed the controls deftly enough for Chris to challenge her to a race. Chris took the larger engine, Alec noted with a faint smile. But Zelda would have let the boy win, he expected, regardless.

He felt at ease. He'd only met her yesterday, but somehow

her presence offered him a much-needed respite from all the inconvenient demands that circumscribed his life. He had no idea why, nor was he likely to overintellectualize his feelings. Women served a certain function in his life, and while Miss MacKenzie was well outside the norm when it came to females he fucked—she was more delightful in a number of ways—he was too jaded to have expectations. Nor did his situation allow him to contemplate more than a few days of amusement. A prospect, however, that filled him with delight. She was really quite amazing—sexually and otherwise.

For instance, here she was comfortably at play with a boy of six, the two of them head-to-head in conversation, Chris animated, talking fast, Zelda nodding in agreement, smiling from time to time. She had perfect instincts and the necessary warmhearted temperament to indulge childish whims. And not just childish whims, he pleasantly recalled. Zelda didn't just make Chris happy, but himself as well.

And once lunch was over, she'd make him very happy indeed.

A shame he couldn't have her for himself alone.

A novel thought for a man who wasn't averse to sharing the ladies in his life, nor generally interested in anything but brevity in his amorous affairs.

How juvenile, he thought. As if life allowed such pretty fantasies. He dismissed visionary ideals for less auspicious reality, although reality at the moment was extremely fine with his picturesque houseguest in full view.

In boots, leather breeches, and a short black jacket, Miss MacKenzie's ripe, shapely body was a delectable sight to behold. She seemed indifferent to her appearance, at ease in her unconventional garb. One of her many charms, he thought, that nonconformist attitude to the world. As for his reaction to her charms—they were predictable and unfortunately, at the moment, impractical. He consoled himself with a quick glance at the clock and the knowledge that his irksome celibacy would soon be at an end. An hour, perhaps . . . or less and he'd be assuaging his lust.

There. Everything was nicely compartmentalized and entrained.

A short time later when a servant came up to announce luncheon, Dalgliesh rose from his chair with a casualness bred in him from a young age. He rarely showed his feelings. "Time to go," he said with a polite smile. "Should I turn off the main switch?"

"Do we *have* to go? I'm not hungry yet." Chris looked at his father with an imploring gaze. "I want to play some more."

"You may have a tray brought up if you wish."

"Can Miss MacKenzie stay with me? I haven't shown her all the fueling stations yet or how the engine fire box turns real red when it gets hot or—"

"I'm afraid Creiggy's waiting for us," Alec gently interposed. "You know how she likes us to be on time."

"May we come back later and play?" His father's warning was sufficient. Creiggy was a stickler for punctuality.

"Certainly."

"When?"

"We'll have to see."

"When you say *we'll have to see* that means no," the young boy grumbled. "And I want to play with Miss MacKenzie some more."

Good God, his son was a rival for Zelda's attention. "Why don't we come back before dinner and play with your trains? How would that be?"

"What time?"

Alec recognized that dogged little jut to his son's chin and offered certainty. "Why don't we say half past six. Miss MacKenzie was up late last night at the Grovelands'. I believe she's going to nap this afternoon. Isn't that right?" He turned to Zelda, his expression choir-boy innocent.

"I was rather planning on it," she said, trying not to turn cherry red. Not succeeding.

"Then half past six it is," the earl noted. "Allow me to escort you downstairs, Miss MacKenzie." He offered her his arm with studied nonchalance. Restraint was the order of the day. A constant in his relationship with Zelda. An ordeal for a man of unfettered principles when it came to sex. But then he didn't bring his inamoratas home, nor introduce them to his son—or, more saliently, to Creiggy—so he'd never been obliged to curb his libido before.

Although the strain was beginning to tell—rationalizing aside—and luncheon proved difficult. Zelda was too close, too enticing, too explicitly sexual. Alec resorted to the time-honored expedient of drink in lieu of conduct unbecoming a gentleman.

As for Zelda, she found Dalgliesh's presence beside her the most lurid of aphrodisiacs. The scent of his cologne was pungent in her nostrils, his soft breathing audible, his smallest movement triggering a discernable jolt to her senses. Without the distractions of the playroom, she was susceptible to every shifting nuance of his body, making her even more keenly aware of the imminent pleasures in store for her after lunch.

Unaware of the edgy tension, Chris busily chatted with the footmen, who treated him with casual affection. Creiggy appeared immune to the undercurrent of nerves, tucking into her food with seeming disregard for her surroundings.

Alec, who never watched the clock, watched the clock, drank his lunch, and came to the conclusion that the phrase *time stands still* was not simply poetic license.

Zelda tried to eat, tried to keep from looking at Dalgliesh, tried to think of something other than her impending gratification—and in this instance, failed miserably. Lost in lustful contemplation, she ate without tasting, drank Dalgliesh's vintage champagne with no more regard than she would water, and viewed each dish set before her with the mild surprise of someone coming awake.

The numerous servants exchanged telling glances as they served the various courses to a largely silent table, Chris's boyish chatter notwithstanding. The staff all knew that the earl had never invited a lady to Crosstrees. Seeing him essentially mute and drinking hard suggested he may have regretted his impulse. The lady was equally speechless, a far cry from the usual flirtatious coquettes favored by the earl. Below stairs gossip being what it was, Dalgliesh's lovers were well-known and much discussed.

As for Creiggy, none dared speculate why she chose not to speak. She was a force to be reckoned with in the household. Best not try to decipher her mood.

And so the strained atmosphere persisted until a servant happened to lean in too close to refill Zelda's champagne glass.

Startled, she recoiled, squealed.

Creiggy looked up.

Alec glanced her way.

Chris grinned.

And Zelda turned bright red.

"I'm afraid I was daydreaming," she quickly explained. "I tend to do that when I'm tired. Not that I'm *particularly* tired—well perhaps just a little, what with the hunt yesterday and the busy evening at the Grovelands'—not that it was *especially* busy," she swiftly added, not wishing to allude to her evening with Dalgliesh, "but perhaps just—"

"A day of hunting would make anyone tired," Creiggy kindly interposed to mitigate Zelda's embarrassment. "I've never understood the attraction of putting one's life at risk when one could enjoy the scenery from the comfort of the terrace windows and avoid those treacherous fences. Pass Miss MacKenzie one of those apple tarts, William. They're a specialty of the chef, my dear. You must try one."

Alec smiled his thanks to Creiggy. He didn't dare look at Zelda again. Instead, he pointed at his empty glass.

His old nanny said, "That's your sixth whiskey," and waved off the servant who'd jumped to comply to the earl's gesture.

"Surely you're not counting my drinks?" Alec softly said.

"I always do."

"Well stop." He pointed at his glass again.

"It's not a remedy."

"Thank you for the advice," he coolly said and jabbed his finger at his glass.

The servant didn't budge, deterred by Creiggy's sharp gaze.

Alec glanced over his shoulder. "May I remind you who pays your wages, Henry."

"You do, sir." But the man didn't move.

"God almighty." Spinning around in his chair, Dalgliesh plucked the bottle from the footman's hand.

"Papa swore!" Chris cried. "You're not supposed to, Papa!"

"Hell if I can't." Pulling out the cork and tossing it aside, he raised the bottle to his lips and drank deeply.

"Papa swore again!" Chris's gaze flicked back and forth between his father and Creiggy. "You owe money to the poor box, Papa. Doesn't he, Creiggy?"

Leaning his head against his chair back, Dalgliesh briefly shut his eyes. This was what came from inviting an extravagantly sensual creature like Miss MacKenzie into his life. Complete chaos. And the most glorious, mind-fucking pleasure as well, he thought—that prodigal exception effectively vindicating all else.

Opening his eyes, he set the bottle on the table. Understanding that the situation required a conciliatory gesture, perfectly capable of humoring people when necessary—in this case, the highly motivating prospect of sinking his cock into Miss MacKenzie's hot cunt the requisite necessity—he addressed the table at large. "I apologize. You're right, Creiggy, I shouldn't drink so much. And, Chris, remind me to put some money in the poor box tomorrow. I shouldn't have cursed. Now then is my atonement complete? Is everyone happy? Are you happy, Miss MacKenzie?" he added at the last because he couldn't help himself once he'd uttered the word that had become so relevant to his life since meeting Zelda.

"I am," she simply said, turning pink to the roots of her flaming hair.

"Good. Do you like the apple tart? As I recall," he softly said, referring to their breakfast in Fitz's hamlet, "you do." Having succumbed to temptation, he couldn't keep his eyes off her.

"Yes. It's excellent."

"Good," he said again, byzantine implication in the single word. "And is the champagne to your liking?" Lord, she was beautiful. Happiness took on a corporeal form.

"Yes."

His gaze traveled over her black serge–covered breasts. "We mustn't forget your wardrobe."

Creiggy looked up from her apple tart at that.

"Please, don't give it a thought," Zelda whispered.

He finally noticed the extreme softness of her voice, noticed as well the rigid set of her shoulders. He was embarrassing her. He must stop. "If you'll excuse me." Pushing his chair away from the table, he quickly rose. "I have to finish some correspondence. Someone will see you to your room, Miss MacKenzie, when you wish to nap."

"I know the way."

Something in her voice stopped him midturn—a sultry undertone, undeniable and familiar. He turned back. "Are you sure?"

"Very."

He smiled; he'd said as much in answer to her not so long ago. "I'm glad," he said. "Pleasant dreams, Miss Mac-Kenzie."

The room was quiet as a tomb after Dalgliesh walked out.

Morbid curiosity, astonishment was writ large on every retainer's face.

Conjecture lifted Creiggy's brows.

A warm, celebratory glow melted through Zelda's senses and effectively nullified puny reality.

"Now what?" Chris said into the hush, boyish issues quite separate from adult concerns. "I don't have school today, do I?" He sensed a break in his routine. His gaze on Creiggy was hopeful.

"No, not today," Creiggy affably said. "Perhaps you'd like to go to the toy shop instead."

"Would I ever!" Chris leaped to his feet, his face wreathed in smiles.

"Then run upstairs, wash your hands and face, and I'll

meet you in the front hall. Don't let me keep you, Miss MacKenzie," Creiggy remarked as Chris raced away. "And I apologize for the little scene. I tend to speak my mind."

"Alec seems relatively tolerant of plain speaking."

"He's remarkably patient with all of us." Creiggy smiled. "He always has been. Now, dinner's at seven so Chris can join us. We keep country hours at Crosstrees."

Zelda came to her feet. "Chris is such a sweet boy."

"They both are."

"Yes, I know." Zelda's smile warmed her eyes. "It's very agreeable here. Snug and homey. Surprising in such a grand establishment."

"Alec dislikes pomp and pretense."

"All this splendor aside." Zelda indicated her sumptuous surroundings with a sweep of her hand. A room for every occasion, she thought, the breakfast room having given way to another cozy sun-filled chamber, as if the architect had planned for family meals to follow the sun. Portraits of beautiful women and large, dark men like Dalgliesh lined the walls, the gilding and handwrought paneling softened with the patina of age, a colorful, lavish carpet from Persia soft underfoot.

"Most of the artifacts are from generations past," Creiggy said. "Although the dowager countess collects antiques and paintings on occasion. She recently bought the Van Dyck over the mantel and the small Rembrandt in the corner and that pretty chair"—Creiggy pointed—"was in the Trianon during Pompadour's sojourn."

"Alec's an indulgent son." The items were costly.

"He always has been."

"More of his kindness."

"Some of it born of necessity. Perhaps he'll tell you about it."

"I wouldn't dare to presume."

"But you already have. Most charmingly, my dear. Don't take alarm."

"Thank you then. I won't."

"I suggest you leave before Chris returns. He's going to

insist you come along if you're still here, and I can't guarantee you'll get away without a fuss."

Zelda dipped her head in acknowledgment. "I understand. I had four younger brothers. Until dinner then."

If she was a betting woman, which she was, Creiggy thought, watching Zelda walk away, she might be tempted to wager a tidy sum on the possibility that Miss MacKenzie had seriously breached Alec's long-standing defenses.

That the bonny lass happened to be a beautiful, intelligent, equestrian Scotswoman was more than a body could have hoped for.

She was a veritable gift from the gods.

She even dressed like an Amazon.

Leaning back in her chair, Dalgliesh's old nanny smiled. It almost made one believe in the wee folk.

CHAPTER 15

ON ENTERING HER bedroom, Zelda shut the door and smiled at the man lounging on her bed. "I was hoping you'd be here." She moved toward him, unbuttoning her jacket as she went.

"Did you doubt it?" His tone was easy; sex a constant in his life.

"I wasn't entirely sure when you mentioned correspondence."

"A polite lie. I barely made it through lunch."

She grinned. "Is that what you call drinking half a bottle?"

"I call it hell on earth. All I could think about was being alone with you. Here, let me help you." He sat up and swung his legs over the side of the bed.

"How much time do we have?"

"Oh Christ." An almost imperceptible sigh. "I forgot. Mrs. Drewe is waiting for us."

She didn't ask who Mrs. Drewe was; she didn't care. "Let her wait."

"It won't take long." His voice was gentle, conciliatory as he came to his feet. "A brief detour, no more."

"Postpone whatever it is."

She was very close, inches away, looking up at him, her violet gaze hot, impatient. He hesitated for a fraction of a second, debating. Then he took her hand. "I'd rather not." Both out of courtesy and because he had a mind to see her in something other than pants. But he didn't say that. "Give me ten minutes. That's not so long." Without waiting for an answer, he pulled her toward the door to his dressing room.

"I don't want to," she protested. "Really—I don't." She tugged on his hand. "Alec—I'm not sure I can wait!"

He heard the breathlessness in her voice at the last and came to a stop. Turning back, he took pains to speak calmly. "Ten minutes, no more, darling, and after that I promise you can have anything you want."

"Sexually you mean."

"Of course." He smiled faintly. "Although ask for anything. You'll find me very agreeable."

Her gaze narrowed slightly, resentment in her glance. "This Mrs. Drewe must be damned important."

He swallowed a grunt. Good. She was less breathless now, back to her usual willful self. Keep talking. "Katy—Mrs. Drewe—is our seamstress at Crosstrees. She's very good. She trained at Worth's. And while I adore you in your breeches, I'd adore you more in a gown this evening."

"But need we do this now?" Although timing was no longer the primary issue; it was the warmth in Dalgliesh's voice when speaking of this seamstress. Worth's in Paris? They didn't employ plain women.

An escalating argument implicit in her pettish tone, his in contrast was soothing. He wished to avoid a contest of wills. "Humor me, darling. You might even see something you like. Please?" And without waiting for a reply, he shoved open the door and hauled Zelda into his dressing room before she could dig in her heels. "Sorry to keep you waiting, Katy. Lunch took longer than I anticipated. Allow me to introduce Miss MacKenzie. Zelda, Katy." He dropped Zelda's twitching hand rather than engage in a public struggle. "I see you've found some things," he pleasantly said, hoping to divert his sulky companion's attention. Several doors of the mirrored wardrobe lining the walls were open, and dresses had been hung on the interior hooks. "More than I thought possible. Good work."

"Mrs. Elliot was happy to accommodate you. Lucy Winthrop will just have to wait for a few of her gowns, she said. She finds Lucy more annoying than usual since Harry got his knighthood, so it was no imposition. And you know Mrs. Elliot's always been partial to you. Her exact words were, 'Alec is *such* a dear boy.'" The seamstress grinned. "Naturally I agreed."

Alec grinned back. "And why wouldn't you?"

"Why indeed?"

"Actually, she's a great friend of my mother," Dalgliesh explained, with a glance for Zelda. "I'm simply included within Mother's charitable sphere."

Meek as a lamb. *I doubt it,* Zelda thought. Mrs. Elliot had worked for him before, she expected. And Mrs. Drewe—all rosy-cheeked and smiling—was a pretty country maid fresh as the dew. And damned friendly as well. She'd bet one of her hunters that little Katy and Alec were *more* than friends.

With the reason behind such an array of gowns accounted for, Katy addressed Zelda with a polite smile. "It's a pleasure to meet you, Miss MacKenzie. Crosstrees doesn't often have company."

Was she being warned off? "The pleasure's mine," Zelda replied with forced civility and the barest of smiles.

"Did John find someone to watch the children?" Best to clarify Katy's status with that coolness in Zelda's voice.

"Liz came over, thank you. The children like her."

Whose children? Zelda suspiciously wondered when it was no business of hers if Dalgliesh had by-blows by the dozens.

Now a frown. "I hope Will's feeling better. Katy's husband," Dalgliesh offered in an attempt to erase the frown. "He sprained his ankle badly."

"Will's nicely on the mend. We're most grateful to you for sending the doctor over. By the way, I have orders to especially thank you for the whiskey," Katy added. "Will's the sweetest dear, but he's not used to being home all day with the children underfoot."

"Especially with your wild bunch. They're darling children but hellions, as you well know. Katy and Will have five youngsters under ten, my dear. Miss MacKenzie raised four brothers and a sister, Katy." His gaze swivelled back and forth between the women. "You two could compare notes."

Katy smiled at Zelda. "I'll bet you never had enough sleep."

"Not when they were young. Someone always stayed up late or woke up early."

"And one eats porridge and one don't, and one likes eggs and one don't."

"And none ate stewed fruit," Zelda said with a real smile, her jealousy of Mrs. Drewe having dissipated when she'd spoken of her husband with such affection. It hadn't been enough that she was married; not with Dalgliesh's amorous record.

"Don't even mention stewed fruit," Katy said with a laugh. "You'd think I was trying to poison them."

"Sometimes if you disguise it with a large amount of Chantilly cream, they—"

Katy shook her head. "I tried."

Feeling that fences had been nicely mended, the earl interrupted. "Since I have orders to expedite this fitting"— he tapped his wristwatch and smiled—"might we find something that can be pressed into service for dinner tonight?" He frowned slightly. "You may have already heard. Violetta destroyed Miss MacKenzie's clothes at Groveland Chase. Hence, our dilemma."

"Liz mentioned it. Dreadful thing. I'm so sorry, Miss MacKenzie. She's a wicked person, she is. I doubt our village gowns can make up for those you lost. But perhaps—"

"They'll suit for now, Katy. We can shop later in London"— Dalgliesh glanced at Zelda—"or Edinburgh."

His use of the word *we* as well as the allusion to shopping later was inexpressibly sweet. Although Zelda cautioned herself about misinterpreting a few casually uttered phrases. "Anything will do," she graciously said. "So long as it's quickly done," she added with a pointed glance at the earl.

He looked amused. "You see, Katy, I have my marching orders. We'll settle for one gown now. After you fit it, the other frocks can be altered without us."

Us again, Zelda noted. How perfectly lovely.

And sheer folly, of course, to inject undue meaning into the earl's words.

Having effectively silenced the bluebirds of happiness singing in her brain, Zelda pointed at a long-sleeved, high-necked wool gown. "I like that one. It looks cozy and warm."

"I've had central heating installed, darling. Pick something more elegant for evening."

She looked at Dalgliesh, one brow arched. "Am I being overruled?"

"Of course not. We'll take the green wool, Katy."

"Do other women allow you to speak for them?" Zelda inquired in gelid accents.

The earl grinned, put his fingers to his mouth, and made a locking motion.

"Thank you."

"You're entirely welcome." With a polished bow, Alec wisely took himself away to one of a pair of leather chairs, where he sat, slid down on his spine, stretched out his booted feet, and made himself comfortable.

"Troublesome man," Zelda said with a sniff.

He didn't answer; he only smiled. Women liked the last word.

Zelda turned to Katy. "Is he always so overbearing?"

Since Katy had never seen Alec with a woman at Cross-trees and the rumors of his amorous liaisons suggested they were primarily physical, she rather doubted he'd ever aspired to anything other than sexual proficiency.

"Acquit me, darling," Dalgliesh gently said. "I humbly yield to you in all things."

Zelda smiled. "Liar." Although his admission, false as it

was, was nonetheless charming. "Oh, very well," she said with a sigh. "You might as well tell me which gown you prefer because I really don't care."

He told her with exquisite courtesy.

She gave in with equal grace and prepared to politely accommodate the earl and the seamstress.

Alec was surprised he cared whether Zelda had a dress for dinner. He'd always taken little or no interest in his paramour's gowns; in fact, he preferred his lovers nude. Not that he didn't understand what was expected of him when it came to his lady loves' wardrobes. But he'd never escorted any of them to a dressmaker or, like now, actually anticipated the role of observer. *Get what you want and send the bill to my man of business*, he'd always said in the past. That had been the extent of his involvement.

Violetta's wickedness had unwittingly given him the opportunity to do what he'd never done before—or more to the point—cared to do. The thought of taking Zelda to Worth's in Paris suddenly leaped into his brain; he found it beguiling.

Christ, he must have drunk too much at lunch if he was thinking about taking Zelda to Worth's. He scoffed at men who treated their lovers like some pretty pet to be flaunted. And Zelda wasn't a pet—far from it. Even if she had been, he wasn't in the market for a pet. The only thing he was in the market for was sex and more sex—until such a time as he wasn't.

There now. Having marshaled his personal defenses, he watched with relative equanimity as Zelda's riding clothes came off—jacket, blouse, boots, breeches. Only at the last, when she was divested of all but her silk drawers and chemise and his gaze was focused on her large breasts straining the soft white silk, did he find it necessary to cross his legs to hide his erection. Then Zelda shifted her stance, drawing his attention to the small rise of her mons visible beneath the sheer silk of her drawers. He slowly surveyed the slight elevation, then his gaze drifted lower to the shaded juncture of her thighs, and his fingers involuntarily flexed against the urge to reach out, push aside the silk, slip his hand between her legs, and slide his fingers in just so . . .

He almost ordered, *Stop! We're done!*

But Katy suddenly moved into his line of vision, holding out the violet-shaded moiré gown for Zelda to step into, and that brief respite was enough to rein in his surging lust. A barbaric thing, lust. He exhaled softly, looked away, deliberately counted to ten, then ten again. At which point, having disciplined what needed disciplining, he was able to contemplate the pinning and tucking, the snipping and ripping—with, if not patience, stoic resignation.

The gown's bosom as well as the hem had to be let out appreciably. Lucy Winthrop was neither tall nor curvaceous . . . more's the pity for Harry. Although he'd always liked Harry. They'd played together as boys and later, too, in different sport.

Before long, Katy stepped away and offered her handiwork for Alec's approval. "Well?" She indicated the pinned gown with a sweeping gesture. "Will that do?"

Is Venus de Milo *acceptable?*

With any other woman, he immediately would have said yes. With Zelda, he said, "Ask Miss MacKenzie."

Zelda smiled at her astute lover and, without so much as a glance at any of the mirrored doors, pronounced the gown perfect.

"I'll have it ready by six, then." Katy began unpinning the back of the gown.

Alec smiled. "You're a dear."

"Liz is the one who's a dear," she said with a flicker of a glance at Alec. "I hope you're paying her well."

"I had John tell her she can name her price, including a bonus for watching your mischievous brood." He grinned. "Battle wages."

"For my darlings," Katy said with a mother's pride.

"But they're always perfect angels when they're sleeping, aren't they?" Zelda observed.

"Absolute angels," Katy agreed, sliding the last pin free. When Zelda stepped out of the gown a moment later, Katy picked it up and folded it over her arm. "I'll be back at six. Now make sure Alec shows you Will's coops while you're here, Miss MacKenzie. He's right proud of them."

"Will's my gamekeeper," Alec explained, rising from his chair and moving toward Zelda. "Thanks to him, I'm the envy of every pheasant-hunting noble in England. My thanks again, Katy. I'll have someone bring over the other frocks. Or if you prefer, take some of the servants with you."

"I might do that." The dressmaker began gathering up the sewing supplies she'd brought over.

Having reached Zelda, Alec held out his hand and quietly said, "Ready?"

"Need you ask?" She, too, spoke in an undertone.

He smiled.

"Don't be smug."

"Me?"

She sniffed. "Insolent man. If you hadn't kept me waiting so long, I'd walk away."

He lowered his hand. "But you're not going to."

"I might."

"And I might become king of England, but"—he grinned—"we both know neither of those things are going to happen. So let's not fight. I can get that anywhere."

"I didn't think all the fawning women would fight with you."

Nor would they. "Let's just say they can annoy me."

"And yet?" A steady stare.

"You can't masturbate all the time."

"I don't know about that."

He softly laughed. "May I watch?"

"If I can watch you."

"We'll work something out. Later."

"And now?"

"I think we should retire next door."

"Oh good and finally and thank you," she said, moving close, sliding her arms around his neck, melting against his body. "Be warned. I'm in a greedy mood."

He tensed. Katy was still in the room.

"I don't care about her."

"I see that." He, on the other hand, disliked public displays.

"Are you afraid of her?" Zelda rested her chin on his chest and smiled up at him. "You should be more afraid of me."

"Or you of me," he growled, still not touching her.

"How afraid?" A soft, feline purr.

Swearing under his breath, the question of an audience summarily dismissed, he finally moved, placed his hands on her bottom and dragged her hard against his body. "How afraid, you ask? Sound-the-alarm afraid. Pillage-and-loot afraid. Don't-look-for-help afraid." It was threat and warning, however softly put.

"I don't know if I should be frightened or excited," she whispered, a small tremor in her words as her breathing quickened. His cock was like a post between them.

"You just have to be submissive, darling," he quietly said as the door closed with a click on Katy. "I'll do the rest."

For a flashing moment, carnal expectation hovered dangerous and flame hot in the wake of his words. Was he serious? she wondered even as her senses, immune to intellectual conundrums, feverishly responded. Was he serious? he thought, surprised. Since when did he require submissive with his sex?

But astonishingly, he found he did with her. And why not? He didn't require dispensation for his actions. He never had.

Spreading his fingers wide, he exerted sufficient pressure for her to feel the full extent of his erection—the means, as it were, of his oppression. "I can keep you prisoner if I want. Did you know that?"

She began to shudder, his stark, unyielding erection hard against her belly a graphic promise of pleasure. Whether she'd heard him or not was a matter of indifference to her necessitous cravings, to every ripe nerve quivering with longing. Her body opened in welcome. "Please, Alec," she whispered. "I've waited long enough. Please!"

"Soon." His novel need for mastery prevailed.

"Don't do this," she wailed, moving her hips against his erection. "I need you!"

"You want this?" He matched the rhythm of her lower body. She whimpered; he was huge. "Yes, yes, oh God, yes . . ."

For a jaded man, he'd forgotten satisfaction could be so sweet. "Yes to anything?" he quietly said as she shivered in his arms.

"Yes—yes . . . anything." Disjointed, breathless words.

"I can't hear you." It was cruel to ask for abject capitulation, a perverse quid pro quo perhaps for his own irrepressible need.

His words were half muted by the lustful pounding in her ears. "Whatever you want," she gasped.

He wanted everything, he thought. He wanted to exhaust himself in her. He wanted to possess and occupy her like the lord of the manor he was. He wanted to put his *practice makes perfect* sexual credo to maximum use. "I'll show you what I want," he said, forcing himself to speak mildly. "In a minute." Then he lowered his head and kissed her like he felt—brutish and afflicted.

This from a man who'd always viewed amour as casual play—a man who often wasn't sure whom he was kissing or fucking after a bottle or two, a man who'd cultivated a masterful lack of involvement.

Now, suddenly, sex was no longer sex as entertainment. It was gut-wrenching and primal, a force majeure impulse without mercy. A full-scale burning of bridges and taking what he wanted.

And he knew about that.

Having lived a less troubled life, Zelda was immune to mind-wheeling tumult. She wanted only orgasmic surcease, now, immediately—then again and beyond again. She'd been craving Dalgliesh since before she'd reached Crosstrees, lunch had been almost unendurable, and how she'd survived the dress fitting was testament alone to her indomitable will.

And now, headstrong and determined—enough was enough!

She broke his grip easily or he let her, and as she reached for his trouser buttons, she snapped, "Play tyrant *after* I climax."

He suppressed his urge to laugh. He could play tyrant anytime he wanted. But charitable *and* horny—perhaps not now. "Here, let me. I'm faster."

"You'd better be." Spinning away, she strode toward the bedroom. "Or I might go on without you."

He looked up, one booted foot in hand. "You think so?" he said in a tone that would have warned off anyone else.

"I know so." Having pulled her chemise over her head, she dropped it behind her.

"We'll see," he said under his breath. The boot off, he flung it. A second later, the other boot joined the first. Stripping off his trousers and underwear with record speed, he slid off his jacket and discarded it before he reached the doorway to the bedroom; his waistcoat and shirt were left behind a moment later. Catching up with Zelda in three long strides, he swung her off her feet just as she reached the bed.

"Finally," she said, her smile close.

"Your finally or mine?"

"Does it matter?"

"I find it does."

"Then yours naturally. Or I'll never get what I want," she said, sultry and low.

"Which is?" He dropped her in the middle of the bed.

"Your glorious, extremely talented cock inside me," she murmured, spreading her thighs wide and lifting her arms to him. "My ambitions are rather fixed."

His were rather more comprehensive. "Do you know what I want?" Midway through his question, he thought about stopping. But he didn't.

"Whatever it is, you can have." She wiggled her fingers.

He took a small breath at such largesse. Then the practiced libertine regained control, the most cynical force majeure was locked away, and he said with a slight smile. "In that case, come here." He patted the side of the bed where he stood.

"What if I say no."

"Don't."

"Ummm. I adore that rough authority."

He laughed. "Christ, you like everything."

"Everything about *you*. My interests are quite specific. I don't regard every man as fuckable as you do women."

How to answer that?

"Don't bother," she said.

"I'm not so foolish." He patted the bed again. But when she responded to his summons, he lifted her down, took her hand, and drew her to the windows overlooking the parkland. "We'll do your finally first because I know how impatient you are," he said, having repressed his strange authoritarian impulses. "Then I'd appreciate my finally next."

"Of course."

It annoyed him that she didn't ask what he wanted. Had she no boundaries? This from a man who had never considered the word before in relation to sex. "No questions?"

"How soon can I come?"

He experienced a ridiculous surge of anger, instantly curbed. "If you'd care to lean over this"—he pulled a small upholstered chair up to the window—"you could enjoy the view while I enjoy your tight little cunt."

She smiled faintly. "A mutual enjoyment, Dalgliesh."

"I expect so." He indicated the chair with a nod.

She obligingly leaned over the chair back, and he thought for a moment of the complaisant females at Margo's in London. "Have you ever considered working in a brothel?" he crisply inquired.

"Have you ever considered hurrying?" She knew male affront when she heard it. It never failed to amaze her that men expected resistance from women, as though that in itself stamped them as virtuous. "I was under the impression neither of us were novices. Was that unclear somehow?"

It occurred to him to hit her, an astonishing impulse. "Jesus, you're a bitch," he said instead.

Abruptly coming upright, she spun around. "Does that affect your interest in me?" With a contemptuous smile, she surveyed his rampant erection pulsing against his stomach. "It rather looks like it doesn't."

He stared at her narrow-eyed, a tick fluttered across his cheek; he visibly brought himself under control. Then he took her by the shoulders, swung her around, pushed her down, kept her in place with a hand on her back, and said very softly, "My interest is the same as yours."

Her hands braced on the chair seat, she glanced over her shoulder. "Only our timetables differ," she said, sarcasm light in her voice.

"A little patience, darling." He ran his palms down Zelda's back, slender waist, over the plump curve of her bottom like a rider gentling his mount before settling in the saddle. "Although you're always ready, aren't you? An attractive asset in a woman," he whispered, sliding his fingers between her legs, testing her readiness like one would a mare about to be mounted.

She quivered, feverish with need after waiting half the day.

"Would any cock do, I wonder?" he softly said.

"Right now, I'd prefer yours, if you don't mind. And a little less challenge."

"My, my—how demanding. Do men like that?"

She bit back the temptation to respond. He was unpredictable. And she needed him at the moment.

He gave her points for restraint. But then she was ripe for mounting. His fingers were drenched, her sex slick, needy. He slid his fingers gently up and down her moist cleft, once, twice, three times while she softly panted. When he turned his attention to her distended clitoris, her gasp brought a faint smile to his lips. "Now in terms of timetables," he murmured, continuing his delicate massage, "how fast is fast for you? Should I just ram it in or should I take my time? How rough would you like it? Or not rough at all? How much do you want my cock in you? You must tell me." He allowed a pause to develop. "No more insolence?" he murmured, conscious of her tenseness, her erratic breathing as he stroked her silky tissue. "How easy it is to silence you."

That Miss MacKenzie's ready passions were an issue disturbed him briefly. But the lady took the initiative as she was wont to do, swung her hips backward a considerable distance, his fingers slipped deeper inside her, and suddenly he had other things on his mind. The splendor of her shapely, alluring bottom for one, her hot, moist sex engulfing his fingers secondly, and of course, what was most notable—his cock was in full rut and aching like a son of a bitch.

Time enough for introspection later.

He slapped her bottom out of sheer truculence and ordered, gruff and peremptory, "Up, up—higher. Higher. I can't quite reach you." He could reach her perfectly well. But she'd wrought such signal changes in his life, he required retribution, he supposed. As she quickly rose on tiptoe and made herself more available, he smiled, and when he plunged into her and she instantly climaxed, his smiled widened.

One could forgive a woman like that almost anything.

Adjusting his grip on her hips, wanting better purchase, he didn't wait for her orgasm to diminish but tested the limits of her glorious cunt with gluttonous zest and a level of gratification previously unknown to him. Meanwhile, the lady indulged in a gratuitous number of orgasms while he chose to extend the sybaritic, obscenely stunning rapture bombarding his senses. Until, after what seemed a shimmering endless interval, he reached the proverbial point of no return and was faced with a notable dilemma.

Notable for a number of reasons. He'd never faced the dilemma before. Nor would a rational man have debated the issue at all. No more than a rational man would have invited Miss MacKenzie to his hunting lodge. Since he had, however, it begged the question whether reason was in any way involved.

The answer wasn't reassuring.

The fact that he'd not withdrawn from her exceedingly welcoming body when his climax was fast peaking suggested prevailing custom hung in the balance. Perhaps if she hadn't slid her hand between her legs, taken his testicles in a soft, tender grip and gently stretched them, his habits of a lifetime might have continued to hang in the balance.

As it was, he began to ejaculate the moment she tugged on his testicles, and he continued to gush into her sweet, tight, frictionless cunt for endless moments, eyes shut, his heart pumping wildly, his brain convulsed with ecstasy.

He was, of course, sorry he'd done what he'd done the moment his orgasm was over and cooler counsel held sway. But his semen was running down her thighs at that point and his erection was still only mildly diminished, and that proved to be even more of a problem in terms of cooler counsel. Then she said, "Is that all?" and smiled at him over her shoulder.

Really, there was no question that Miss MacKenzie was a most delightful houseguest, nor was there any question of removing from his current location. Until much later, she finally said in that frank way of hers, "My legs are tired. Do you mind doing something else?"

He didn't.

He took a seat in that same chair, lifted her onto his lap, politely said, "Is this better?" and was delighted with her sweet smile and her even sweeter cunt sliding down his cock. After that no one talked for some time.

He'd decided after that first mishap that he might as well indulge himself when it came to ejaculating. Whether he came in her once that afternoon or more than once surely no longer signified. She agreed. She was most agreeable in every other way as well, and he said as much later when they'd moved to the bed.

"I'm so very pleased we met," he said, gazing down on her after their latest orgasm, the faint warmth of her skin light against his.

She laughed. "Is that what you call this?"

"You delight me in body and spirit," he said with a boyish smile. "You bring sunshine and joy in your wake. Is that better?"

"If you mean it."

"Of course I do." A deep, leisurely tone. "I don't invite women home."

"Well, then, I'm flattered, my lord," she teasingly replied. It would never do to believe a faithless rogue like Dalgliesh. But she liked that she was the first, at least, when it came to his guest list.

He frowned. "Flirtatious women I know by the score."

"More than a score from all reports."

"Stop."

"Or?" A seductive smile, challenge in the faint arch of her brows.

He grinned. "I'll make you stop."

"Do tell," she said with a dazzling grin of her own.

He did then at some length, his feelings left in limbo. He didn't know how to explain the novel sensations, in any case. Nor was he willing to pursue such perilous concepts when it came right down to it. He understood why she was here, she understood why she was here. Best leave it at that.

But much later that afternoon, with the lush, captivating Miss MacKenzie lying beneath him, matching him stroke for stroke in a hard, pulsing rhythm, with pleasure prodigal and a wistful fervor infusing his senses, he found himself unmaking his life without a qualm. "What if I gave you a child?" he whispered. "Would you like that?"

She didn't answer. She was panting.

"Good," he said.

CHAPTER 16

WHILE THE TWO lovers were navigating the physical
and emotional limits of carnal sensation, a spirited discussion was taking place in the kitchen. Katy had described in
lively detail what had transpired in the earl's dressing room
as she was leaving.

"I wouldn't expect to see hide or hair of either of them
'til dinner," Katy cheerily said. "He's sweet on her. It's plain
as day."

"I wouldn't go that far," a footman cautioned. "He's not
the type. Love 'em and leave 'em, that's his game."

The housekeeper, who'd known Alec from childhood,
who wished him the happiness he deserved, softly sighed.
"Even if he is sweet on her, his wicked wife stands in the
way. Poor boy."

"Then it's time he divorce her." Even Rowan was surprised at the vehemence in his voice; he wasn't, by nature,
strident.

The staff in Dalgliesh's various establishments were
privy to every nuance of their employers' lives, and save for
the old earl, they'd served the Munros with affection. The

retainers had always protected the dowager countess, too, as best they could. And they viewed the young boy who'd matured into the admirable man he was today as partly due to their fostering.

"You know that bitch'll fight a divorce to her last breath," the steward muttered. "She spends a fortune on herself every year."

"There's other ways," one of the upstairs maids softly attested.

A hush descended in the kitchen, everyone's thoughts on the dowager's illness four years ago that had brought Alec home.

"Time enough for that," the housekeeper flatly said, fingering the cameo at her throat. "If all else fails."

"The flame-haired beauty might be just a passing fancy like all the others," the hall porter cautioned. "Best wait and see."

"If'n she ain't though," said a young groom who'd just come in for his lunch. "We can always help things along."

A wholesale nodding of heads acknowledged his statement, and the silence lengthened as all thoughts centered on their young lord's plight.

Until Rowan suddenly clapped his hands. "Back to work everyone. There's nothing we can do today."

"Except tiptoe by the lady's bedroom so as not to break their rhythm," a young lad quipped.

"That's enough, Matthew," the housekeeper sharply reprimanded. "I won't have any lewd talk about his lordship or his guest."

"Yes, ma'am."

But the lad beside him whispered in his ear, "As if she don't know Dalgliesh is known far and wide for vice and debauch, lucky dog."

As the housekeeper's glowering gaze skewered him, the boy quickly murmured, "I was just sayin' that Lord Dalgliesh deserves all our help and support, ma'am."

"Humph. I should hope so. Now, I won't hear any ill spoken of the earl. Do you hear? He survived a childhood that would have turned any other boy into a monster, bless his soul. And he's taking care of his mother and that evil woman's children with the unselfishness of a saint. So if he kicks up his heels now and again," she said, referring to Alec's dissipation in euphemistic terms, "he's allowed. Is that clear?" She swung her dour gaze over the crowd. "Everyone. Clear?"

Murmurs of affirmative echoed round the room.

"Now off with you." She waved her hand vigorously. "The chef and I have a dinner to deal with. His lordship must have all his favorite foods tonight."

AT THE SAME time her husband was randomly and perhaps involuntarily transforming his life, the Countess of Dalgliesh was having tea with the ladies at Groveland Chase. The men were still out hunting, although the afternoon light was beginning to fade, the thin grey mist outside the windows muting the landscape into blurred shapes and shadow.

In contrast to the muted, grey day outside, the ladies lounging about the room looked like so many hothouse flowers in their colorful tea gowns trimmed and festooned with ribbons, lace, and endless ruffles. Fires crackled in the fireplaces at both ends of the sitting room, the chandeliers had been turned on, and soft-footed servants moved about the room, offering champagne and sweets to the ladies, refilling glasses, lighting cigarettes for those who partook of the Turkish weed, and taking note of Neville's unobtrusive nods or raised finger as he directed the ritual of tea from his position near the door.

Violetta and Bella were engaged in a tête-à-tête over champagne and a plate of plum comfits set on a table between them, their conversation predictably about men. Both were beautiful, thoroughly self-centered, and shamelessly wanton. That their fashionable milieu regarded fidelity with amusement allowed them such license.

From a very young age, both women had learned how to use their beauty to advantage. Bella's husband was charming and rich and involved in his own pursuits; they lived a civilized life. As for Violetta, her first husband had unfortunately gambled away a fortune, and when his life had come to an end in a fit of drunken despair, she'd been left with a young child and her husband's mountain of debts.

But she'd recovered nicely as everyone knew. And so Bella said with a sly smile, "Darling, your position is secure. You're married to Dalgliesh. It can hardly matter if he ruts with that Scottish woman at midday in Piccadilly Square so long as you're his wife. Does that MacKenzie woman affect your allowance? No. Does she affect your, shall we say, amusements? No. Does she affect your place in society? Not in the least. And really, dear, you know Alec. He'll forget her name in a day or so."

"That may be, but he embarrassed me last night," Violetta said, fretful and sulky. "You saw him. He practically hovered over that hussy before dinner, when everyone knows he's the last person in the world to give that sort of attention to a woman."

"He's just temporarily infatuated. You have to admit Miss MacKenzie has presence. And she adventures around the world. Men like that sort of exotic female. He'll tire of her soon enough. Doesn't he always?"

"The strumpet's not only fast and loose, she's utterly brazen." Violetta schooled her face to a mendacious apprehension. "She actually threatened me, you know."

"My heavens! What did you do?" Exchanging lovers and husbands was normally done with well-bred urbanity. Everyone understood the rules.

"Naturally, I walked away. I was terrified," Violetta said with a little dramatic shiver. "Who knows what the fiendish bitch might do?"

"Well, she's gone now," Bella said with a shrug of indifference. "And so much the better, if you ask me. She didn't appear to have any conversation. I tried to talk to her once after dinner and she barely replied."

"The Highlands are hardly the place to learn fine manners."

"I doubt Alec's interested in her manners," Bella sardonically noted.

Violetta's fine nostrils flared, feeling the slight. It was humiliating that Alec had so brazenly played court to a woman. Especially when he was notorious for avoiding all but the most idle flirtations. *Everyone* had noticed his arresting interest in Miss MacKenzie. "I want her to pay," Violetta bitterly declared, the shift in her domestic affairs unacceptable. "And I intend to see that she does."

"I understand your frustration, darling. You're angry. But don't we all want what we want? *I* came to this godforsaken place hours from civilization in the hope that Jamie had tired of his wife. It's been over a year, and she's been breeding for a good deal of that time. I thought he'd be looking for other playmates by now. Alas, no. And she's actually nursing their son. Did you know that?" The blond beauty made a face. "I can't imagine that can be attractive. You'd think dripping breasts would be rather messy, if not completely off-putting to any thought of passion."

"I wouldn't know. I had a wet nurse for Chris."

Bella smiled faintly. "A sensible woman. Speaking of sensible, darling, rather than dwell on revenge, why not enjoy Freddy's company. He obviously adores you, and God knows he's in no hurry to return to his wife. Who would? Have you seen her?" Countess Minton made a little dismissive gesture with her ringed fingers. "Plain as a sparrow, no breasts, and thin as a rail. A shame his father had the ill fortune to invest in that railroad venture in Argentina. With Freddy's good looks and title, he could have had an heiress *without* the taint of the steel mills. As for Dalgliesh, darling, really you must count your blessings. He allows you carte blanche. What more could you want?"

Violetta couldn't say what she really wanted. She'd learned very young not to do that. It frightened people. "I'm sure you're right," she sweetly said. "Alec does allow me freedom."

"And an unlimited allowance," Bella pointed out.

"Yes. He's very generous."

"Come, now, enough useless spleen. They say it's harmful to one's looks—frowning. I prefer being amused. Do let's put our heads together and see if we can deduce who's father to Cressidia's coming child. It's not her husband. Everyone knows he's incapable."

"With women."

"That's what I meant. So then—who tops the list?"

Violetta answered, gleeful and vivacious, but behind her bright smile and convivial reply, she was planning her revenge. On her husband. On the woman who'd disrupted the habitual pattern of his life, and in so doing—hers. She didn't believe for a minute that this was just another sexual romp for Dalgliesh. If it had been, he would have remained at the Chase for the weekend, he would have treated Miss MacKenzie with his usual indifference. He never would have taken the time to warn her off like he had last night.

And he'd warned her and Freddy both—in no uncertain terms.

She knew what he was capable of, too; she'd taken his threats to heart.

But she also knew that she wouldn't allow her title of countess to be put in jeopardy. She'd worked too hard for that coronet. "Oh, really? Bunny Lisle? Do you think so?" Violetta gave her full attention to Bella. "Even when he already has that little family in the country with that actress or singer or whatever she is? I rather prefer Max Baring as candidate for father. He and Cressidia were seen together in her husband's box at the opera. And they weren't listening to the music."

And so teatime continued, the two ladies blandly exchanging malice, drinking champagne, then more champagne. Bella gossiped about the latest on-dits from London. Violetta listened with half an ear, automatically responding to the tittle-tattle, when in fact, she was planning on leaving in the morning. She couldn't wait until Monday. She had much to do.

CHAPTER 17

At half past five there was a light knock on the dressing room door.

Dalgliesh glanced down at Zelda sleeping in his arms and spoke in a voice calculated to reach his valet's ears with minimum shock to Zelda's. "Thank you, Jenkins."

Zelda stirred.

"It's nothing, darling. Sleep." For a few minutes more. Then they had to get ready for Katy, Chris's playtime, and dinner. Life went on no matter how unquenchable one's desires. He smiled. Not that he had any complaints concerning his insatiable appetite for the lady. A streak of good luck, he'd say.

He should have wakened her; there was still much to do. But she was soft and warm in his arms; he felt at peace—a pleasant sensation for a man who hadn't known much peace. Or it could just be orgasmic surfeit drugging his senses, he thought with another smile. And that had nothing to do with luck.

But however agreeable it was to let the minutes slip away,

as six o' clock approached, their commitments could no longer be ignored. Bending his head, he touched his lips to Zelda's forehead. "Duty calls, darling."

"Ummm." The silky sweep of her lashes fluttered upward, then fell.

Her low throaty murmur resonated in all his susceptible, oversexed pleasure centers. A shame they were under time constraints. He sighed. But they were. "Ten minutes before your dress fitting. Nine minutes, fifty-five seconds, fifty-four, fifty-three—"

Zelda groaned.

"I have a present for you if it helps."

A shake of her head, eyes still shut.

"You'll like it. It's not diamonds."

Her lashes slowly lifted and she looked up, amusement in her gaze. "Is there a woman who could resist a remark like that?"

He grinned. "Exactly my point. And for your information, I don't buy jewelry for women. You're the first. So my feelings are very fragile," he shamelessly asserted. "Pray don't trample them."

She laughed. "Liar. But I promise to be gentle."

"I'm relieved," drawled the man known far and wide for his indifference to tender emotion.

"While *I'm* divinely happy." How could she not be after the past hours with Dalgliesh, who had set out to please her, who always left enamored women in his wake. "Pray tell *me* not to be so juvenile."

"Be anything you want, sweetheart. I'm happy, too," he said with practiced charm and an open, generous smile. "And we'll make each other happier in about"—he glanced at the clock—"four hours. But at the moment, we're pressed for time." Sitting up with fluid grace and finely tuned muscle, he tossed the ivory silk quilt aside and lifted her into a seated position. "So what do you want to see first?"

She grinned. "First?"

"I told you I was besotted," he said, sliding from the rumpled bed. "Didn't you believe me?"

"No."

He shot a teasing glance over his shoulder as he strode away, unashamedly nude, splendidly male, casually libertine. "Maybe you will after you see what I bought you."

"How did you manage in such a short time?" It was a woman's question. She wanted to know why he'd done what he'd done, what he thought and felt, every little emotional nuance motivating him.

"I have a telegraph line to the house. An efficient secretary. The London train comes into Crosstrees Station at half past four. That's about it." A man's answer.

While she'd gleaned nothing from his reply, his thoughtfulness couldn't be faulted. She, on the other hand, had considered only her own pleasure in coming to Crosstrees. "I feel guilty." She bit her lip. "I should have brought something—at least for Chris." A small courtesy gift from a guest *was* customary. "I apologize."

Dalgliesh stopped, half turned, a fleeting look of surprise on his face; women in his world took not gave. "Don't be silly. Your visit is gift enough for Chris. He's thrilled. As for me, you brought me something I hadn't known existed. Joy. And that, my dear"—he caught himself; he'd safeguarded his emotions too long to expose himself completely—"is like the chimera of myth," he finished lightly. "Now shut your eyes and prepare to be amazed."

When he opened his dressing room door, a smile lit his eyes. His valet was a man of orderliness and precision. A number of boxes were neatly piled on a table, in an ascending order of decreasing size. And the smallest at the top was a distinctive ivory white, holly wood box from Fabergé.

Picking up the serried packages, the earl reentered the bedroom, kicked the door shut behind him, and bore his gifts to the first lady to occupy his bed. Not that he viewed Zelda in those terms; he was conditioned against such dramatic symbolism. "You can open your eyes," he said, setting the stack on the bed, taking a seat beside her, and pointing. "Start with this one."

Zelda recognized the white wooden box as well. "You

shouldn't have." She cast him a playful, coquettish look from under her lashes. "Was that demure enough?"

She wasn't even remotely demure, with her tousled hair and breathtaking beauty, with her sporting blood and wild passions. "If I was looking for demure, I wouldn't have invited *you* to keep me company."

She grinned. "I'm not sure that's a compliment."

"Of the highest order, my dear, believe me." In fact his secretary had said that morning with what could only be characterized as shock, *Are you sure, sir?* when Dalgliesh had dictated his detailed list of items. It was an unprecedented event; Dalgliesh had always delegated his gift-giving to his secretary with a casual, *Send whatever you think appropriate.* "Open it," Alec said, tapping the box in Zelda's hand. "I'm not exactly sure what they sent."

"Who handles Fabergé here?" Zelda asked, unfastening the gold clasp.

"A dealer I know. I order Fabergé cigarette cases in my racing colors through his shop. He usually has a few Fabergé items on hand."

Zelda lifted the lid on its gold hinges, drew in a small breath, then turned to Dalgliesh. "It's beautiful," she murmured, running her finger over the polished stone. "It's even the right color." A lapis lazuli miniature hunter with diamond eyes and gold bridle and saddle was nestled in white velvet; a Fabergé specialty—animals created from semiprecious stones.

"I didn't know what Beckworth had in stock. I just ordered a horse."

"And Lady Luck was on my side." She leaned over and kissed him. "You shouldn't have, but thank you."

Giving presents should always be like this, he thought, feeling pleased and gratified, basking in the sunshine of her smile. "Here's the one that's not diamonds." Taking the wooden box from her hand, he held out a green leather jewelry case.

She opened it and gasped.

It gave him pleasure to hear her sharp intake of breath,

his satisfaction quite out of proportion to the small utterance. "Try it on."

"It's too much." She met his gaze and held it. "Seriously, Alec, it's outrageously too much."

"Nonsense." Coming up from his lounging pose, he lifted out the single strand of large pearls from which a sizeable violet-hued pendant hung. "It's only an amethyst." It was, in fact, an extremely rare, extremely large purple diamond. He'd seen the piece displayed in the window of a Mayfair jeweler not long ago and, recognizing its value, he'd suspected it had remained unsold.

Slipping the pearls around Zelda's neck, he locked the jeweled clasp and leaned back to survey the stunning piece and the stunning lady in whose impressive cleavage the diamond nestled. "It's the same color as your eyes. Although not nearly as beautiful."

"You're spoiling me." Zelda touched the large tear-shaped jewel. "Really, Alec, I shouldn't accept something so fine."

"You have to."

She lifted her brows at the casual authority in his tone. "Or?"

"Or I won't let you climax again," he lazily drawled. "And we both know how much you like to come."

"Maybe I don't need you," she smoothly countered. "Have you thought of that?"

He grinned. "Bet?"

"So I'm captive to my lust? Is that what you're saying?"

"Pretty much. Look, darling," he gently said. "We both are. I'm only teasing you. I could no more leave you than you could resist your desires. We're prisoners to this"—his smile was indulgent and sweet—"glorious insanity. So why not enjoy it? We'll worry about tomorrow, tomorrow. Wear the necklace as a token of my affection. It would please me. Now before I sink into a stew of maudlin sentiment," he said on a small exhalation, "open the other boxes. Katy should be here soon, and after that Chris'll be waiting."

"So I must hurry?"

He grinned. "As I recall, you do that well."

She punched him in the arm.

"Ow, ow! Ow!"

"You didn't even feel it," she playfully rebuked.

"I might have. Maybe I did." He grinned. "I'm sure I did."

She smiled; his arm was as unyielding as steel. "You're so much fun. Gratifying, too, I might add—in every conceivable way."

"The feeling's mutual, darling." *And wondrous and stupefying.* "But at the moment," he said, aware of the members of his household awaiting them, equally aware that words like *wondrous* and *stupefying* were at best diversions in his hindered life, "we really have to hurry. Katy's next door by now. See what you think of this one last item. The rest can wait." Sitting up again, he shoved aside several of the boxes, pulled out the large box on the bottom, flipped open the lid, and hauled out a shimmering length of golden sable with a sweep of his arm. "I thought you'd like the color."

She was speechless. It was gorgeous; it cost a fortune. It was the most extravagant gift she'd ever had. And when she met his warm, tender gaze and he said, "Try it on. Make me happy," tears welled in her eyes.

"Darling—don't take it if it'll make you cry," he whispered, brushing away the wetness that had spilled over and was trailing down her cheeks.

"Tears of happiness," she sniffled.

He exhaled the breath he hadn't realized he was holding. Tears unnerved him. No, Zelda's tears unnerved him because he wanted nothing more than to give her the sun, the moon, and the stars for the pleasure she brought him. "Let's see if it fits," he quickly said, hoping to curtail her tears, his impossible aspirations, why not the passage of time while he was at it? Tossing the glossy fur around her shoulders, he lifted her into his arms and rose from the bed with an effortless strength. Carrying her over to a cheval glass in the corner, he set her on her feet, slid her arms into the coat sleeves, and buttoned up the front like an attentive parent dressing a child. Then he brushed her lips with his and, standing back, smiled. "It's lovely. Like you."

"Keep being this nice and you'll never get rid of me."

"That's the idea."

Her eyes flared wide.

"That's the idea," he softly repeated. "Although I dislike explanations if you don't mind. Particularly with—" He broke off. "Do you suppose we could talk about this later?" Presumably when he'd recovered his wits. "Do you like the coat?"

She knew better than to press him; he labored under uncompromising restrictions. "I adore it. It's magnificent"— she smiled—"stunning, and every other superlative known to man." The sumptuous fur was almost weightless on her shoulders, the lining a jade green tissue silk, the golden sable tailored for riding like the coat Violetta had destroyed. "How did you find something so perfect? Especially with my height."

"My secretary took the measurements when I said, *She comes to about here on me.* James did the rest. Then he hounded all the vendors mercilessly today to see that everything made it to the train on time. You may thank him at dinner. He's joining us."

She hadn't realized the full extent of the authority wielded by a man of his wealth, nor Dalgliesh's casual expectation that his orders would be fulfilled. "Do you always get what you want?"

"I generally do. My marriage aside, of course," he coolly said. "Now then, I hear Katy next door," he added, deliberately changing the subject. "We probably shouldn't walk in naked."

"Am I one of your acquisitions?" She didn't want to change the subject.

"No. Could we talk about this later?"

"What am I?" She shouldn't ask; anyone with any sense wouldn't.

"You're the best thing that's happened to me in a long time," he said. "Now may we get dressed? It's getting late."

She smiled. "How long a time?"

He looked at her, a pause, no smile. "I'd have to add it up."

"That's very sweet."

"No, it's a huge fucking problem." He dragged in a breath, exhaled, then spoke in a normal voice. "I'm putting on a robe. I suggest you find something to wear or I'll carry you in like that."

Watching him walk away, she was overcome by a rush of compassion. Clearly there were unknown reasons why he suffered the indignity of a wife like Violetta, she thought, unbuttoning the coat and dropping it on a chair. Equally clearly, she had no right to meddle in his affairs. She was sensible of the limitations of their relationship; she wasn't an innocent.

But who wouldn't be tempted to wallow for a time in the blissful realization that *she was the best thing that had happened to him in a long time*? And who wouldn't be tempted to revel in every pleasure, sensual and otherwise, during one's brief sojourn in Dalgliesh's inimitable paradise?

Certainly not she.

"Leave the necklace on."

Roused from her musing, she looked up to find Alec, clothed in a grey silk robe, a short distance away. "Orders?" It was an automatic—trifle testy—response from a woman too long her own mistress.

"God no. But leave the necklace on anyway."

She sniffed. "You're impossible."

"And *you're* impossibly tempting," he muttered. "God in heaven, put something on." Spinning around, he strode away, picked up her chemise from the carpet, and tossed it at her. "If Chris wasn't waiting, everyone else could go to hell," he said, tautly. "They're old enough to understand." Scooping up her drawers a moment later, he came and set them on top of the coat. "Hurry," he said curtly and took himself well away from temptation.

He kept his distance while Zelda donned her chemise and drawers, although the cost of his restraint could be glimpsed in the frequent clenching of his jaw. But by the time she joined him at the door to his dressing room, he'd reduced his lust to a manageable level. "Katy was supposed to find you some lingerie," he said in an ordinary voice. "We have to remember to ask for it. Although," he added with a small smile because he'd never been particularly saintly, "perhaps that's not entirely necessary."

"Under different circumstances, I'd agree. Unfortunately—"

"I have a houseful of encumbrances. Retribution, no doubt, for my many sins," he sardonically said.

"I'm more than willing to be patient."

His mouth quirked in amusement. "Since when?"

"Well—moderately patient. Four hours, I believe you said."

"Or less. I'll see that it's less," he brusquely amended, took her hand, and opened the door.

As they entered his dressing room, he informed Katy that they were slightly behind schedule, and if she'd deal with the fitting speedily, he'd be in her debt. Then rather than take a seat as he had last time, he took up a position across the room, rested his shoulders against the walnut paneling, and prayed for swift action on Katy's part.

There was no safe range with Zelda half naked. It was impossible to look at her and not want her. In further effort to avoid an embarrassing erection, he focused his thoughts on his looming court case in South Africa. A problem having to do with a corrupt judicial system and rivals trying to nullify his mining claims. A serious enough problem, it turned out, to effectively curtail immediate issues of lust.

Once Zelda was fully clothed in the fashionable evening gown: the moiré skirt and velvet bodice accented by a pale rainbow of lace and ribbons at the shoulders, the low décolletage perfect foil for the purple diamond, he was able to speak in a normal tone. "You look enchanting, my dear. Thank you, Katy. Your work is masterful as always. I'm afraid we'll need something wearable in the morning—if that's possible."

"I'll send over a frock by seven. The necklace is perfect, isn't it?" the seamstress added with a smile. It was apparent now why Alec had selected the violet gown.

"It is. We must thank Lucy's fortunate taste in fabrics." The earl pushed away from the wall. "Now if you'll excuse us, Chris is waiting." Offering his arm to Zelda a moment later, he took the package Katy held out to him.

"Lingerie," she said. "You'll find a corset in there suitable for the gown. Not Parisian but serviceable."

"I'm sure everything's adequate. Thank you again."

On their return to the bedroom, Alec helped Zelda out of her gown, reminding himself all the while that he was capable of controlling his impulses. But he suggested they bathe separately; there was only so much a man could take.

Having bathed and outfitted himself in another suite with Jenkins' admirable assistance, Alec was waiting in his bed-chamber before Zelda emerged from his bathroom. He wasn't surprised he was first on the scene. Women always took an inordinate amount of time readying themselves; not that he was about to mention that. Nor take issue with Zelda's refusal of a maid to help her dress when he would have preferred not being involved. Instead, as she walked into the bedroom, nude and flushed pink from her bath, her curling hair pinned up in charming disarray, he sternly reminded himself he was well past adolescent impetuosity. Rising from a chair near the bed, his voice was calm when he spoke. "What can I do to help? Chris is impatiently waiting, I presume, and Creiggy insists on punctuality."

"You don't actually listen to her, do you?" Zelda had seen him in action.

"I try," he said, ripping open the package on the bed and lifting out the white satin corset Katy had purchased as underpinning for the gown; they could chat about Creiggy's position in his household later—or never. "This looks like a two-person operation."

She grimaced; she disliked corsets as a rule. "I wouldn't *have* to wear it."

"You do with that neckline."

"You know that, do you? Naturally you would," she petulantly said before she could stop herself.

"Could we not argue about things I can't change?" He lifted one brow in a flicker of impatience. "Time's short. Be a dear—humor me."

"Don't I always?"

"*Sometimes* I believe is the appropriate word."

"Sexually I mean."

He smiled. "Then, yes, always—for which I'm most grateful."

"But I still have to wear that?" She wrinkled her nose.

"Unless you prefer a gaping décolletage."

"It wasn't gaping badly."

"Yes, dear," he said with quiet resignation. "Why don't you tell me what you want to speed up this operation. I'm ready to bargain." In fact, he was quite ready to do anything to see that she was no longer standing nude before him. His libido was barely under control, and even if she hurried, they were going to be late for Chris. "Name your price."

"A nap tomorrow?"

"Done." Somehow.

As she walked toward him, he carefully focused his gaze on the wall over her shoulder and silently counted the number of deer in the landscape depicted on the century-old, handpainted wallpaper. He was on ten when she reached him, on twelve when he handed her the corset, and on fifteen when she said drily, "If this is what Katy calls serviceable, she must have been dressing courtesans in Paris."

A comment he had no intention of responding to verbally or visually. He remained studiously counting as she bent over, adjusted her breasts into the largely nonexistent cups, and holding the boned bodice in place, turned her back to him. "Not too tight," she said a trifle sullenly.

He finally looked then, drew in a small breath, and hoped he could do what he had to do without disgracing himself. There was something about a woman being laced into a corset that triggered every male fantasy of domination and control—crude and reprehensible as that might be. Which lewd thought required he caution himself against indulging in that little perversity when he'd not always in the past. But the circumstances were different tonight; he had responsibilities to his household—his temperamental chef most prominently. Baptiste threw tantrums if delays caused his haute cuisine to suffer, and he was worth keeping for his way with a pineapple soufflé alone. Although his superb white pepper beefsteak was a close second.

So—another smothered breath of constraint, and Dalgliesh began to swiftly lace up the back of the corset. He centered his gaze on the lacing, looking neither up nor down, Zelda's silken shoulders and bare bottom a temptation he daren't contemplate. In, out, in, out, pull, in, out, in, out, pull—not too much pressure. He actually congratulated himself as he finished tying the silk cording into a bow and stepped back; it wasn't often he had the morals of a Methodist. "Is that all right?" he politely inquired. "Not too tight I hope?"

How affable he was when she was sulky. How silly she was, too, to grumble over such nonsense as a corset when he showered her with gifts and boundless pleasure. When she was where she most wanted to be. "Not too tight at all. You're an excellent lady's maid. And forgive my petulance," she said, turning around, arms outstretched and smiling. "What's next?"

Lock the door and lose his chef. There was no other answer with the showy, quintessential image of ripe, succulent womanhood scorching his retinas. Zelda's large breasts, pushed high into soft, fleshy mounds were still quivering slightly from her swiveling turn. Her tightly laced waist was even more slender—male power perhaps measured in its reduction—while her sumptuous form was molded by the corset into a fashionable hourglass shape.

The resplendent totality was a triumph of fuck-me femaleness.

And if he wasn't horny enough already, the curved base of the corset served as perfect frame for her gleaming pubic hair—intentionally he assumed. And to powerful effect.

When he didn't answer, she glanced downward and whispered, "Oh my."

"Indeed." His voice was barely audible, his gaze like hers significantly placed. Then his glance lifted, and raising his hands, he lightly caressed her nipples available to the touch with only a small scallop of satin supporting her upthrust breasts. "A slight change in schedule, darling," he said, his voice husky and low as he gently stroked her turgid nipples. "If that's all right with you." A cultivated, meaningless addendum.

"Just so long as I have this," she said on a caught breath, gripping his erection through the fine wool of his trousers, his fingers triggering every salacious nerve in her body, "inside me."

He began propelling her backward toward the bed; an answer of sorts.

"We'll have to apologize to . . . everyone." A portion of her brain was still marginally functioning beyond her fierce desire.

He heard her through the white heat of lust, dismissed her comment out of hand, his brain focused on consummation, his cock ramrod stiff and in command. As he shoved her down on the bed with one hand, he was unbuttoning his trousers with the other. Driven, relentless, his gaze opaquely intent—as if he saw only her or, more likely, didn't.

Perhaps someone less sexually greedy might have noticed his benighted gaze and taken alarm, but Zelda's attention was riveted on Alec's nimbly moving fingers, her world view narrowed to the partially unbuttoned trouser placket from which his rampant cock would emerge. She was softly panting, her body already wildly throbbing, as if she'd become a nymphomaniac overnight. As if through some masterful wizardry Dalgliesh had turned her into a fervent sexual devotee, eager, compliant, frantic for his touch, willing to do *anything* to feel him inside her.

If she wasn't so frantically aroused, she might have had misgivings about so servile a role. But she was at his mercy, her impossible cravings swamping even issues of female independence. "Hurry, hurry, hurry," she pleaded, wiggling upward on the bed to make room for him. "Hurry!"

One of his trouser buttons suddenly stuck, and for a flashing second, Alec debated ripping it off. Then it slid free and he sucked in a horrified breath. Christ, since when had he become desperate for sex?

"Alec!" Zelda wailed, trembling, wanting what she wanted, desperation in her case an uncritical compliment. "For God's sake!"

Wrenched from his calamitous thoughts, he quickly reset his priorities, a familiar coolness entering his eyes. "Give me a second," he said with a practiced smile, freeing the last few buttons on his underwear. "There now." His cool gaze was directed at her as he extracted his erection from his clothing and measured its length with a fingertip. "Is this what you're waiting for?"

Like they all did and he knew it. "Bastard," she hissed, hot tempered and hot-blooded and not sure which took precedence.

He looked amused. "I feel confident you might overlook that. Am I right?"

No matter how softly spoken, it was a challenge.

She glared at him. "Am I supposed to beg?"

"Did I say that?"

"That's what you meant."

He shrugged. And didn't move. And waited.

It was for her to decide. Although her raging desires and newfound addiction rather put her at a disadvantage. Particularly with his towering cock, splendid and imposing against the dark fabric of his evening clothes. "Forgive my outburst," she said. "I'm a bit on edge." She smiled then, and her voice drifted lower, turned sultry. "If you'd be so kind as to *accommodate* me, I'll endeavor to accommodate you, then we'll accommodate each other. You know the drill."

His nostrils flared at her words, her seductive tone. "You know the drill as well."

"I doubt I'm in your league," she sweetly said.

"Allow me to be the judge of that," he said not sweetly at all. He'd never known a woman so insatiable, so wanton, so *accommodating*.

With his engorged cock tantalizingly near, she bit back her caustic reply. "Could we discuss this later?"

"What if I want to discuss it now?" he said with equal politeness. "Your, shall we say, sexual talents in particular. For instance who taught you—"

"Have you no manners at all?" she tartly said as he finished his sentence.

"I'm afraid not. Who was he?"

"You wouldn't know any of them."

"Them?" Ice in every syllable.

"Like your thems," she fired back.

"I'm allowed. You know the rules."

"I make my own rules."

"We'll see," he said, sounding bland and reasonable if you didn't look at his eyes.

"No, we won't *see*." A woman of beauty such as she was rarely thwarted and *never* in situations like this. "I don't need *any* man that badly," she said, bristling at his divine-right presumption and perhaps more for the reason he was so assured. *Women never said no.* "If you'll excuse me. There must be something here I can use for a dildo." She began to roll off the bed.

He stopped her in midroll, grabbed her ankles, flipped her on her back again. "You're not excused," he said, curt, autocratic, deeply autocratic. "And I happen to have something you can use for a dildo." Each word was clipped and cold, his mind overcome by a pure, high white fury, the sound of those words—*You wouldn't know any of them*— crashing in endless waves through his brain. His eyes half shut, his rage concealed behind the shield of his lashes, he hauled her by her ankles to the edge of the mattress, shoved her feet back so her legs were bent, so her sex was exposed. So she was available. *For him alone.*

Then he drew in a ragged breath and undertook to suppress his monstrous jealousy.

And failed.

Struggling against his punishing grip, Zelda muttered, "You're hurting me."

"Forgive me," he said without looking at her, and tightened his grip.

"Maybe the others like bloody male domination," she hissed. "But I *don't*!"

Dalgliesh's gaze lifted from the small trail of pearly fluid glistening in her pubic hair. "Really? You should tell that to your cunt."

"I'm quite capable of restraining myself," she huffily replied.

His lips curled in a detestable smile. "Care to wager on that? I can practically see your heartbeat in your clit."

"Screw you," she spat.

"Is that an invitation?" His voice was soft as silk.

"It most certainly is not!"

"Really," he said again in that same unconvinced tone. "From my vantage point, you look damned inviting." Sliding his hands up her legs, he forced her thighs wider effortlessly as if she'd not been resisting and contemplated the lodestone of his lust: her pink, pouty, glistening labia; her bright pubic hair; that enticing pulse visible in her prominent clitoris; the increasing flow of pearly essence wetting her genitalia and those areas susceptible to gravitational forces.

He was going to fuck her.

Regardless of what she said or did or thought.

He was almost smiling as he let go of one leg and placed his hand palm down on the inflexible, boned satin covering her stomach. Slowly splaying his fingers in a deliberate, willful gesture, he exerted a small, decisive pressure. Making it plain that he was in charge, she was not, and she'd service him whether she liked it or not. The bewitching Zelda had shattered the established patterns of his life, and at the moment, he was very much inclined to exact payment for the anarchy she'd sown, and more primitively—demand a price for all the men she'd fucked.

She saw the cold ferocity in his eyes, knew she was powerless against his size and strength, and instead of terror, she was shamefully aroused, excited, overcome with a deep and terrible craving. Fevered and frenzied, she began to tremble, her desire for him an ache of longing, a sick, melting ache.

A sudden, knowing warmth infused his eyes. "I thought you weren't excited," he said, husky and low, a smile in his words. "I thought you didn't like male domination."

"I'd slap you if I could," she muttered.

"No, you wouldn't." His grin was condescending. "You'd open your legs wider so I could give you what you want."

She should hate him for his arrogance and assurance, for his cheeky insolence, for all the women before her. Instead, delirious with longing, flame hot and seething, heedless to all but her desperate need, she opened her legs wider while he watched, a faint smile on his face. And she almost said, *I love you,* too, despite that smile, because he was the most beautiful, desirable man she'd ever known. But she wasn't completely lost to all reason, and he'd probably walk away if she did, which wouldn't do at all. So she addressed him with similar cheekiness. "Give me what I want, and I'll decide if you're accommodating enough."

His smile widened. "Am I being graded?"

"Did I say that?" she replied as he had earlier.

He laughed. "I'm going to have to pick up my game." He adjusted her bottom minutely on the bed as if half inches mattered and, looking up, met her gaze with a look of innocence. "I'm hoping for a high score."

"I'm hoping for a little more speed."

"You always do. Have you ever considered a change of pace?"

"Have you considered how it might affect your score?"

"I'm planning on it. Stop wiggling." He was guiding his erection into her liquid cleft.

"I'm not wiggling, I'm trembling. There's a difference."

"Here's another difference," he murmured, entering her only marginally and stopping. "Now do your multiplication tables," he drolly said, intent on inhibiting the lady's normal tempestuous rush to orgasm. "We're going to slow this down."

"Don't be cruel," she panted.

He was unprepared for his cock's sudden independence,

and as his erection surged and another small measure of her sleek, silken warmth engulfed his rigid length, a brief question of who or what was in charge ensued. And was quickly settled.

Fornication was, after all, Dalgliesh's speciality.

Zelda's breathing had quickened at the increased penetration; she softly moaned, whimpered, wanting more. "God, Alec, don't do this to me," she pleaded, trying to raise her hips to lure him in more deeply.

"Wait," he whispered, holding her down.

Another whimper, her body was melting, turning liquid with longing. "I can't."

"Try . . . for me." His voice was gentle. He felt her relax under his hand, felt her yield. "There now," he murmured, sliding his massive cock in another small distance. "Better?" He was watching her, an unreadable expression in his eyes— an exile in a strange land questioning custom and usage and moral equivalent.

Her lashes lifted fractionally. "More." A pouty little sound.

His sigh was imperceptible; was there a prorated price for anarchy? "What do I get if I give you more?"

"My gratitude." *My undying love.* The last forbidden words.

He glanced at her with a small smile. "I'm not sure that's enough."

"Then what do you want?"

I want to own you and keep you like some goddamn benighted sultan. "Let's start with a kiss." He sighed aloud this time. "Damn witch."

But their kiss was brief, the merest token. They were both too ravenous and far beyond sweet caresses. Although he could wait longer than she. He smiled. Perhaps anyone could. In the end though, he didn't make her wait because he wished to please her more than he wished to punish her. An aberrant concept—punishment—in any event, prior to his meeting Miss MacKenzie. Furthermore, he wasn't particularly self-denying, his cock was aching, and time was at a premium.

There was no time in fact; they should be next door right now.

"Try not to scream," he whispered, sliding his hands around Zelda's corseted waist. "Katy's next door." His grip was firm but gentle now, without prejudice—a temporarily tamed bluebeard who understood with the clarity of the morally degenerate that his life was going straight to hell. He should leave, he should send her home, he should return to his bluebeard castle and pull up the drawbridge. Instead, he slowly, deftly, with highly professional skill, penetrated her hot, welcoming body while she panted and shivered and arched up to meet him. And when he reached the deepest depth, when his cock had nowhere else to go, he flexed his legs and, with a low animal sound, pushed.

Gorged, glutted, crammed full, she gasped, pleasure exploded and shuddering, and softly moaning, she surrendered to the raw, wild ecstasy rippling outward from her overwrought vaginal tissue.

For protracted, heart-stirring moments, the world disappeared and the lovers absorbed the seething, tumultuous, transcendent impact of cock to womb. Perhaps their nerves were overstimulated after hours of sex, or sensation was amplified by excess; perhaps the depth of Dalgliesh's invasion was to blame for their disorientation.

But inherently attuned to female responses, he'd heard her gasp, recognized the nature of the sound, and given his size, understood he might have done damage. Moments later, rallying first, he kindly asked, "Did I hurt you? Should I stop?" The last a magnanimous offer, considering the state of his arousal; perhaps an impossible offer.

Zelda's eyes opened so slowly he braced himself for affirmative answers and the personal dilemma to follow. Then she smiled a familiar, sensual smile; he nodded and smiled back. "I'll be gentle."

"Not too gentle."

His grin was warmly boyish. "Yes, ma'am." And he proceeded to give the lady what she wanted in range, scope, pacing, and carnality. He knew what *not too gentle* meant for her.

She began to climax quickly like she always did.

After a swift, cursory debate that only briefly considered consequences, he climaxed with her and in her.

"Sorry," he said afterward, clearly not meaning it, not knowing what he meant, cavalierly shrugging off his indecision. Applying himself instead to more practical functions like withdrawing from a saturated cunt without staining his trousers. Pushing himself upright, he carefully eased out. "I didn't want to change again," he said, although added reason for his fully clothed performance had to do with complicated, untidy sovereign power.

"So practical," Zelda murmured. "And you needn't worry about climaxing in me. I just had my menses."

He suppressed his surprise. *Why hadn't she said that before?* "I might do it again then."

"I'm extremely amenable right now."

He looked up from wiping himself with his handkerchief. "You probably shouldn't say that."

"Do we have time?"

He hesitated for a fraction of a second, then sighed. "I wish." Dropping the handkerchief, he began buttoning up.

"In that case, I need a towel."

He stopped for a moment, his fingers arrested; he didn't take orders well, particularly from women.

"Please, your lordship, sir," Zelda playfully said. "Is that better?"

"Sorry. You're different." He abruptly grinned. "In so many charming ways."

He turned out to be extremely versatile as a lady's maid. But then he'd had considerable experience—generally taking off clothes, but reversing the procedure wasn't demanding. After his fetching and carrying, hooking and tying bows, slipping on shoes, clipping on jewelry, handing over hairpins, they were only ten minutes late to the nursery.

They arrived hand in hand, breathless and laughing.

Chris looked up, then instantly raced toward his father.

Alec picked him up, swung him into his arms, and cheerfully said, "First, I think you should show Miss MacKenzie how to stoke those fire boxes. She's going to be amazed."

"It's real fire!" Chris exclaimed, swinging his gaze toward Zelda, his eyes wide with excitement, pleased he had his playmates back. "Put me down, Papa, and I'll show her!"

Zelda *was* amazed and mildly alarmed as the coal-stoked engine box turned bright red and little puffs of smoke erupted from the engine. She glanced at Alec in silent query.

"Only under supervision, darling," he murmured. "No one wants the house to burn down."

A servant came in with drinks for the adults—whiskey from Alec's Scottish estate, although he didn't say where it was and she didn't ask. They were both more guarded when not in full rut. While Chris kept up a running commentary, Alec and Zelda sat side by side on a wooden bench pulled up to the train table, kept Chris company, exchanged fondly benign glances when Chris wasn't looking, and drank their whiskey.

A garrulous six-year-old didn't require more than the occasional word of agreement or encouragement from his audience and he was happy. Although Alec did say once, "That's enough coal, Chris. I don't want another engine to explode. It did once," he said to Zelda under his breath. "Chris was thrilled. I was less thrilled. The servants weren't thrilled at all. The draperies caught on fire, then the carpet, then—Chris, no, stop—that's quite enough."

When a servant came to announce dinner, Alec turned off the main switch, Chris ran ahead to announce their arrival, and Alec and Zelda walked downstairs hand in hand. Like lovers. Like lovers who'd known each other longer than two days. Like lovers in love, those at the table thought with varying degrees of interest as they observed the couple enter the dining room.

Creiggy pleasantly thought, *Will wonders never cease?*

James was amazed. Presents were one thing. But this?

Having served Dalgliesh both in South Africa and England, having always opened all the earl's mail, having been instructed to use his own judgment with regard to the perfumed billets-doux arriving at Dalgliesh's door, he considered himself privy to his lordship's attitude toward women. And now, this sudden breach of custom.

As for the servants in attendance, since their employer's affections had already been thoroughly discussed below stairs, they viewed their newly enamored lord and his guest with less surprise. Actually—no surprise at all.

CHAPTER 18

IN CONTRAST TO luncheon, the earl was in a conspic-
uously good mood at dinner. He was charming, affable, fully
engaged, offering up topics of interest, introducing bits of
local gossip, conversing with grace and wit—his attentions
extending to Chris, whom he entertained with several edited
stories of his boyhood. All the while casually monitoring
Rowan's management of the dinner with a glance, a lifted
finger, a smile. As for his lover's comfort, he took particular
pains to see that Zelda enjoyed herself. Including ordering
a special champagne.

"For you, darling," he said, looking down the length of
the table to where she sat in the hostess's chair, elegant and
beautiful in her violet gown, his diamond sparkling in her
cleavage. "I hope you like it." His heated gaze could have
ignited wet elm.

Zelda's face turned cherry red. She'd never been able to
overcome the inconvenience of her pale complexion.

"You're embarrassing Miss MacKenzie," Creiggy chided.

"I'm so sorry," Alec blandly said.

Creiggy sniffed. "If you sounded like you meant it, it might help."

"Should I get down on my knees?" Alec roguishly queried. "I'm more than willing."

"Alec, please," Zelda murmured.

His smile instantly disappeared and, sliding up from his lounging pose, he quietly said, "I'm truly sorry, dear. I'll behave."

James muffled a gasp.

The servants stopped what they were doing.

Even Rowan lost a modicum of his dignity.

Chris opened his mouth, then shut it as Creiggy's fingers bit into his arm.

"There now, that's better," Creiggy briskly said into the silence. "I'll have a wee dram more of that whiskey, Rowan. It's a right fine bottle."

From that point on, Dalgliesh was circumspect and discreet, never overstepping well-mannered convention.

His gallantry and kindness had a predictable effect on Zelda; she was even more enamored, more in love. How sweet he was, she thought, how unselfish. How utterly charming. Not that she didn't understand that falling under his spell was the height of foolishness. That he seduced and enchanted with careless goodwill. That a man of his reputation only played at love.

Yet she was drawn to him like every other woman he toyed with, she sternly reminded herself. She must remember this Crosstrees paradise had a definitive limit. Once their holiday was over, they'd both return to their former lives.

She understood the rules.

Amorous amusements were countenanced in the fashionable world, even viewed with leniency, provided one adhered to the orthodox canons. Men, as Dalgliesh had alluded to, were allowed more freedom in their carnal amusements. Married women were expected to provide their husbands with an heir and a spare before embarking on an affaire. Unmarried females were in theory taboo; in practice, they, too, were susceptible to passion. But always, always, the end of an affaire required a civilized adieu.

The world of the haute monde was small and incestuous, socializing restricted to a narrow coterie who met at the same receptions, parties, dinners, and country house weekends. Husbands and wives, their lovers, ex-lovers, and future lovers, young ladies and gentlemen, those of a certain age who only observed the modish in their pleasures—all repeatedly rubbed shoulders or elbows or other more intimate body parts. Discretion was key, undue emotion was considered bad taste, and agonizing over a love affaire was embarrassing for everyone.

Zelda was perfectly aware of prevailing custom. Nor did she wish to be viewed as one of Dalgliesh's lovesick discards. She refused to play such a profitless role.

In the meantime, however, she intended to fully enjoy the sweet enchantment of this rare, golden idyll. To that purpose, she upended her champagne glass, quickly drained it, and took pleasure in the sparkling bubbles sliding down her throat.

Dalgliesh had been watching her and smiled. God in heaven, she made him happy. He signaled to have her glass refilled.

In the course of dinner, James and Zelda found that they shared a cousin twice removed and exchanged stories of the globe-trotting George Hamilton. Which brought up Zelda's globe-trotting travels, which in turn offered a further glimpse into the man she'd come to love. Alec had traveled extensively beyond Europe. He'd surveyed the diamond fields in India and Brazil, hunted in Persia and with the Bedouins in the Sahara, sailed to Antarctica, climbed in the Himalayas, and spoke six European languages and numerous African dialects from his travels on the continent. And had been to a great many places most people hadn't.

"I'm impressed," Zelda said, lightly. "I feel quite provincial."

"On the contrary, darling," Alec replied, his voice smooth

as honey, "you're the most enlightened, adventuresome woman I know." With an affectionate smile, he raised his glass to her in salute.

Zelda raised her glass to Alec; their eyes met.

A small heated silence fell.

"I'm pleased to see you children are getting along," Creiggy said into the incandescent pause. "Now, are we all ready for dessert?"

As dessert was being served, a servant came in and whispered in James's ear. He excused himself, and when he returned, spoke quietly to Dalgliesh, then handed him a telegram. The earl scanned it quickly, crumpled it in his hand, stuffed it in his pocket, and dismissed his secretary with a nod.

Dinner resumed as if the interruption hadn't occurred. Dalgliesh artfully brought up the matter of Chris's jumping lessons, after which there was no end of childish chatter over a Bavarian cream, a pineapple soufflé, macaroons, and a plum tart still hot from the oven. The telegram, as intended, was forgotten.

It wasn't until the women and Chris were preceding the men into the drawing room where tea was being served, that Alec had an opportunity to speak quietly to James. "This situation bears watching. Keep me informed. Not that Knowles isn't fully capable of dealing with their maneuvers. Still."

"Judge Felden has a price," James said, flatly.

"We just have to make sure ours is higher. See that Knowles understands that. Tell him no half measures. I'm not losing my mining claims for the price of a judge."

"Yes, sir. I'll see that Knowles is informed."

"Isn't she lovely?" At his secretary's blank look, the earl added, "Miss MacKenzie."

"Oh, yes, sir. Quite, sir. A stunning woman, sir." James was stunned himself at the tenderness in Dalgliesh's voice when he spoke of the lady. Especially since his lordship often didn't know the exact name of the woman to whom James was supposed to send one of the earl's customary gifts of appreciation.

"If you could monitor Knowles for me, I'd be grateful. Miss MacKenzie and I will be busy for a few days."

"Certainly, sir." A slender man of middle height, James hastened to keep up with the earl's long stride.

"If an emergency comes up, by all means inform me. Otherwise, take care of things yourself."

James Armitage, of the Yorkshire Armitages who'd lost the bulk of their estate two generations ago after a series of bad investments on the exchange, had been secretary to the Earl of Dalgliesh since the earl had come into his majority and his grandfather's fortune at eighteen. Five years older than Dalgliesh, they'd first met when James had been suggested for the post by the Crosstrees steward. Even at eighteen, Dalgliesh had presence and no visible vulnerabilities. Because of his mother's estrangement from his father, because he was his mother's protector, he'd been educated by tutors at home. He was well-read, well educated, already linguistically agile in several languages. He was reticent at times—due to his experience of human nature observed at close hand in his family—but he was also disarming and eminently capable, and James had been warmly welcomed into the hospitable sphere of Alec's company. Initially at the splendid Dower House where Alec and his mother lived, soon after in South Africa where Alec had gone to find some purpose to his life beyond resistance to his father. Now back in England again, and in all those ten years, James had never so much as seen the earl look at a woman with fondness— his family aside. Certainly, he'd never heard the earl speak of a woman in the tone of voice he reserved for Miss MacKenzie. And most startling, the earl who was normally obsessed with his businesses, mining and otherwise had said, *I'll be busy for a few days.* It was such a departure from the norm, James momentarily questioned the earl's soundness of mind or, at the very least, his sobriety.

Tea and liquor was served in the drawing room, and the evening continued its agreeable course. Chris was entertained with a game of cards, Creiggy playing for blood like she did, Alec cheating so Chris won anyway. He was rewarded for his efforts by his son's gleeful jubilation, Creiggy harrumphed in defeat, and James marveled at the earl's deft of hand. Not that Dalgliesh hadn't honed his already formidable skills in the mining camps, where drink and gambling were the major entertainments. Still, it took a practiced eye and amazing technical skill.

Creiggy, grumbling, had her whiskey glass refilled.

Alec grinned and spoke to her under his breath, "He's only six. He has plenty of time to learn about losing."

She sniffed. "I'm not so sure some people have ever learned that lesson."

"Learned what lesson?" Chris chirped.

"It's more blessed to give than receive," Alec mildly said. "Isn't that right, Creiggy?" He glanced at her, mischief in his eyes.

"Indeed. Listen to your father. He's a right religious man."

After another game that Chris won, thanks to his father, Alec and Zelda accompanied the boy up to the nursery, tucked him into bed, read him a story, and sat with him until he fell asleep.

Traversing the maze of corridors from the nursery to Alec's apartments, the swish of her skirts an accompanying whisper of sound, Zelda glanced up at Dalgliesh with a quizzical lift of her brows. "How old were you before you won a hand of cards against Creiggy?" She'd watched the interplay between the nanny and her former charge with interest.

"Five. But then I had an Italian tutor who'd sharpened his German with a year at the casino in Baden." He smiled. "And Creiggy annoyed him—as you can see she might."

"Your mother didn't mind you gambling at so young an age?"

"She probably didn't know. She was busy matching wits with my father at the time. Later she chose to ignore him. But it was early days in their marriage, and she still labored under the illusion he might be redeemable. So Creiggy and my tutors were given free rein. You'll have to meet Maman someday. She'd like you."

"She's better then? Fitz said she'd been ill."

He glanced at her, a sudden sharpness in his gaze. "Ill? I suppose you might say that," he said, sarcasm soft in his words. "She almost died."

"I'm sorry. Fitz didn't mentioned that."

"He wouldn't have known. Here we are." Not about to discuss his mother's ailment, he opened the door to his suite, bowed her in, and shut the door behind them. Neither had slept much the night before, the day had been busy as well, carnally and otherwise; Zelda had almost fallen asleep twice in the nursery. As they walked through the sitting room to his bedchamber, he graciously said, "If you're tired, darling, I won't bother you."

She stopped and turned. "I'm not *that* tired. Are *you* tired?" Oh God, he was bored already and she was acting like every other infatuated woman he knew.

"I'm never that tired," he said, taking her hands and drawing her into his arms. "In fact, I want you every hour of the day and night. It's amazing and mystifying, but altogether delightful."

Her world having righted itself again, she gazed up at him with open adoration. "I find it terrifying, wanting you the way I do."

"No, darling. It's heaven on earth." His smile warmed his eyes. "And I'm the least religious man in the world."

She laughed. "So I've wrought some miracle."

"Or I'm in favor with the gods for the first time in my life. Either way, I'm pleased. More than pleased. We'll cancel Fontainebleau, stay at Crosstrees, and enjoy these celestial pleasures."

"We?" A playful arch of her brows.

"You can't go."

She wasn't so foolish as to believe him. "I have to, of course."

He smiled. "You can try."

"I won't tonight, at least."

"Then I must endeavor to entertain you so you won't go at all."

"How nice," she murmured, sliding her hands up the

lapels of his evening coat, then higher, cupping his face in her palms. "How exactly does this entertainment begin?"

It began with Alec making sure Zelda had what she wanted, along with her choice of a thousand variants on pleasure he'd learned and knew and executed with ease. In time, he undressed her and then himself while she lay sprawled in bed, trying to catch her breath, watching him with avidity and affection, with her perpetual impatience. "I don't suppose it would help to say don't scream so loudly," he said, grinning as he approached the bed once again.

"I'm so sorry." She didn't sound sorry at all; she was smiling. "Am I embarrassing you? Would you like to gag me?"

A wicked gleam entered his gaze. "Would you like to be tied up? Is that what you're saying?"

So the devil would have looked in the Garden of Eden, she thought, offering sweet temptation. "I'm not sure."

"Should I decide?" He had already.

She shook her head.

"No, I shouldn't decide, or no, you don't wish to be bound?" He was stripping a braided tieback from the bed curtains.

"What are you doing?"

"I thought it was obvious," he said, moving to the next corner of the bed.

"Alec, don't. I don't think so."

"You like me to take charge, darling." A third tie came free in his hand. "Or at least your hot little clit does, as I recall. Why don't you show me I'm wrong if I am. It'll put the matter to rest."

"No."

He'd heard that kind of no before, from women who meant the opposite. From teasing women and women who found repudiation arousing. Or in this case, from a woman who liked to think she was in charge. "Why don't I look for myself?" he said, with extreme urbanity, turning to her with three silk ties looped over his hand.

"Alec! No!" She shoved herself upward on the bed as he reached for her.

But she was smiling, so he said, "Yes," grabbed her foot, and dragged her back. Although it wouldn't have mattered if she wasn't smiling. He knew how to bring a smile to a woman's face.

"Now mind your manners and you'll be rewarded," he said in a low tantalizing murmur. "I promise." Quickly seizing her pummeling hands, he smoothly trussed her wrists. "That's better." He tested the knot, then smiled faintly. "I prefer a little more obedience."

It suddenly occurred to her that a good number of obedient women had proceeded her. "I didn't know you were looking for obedience," she said in an unmistakably pettish tone.

He grinned. "Now you know." He slipped his fingers under her back. "Lift up a little." She didn't, of course, nor had he expected her to after hearing the umbrage in her voice. But he *had* done this a few times before—instructed originally by his little duchess next door to Munro Park. He knew Zelda would enjoy it. As would he, for the usual reasons and for other less benign reasons. Those having to do with Zelda's unbridled sexuality and his continuing struggle with her past exercise thereof. At which unpleasant thought, he took the slack out of the cord he was wrapping around her waist and jerked it taut.

In the grip of her own resentments, Zelda only saw a dégagé man tying an intricate knot at her waist, managing this little sexual performance as effortlessly as he dealt with every other aspect of carnal play. It shouldn't matter; if she was sensible, it wouldn't. She'd ultimately profit from his expertise. But the manner in which he'd acquired his professional skills, all the women he'd pleased and who'd pleased him, brought her temper up. "Even with my hands tied, I could still kick you," she said, sulky and sullen, green-eyed with jealousy.

"Give me a minute and you won't want to." He was forming a more complicated knot in the third tie and didn't look up.

"So sure, Dalgliesh?"

He smiled faintly and looked up. "Pretty damned sure."

"You're really irritating me."

"Not for long, unless I've lost my touch," he murmured, intent on his task, his long slender fingers deftly manipulating the braided silk.

"Have I mentioned how I dislike arrogant men?"

"Actually, you have."

"Well, perhaps it bears repeating. Damn you, look at me!"

"There now," he said as if she'd not spoken. He lifted his head and deigning at last to give her his attention, met her heated gaze with an agreeable one of his own. "Let's see how this fits." He held up an intricate, sinuous, oval design of blue silk cord like that used as ornament on regimentals, the decorative knot work set midway down the length of the tie. Without waiting for an answer, indeed, already preoccupied, he slid one end of the tie through the bowline loop at her waist, and handily brushing aside her flailing fists, fastened it to her wrist bonds.

"Stop this, Alec!" She wrenched her hands upward and the end of the cord he was holding slipped from his grasp.

"Hush, darling. You don't mean it," he said, calmly retrieving the braided strand left dangling.

"I can't imagine how you know whether I mean it or not!"

Surely not a comment he cared to answer. "Just give me a few minutes of your time, sweetheart," he affably said.

"Do they all say yes when you ask them like that?"

Again, a question best not answered when she was glaring. "Darling, your jealousy is misplaced," he said, instead, and holding her wrists in a firm grip, ran the length of the silk braid down her stomach with his other hand.

"Allow me to disagree," she said with a sniff, damn his smooth penitence. "Now untie me. *Alec*, do you hear!"

He agilely sidestepped her kick and stood breathing softly, the loose end of the silk tie draped over one finger. "You're being childish."

"I am not!" Even as she said it, she realized how juvenile she sounded. But she jerked on the cord tied to her wrists anyway.

He laughed. "Brat. You don't know what you want." This time the cord was firmly trapped between his fingers. "I'm offering you unlimited orgasms," he said expansively. "I don't see the problem."

"The problem is the countless women you've offered them to before me."

He was smiling faintly. "Am I questioning your orgasms with other men?" He was, of course, but he was making a point, and to admit to jealousy was unthinkable. "Now don't be obstinate. You'll like this." Either reading her hesitancy as consistent with female behavior or perhaps simply indifferent to her reply, he took advantage of her momentary stillness and moving a step closer, swiftly slid the braided cord between her legs, eased her pouty flesh open with his fingertips, properly positioned the ornamental knot, and at her small gasp, quickly rolled her on her side and nimbly attached the other end of the tie to the one circling her waist in back.

Seconds elapsed—five.

His satisfaction—immeasurable.

Returning Zelda to her former position, he serenely surveyed his handiwork. "Now, how does that feel?" He was pleased to see her breathing had changed, a slight flush was rising up her throat.

"I might ask the same of you," she said, giving nothing away, her glance on his upthrust erection lying hard against his stomach, the distended veins visibly pulsing.

"As you see." Amusement warmed his gaze.

"Then at least one of us is enjoying ourselves. For your information, I don't like this game. I don't like that you've probably done this a thousand times before. I particularly dislike the fact that—" She sucked in her breath, stunned at the hammer blow of lurid sensation that imploded outward from the targeted knot crushed against her clitoris.

Alec, smiling, was holding her wrists immobile in order to maintain the pressure on the knot. "Perhaps two of us are enjoying ourselves now," he softly said, making a small adjustment with his free hand to the ornamental knot. "Or do you find this more pleasant?" He tugged on her wrists, lifting them a fraction higher.

Her wild, frenzied scream exploded, echoing in shimmering waves up the walls, flaring across the ceiling as hotspur, rampaging delirium shuddered unchecked through her body, seared every sexual receptor and nerve in passing. Left her a moment later, half dazed, without breath, gasping for air.

"You seemed to like that," the earl mildly said, a modicum of his unwonted jealousy assuaged, the matter of supremacy clarified. "Try this." Leaning over slightly, he placed his palm over the knot and exerted a precise, masterful pressure learned in his youthful apprenticeship under the tender tutelage of the charming duchess. "What do you think?"

She'd gone tense under his hand, so close to orgasm she couldn't force her brain to deliver the required response.

"Answer me, darling, or I might take away my hand." He began lifting the weight of his hand.

"No, no—don't!" A breathless rush of words, impassioned, humbling.

And particularly gratifying to a man who, personal vanity aside, wouldn't have cared three days ago what a woman liked. Nor that he have dominion over her.

With the ultimate pleasure trembling on the brink, Zelda had long since abandoned herself to the passion-filled fervor of glorious sensation. Reality had been replaced by soul-stirring ardor, and softly moaning, she sought orgasmic surcease. Restless, impatient, she moved her hips to magnify the erotic pressure of Alec's hand, eagerly lifted her pelvis into his palm, frantically reaching for the blissful curative to her lust.

The silk knot was soaked through. Zelda's liquid arousal was drenching his palm and fingers, his skin slippery, slick—like her cunt. The bitch was unforgivably carnal, he indignantly thought, ravenous, lustful—qualities that in any other woman would have been welcome.

Qualities that never would have provoked his resentment.

Or jealousy.

With the inconceivable word finally emergent, he sucked in an incredulous breath, immediately dismissed such aberrant thoughts, and swiftly brought Zelda to orgasm. As though to underscore the ordinariness of the transaction. The casualness. The fact that this was sex and only sex.

But the wanton hussy didn't just come once but twice more in rapid succession before he irritably removed his hand. Then, when she finally opened her eyes and lazily gazed up at him from under the lacy fringe of her lashes like some sumptuous courtesan, she had the audacity to murmur in an outrageously sultry purr, "Damn you, Dalgliesh, I should hate you for your boorish ways. And if it didn't feel so good, I would."

He stood very still for a moment. Then he said, "Care to go for some records in feeling good?" His smile was offensive.

"How tempting. Under other circumstances I might be inclined to agree."

"Meaning?"

"Meaning, I like men who actually smile when they offer me sex."

It was the worst possible thing to say when he was choking on jealousy. *"Men?"* he said in a dangerous voice.

"Is that a problem?"

He didn't answer for so long she opened her mouth to speak again. "It might be," he said, arresting her comment.

"I'm so sorry," she said in a tone that wasn't in the least sorry.

"A pity, I agree." A tight smile, followed by a tick over his cheekbone, followed by a small breath of restraint. "If I can't offer you sex, perhaps you'd like to bring yourself to orgasm. You said you liked to masturbate." His cool blue eyes were expressionless. "And I like to watch."

"No, thank you." Her response was neither cool, nor expressionless. She was less skilled in artifice.

"Perhaps I can change your mind. Actually, I know I can."

"Really, Alec, you're much too familiar with willing women bent on pleasing you. We aren't all submissive. In fact, I don't—" Her sentence ended in a long throaty moan. Alec had elevated her wrists slightly, exerting a deft pressure on her clitoris, maintaining the contact—with professional finesse—just short of discomfort or climax.

He knew the exact equation.

"Submission can have its rewards," he whispered, a faint smile on his lips with her breathy moans resonating in the air. "Come, darling, you can do it yourself. I'll show you." He slowly raised and lowered her wrists in a smooth, gentle rhythm, his gaze on her face, triumph in his eyes. "See . . . like that—not too fast." He watched her take a deep breath, then he gently stroked the slippery knot just enough to make her tremble. "Now try it yourself. There—that's the way."

She was sick with humiliation as she obeyed; sick with longing, too, and insulted and disgusted and awed by the inexpressible magic. Desire, hot and insistent, flared deep within her, a kind of desperation melted through her body and brain, all her senses overwhelmed by an impossible craving. No other man had ever made her feel this way: insatiable, consumed with longing, mindlessly compliant. But then no other man rivaled the earl's stark beauty, sexual ingenuity, and matchless capacity for pleasure.

A shame he was utterly faithless.

"I'm going to watch you now. Don't stop," he said, exacting his own form of punishment for the jealousy he couldn't escape.

It was an order no matter how softly put. She should stop. She should refuse. She should open her eyes, tell him she wasn't like all the others, that he was the least redeemable man on the face of the earth and she was done. But he bent down just then and gently kissed her and stroked the knot over her clitoris, and she wasn't offended anymore, she was shaking. Then he set her hands into the appropriate rhythm again, whispered, "Show me what you can do," and she did.

Pulling up a chair, he dropped into it, slid into a sprawl, and eyes half shut, contemplated the obscenely sensual lady in his bed pleasuring herself. Her nipples were erect, her large breasts soft, pinked, made to suckle babies, her voluptuous form made to bear babies, and he half swore under his breath at the infinite and dangerous possibilities. He shut his eyes briefly, waited for the hair at the nape of his neck to subside, and setting aside his indefensible train of thought, resumed his survey with a more familiar dispassion.

An abbreviated dispassion as it turned out.

At first, he told himself that it couldn't possibly matter that she came so swiftly and often. He liked lascivious women. But by her third orgasm, his frown was in place and his lips were set in a grim line. After her fifth orgasm, he forcibly reminded himself that Miss MacKenzie was no different than any other woman—a transient pleasure, no more.

He tried to warn himself off. But the pulse beating at his temple negated casual and not so casual reminders, and his cock was so stiff it was seriously affecting his judgment. So much so that he surged to his feet when he hadn't meant to and grabbed her wrists to stop her.

In the afterglow of a particularly satisfying orgasm, Zelda lifted her gaze and sweetly smiled. "My, my, do I detect some ill humor? Was it something I did?"

A mutual resentment vibrated in the air.

Two intractable individuals crossing swords.

Dalgliesh studied her for a moment where she was lying splendidly female, ripe and yielding, her skin flushed from passion, her eyes still half lidded from orgasmic surfeit, and realized he was about to succumb to savage impulse for the first time in his life. "It wasn't anything you did," he said, in a deliberately calm voice. "It was rather something I didn't do. But that can be remedied." Leaning over, he picked her up with a powerful sweep of his arms and dropped her face down on the bed.

She was momentarily speechless. Then she glared at him. "Must you be such a brute!" The words were scathing.

"As if you're some goddamned tender maid," he said with irritation. "Instead of—" He stopped himself. It didn't matter.

"A libertine like you?" she insolently returned, beginning to scramble up on her knees.

"Yes, that's exactly what I mean." He checked her upward movement, his palm hard on the small of her back. "I shouldn't try to rise any higher," he said, holding her in place. "Although it's up to you."

"I appreciate your advice, but I'll do as I—" She gasped and dropped back on her forearms, the shock to her clitoris stunning.

"Very sensible." He sounded impatient. "Now lift your bottom. It's my turn."

"No." A venomous hiss.

"You must."

"I won't!"

"Of course you will," he said.

"I will not!"

"Would you prefer my help?"

He spoke in a low, brutal tone that should have frightened her but instead aroused her, as if some barbarian had come to claim her as his conquest of war.

"Must you humiliate me?" Although the shimmering heat stirring between her legs contradicted her snappish query.

"You find fucking humiliating?" A sardonic smile of disbelief. "Since when?"

"Since I feel a certain repugnance at the moment. To you."

"You're not allowed."

"*You* won't allow it?" Soft as silk mockery from a willful woman.

"Yes—me." He made a dismissive gesture, as though to forestall his inconvenient obsession with who she'd fucked. "Consider, darling. You're in my home, in my bedroom, *tied up*, in case you haven't notice. You're hardly in a position to oppose me." His brows lifted slightly. "Have I made my point?"

"Very well," she retorted with a huffy little sniff. "You have the whip hand. Do what you must, you fiend."

He laughed so long if she hadn't been angry before she would have been now. "Such lovely theater," he finally said, still chuckling. "Whip hand? Nice touch from a woman who likes to climax a dozen times in a row. Or are you really interested in whips?" Suddenly reminded that other men might have wielded whips with her, his amusement abruptly vanished. "Now then," he said in a different tone, "this shouldn't take long. Feel free to participate, or compose a list of my lamentable sins while I'm fucking you, if you prefer," he added, climbing up on the bed. "But I wouldn't suggest you resist. It could be uncomfortable."

Nor would she resist, she decided. No more than she'd move. She wouldn't respond in any fashion whatsoever. He could play the damned lord and master to his heart's content.

Bent only on swift consummation at the moment, Alec took no notice of her inertia other than to acknowledge it as sensible. Quickly positioning himself behind her, he raised her to her knees, smoothly adjusted her bottom so her moist, swollen cleft was conveniently in position, slid aside the silk cord with a twitch of his fingers, and after guiding his erection into place, plunged forward without preliminaries.

Not that a liquid cunt like hers required priming.

Bottoming out in her slick flesh a second later, he gave voice to a low, raspy groan, the radical pleasure spiking up his spine and exploding in his brain a true wonder of wonders. God in heaven, she was amazing: hot, wet, smooth as silk, a perfect fit like a well-tailored glove. That perfect fit divinely tight and pulsing around his cock.

He felt his erection swell in appreciation of Miss MacKenzie's superlative cunt and her readiness to accommodate him. As a connoisseur of both qualities in a woman, he was capable of recognizing her exceptional fuckability. And had he been less disapproving of the other men she'd entertained, he might have been more grateful.

He might have noticed as well that the lady was trembling, inside and out.

As it was, sulky and discontent, he was only interested in a precedence-setting retaliatory fuck. For all the worst reasons. For alarming reasons, had he been in the mood for reflection. But reflection wasn't on his agenda at the moment.

That the resplendent, oversexed Miss MacKenzie was at his mercy was resolutely front and center in his brain.

"Can you feel me?" A rude, meaningless query with his cock stretching her tissue taut and her breathing labored. When she didn't answer, he rammed in deeper, forcing a response. "Tell me."

"Yes, yes, yes, yes . . ."

Her voice was breathy with passion, damn her. "Do you want more? If you don't, I'll stop." He waited for her reply, knew what it would be, was enraged because he knew what it would be.

"Don't stop," she whispered, the words barely audible.

But he heard, had predicted her reply. "Don't say you didn't ask for this," he growled like an angry, newly virtuous clairvoyant and, holding her tightly pinioned, pushed deeper.

Her scream was one of pure ecstasy.

With his normal self-restraint already pricked and goaded, her sensual cry was like a trip-hammer to his seething impulses. Suddenly beyond caution and thought, he plowed into her silken heat with uncompromising fury, thrusting and withdrawing, roughly, violently, marking her as his in the most unjustified manner, like a savage, an animal, his lower body plunging in over and over again in primitive, renegade aggression.

When he felt her moving to meet him, matching his pace, heard her feverish breathing, he thought of all the other men who'd done what he was doing to her and clenched his teeth to keep from calling her all the rude, indecent names that came to mind. Names he never before would have considered calling a woman. Base, obscene names provoked by raving jealousy.

How many had there been? What had they done to her and her to them? Did it matter or didn't it? Of course it did.

Then a delirious jolt of sensation put period to further reflection. The edge of the knot jammed against Zelda's clit was raking the length of his cock with each powerful thrust and withdrawal. He felt it vividly coming and going, more so a second ago. He knew she felt it coming and going, too.

His reaction was instinctive perhaps with the question of Zelda's intemperate libido perversely affecting him. Or perhaps it was nothing more than the fact that he'd recently spent some time with his little duchess who was still very beautiful. Were the ladies the same or different when he put his fingers . . . just so?

Zelda jerked under his hand, screamed, and instantly climaxed.

Fuck. As if he hadn't known.

She came on command.

Which was a problem when it shouldn't be, when it never had been before, when a woman's promiscuity had always been an asset. But rather than face the reasons for his incoherent anger and recently acquired righteousness, he chose to ride roughshod over all the baffling enigmas. Forcing her thighs farther apart with the pressure of his body, he rammed in farther, penetrated deeper, made it clear who was helpless and who was not. Who was directing the carouse, the sport, this particular roll in the hay.

Damn her—she was feverishly panting, catching her breath at each brutal downstroke, meeting his rhythm like some obliging, harem-trained cunt.

Zelda was trying not to think about how shamelessly she wanted him, how she was utterly without pride. How he had but to touch her and her body responded like an enslaved addict waiting for her next allotment of pleasure.

She could feel the heat of his breath on the back of her neck, hear his muffled grunts at the depth of each powerful thrust, feel him move and swell inside her, and felt helpless, overwhelmed, and damn him, desperately aroused.

Equally resentful of his bondage to the passion that Zelda so freely offered, Dalgliesh chose to obviate the emotional chaos in his brain in a predictable fashion. Substitute sex for feeling, quickly climax, and put an end to senseless introspection.

Fornication was the path to Nirvana after all.

And he knew every signpost on the road.

Sliding his hand over Zelda's left hip and stomach, he

neatly disposed his fingertips over a particularly sensitive area. His right hand was installed with his fingers lightly touching the decorative knot. This he knew well, this artful arrangement of his hands. He now controlled the lady, her passions, her randy cunt and randier clit. Marginally adjusting the pads of his fingers, he exerted a modicum of pressure in preparation for his long-delayed orgasm. Then, moving with dispatch, impatient now with any further delay, he settled into a wild, selfish drive to orgasm like some customer doing business in a whorehouse. He no more heard Zelda's screams—as she climaxed over and over again with his fingers deftly placed for a simultaneous vaginal and clitoral orgasm—than he heard his voice of reason reminding him not to ejaculate in her.

So he did.

Ejaculate in her.

Rather quickly and profusely as it turned out.

Like a customer in a whorehouse.

Then, postcoital, his reason was instantly restored and he was scandalized by his actions, contrite, remorseful, and God help him, in too deep. Quickly untying Zelda, he lifted her into his lap and held her while she trembled like a leaf. He apologized in all the ways he'd learned in his dealings with women and in more sincere, abject ways particular to Zelda. He was a brute, a beast, an inhuman knave. He'd make it up to her. He'd do anything. She had but to tell him. He actually meant it when he never had before. He actually cared for her more than he wished as well—more than he comfortably could afford.

When Zelda finally stopped shaking and found her breath, she touched his cheek. "Stop apologizing. You didn't hurt me. On the contrary, as you could tell from my screams," she said, smiling. "I must have wakened the house."

"I'm sure you didn't," he politely replied, knowing Miss MacKenzie would be the topic of conversation below stairs for some time. Not that it mattered; his servants were discreet.

"I should apologize, too," she surprised him by saying.

"I'm sorry I'm so beastly jealous about all the women you've known. I wish I could help it, but I can't. Forgive me for being so foolish."

"We'll be foolish together," he kindly said.

"Oh good. I don't want to fight. I adore you too much." She gazed up at him with a luscious courtesan's smile. "And naturally, your glorious cock as well."

He laughed. "Little wanton."

"I'm not little."

"You are to me."

It wasn't often she heard that. Or ever. "How very nice. Then I may continue to adore you and your, er—lovely assets?" she purred.

"Christ, who would say no to that? Don't tell me," he quickly said. "I don't want to know."

"Since I rather immodestly declared my love for you a day after we met, you may rest easy. I'm not in the habit of adoring penises at random."

Her plain speaking always charmed him. No subterfuge with Miss MacKenzie. You knew where you stood. "I consider myself very lucky then. And you're adorable as well." He wouldn't be making any declarations of love even though she'd given him some of the most remarkable moments of his life. "Every delectable part of you is adorable," he pleasantly said.

"Some parts more than others?" she teased, having no expectations other than sex from Dalgliesh.

He grinned. "It depends."

"On?"

"Whether my heart is still beating," he drolly replied.

"I know what you mean. We *could* just stay here until we expire from passion."

"It's definitely a thought."

"Lord, Alec, I don't know what's happening to me. I'm completely mad and infatuated, mindlessly obsessed. I can't get enough of you." Stretching up, she kissed the line of his jaw.

"Ready again, are we?" He knew that look.

"We don't have to if you're tired."

"In your company, darling, my cock will be the last thing to give up the ghost." He glanced down. "As you can see."

"How wonderful, how very, very wonderful," she murmured, swinging around on his lap and coming up on her knees. Drawing his erection away from his belly, she arranged herself with his help, then sank downward with a contented sigh. "I do thank you from the bottom of my heart and from other more susceptible regions as well," she murmured, wiggling slightly to better experience her gratitude. "I feel as though I have to gather my rosebuds while I may with you. I hope you don't mind I'm sticky."

"Not in the least," he said with an amiable smile. "And gather away to your heart's content." He offered up a prayer to all the gods in heaven and elsewhere who'd brought the delicious Miss MacKenzie to his attention. Then, he embarked on his countless journey to orgasm that night. His lovely houseguest was, as always, wild and untamed, offering herself completely, opening her body to him to ravish and possess. Until very late, finally exhausted from fatigue and sensory overload, she whispered, "No more."

Holding her close, he watched her doze off quickly, like a child does who's played too hard. She was flushed from her exertions, her skin hot against his, her damp hair cool on her shoulder, her breath soft on his chest.

Resting against the pillows, Alec relaxed after two days of Zelda's passionate, occasionally strenuous demands. Contentment seeped into his bones, a comforting stillness crept into his consciousness, the strife and dissension in his life momentarily obscured by deep-felt bliss.

The notion of bliss registered in his brain with shock and reduced him to a breath-held silence. Feelings of bliss were so far removed from his life that he surveyed the scene of this strange happening with wonder, as if some clue to his extraordinary emotions were visible in this room he'd slept in since childhood. But nothing had changed: the furniture, draperies, carpet, the paintings on the walls, unchanged. He started breathing again.

Perhaps it was just that Crosstrees had always been a refuge. Perhaps it wasn't bliss so much as the simple comfort he'd always found here. Or perhaps he was overtired, overfucked, and too exhausted to think straight.

Apropos his flagging reason, another freakish thought entered his mind. A thoroughly ludicrous, ill-advised thought, considering the fact that he was married, his mother was frail, and God knew where Violetta was.

He should introduce his mother to Zelda.

Christ. There it was again. *Not the why, just the blinding impulse.*

Of course, he'd mentioned as much to Zelda earlier, but his remark had been mere courtesy—the kind of thing one said but didn't mean. Then, defying common sense and good judgment, the idea took on substance, took on a matter-of-fact life of its own. *They'd like each other. They both like children and horses.* And him. None of which was sufficient reason to complicate his already complicated life.

Yet . . . the thought remained.

His heart raced for a moment, issues of witchcraft briefly considered.

Only briefly.

He was, after all, a man of measured disposition. The reason why, he supposed, he'd struggled so with his powerful response to Zelda. He wasn't by nature capricious. He'd faced too many difficult choices in his life.

But now strangely, in this same room, in the same house where he'd always felt the weight of responsibility, his burdens had miraculously lifted. He no longer despaired that he'd sold his future at great cost. He felt instead, a pleasant triumph, as though he were in possession of the field, the battle won.

As though he'd reached safe shores.

An impractical whimsy, of course.

But whimsy or not, real or not, it felt good—like a fresh wind of freedom.

Smiling to himself, he took pleasure in that newfound sense of freedom, however fanciful, delighted in the sweet illusion, gave a grateful nod to accident or fate or Lady Luck—whichever had sent the ravishing Miss MacKenzie his way.

Now he must find some way to keep her. For however long he could. She'd fuss, of course—a pale word for her dissent, he knew. But he'd deal with that, too.

Much later, with nothing resolved other than the inclusion, somehow, of Zelda in his life, his breathing slowed, his eyelids slowly shut, the challenging pressures he faced ceased to trouble him, and the Earl of Dalgliesh drifted off into a deep, unafflicted sleep for the first time in years.

CHAPTER 19

ALEC CAME AWAKE first. With morning, reality once again intruded, and with it, all the impossible strictures of his life. Swearing under his breath, he grimaced—all his liabilities preying on his fragile hopes. Then he glanced at the clock, viewed the time with surprise, and leaving Zelda sleeping, quietly vacated the bed.

A moment later, he entered his dressing room. "'Morning, Jenkins." As usual, his valet was waiting for him with his morning coffee and the day's first mail. "I'm afraid I'm late. Is the coffee still warm?"

"Yes, sir. I had the chef send up a pot I could put on the grate. Your robe, sir."

Alec slipped his arms into the robe Jenkins held out and smiled. It was warm from the grate as well. "I hope the coffee's black."

"Very, sir. I thought you might like it stronger than usual this morning." A man of indeterminate age with the muscular, wrestler's physique of his native Wales, Jenkins had valeted Alec since boyhood. With her son's safety in mind, the dowager countess's decision to hire Jenkins twenty-two years ago had factored heavily on Jenkins' athleticism. "The first delivery, sir." Jenkins held out Dalgliesh's correspondence. "James said there are two telegrams of note."

Knotting the tie on his robe, Dalgliesh took the small stack from his valet and, without looking at it, inquired, "Did the information I requested arrive?"

"Yes, sir. The countess left early this morning. John spoke to the maid who packed for the countess. Lord Mytton left as well."

Dalgliesh frowned faintly as he listened. "They're being followed?"

"Yes, sir. Six men. Just in case they're needed. They'll telegraph throughout the day, as you wished."

"I want to be informed discreetly when the telegrams arrive. Miss MacKenzie's not to know."

"Naturally, sir." As a pause developed—the earl momentarily preoccupied in thought—Jenkins said, "Your bath is prepared in the Adams' suite. I could bring your coffee there."

Dalgliesh looked up, glanced at his bedroom door, at the clock, then back to Jenkins. "Why not."

"The maid will inform us if Miss MacKenzie wakes, sir."

Dalgliesh smiled. "Ever efficient, Jenkins. Thank you. Do we have a sweet pastry of some kind for the lady's morning tea?"

"Of course, sir," Jenkins replied, looking pained.

"Excellent. Thank you again." Alec smiled at his invaluable valet who anticipated his every whim. Then he turned and strolled toward the hall door.

"Will you be riding today?" Jenkins picked up a tray from the grate.

"Probably."

"I thought as much. The weather is excellent. A light breeze from the west, sir, but clear and sunny."

WHEN ZELDA WOKE, Alec was dressed and sitting in a chair by the windows, a cup of coffee in one hand, a recently delivered telegram in the other.

"Business?"

He looked up and smiled. "Morning, dear. Yes, business. Nothing important." He set aside his cup and the latest telegram from Knowles. "Would you like to bathe first or have breakfast?"

"Are we expected downstairs?"

"Not necessarily. Chris eats in the nursery if I'm busy."

"Will you be busy?"

He laughed. "I just got dressed."

"I could help you undress."

"In that case, I'd be delighted." He rose. "Let me have Jenkins deliver a message to the nursery. Should we say eleven for Chris's lessons?"

"That would be lovely."

"It always is," he said with a grin. "I'll be right back. You need a bath, don't you?" he said over his shoulder as he walked away. "I could help you with that."

"Ummm . . . how nice. Do hurry, darling."

"That's what you always say."

"Are you complaining?"

He turned and flicked his hand downward. "Does it look like I'm complaining?" His massive erection stretched the soft chamois of his riding pants.

She felt the hot libidinous jolt down to her toes. "My God, Alec," she breathed. "I'm going to die for want of you. I have no restraint—none at all. It's terrifying."

"I, on the other hand, find it deeply gratifying." He smiled, then put a finger to his lips. "Jenkins is tidying up next door." Opening the dressing room door marginally, he issued a few brief instructions before shutting the door and turning back to her. "There now. We have two hours. Are you undressing me or am I?"

Her bath was all she wished and more. Alec played lady's maid with much more tenderness and considerably more pleasure. And when they left the bathroom, the water that had splashed over the sides of the large marble tub in the course of Zelda's bath required a few words with Jenkins.

"I'll be right back, dear. Decide what you're going to wear and I'll help you dress."

She smiled. "Really?"

"Or do something else." He grinned. "You decide. But that water needs taking care of," he added, moving toward his dressing room door, clothed only in his underwear. He was too hot and wet to even think about dragging on tight chamois riding pants. And Zelda might change her mind about dressing in any event.

His dressing room was empty, but he rang for Jenkins, and when his valet arrived, quickly explained the situation. "The bathroom's a mess. There's water an inch deep on the floor. If you'll see that someone cleans it up, I'd appreciate it."

"Certainly, sir." Not a flicker of surprise greeted the news. Although, Crosstrees as an amorous retreat was unique.

"I apologize for the flood in there," Alec said, knowing as well as Jenkins how unusual the circumstances. "I'm afraid there might continue to be extra work for the staff with Miss MacKenzie visiting. I hope no one minds."

"I'm sure they don't, sir. Miss MacKenzie has brought Crosstrees to life, if I may say so. The staff enjoys the change of routine."

Alec smiled. "You're very kind, Jenkins. I'll tell Miss MacKenzie that she's appreciated not only by me but by everyone."

"Very good, sir. Would the lady wish for breakfast anytime soon?"

Alec hesitated. Zelda's sexual appetites took precedence. "Why don't I ring when Miss MacKenzie's ready for her breakfast. We have our appointment with Chris at eleven. Presumably she'll eat before that."

"Yes, sir. I'll tell Baptiste."

Alec grinned. "Is he raging already?"

"I'm afraid so, sir."

"Perhaps his mother would like to come and visit him or take a trip somewhere. Rome perhaps. She's religious, is she not? You could suggest a private railcar for her from Paris to Rome. Would that soothe Baptiste's artistic temperament?"

"I'll mention it, sir." He wasn't so sure, with the deafening level of shouting and pot banging coming from the kitchen.

"Better yet, just ask Baptiste what he wants to deal with what looks to become an irregular schedule. Miss Mac-Kenzie is of rather a capricious nature," Alec blandly said in lieu of the more prurient truth. "Breakfast is likely to be ad hoc. Luncheon slightly less uncertain, I suspect. And tell Baptiste, his sacrosanct dinner hour will be preserved save for, shall we say—some personal emergency." The earl smiled faintly. "See that Baptiste is rewarded for his patience and understanding in whatever fashion he prefers. I can't guarantee regular mealtimes for the foreseeable future. I'll talk to Creiggy myself about the changes."

Both the words *foreseeable future* and Creiggy's possible reaction to a reversal in the settled meal schedule, when repeated by an awestruck Jenkins on his return to the kitchen, served to fuel wild speculation. All the servants wondered what the earl's intentions were apropos the beautiful Miss MacKenzie. And where they might lead.

As it turned out that morning, Alec and Zelda barely made it out to the stables in time for Chris's lesson. And a day that began with such unalloyed delight, continued in the same vein. The jumping lessons were both instructive and playful. Baptiste had been mollified with an expensive trip for his mother to Rome and had shown his appreciation by serving many of Alec's favorite dishes for lunch as well as several more appropriate to a lady's palate.

After lunch, Alec, Zelda, and Chris rode to a hamlet on Alec's estate that was as well cared for and attractive as that on Groveland lands. They partook of cookies and cider, sweet cider for Chris, hard for the adults, and on their return to Crosstrees, Alec saw to it that Zelda was accorded the nap time she'd requested. In which no one actually napped.

Katy had supplemented Zelda's wardrobe with a tailored day dress in dark silk bouclé as well as an evening gown in cream satin that set off Zelda's flaming hair beautifully. Dinner was lighthearted and convivial, the conversation quickwitted and merry. Embraced in the bosom of the small family—welcomed and made to feel at home, Zelda felt an undiluted joy. She even allowed herself to indulge in the fond illusion that Alec and Chris were hers; pure fantasy, of course. But she was deep in love; allowances must be made.

Very late that night, with Zelda at last sated and sleeping in his arms, Dalgliesh engaged in reflection of his own. Although his had nothing to do with fantasy. He was rearranging his schedule. No longer dégagé about Zelda, no longer considering her a temporary amusement, he was averse to her leaving him. He wouldn't go so far as to contemplate the word *love*. Coming from his background, perhaps he could be excused.

But he was keeping her.

And the necessary logistics required some planning.

A woman like Zelda wasn't looking for a protector, nor did she deserve to be treated as though she was. She'd object to his plans, of course; he didn't relish the impending argument. Although any other woman he knew would greet his proposal with squeals of delight. Then there was her family. They, too, would take strong exception.

But he wouldn't be deterred.

And if one plan didn't work out, there was plan B. And if that didn't work out, there was always the rest of the alphabet.

He was determined.

CHAPTER 20

MONDAY MORNING AT breakfast, a servant delivered a note to the earl. Setting down his coffee cup, Alec took the envelope from the footman and glanced at the coat of arms gracing the top-left corner "Groveland," he said to the table at large and, taking out the enclosure, quickly scanned it before looking up. "Company for lunch. I forgot I'd invited them."

"Oh dear," Zelda murmured. She'd forgotten, too. Any number of embarrassments could be in store.

"It's strictly informal, darling," Alec said to mitigate her obvious alarm. "They're bringing the children. And you know everyone. I doubt they'll stay long."

"Chris will enjoy seeing the children," Creiggy interposed, thinking if Alec had invited children to his house for the first time in his life, there was no reason not to facilitate the miracle. "Chris, you can show little Monty your puppies. I'll see that we have plenty of nursemaids on hand for all the wee ones and food for the childers."

"There, darling," Alec said. "Everything's taken care of. Thank you, Creiggy. Do you need us to do anything?"

"Be on the drive to greet them," she said, giving her employer a hard look.

"Yes, ma'am," Alec said with a grin.

"Just see that you are. No excuses." And everyone, save Chris, knew to what she was alluding.

The adults rode over, along with Monty and Celia, who sat perched in front of their fathers. The younger children and their nursemaids were driven over in a carriage, and after everyone dismounted and the carriage emptied, greetings were exchanged. Then all were invited in. Oz carried Celia, Monty roosted on Fitz's shoulders, both children talkative, inquisitive, and clearly indulged by their fathers, who replied to their questions easily and with endless patience as the party proceeded to the dining room.

Baptiste and his army of subordinates had, on Creiggy's orders, outdone themselves in offering children's fare in colorful display: macaroni formed into rabbit shapes with olives for eyes; buttered bread cut into star shapes and spread with pâté or jam; cheese balls piled high into a pyramid topped with a spray of succulent red grapes; huge strawberries from the hothouse; rice pudding with raisin faces; little decorated cakes in every color of the rainbow. Meanwhile, the adults partook of a tour de force of haute cuisine from Dalgliesh's masterful chef, who was beside himself with joy at the prospect of an actual luncheon party in the house. The earl never entertained.

It was a noisy gathering with the children, adults, and even the nursemaids seated at the table. The parents were immune to the raucousness. They all subscribed to a hands-on approach to parenting, unlike many in the aristocracy, who preferred their offspring remain in the nursery until such a time as they were capable of making intelligent conversation.

Zelda found herself not at all embarrassed, instead delighted in the circus atmosphere. It reminded her of past mealtimes at home with all the children talking at once. Although, the babies particularly drew her attention—Oz's Raj in his mother's lap, dark like his father, plump and happy, even at three months riveted by the activity around him. Jamie's boy, Davey, was walking at ten months and a handful even for his father, who was trying to keep him from crawling up on the table to get a closer look at the spectacular pyramid of cheese. Fitz's Sibyl had her mother's coloring, and while only a month older than Davey, sat quietly next to Rosalind in a high chair and daintily ate her bread and jam without smearing her fingers or face. A meticulous child, Zelda thought, smiling faintly; she'd find the world more messy than she'd like. Although with competent parents like hers, she'd likely have the talent to fix whatever needed fixing.

Meanwhile, the two toddlers, Monty and Celia, were chattering like magpies to Chris, who, beaming, was serving as their youthful authority.

Dalgliesh observed the alien scene with good-natured complacency, his arm laid along the top of Zelda's chair, his fingertips idly brushing her shoulder from time to time. He was pleased that she was enjoying herself, that he could do this for her.

At his direction, she'd been placed beside him. He liked her near—liked the scent of her, the lingering warmth from her body, the knowledge that she was his. Not that he'd discussed his proprietary instincts with her. Nor would he.

Oz's daughter, Celia, sat on her father's lap while she ate. An incongruous sight, any of his former companions in vice would have reflected. But Oz wasn't only a fond father but a fond husband as well, his attention to Isolde who sat beside him one of undisguised affection. Raj had fallen asleep like babies do—his eyelids fluttering once, twice before he'd abruptly dozed off.

Observing the precious image of mother and sleeping babe, Zelda felt tears welling up in her throat. Since meeting Dalgliesh, she was more vulnerable to such tender scenes. Envious.

Alec took note of Zelda's look of longing, understood. Perhaps even agreed at some primal level. Leaning over, he kissed her cheek lightly. "Would our baby have red hair or black?" he whispered. "Your eyes or mine?"

Blushing furiously, she looked away and quickly reached for her wineglass. But her hand was trembling so violently, she jerked it back and dropped it into her lap.

The adults witnessing the scene were shocked.

Dalgliesh was not a demonstrative man, nor given to tenderness.

He was, in fact, considered by some, callous to women.

Fortunately at that moment, Monty asked Chris in a high-pitched toddler lisp if he could see his pony, his father beside him said, "After lunch, Monty," and the dangerous moment passed.

Alec turned to Rosalind on his right and asked her when they planned to return to London. Not because he cared, but because his heart was suddenly thudding in his chest and he needed time to recover.

"Not until after the New Year," Rosalind replied in a comfortable tone, having seen that same stunned look in her husband's eyes long ago. "Fitz likes to hunt this time of year, and we generally spend Christmas in the north. The children enjoy the outdoors. Don't you, Sibyl?" she said to the little auburn-haired girl seated beside her in the chair brought down from the attic.

The pretty bright-eyed girl looked up, smiled through a mouth full of bread and jam, and vigorously nodded her head.

Jamie, however, in his cousinly capacity, viewed Dalgliesh with mistrust. Everyone knew he saw women as sport. "Are you leaving for home soon?" he asked, addressing Zelda, two places removed down the table. "You should travel with us."

Sofia looked at her husband in surprise. That was censor in his tone.

Zelda welcomed the distraction from more perilous issues of babies with Dalgliesh. Although she objected to her cousin's oversight. "Surely you're not playing chaperon, Jamie," she silkily rebuked.

"I'm just asking."

Her gaze narrowed. "Asking what exactly?"

"My intentions, dear," Dalgliesh calmly said. "He has every right."

"He certainly does not," she crisply replied. "Really, Jamie, you overstep. Papa knows I'm here. I told him before I left Groveland Chase." She smiled. "So you needn't concern yourself with my affaires."

"I might anyway." A gruff rebuttal.

"No, you certainly will—"

"Let me assuage your concerns, Blackwood," Alec gently interposed, holding Jamie's gaze. "My intentions toward Zelda are honorable insofar as my circumstances allow."

"Which is the problem," Jamie returned, as gently.

"Do you two *mind*?" Zelda was controlling her rising temper with effort. "This is *not* a matter for discussion."

"Perhaps later," Alec murmured with a telling glance for Jamie and a smile for Zelda.

"No, not later," Zelda snapped. "Not at all. Do you understand?"

"I'm sure the childers would rather talk about puppies," Creiggy proposed in her familiar role of referee. "Chris tell everyone how many new puppies we have in the stables." She looked up and surveyed the table with a bland glance. "Fox terriers," she said. "The sweetest wee things."

The children all started talking at once.

Zelda offered Creiggy a grateful smile.

Dalgliesh sat back and contemplated the charming chaos brought on by Creiggy's helpful meddling; he'd mollify Blackwood later. And he really must see that Chris had friends to play with, he decided. The boy was clearly enjoying himself. Having spent a solitary childhood, he wished something better for Chris.

Although in terms of *better*, his life had much improved since meeting Zelda. The idea of Worth's suddenly appeared in his consciousness—foolishly perhaps. But the thought of watching Zelda while she was being fitted for a wardrobe charmed him. Perhaps he could coax her into shopping there if he promised to take her hunting at Fontainebleau.

Then Fitz asked him whether his gamekeeper's leg had

healed, and Paris and Worth's was summarily dismissed. Many on the staff at Crosstrees and Groveland Chase were related, the local community a tangled web of shared ancestry and kinship. Fitz's and Alec's families, resident in the area for centuries, had long been interested in preserving the region, both in terms of the human and animal populations.

After a time, the party removed themselves to the stables so the children could play with the puppies, and once everyone was focused on the wee fox terriers, Dalgliesh took the opportunity to draw Jamie aside into a vacant stall.

"I understand your concern for Zelda," he quietly said. "I'm not unaware of my reputation. But she's not like the rest." He took a small breath; he didn't, as a rule, apologize for his behavior. "As for my plans, I haven't told her yet, or rather talked to her about them," he corrected himself and was rewarded with an understanding grin from Jamie. "I'm hoping to however." And he went on to explain his intentions. "So you see," he said, pausing a second before continuing, "the situation is going to be difficult in any number of ways, not the least of which is persuading Zelda to agree."

"She may not. Or she may not, yet."

"I understand, but I want her with me. I'm not a patient man."

"I don't know Violetta particularly well, but she doesn't appear tractable."

"She's anything but," Alec brusquely said.

"I believe this is where I say if there's anything I can do to help."

Alec smiled. "Violetta's not likely to listen to you any more than me."

"I meant in other ways. I know people who can say, nudge someone along. I can do as much myself, if it comes to that."

Dalgliesh knew Jamie's history as a mercenary. The men met in their clubs over drinks from time to time. Blackwood had almost died saving Sofia from a murderous thug not long ago. Alec also knew he wasn't about to mention what Violetta had done to his mother. It would open up a scandal he'd been at great pains to conceal. "Thank you, but I can manage Violetta. And if I must, I'll send Zelda home until I can resolve the situation."

"Your marriage, you mean."

"Yes."

"You're serious then."

"I find that I am." The earl smiled wryly. "I have no idea why, but I've given up trying to deal with this logically.

"Love does that to you."

"So I've heard."

"And now you know."

"Do I?"

Jamie laughed. "Ask any of us here—we men at least—and you'll find that your feelings aren't unique. We all questioned what love was—stupidly, I might add. In fact, it was Sofie who came looking for me in Dalmia—for which I'm eternally grateful. So I sympathize with your skepticism. I was willing to die for Sofie and yet couldn't recognize why."

"Perhaps we're not schooled in such feelings."

"Apparently not," Jamie sardonically noted. Then he smiled. "Although the resulting revelation is without parallel in terms of pleasure."

"Amen to that—the pleasure part."

Jamie frowned. "She's my cousin."

"Of course. I apologize."

"I'd prefer your apology take the form of dispatching your wife."

The tone in which Blackwood said *dispatching* gave Alec pause for a fleeting moment.

"Legally I meant." Jamie recognized Alec's hesitation.

"Of course. Although the price of Violetta's leaving is going to be a helluva lot more than she's worth."

"But not more than Zelda's worth."

"Agreed. Although I'd appreciate your discretion until I've arranged my affairs. I don't want to give Violetta an opportunity to prepare a defense."

"Naturally. You have my word." Jamie grinned. "Best of luck with Zelda. She's going to give you trouble."

Alec hadn't revealed all he planned to do—only enough

to relieve Jamie's concerns. Nor did he disclose what he was willing to do should Violetta prove difficult. Blackwood wasn't alone in his capacity for violence. One didn't survive the mining camps—where drink was a way of life, tempers were volatile, where claims were often disputed at the point of a gun, and people were willing to die over a diamond— without certain skills.

Skills that Alec had been forced to acquire as his father's son.

IN THE END, it was Alec's escalating commerce in telegrams that won him his way with Zelda.

After their guests departed, another telegram was delivered, the message so disquieting that he went utterly still for a moment. Recovering, he folded the small sheet with one hand and slid it in his pocket. "A slight problem. Nothing untoward," he said, then smiled his usual smile.

"It's more than that." Zelda held his gaze, hers concerned. "Is it your mother?"

He almost said yes, expecting she'd be more sympathetic, more likely to come with him. But he didn't for a variety of reasons, none of them necessarily virtuous. If it would have helped, he would have lied through his teeth to keep Zelda with him. But Knowles was beside himself, his panic came through even on paper, and Alec knew he'd have to deal with a new crisis immediately when he reached home. So he answered with a half truth. "An approaching court case in South Africa requires my attention."

"It must be serious."

"I'm afraid so. My mining claims are being challenged, and with them, my mines, of course. I have to go home."

"To *South Africa*?" She couldn't disguise her alarm.

"No. To Munro Park. I have a fully staffed office there. I'd like you to come with me. Once I deal with this issue, we could go hunting at Fontainebleau, if you'd like. Please, say you will."

Having thought she might never see him again should he

sail for South Africa made it very much easier to say yes. "I'd like that, if you think it's quite all right."

He wanted to say whatever he chose to do was quite all right; men of wealth made the rules. But he was well mannered and said instead, "I'm sure it is. Chris will be as pleased as I."

"Will your mother approve?"

Had she ever disapproved of anything he'd done? "She'll be delighted."

"You're sure now."

"I'm positive. Although I'll beg your pardon in advance. This difficulty will demand my full attention at first. John could take you riding and show you Munro Park." He smiled. "You'll enjoy my stables. Two Derby winners and a Newmarket Stakes winner, along with fifty other thoroughbreds. Take your pick."

"How can I refuse?" she lightly said.

"How indeed, and I'll entertain you at night once the offices close in Johannesburg."

"Then, naturally, I most eagerly agree."

She thought afterward that she should have been more reserved, not so impetuously willing. But South Africa had frightened her badly. And even knowing she must leave Alec some day, she couldn't quite bring herself to give him up just yet.

CHAPTER 21

ALEC TRAVELED BY private railcar, a luxury given to those of great fortune; a convenience as well, since he generally had Chris, Creiggy, James, and servants along. Two carriages awaited them at the station for Munro Park, and fifteen minutes later, they were being deposited at the Dower House—a magnificent, well-maintained Tudor structure considerably larger than most dower houses. But then the Dalgliesh wealth allowed such extravagances.

It was nearly ten o'clock, yet the main block was all alight in anticipation of their arrival; James had telegraphed ahead. Chris was sleeping in Dalgliesh's arms. Alighting, he handed the boy to a waiting footman; Creiggy followed and hustled the man into the house.

Turning back to Zelda, Dalgliesh helped her down. "Welcome to my home, darling." He'd never said that before, although it pleased him to say it. Just as it pleased him to know Zelda was near even though he'd be busy dealing with the newest crisis jeopardizing his mining interests.

Zelda surveyed the towering redbrick facade, its rows of

windows glowing golden against the starless sky. "What a lovely home."

"It's comfortable," he said in gross understatement. "Come, darling, meet my mother." Taking Zelda's hand, he moved forward.

The front door was open, the light from within flooding out onto the gravel drive—an inviting sight on a chill night. As was the tall, slender woman with pale hair and a welcoming smile who hurried out to greet them.

"Darling, what a wonderful surprise! We weren't expecting you until Thursday."

"Business, Maman. There's always something pressing. May I introduce Miss MacKenzie. Zelda, my mother, the dowager countess, Louisa."

"Lulu, please. No one calls me Louisa save the Queen. What a pleasure to meet you, Zelda. Do come in. I have your whiskey waiting, darling," she said, taking Alec's free arm as he walked toward the doorway. "By the way," she said, looking past Alec and smiling at Zelda, "I met your father, Sir Gavin, at the Turlingham hunt years ago. A superb horseman, as you are, I hear."

Alec must have telegraphed a short biography, Zelda thought. Nor did his mother have the look of an invalid. She was very beautiful, vivacious, and as charming as her son.

Moments later they were seated in a cozy sitting room with original linen-fold paneling, the fire on the hearth fragrant with applewood. After Crosstrees, the opulence of the setting no longer surprised Zelda. A profusion of notable paintings hung on the walls, the furniture was partly Tudor along with a luxurious mix from other centuries, the rugs underfoot were plush and thick, the tabletops strewn with a glittering display of bibelots. One sofa and several chairs were scaled to a man of Dalgliesh's size, and he was currently lounging on a long leather sofa, his feet up, his head resting on the rolled arm, his drink balanced on his chest.

"One whiskey, Maman, and I have to meet with my office staff. They're waiting."

"I know. I've been hearing the bustle and rumors all day. Such a shame you had to cut short your hunting holiday. But Zelda and I will manage quite well without you though, won't we, dear?"

The dowager countess was fair in contrast to her swarthy son, her eyes a brilliant green although they held a similar warmth like her son's when she smiled. "We certainly will," Zelda politely replied before turning to Alec. "Do go whenever you must. I'm perfectly fine."

"John will entertain you tomorrow. I've offered Zelda a tour of the estate if she wishes," he explained to his mother. "Provided the weather cooperates."

"You forget I live in the Highlands," Zelda said. "I'm comfortable in any kind of weather."

"Might I suggest you ride Valour. He literally walked in eight lengths ahead at the Hardwicke Stakes. He'll give you a bloody good ride."

"Thank you, I will. He sounds intriguing. Do you ride—" She hesitated.

"Lulu, please. I so hate to stand on ceremony, as Alec will attest. As for riding, I haven't of late. Alec may have mentioned, I've been recuperating from a beastly little illness that's much improved now. But I'm still not quite as strong as I was."

Zelda noticed Alec's swift glance—instantly extinguished—light on his mother when the dowager countess mentioned her illness.

"I'll have the kitchen pack a lunch, should you need it," Alec said. "But feel free to arrange your own schedule." Although he'd already sent instructions to John to keep her away from the main house where Violetta lived when she wasn't in London or visiting friends. "I should be available anytime after seven." He quickly tipped the whiskey down his throat and came to his feet. Setting the glass on a table, he sketched a small bow. "Until later, ladies."

As the door closed on him, the dowager countess softly sighed. "Such a difficult time for Alec. The office has been in turmoil since yesterday. Nevertheless, I'm so pleased you came. Alec never has visitors. You're important to him, I can see. I do hope you like my boy."

Zelda's blush was masked by the shadowed lamplight. "I do. He's very easy to like."

"I think so, of course, but then I'm his mother," Lulu cheerily noted. "Would you like another whiskey or would you prefer champagne?" The dowager had been sipping on her champagne, although she'd drunk very little.

"I think I'll have one more whiskey, but don't get up. I'll help myself." At the drinks table, Zelda half turned to say, "I thought I recognized the taste. This whiskey is bottled in the valley next to ours."

"I expect Alec knew that." He had, in fact, had James telegraph a detailed list of instructions for the comfort of his guest. "Creiggy taught Alec to appreciate good whiskey. She's Scots, you know."

"One can't mistake the soft burr in her voice," Zelda remarked, returning with her refilled glass. "She has relatives not far from us."

"Is that so? So when Creiggy and Alec were on holiday in the Highlands years ago, you might have seen them. They often spoke of their visit there. Creiggy was always good to Alec."

"They seem to have a wonderful rapport. Even though she's quite outspoken, he doesn't seem to mind."

The dowager chuckled. "I doubt she'd notice if he did mind. Creiggy has always been forthright. In fact, when I first hired her, she told me she'd insist on her own schedule in the nursery and the freedom to train Alec in her own way—with my support, of course." She laughed. "Which she really didn't mean. But as you see, my son has prospered under her care."

"Indeed."

"I was very young when I married and soon with child," the dowager said. "I'm sure Creiggy recognized a green girl when she saw one." Her pale brows drew together briefly at recall of her husband's explosive temper that had come as a shock on her wedding night. Then she suddenly smiled. "I knew I needed a strong woman like Creiggy for my baby. Alec and I have been most fortunate to have her. And now Chris has her as well."

"He's a darling little boy. We were teaching him how to jump his pony. He's very quick to learn."

"And so adorable. Alec dotes on him, as do I. It's quite wonderful to have a child in the house."

Zelda didn't inquire whether Chris's mother lived in the house, but she rather thought not. Nor did the dowager enlighten her. "I couldn't agree more," Zelda said instead. "I raised my four brothers and sister so I'm used to having children about. In fact, I miss the tumult now that they've all grown. I've been traveling a good deal in order to keep busy."

"Alec mentioned you'd spent time orchid hunting in Brazil. You must see my orchids."

Good God, he'd apparently sent his mother an extensive biography. She didn't know whether to be flattered or concerned. Did she require vetting by his mother? Did *he* require that she be vetted by his mother was more to the point. On the other hand, the dowager appeared to be extremely pleasant, and Zelda had no intention of impinging on their lives for long. How could it matter who needed vetting or why?

WHILE THE LADIES chatted over drinks, Alec swiftly made his way to the back of the house where his offices were located, his thoughts on the latest catastrophe in the making. It was bad enough that he was dealing with a corrupt judicial system, now Rhodes was recruiting a militia and preparing for an insurrection in the Transvaal. The last telegram he'd received at Crosstrees had relayed the information in code. Not that he wasn't aware of Cecil Rhodes' vision to incorporate the Transvaal and the Orange Free State in a federation under British control. But he risked losing his mines if things went wrong—if the insurrection failed, if Germany intervened, if some jingoistic politician in London wanted to make a name for himself and hostilities escalated. Damn greedy bastards. He got along just fine with Paul Kruger, president of the Transvaal Republic.

Swearing under his breath, he shoved open the office door, came to a halt on the threshold, and quickly scanned the room. Everyone was still at their desks.

"I hear we have trouble," Alec said.

A collective groan went up, and Fulton, his office manager, came forward to meet him, his broad face unmarked by anxiety. "Not if you want to finance your own army," he said with a cheerful roll of his eyes.

"We may have to." Alec shut the door behind him. "How many days do we have before these idiots go to war?"

He spent the remainder of the night with his staff, planning for every possible contingency, ordering up men and arms to protect his mining properties, sending pointed messages to various politicians, preparing for additional supplies to be brought up for his miners should they come under siege. Debating how far to publically involve himself in the imminent disaster.

Toward dawn, he and Fulton were the last men left; everyone else had gone off to bed. Maurice—mention the name at your own risk—Fulton was lying on the conference table in the middle of the room, his hands under his head, a whiskey bottle at his side. An ex-sergeant in Her Majesty's grenadiers, Fulton was a large man like Dalgliesh, with iron nerve and the instincts of a coldblooded killer. Both of which had come in handy more than once in South Africa. Alec and Fulton had prospected together and survived a scrap or two or ten. Standing back-to-back, they could take on a platoon, in fact, had once out in the bush and lived to tell the tale.

Alec's feet were parked on his desktop, his head rested against the pleated leather of his chair back, a silver flask held loosely in one hand. A hint of exhaustion softened his voice as he spoke. "Can this be handled without my sailing south, or must I carry the message in person? I'd prefer not going."

Fulton turned his head. "Knowles can take care of it."

He smiled at his employer. "I saw her. I can see why you wouldn't want to leave England."

A slight widening of Alec's eyes. "You saw her?"

Fulton grinned. "Had to see Rhodes' competition for myself." Alec hadn't responded to all the earlier warning telegrams save for a repeated, *Keep me posted.* "Your wife's going to froth at the mouth."

"She has already. Which reminds me. I need more guards on the premises."

"Good idea. I'd suggest a good barrister, too."

Alec's gaze narrowed. "For?"

"For your divorce, of course. Don't tell me you brought this ravishing woman to your home only to ravish her. You could have done that anywhere. Or left her at Crosstrees."

The flask halfway to Alec's mouth was checked. "You know that, do you?"

"Let's just say I've watched you roger your way around the world, and not once have you invited one of the little coquettes home to meet your mother."

"I suppose you have a barrister in mind," Dalgliesh drawled before putting the flask to his mouth and drinking deeply.

"Damn right. No one better than Fitzwilliam. He's the biggest gun of the day, the best hatchet man in the business, a real human hawk in court. And he has charm aplenty. He can even charm the mirthless, pigheaded Queen."

"How's he in bed?" Alec asked, snapping the lid back on his flask. "Violetta prefers to be charmed in bed."

"He's a dedicated lecher and self-confessed amorist who doesn't mind doing a little business in the boudoir if it comes to that."

Alec laughed. "Christ, he's perfect. Do you get a finder's fee?"

"Of course. A fair exchange, n'est-ce pas?"

"Hell yes. Send him a message. Have him come up."

"When?"

"As soon as possible. I've finally reached the end of my rope."

"No, you finally found someone who mattered."

"Yes. I did. Which reminds me." Dropping his feet on the floor, Dalgliesh stood and nodded at his cohort. "Wake me if you have to. Otherwise, I'll come down in a few hours. You'd better get some sleep, too. God only knows what these greedy pricks will do next."

CHAPTER 22

THE FOLLOWING DAYS were lovely and bewildering and unthinkably sad for Zelda because she knew eventually her season in paradise would end. Alec was sweetly solicitous, coming to her whenever he could, making excuses to everyone when he shouldn't be leaving to see her and did anyway, making love to her with a kind of feverish impatience, with tenderness, with explicit lust and disarming affection. Insisting she stay when she talked of going. Telling her he was going to divorce his wife and marry her. That said near dawn one morning when he'd finally come upstairs to bed.

Pushing herself up on her elbows, Zelda gazed at Alec, who was rapidly stripping off his clothes. "Is that a proposal?"

"A proposal?" Preoccupied with Knowles' last wire, he wasn't sure what she meant. He paused in his unbuttoning.

"A marriage proposal."

Ah—enlightenment. "Yes, as a matter of fact it is. Say yes." He went on unbuttoning his trousers. "Make me a happy man."

Her heart was beating like a drum, but she was a woman first. "Might you be a bit more romantic?"

"Sorry, darling. Everything's in chaos right now. Now, then," he briskly said, kicking aside consideration of Knowles' message along with his trousers and moving toward the bed, splendidly nude and aroused, "I'd be honored and delighted if you'd consent to be my wife, my love, my partner, my friend." Pulling aside the covers, he lowered himself between her legs with practiced finesse, slipped his hand under her elbows so she tumbled back, and bending his head, brushed her lips with his. "I promise to adore you forever. I promise to make you happy. I promise to give you babies. Say yes. You have to say yes." He was focused now, his heart in his eyes.

How could she not when she loved him beyond reason. "Yes, even if I can't. Even if you can't. Even if it's impossible."

He shook his head. "Just yes."

Tears filled her eyes. "Then, yes."

"There now, that wasn't so hard," he said with a grin. Then he kissed away her tears, made her happy in ways he'd perfected long ago, and recklessly gave himself up to the wonders of love. For a man who'd learned long ago to control his emotions, who'd managed his life with circumspection, who only took calculated risks, it was a huge sea change.

But he wanted this. And he'd have it.

One way or the other.

In the days that followed, while Alec was feverishly involved in plans to avert disaster in Johannesburg, Zelda filled her hours with riding or entertaining Chris—in the nursery, schoolroom, or at the jumps—often with Alec, who always took time out of his day for Chris. He was a conscientious, loving parent, unlike his own father or because of it. Or simply because he loved the boy.

Although Alec's mother was often in the schoolroom with Chris, he and Zelda would also visit with her as well during the course of the day. Due to the dowager countess's delicate health, she kept a light schedule—sleeping late, resting in the afternoon, ordering her household from her desk in her sitting room with the help of a secretary and two assistants. And while she rarely went out in society, she had a vast friendship, all of whom kept her up-to-date on the latest gossip. She was an amusing conversationalist, an excellent mimic, and an insightful observer of the human condition. But Zelda liked it best when she related boyhood stories of Alec.

"In fact," the dowager countess said one afternoon over tea, after recounting a tale of her son's youthful escapades with his friends and, of all things, an elephant, "once this crisis in South Africa has passed, I wouldn't be surprised if Alec has a dinner party so some of his friends can meet you. They're all quite entertaining. You'd like them."

Which comments prompted a question Zelda didn't vocalize: *Would Violetta concern herself with her husband's dinner party?* But the dowager countess never spoke of Violetta, nor did Chris. It was almost as though she didn't exist. Unfortunately, she did, as she'd made clear to Zelda at Groveland Chase not long ago.

But demons were verboten in paradise.

Just as lovesick inamoratas were forbidden to think of the future. It was more gratifying to live in the dream.

Alec, on the other hand, was fully intent on the practicalities, and that afternoon Fitzwilliam was seated across his desk from him.

Fulton had met the barrister as he stepped down from the carriage that had been sent into London for him since the weather was too chill for Dalgliesh's new Mercedes motorcar and the train schedule was unfavorable. The men had chatted on the way to Alec's study, where Fulton had introduced the earl, declined the coffee that was being served, and returned to the office, where a betting pool was generating excitement. Everyone was laying odds on how much it was going to cost the earl to shed his wife.

"I don't care how much it costs," Alec was saying to Fitzwilliam at the moment as though in tune with his wagering employees. "I suppose you hear that often."

"Actually, no, I hear the opposite. Most men want to pay as little as possible."

"Perhaps most men aren't married to a wife like mine."

The barrister smiled faintly. "Now that I do hear quite often. I'm assuming another lady is involved." At Dalgliesh's obvious surprise, Fitzwilliam added, "There generally is, my lord. Otherwise a man would continue muddling through."

"No doubt. I, however, have come to the point where muddling through, as you put it, no longer appeals. So the question is, how quickly can you get me a divorce?"

"It's a rather drawn-out affair I'm afraid."

Alec held the man's gaze for a telling moment. "I don't want it to be drawn out."

The barrister pursed his lips. He was a diplomatic man. That was why Wales confided in him, why peeresses whispered their secrets to him, why prime ministers sought his advice.

"I don't know whether the courts in England operate like they do in most other countries," Alec went on, ignoring the man's silence, "but if they do, pay whomever you have to pay to expedite the proceedings. Money's no object."

Now *that* he never heard. "Maurice said you were in earnest."

"You mean you have clients who aren't?"

Fitzwilliam shrugged, his fine tailoring accommodating his gesture without a ripple. "Some. Not many mind you, but there's the occasional man who's still in love and can't quite pull the trigger, so to speak."

"I'm quite willing to fire a complete artillery barrage." Alec met Fitzwilliam's calm gaze as calmly. "I trust we understand each other. When you speak to my wife's counsel, I wish that point be made perfectly clear. I'll go to any lengths to end this marriage. See that she understands that." He lifted his hand from his chair arm and signaled his next remark with a flick of his fingers. "I don't care to know any of the details. Do whatever you have to do."

Fitzwilliam never missed a word or a look or a gesture in any of several languages; his understanding was acute. This unsmiling man knew exactly what he wanted and was coldly determined to get it. "Very well. I'll file the papers tomorrow. One word of caution, my lord. The court proceedings are published. You know that, I assume." Even the venerable *Times* devoted considerable column space to the lascivious details of divorce cases—who said what to whom, who did what to whom, every syllable spoken, every expression worn, every wild, shocking, disgusting, distressing moment revealed.

"I know," Alec crisply said. "And I don't care. Do you need me to sign anything today?"

Fitzwilliam reached inside his coat, fetched out a folded sheet of paper, and slid it across the desk to Dalgliesh. "The order to proceed, my lord."

"Where do I sign—ah—I see." Alec reached for a pen from a splendid silver ink stand—a model in miniature of his yacht. He signed without reading the document; he trusted Fulton's judgment. "By the way," he said, handing the paper back, "I should mention, I'll require custody of my wife's son. I trust that can be accomplished."

Fitzwilliam swallowed hard. When in the past, the husband had always been given custody, since 1873 the courts were allowed to award custody as they saw fit. And in the last decade, it had become morally acceptable to grant custody of young children to their mother. Furthermore, Dalgliesh wasn't the boy's father, although that fact could be overlooked under extenuating circumstances. The barrister asked the crucial question. "How old is the boy?"

"Six."

His fist closed on the paper. Fitzwilliam rarely disclosed his feelings. But this wasn't court, nor a public setting, and the earl's answer was devastating.

"Apparently there's some problem," Alec softly said, watching the barrister flinch.

"The boy isn't yours. Is that so?" *A final check.*

"Yes. But his mother's a danger to him. He's afraid of her. Does that help?"

Fitzwilliam's relief was immediate, but then he didn't like losing. "Indeed, it helps a great deal," he said with a sudden smile, followed quickly by a slight frown. "You have witnesses who will confirm this?"

"Any number you like. The countess sees her son rarely, and when she does, he's disturbed for quite some time afterward."

"I'm sorry to hear it," the barrister respectfully said. "But the boy depends on you, I'm told. An advantage, my lord. And in terms of a custody suit, the boy's fear will be of great value." Fitzwilliam returned the creased paper to his coat pocket. "The judge will require more than hearsay, however."

"The boy's nanny will prove an excellent witness if it comes to that. She's of frightening competence and keeps a definitive diary of, say—useful events. She's a real champion for the boy." About to go on, Alec hesitated briefly. Then having made a decision, he said, "One more thing."

Fitzwilliam braced himself. He'd heard that phrase in that tone of voice before. "It's best to be forthcoming, my lord. Surprises in court tend to be dangerous."

"Violetta's not likely to divulge this information." Alec rubbed his cheek with his fingertips, having reached a point that he'd given four years of his life to avoid. He was about to tell a stranger what he'd long concealed. The irony didn't escape him—he of all people taking this risk for love. "There's another child," he said. "It's essential I have custody of her as well." He went on to relay an account that, if revealed, would be tragic for people who mattered to him. As for Violetta, he'd willingly expose her depravity, he added at the end, if not for the pain it would cause his mother.

"I see," Fitzwilliam replied, his breathing somewhat altered. "As you suggest, we won't bring it up unless it's absolutely necessary." He was rarely shocked, but without question, the earl's disclosures were lurid.

"I'll rely on your expertise in such matters, although you understand it's the last thing I wish the world to know. Our advantage is Violetta wishes the facts kept secret even more than I." As for the information he'd kept to himself, there was no possibility Violetta would bring it to light. Those details, at least, would remain private. He leaned back in his chair, satisfied as far as it was possible with his life about to become even more notorious. "So everything will soon be entrain, I assume?"

"Yes, my lord." Such redoubtable assurance came from possessing enormous wealth. One's wishes were rarely thwarted.

The earl regarded Fitzwilliam with a polite smile. "And I can hope for an expeditious process?"

"I'll do my best, sir, but the Court of Chancery moves at its own pace."

"When you learn of the magistrate assigned my case, give me his name. I'll see what I can do. There's always friends of friends—that sort of thing," the earl said incidentally. "It never hurts to personally put one's case to a judge."

No doubt when one owned diamond mines all things were possible. "I'll see that you have the name, sir."

"I'll thank you in advance then. Let me know if there's anything you need. My secretary can send it along, or should you require my personal attention, please feel free to enlist it. Is that all then?"

Fitzwilliam knew a dismissal when he heard it. He rose when Dalgliesh did, took his extended hand, and shook it. "You can expect to hear from me in a few days."

"I appreciate your help," Alec said cordially. "We all do."

The coffee remained untouched, but then this wasn't a social occasion.

After leaving Dalgliesh's study, Fitzwilliam sought out Fulton before returning to London. He was beckoned into Fulton's office when he appeared, asked, "Whiskey or brandy?" waved to a chair, and a few moments later, handed a whiskey.

"I've never seen a man so inflexible in his resolve," the barrister said. "So defiant of obstacles."

"I told you." Fulton raised his glass in salute and took a seat behind his desk. "The man's without fear. Whether inborn or learned, he never backs down. Add to that the splendid Miss MacKenzie's allure," Fulton murmured with a man-to-man lecherous grin. "Why wouldn't he be resolved?"

"I've seen many beautiful women in my business, but never a man so willfully intent—not to mention indifferent to cost. She must be good. Perhaps the instigator of this divorce as well?" After years of handling rich men's divorces, he held a personal bias in that regard.

"Actually, no. It's the earl's idea. He's in love." Fulton made a wry face. "He's going to present her with a fait accompli, a marriage license, and all his earthly possessions."

"Which are considerable," Fitzwilliam said over the rim of his glass before downing half the liquor.

"To put it mildly."

"Has he proposed in some fashion at least, and if so, has she accepted?"

"I believe so. Not that Dalgliesh much cares once he wants something. He'd have her if she said no."

The barrister's brows rose into his sleek auburn hairline. "In this day and age?"

"And with a woman who's as independent as he, according to his old nanny, who's a commanding presence in her own right."

The barrister relaxed in his chair, the subtext suddenly clarified. "That's why he wants her, of course. Kudos to the lady for playing hard to get. A brilliant move on her part."

"Not from what I hear. I hear she's without subterfuge."

Fitzwilliam offered his colleague an indulgent smile. "When you've been in my business as long as I have, you'd understand that no woman is without cunning when it comes to marriage." The present countess particularly came to mind. "And with a man like Dalgliesh, who can buy and sell a good deal of this country if he wishes, there's not a woman alive who wouldn't scheme and plot to become his countess."

"His new countess."

Fitzwilliam lifted one brow. "Indeed. And he's young yet. They may be more. He can afford it."

"You may be right. Then again you may not be. He's in deep and I've known him a long time. There's never been a woman he couldn't walk away from. That's not the case with this one."

"I won't argue the point. But I hear rumors; I pay to hear rumors. People tell me things. His wife will fight this tooth and nail." Insofar as she can, he reflected.

"He knows that. He knows it better than anyone. He just wants results. That's why I suggested he talk to you."

The barrister heaved a small sigh. "In that case, I'd better hie myself back to London and get my clerks working on this. Not that the current countess hasn't paved the way nicely with her behavior." The law allowed a husband to divorce his wife for adultery alone; a woman needed additional reasons to sue for divorce. "The countess's sexual conduct will be her undoing." He raised his glass, then drained it.

"Good, because the earl wants this divorce yesterday."

"So I understand. Is there some—er—reason for haste?" the barrister delicately inquired, setting his glass aside.

"None that I know of, but I'm not privy to the details of Dalgliesh's love life." Recalling numerous episodes in numerous brothels around the world, Fulton amended, "Let's just say, I'm *no longer* privy to the details of his love life. *You* could ask him, if you like."

Fitzwilliam smiled faintly. "I don't think so."

Fulton shrugged. "He probably wouldn't answer you even if you did. He's a private person. Always has been."

Until he needed a divorce.

Fitzwilliam was familiar with the dilemma, even sympathetic. But there came a time when some pretty female turned some peer's head, he was called in to extricate the nobleman from his insupportable marriage, and lordly privacy was suddenly worth sacrificing.

CHAPTER 23

As IT HAPPENED, the next morning, an incident occurred that even more seriously—and noisily—impinged on the earl's privacy.

Walking to the armoire to select a gown, Zelda was passing by the windows overlooking the parkland when she caught sight of Alec striding toward the woods. She came to a stop. This wasn't the first time she'd noticed him cross the lawn when he'd said he was going downstairs to the office. Twice before she'd seen him disappear into the forest.

He'd seemed more distracted than usual this morning, and now—another mysterious excursion. Her curiosity piqued, she selected a warm tweed skirt and jacket from her newly improved wardrobe and dressed. Since the household was still asleep at that hour, she used the main staircase, knowing there was little risk of meeting anyone so early in the morning. Only the hall porter came groggily awake as she crossed the entrance hall; she waved him back in his chair. "I'm going for a stroll," she said. "I won't be long."

Standing outside the door, she buttoned her sable coat. The mid-November morning was cool, the lawn white with frost. But the sun had just risen, the pale azure sky clear and bright. She must hurry before Alec's footprints melted away. Walking down the drive past the west wing, she turned and made her way toward the point in the woodland where she'd lost sight of Alec. His track was visible as she approached it and easily followed.

The forest path was well-worn between the Dower House and whatever lay beyond. Dappled sunlight penetrated the bare branches of the trees, glinted off the few gold, ochre, and burgundy leaves still left on the oak trees, while the pines in Capability Brown's marshaled landscape scented the air. Zelda fought back a wave of desolation as the familiar fragrance spurred unwelcome memories of home.

Home meant leaving Munro Park and Alec.

Home meant privation and loss.

Home meant the end of the dream.

How easy it was to forget harsh reality when Alec was promising her the moon, when he was tender and loving and infinitely kind. When she was deep in love.

But she knew better; she had from the first. No matter how charming and passionate Alec might be, too many women had preceded her in his affections. None of them for long. On the other hand, no one actually died of unrequited love save in the pages of the penny novels. She'd survive, she bracingly maintained. And at the moment, her life was brimming with happiness. How foolish it would be to indulge in regret beforehand.

Her momentary distress silenced, she continued her course and soon arrived at a pretty green that held a small church, an ancient graveyard, and a parsonage surrounded by the chaste gardens of winter. The house and church were medieval in character, constructed of warm, honey-colored stone, the unadorned design the work of a local mason unacquainted with the ostentatious splendor of the gothic. The church was a private chapel, she suspected, for the Dalgliesh family and its retainers, while the sizable parsonage suggested that the earls of Munro provided generous livings to their clergy.

After following Alec's tracks to the parsonage door, Zelda came to an abrupt standstill. Dare she barge into a parsonage uninvited? Was some plausible excuse required? Or should she more sensibly return to the Dower House?

If she chose the latter, however, the mystery wouldn't be solved.

Nor her curiosity assuaged.

Her decision swiftly made, she approached the door, lifted the brass knocker, let it drop, and waited.

And waited.

And waited.

Impulsive and nervy she might be, but she wasn't audacious enough to simply walk into a stranger's home. Reluctant to leave, yet conscious of the civilities, she hesitated a moment more before surrendering to good manners and turning away.

The door suddenly opened.

Swinging back, she faced a young maidservant staring up at her, wide-eyed and uncertain.

"The vicar and missus . . . ain't at home." The girl's voice was as hesitant as her gaze. "They're—in the village." She took a nervous breath. "It's market day, ye see. Come back anither—"

"I believe Lord Dalgliesh is within," Zelda interjected, feeling as though pagan magic was at play with the door opening so fortuitously. She smiled to calm the maid's apprehension and indicated the footprints on the drive. "His lordship's?" she innocently queried.

"Oh, aye," the young maidservant said with sudden comprehension. "But he don't live here," she added with de facto finality and began shutting the door.

Zelda stuck out her gloved hand to arrest the sweep of the ancient studded door. "Might I see him?" Her tone was infinitely polite and cajoling.

"I don't know, miss—what with the master—gone from home . . . an' all," the maid stammered. "I don't rightly know—if'n I should . . . let you in."

The young girl must be a lower servant unused to making

decisions, or perhaps she'd been left with succinct orders to admit no one. "I'm sure his lordship wouldn't mind." Another friendly smile. "He and I are good friends."

Not that Zelda didn't understand what she was doing was shamelessly bold and pushy. Oh, dear. The unnerving thought gave her pause. What if she blundered in on some church business? What if someone other than the vicar and his wife was inside? How awkward would that be—how embarrassing? Would Dalgliesh introduce her as his newest paramour?

Not likely, or perish the thought—what if he *did*?

Zelda had just decided that perhaps she was being too brazen, that she'd be better served by leaving well enough alone when the maid shrugged and said, "If'n you say you're friends, miss. This way. He be in the nursery."

The blood drained from Zelda's face at the word *nursery*, her heart beat wildly, and for a tentative moment, she felt faint. But the moment passed, the blood rushed back, her face flushed, and her temper exploded. Damn his miserable lying hide! He didn't have children, he'd said, he'd never cared about having children, he'd said! Perjurer! Charlatan! *Like bloody hell he doesn't have children!*

Her voice came out slightly breathy and high when she spoke. "If you could show me . . . the way . . . to the nursery, I'd be grateful."

Following the servant up the stairs, then to the back of the house, Zelda had time to regain a modicum of her composure. She cautioned herself not to jump to conclusions; there might be a perfectly reasonable explanation. The children didn't have to be his. Maybe Alec just liked the vicar's children. Such sentiments came from her heart, of course. Her intellect was less forgiving. Then why the secrecy? She knew why. A man of Dalgliesh's reputation was bound to have love children.

And so it appeared a moment later when she was ushered into a large, sun-filled, toy-filled, richly decorated room quite beyond a vicar's income.

"What else don't I know?" she coolly said, contemplating the scene before her.

Dalgliesh was seated on the floor, a little girl with dark ringlets in his lap, the book they were reading open in his hand.

"You don't know much of anything," he replied, his gaze and voice scrupulously bland. "Rose, will you take Julia to the kitchen and give her some of that warm gingerbread?" Setting the book down, he bent his head, gave the pretty child a kiss on her cheek, whispered something in her ear that made her giggle, and picking her up, came to his feet. He handed her to the maidservant who'd shown Zelda into the room, his smile in place until the door shut on the pair. Then he turned on Zelda, his smile wiped away, his eyes chill. "Who the hell asked you to follow me?"

"How many other children do you have tucked away?" Her gaze was equally frigid. The child's resemblance was uncanny, the same color hair, eyes, the identical smile.

"I don't have to answer that." How dare she invade his privacy, interfere in what was none of her business.

"Yet you want *more* children! You want *me* to have your child!" Her outrage rang to the rafters.

"I didn't hear you refusing." His voice in contrast was softly mocking. "On the contrary, I believe you said—"

"You bloody bastard!" She bristled at his confident half smile. "It's not enough that you're an oversexed profligate, you have a harem, too! How many? How *many*, damn you! How many women and by-blows have you left in your wake? What's the record for a filthy-rich libertine who fucks every woman he sees?" Her voice was shrill, piercing, earsplitting.

He was tired. He would have given anything not to be here. And he wasn't the only one oversexed. "Could you please stop screaming?" he quietly said. "And there's no record. I'm just doing what I have to do, what I've always done. Take care of people."

Damn him—so smoothly perfidious, so calm and mollifying. "Pardon me if I don't believe you." She tried to speak with equal serenity, but her tone was still breathy with hysteria. "Tell me—about Julia—and the others? Where do you keep—them all? South Africa—I suppose . . . where else?"

"There's only Julia. And she's not mine." He shifted his stance. He wanted to say, *Don't be silly.* Instead, he selfishly thought, *Christ, why now?* Why not in a week or so when everything wasn't going to hell in Johannesburg, when he'd have some answers from Fitzwilliam, when his life wasn't so goddamned complicated.

"I'm supposed to *believe* you"—she flung her arms wide, the pitch of her voice escalating again—"after seeing *this*? Does Julia's mother live here? Am I intruding on your *bloody love nest*!"

He hated that screeching tone in a woman. Rose was going to wonder what the hell was going on with Zelda yelling the house down. He'd have to explain to John later. If Zelda didn't matter so much to him—no . . . if he didn't love her, he wouldn't have to even think about appeasing her. He'd never appeased a woman before other than in clichéd ways that were notoriously false. And now he surely must, for any number of reasons that wouldn't have mattered a month ago. "I'm so sorry," he gently said. "Come, let's go home. I'll try to explain." He took her arm.

"Don't *touch* me!" She jerked her arm away.

He put his hands up, palms out, took a step back. "I won't touch you. I won't get within a yard of you." His gaze and expression were warily deferential. "Just walk back to the house with me and listen. There's an explanation. Please?" Jesus, loving someone could be bloody hard. There was something to be said for not giving a damn.

When Zelda finally nodded after what seemed a very long time, he exhaled, then cautiously proposed, "If you'll give me a minute, I have to say good-bye to Julia. She's only three and I promised her we'd finish the book today."

"Oh Christ," Zelda muttered. A pause. A sigh. Another more lenient sigh. "Go finish your book."

Recognizing the hint of forbearance in that last sigh, Dalgliesh was encouraged. "I won't be long. Would you like to come and listen to the story? It's about a princess," he added, smiling faintly. "And there's warm gingerbread in the kitchen."

"I don't want to be charmed." Her gaze held a sea of trouble.

His heart disengaged for a moment. He made a deduction, and it began beating again. "Then I won't," he said. "Wait for me."

Sometime later as they retraced their journey through the woods and Alec finished his explanation, Zelda looked at him with derision. "Do you really expect me to believe that? Tell me again how you didn't want to screw Violetta but you did anyway."

Swallowing a sigh, he spoke with utmost courtesy. "As I said, my mother had been on the verge of death for days. I hadn't slept the entire time. When the doctor said the worst was over, that Mother would live, Creiggy talked me into lying down for an hour. She promised to wake me. I didn't know who crawled into my bed or why or cared."

"But you screwed whomever it was anyway."

"I didn't know what I was doing. I was dead to the world."

"But your cock still worked as usual and Violetta took advantage of you. Pardon me if I find that incomprehensible," Zelda said, crabbed and acerbic.

"Believe it or not, it's true. When the doctors told us that Mother wasn't going to die after all, Violetta panicked. She was already pregnant. She had to do something to remedy her situation."

"And you were the something."

"A very convenient something right next door to my father. From that point on, it didn't matter to me whether she was in my bed or not. I knew I wouldn't be able to return to Johannesburg. Mother would require care for the rest of her life. Not to mention Chris had been vital to Mother's recovery. She'd come to love him when Violetta, presenting herself in friendship, had been visiting every day. Mother responded to Chris's voice even in her coma. When Violetta informed me that she was pregnant a few weeks later, I briefly questioned her statement because I was always careful not to take such risks, but there *was* that time when I was more asleep than awake, so"—his voice took on the equivalent of a shrug—"since I was more or less confined to England, it didn't seem a huge sacrifice to marry her. Mother adored Chris. I'd known Violetta before she'd married Joe Clarke. She'd always been friendly."

Zelda gave him a waspish look. "Your kind of friendly."

"Every man's kind of friendly," he brusquely said.

Her gaze was guarded now, examining. "So you did all this for your mother?"

He nodded. "Mother needed me. She also needed Chris, and a baby would bring her enormous happiness. And I knew I'd have to marry someday anyway. What I didn't know was that I was being cheated." He softly sighed. "My father gleefully informed me the night of my wedding that he was the father of Violetta's child. I was unprepared, of course, shocked, stunned, dumbfounded. *I'll kill him,* I thought. I probably did in the end. We came to blows. We often had in the past, but I wasn't an adolescent anymore, and six additional years of drinking hadn't improved his health. He collapsed while we were struggling over a shotgun he'd grabbed from his gun cabinet.

"He died a week later without fully regaining consciousness. Had the scandal surfaced, it might have killed Mother. She was still very weak." He shrugged. "Although Creiggy thinks otherwise. I'm not so sure. But Mother'd suffered enough at my father's hands. She didn't need this final insult." By that time, too, he'd begun to suspect who was to blame for his mother's illness. Not that he was about to bare his soul on that account. "And if I'd been inclined to question my father's swaggering disclosure," he added, his mild tone tempered by the intervening years, "Julia was born six months later, weighed eight pounds, and was unmistakably a Dalgliesh."

"She is—very much so," Zelda murmured.

"She's also a darling. It's not her fault she came into the world the way she did. John and Lily have been wonderful to her."

"Your mother doesn't know?" Surprise and anxiety tempered her query.

He shook his head. "That was Violetta's trump card. She knew I didn't want Mother hurt. But I'm going to have to explain it all to Mother now that I've begun divorce proceedings. I was going to tell you that I talked to a barrister once I had more definitive news. In any event, Mother will have to be informed about the divorce and about Julia." He grimaced. "Somehow. Creiggy seems to think Mother's stronger than she looks. I hope she's right because the scandal's going to be horrendous."

"Creiggy knows?"

"Everyone at the house knows."

"And yet they've kept your secret?"

"Because of Mother. They worship her."

"Lord, Alec. This is all very confusing and, honestly, unsettling. I'm not sure what to do." Should she believe him? Was he truly divorcing Violetta? Would he actually marry her if he did? A man like Dalgliesh, no matter that he professed devotion, didn't have a record for constancy.

"Give me time to resolve this mess. The barrister, Fitzwilliam, is first rate, Fulton tells me. He'll see to my divorce, then we'll be married." Alec thought about taking Zelda's hand but decided against it. "It shouldn't take too long."

"Violetta's going to fight a divorce," Zelda said, interested in his answer, turning so she could watch his face. For all she knew he could have asked any number of women to marry him before her.

"She can't."

An open, direct look and an unexpected answer. "Why not?"

"Let me rephrase that. Ultimately, she can't prevail."

"You're sure."

"Very."

"But you're not going to tell me why."

"I'd rather not." He blew out a breath, then quietly said, "I'd like you to trust me on this. I know it's asking a lot, considering this unholy mess, but if you would, I'd be grateful." Only a handful of people knew the entire truth. He'd

like to keep it that way for his mother's sake. "There's going
to be scandal enough with the divorce. I'm trying to mini-
mize the humiliation. Not for me. I don't care. But for all
the others," he quietly said.

He looked so afflicted she didn't have the heart to insist.

When he spoke of humiliation, he meant his mother, of
course, and Chris and Julia as well, she suspected. A love
child faced censure even with Alec's wealth. "Of course,
I'll trust you. How could I not?" She loved him.

Taking a chance she wouldn't rebuff him, he gently
grasped her hand and felt both relief and pleasure when she
gave him a sidelong smile dappled by sunlight. "I'll make
this up to you. Fitzwilliam assures me quick success in
court." He hadn't, but then he didn't know what Dalgliesh
knew. "Although," Alec added with a small frown, "you
know the divorce proceedings will be in all the papers. I
suggest you don't read them." He sighed. "Christ, I'm going
to have to warn Mother about that, too."

"At least my family won't care. They're scandal proof.
You haven't met my brothers," Zelda noted. "Three rakish
young bucks who like their whiskey can cause a great deal
of trouble, and Duncan looks to be following in their footsteps in Edinburgh."

Alec laughed. "Good, one less problem. Look, why don't
we go into town and pick out an engagement ring? It would
give me hope that in the fullness of time I'll have my life
back. And I'd love to show you off."

"God no," Zelda said aghast. "Not London. I'd be hor-
ribly embarrassed."

"Then we'll go to Paris for a ring," he suggested. "Just
as soon as the imbeciles in South Africa are restrained."

She smiled. "When will that be?"

He visibly relaxed at the sweetness of her smile. "Not
soon enough unfortunately," he said, his answering smile
warm with affection. "Why don't we have a jeweler bring
out a selection instead."

"Because gossip would probably precede him, that's why."

He quirked one brow. "Since when have you cared about gossip?"

"Since I found myself in your exalted sphere," she replied. "I led quite an uneventful life before I met you."

"If only my life were exalted," he muttered. "Far from it. Welcome to my version of hell."

A prescient comment as it turned out.

CHAPTER 24

ZELDA COULDN'T QUITE envision *any* version of hell at the moment.

She was content, happy, her jealousy assuaged. In fact she was feeling guilty for suspecting the worst of Alec when he was instead taking the time to care for a child that wasn't even his. And doing it despite the absolutely punishing schedule he was under.

He saw Julia every day when he was home, he'd said. When he was away from Munro Park, he sent the little girl notes and presents. Zelda already knew how thoughtful he was of Chris and his mother. As for herself, he was ungrudgingly benevolent in his attentions.

"I feel terrible," she said, glancing at him as they traveled down the woodland path hand in hand. "I'm selfishly taking up a great deal of your time when you have so many other pressing matters needing your attention. I do apologize."

"I want you to take my time." He smiled. "Seeing you is my gift to myself. As for this crisis"—he shrugged faintly—"things should break soon."

She wanted to say, *Which crisis?* The list was long.

Instead, she said, "Maybe you should delay your divorce. You'd have one less problem right now, and everything's fine the way it is as far as I'm concerned," she said with a good-natured smile. "Really."

He looked puzzled and less than amiable. "You want me to delay my divorce?"

"No, I don't *want* you to. It was just a suggestion. You're so incredibly busy now, working eighteen to twenty hours a day, that I thought—"

He was scowling now. "I don't like your suggestion."

"You're angry. I'm sorry."

"I'm not angry. Surprised that's all."

"Because no woman has ever gainsaid you, I suppose," she testily said. "How very nice that must be."

"Now *you're* angry."

Her nose twitched, charmingly, he thought, and then she said, "No—not angry so much as, well—dubious. The truth is that I don't actually believe you mean to divorce. What do you think of that?"

"I don't blame you. I hardly believe it myself."

"There. You see."

She tried to pull her hand away, but he wouldn't let her. "You misunderstand, darling," he said, choosing his words carefully. "What's unbelievable is that almost from the first I've been obsessed with everything about you, how you look, how you smile, how you sometimes"—he paused, thinking of how she'd held him off at first—"care what the world thinks even when you say you don't. I've wanted a child with you almost from the first, too. You know that because I told you even in the midst of that crowd in the kitchen." He finally smiled his beautiful smile that could bring a corpse to life or charm even the most dubious doubting Thomas. "Darling, consider, we're having sex day and night. I'm just being practical. Waiting to divorce might not be an option."

"Oh Lord, don't say that."

"Jesus, Zelda, don't tell me you need a lecture on the birds and the bees."

"Of course not. If you must know, the real, *real* truth is that I'm afraid I might lose you in all the slander and destruction of a divorce." She wasn't so sure he could withstand the storm of public scrutiny when he'd been guarded about his private life so long. She took a small breath before going on, not sure she wished to bare her soul to a man who had, to date, only toyed with women. "You see," she slowly began, her emancipated psyche reluctant to cede the field, "I think, in the end, you might decide it's not worth the long, difficult, embarrassing process. Your entire life will be open to cross-examination in court and in the papers. You don't have to do this for me. Even a child isn't an issue where I live."

In the past he would have smoothly accepted her offer, made promises he'd never keep. But now he meant every word. "You won't lose me," he said. "Not now, not ever. And don't worry about me in court." He assumed that he was paying Fitzwilliam to keep him out of court in any event. But there was no guarantee there, so he didn't offer false hope. "I want to marry you, my dubious darling. I want you to have my children. I want us to live together 'til the end of time." Raw feeling, fierce and passionate, shone in his eyes. "I love you." His smile was achingly sweet. "I always shall."

She wished she'd known him as a boy when he smiled like that. She would have loved him then, too. "Oh good, and thank you," she said on a soft breath of joyful relief, the ferocious sense of fear that had threatened to crush her routed. He didn't ask her if she loved him, but she wasn't jealous anymore of all the women who had. "I love you, too, you know."

He smiled. "I know. And as soon as we get back home, I'll show just how *much* I love you."

She grinned. "What a lovely thought. Forgive me for being so fainthearted. It's quite unlike me. I have no explanation."

"I believe it's called love, darling." He winked in a disarmingly seductive way. "Don't expect logic."

Her senses began to warm as they always did when he

looked at her like that. "I might have other expectations, however," she murmured, her voice sultry and low.

"Don't you always," he said as softly, his gaze taking on a predatory gleam. "It's one of your most—" He glimpsed a flash of light high in a tree where it shouldn't have been and was already slamming Zelda to the ground when the crack of a rifle shot rang out. Tumbling after her, he fired two quick rounds from a small revolver he jerked from his pocket. As they hit the ground, he covered her body with his and hoped like hell his men had heard the commotion.

Three distant shots came in answer. Good. Better odds.

Hoping his men's signal shots had momentarily distracted their assailant, Alec leaped to his feet, scooped up Zelda, and dashed headlong for a nearby pine thicket. Two more shots whined past them before they reached shelter, the last so close it stirred the air in passing.

Alec dropped Zelda on the ground, crisply ordered, "Don't move," and swung back to give chase.

Paralyzed with shock, Zelda couldn't have moved if she wished. She didn't even flinch at the loud, close, rapid-fire shots as Alec emptied his revolver at the distant, fleeing figure.

Coming to a stop a dozen yards down the path, the earl softly swore in several languages. The man had disappeared. Not that his target had been within revolver range. Nor could he continue to give chase and leave Zelda unguarded. No question, though, he would have to see that she was better protected, more to the point, perhaps, that Violetta was more closely watched. It wouldn't happen again, he grimly thought.

Shoving his revolver back in his coat pocket, retracing his steps, he debated what best to tell Zelda. The truth wouldn't serve. *You were the target, not me,* required explanations he wasn't yet willing to supply. Perhaps never if he had his way.

Finding Zelda huddled pale and shaken on the ground where he'd left her, he lifted her to her feet, drew her into his embrace, and began with an apology. "I'm sorry. I'm so sorry," he murmured. "It's over now. You're safe." But beneath the tranquility of his tone, a simmering anger seethed. What the hell did he have guards for? No unauthorized person should have been within a mile of the estate. "If it's my gamekeeper being stupid, I'll have his head," he said. "Creiggy's been telling me Wilson needs glasses."

Zelda looked up, her gaze incredulous. "This was some mistake?"

"It had to have been. These things don't happen at Munro Park."

"You shot back though." Another shock—his lightning-swift reaction as they'd hurtled to the ground. "Why do you carry a weapon?"

"It's a habit in the country." Only a partial lie. "And I shot to scare the damned fool. I have men patrolling the estate," he mentioned in a kind of incidental aside. "They'll find him."

She was startled. "Men patrolling? Why haven't I seen them?"

For good reason. "I suppose because there's only a few." Another lie, but so much was at Munro Park. Since his mother's illness, the estate had been well defended. "They're primarily a deterrent to Violetta. She and Mother don't get along," he said elliptically. "If I'm home, Violetta's welcome in the Dower House. Otherwise not." He shrugged faintly. "It's a long-standing arrangement like everything else in our marriage."

"My Lord, Alec," Zelda said, astonished he had guards to keep his wife at bay. "What a tangled mess. I marvel at your charity. How do you do it?"

He was more than willing to shift the conversation from the shooting, even if the alternative was his noxious marriage. "An arrangement like mine isn't so uncommon," he said, suppressing the old bottled rage automatically now after so long. "I know any number of men who've entered marriages of convenience." He didn't say noblemen weren't required to be faithful, nor that it made marriages like his bearable. "And if you think Chris is sweet now," he said with a fleeting smile, "you should have seen him at two."

"I can imagine."

"One learns to cope," he said.

"By amusing yourself in other ladies' beds."

"Not anymore." There was no point arguing about the past. "You can have that in writing if you want."

"I just might. If nothing else, I could blackmail you with such a promise," she lightly noted. "I doubt you'd like your reputation for vice besmirched."

He smiled. "You must be feeling better. And for your information, I no longer have a reputation for vice."

Her brows lifted in amused delight. "Is that so."

"It is. I intend to be a model husband, attentive to my wife and marriage vows."

"Must I learn to be a model wife?" she playfully inquired.

He shook his head. "You're perfect." Of that he was certain after screwing his way around the world the last ten years. His chin lifted. "Hear that? My men are close." Running footsteps were audible. "And I expect Wilson will have some reasonable explanation for this monstrous mistake."

Zelda brushed his chin with her fingertip. "You were very chivalrous to shield me with your body. I thought it exceedingly romantic."

"I'll be happy to cover you with my body again," the earl sportively offered. "Hopefully soon." Although this incident presaged the end of Zelda's stay at Munro Park. He'd have her escorted home tomorrow.

"How soon?" she whispered.

His smile was warm, tantalizing. "Just as soon as I get rid of my men." But he was already making plans to pay Violetta a visit as soon as Zelda was gone. Apparently, his wife didn't understand she was no longer in a position of power.

He'd have to make that clear.

When the party of armed men reached them a moment later, Dalgliesh casually addressed his lieutenant. "Someone will have to tell Wilson to do his shooting somewhere else next time."

Jed Green, who'd known Alec from childhood, picked up the cue. "I'll speak to Wilson," he said. Although he knew as well as Alec, if Wilson wanted to shoot someone, he wouldn't miss. "It must have been a real fright for the lady."

"Perhaps just a little," Zelda admitted. "But I'm fine now."

"Back to the house then, darling?" Alec's gaze met Jed's for a second before he turned his smile on Zelda and held out his arm.

In the guise of a bantering conversation between Alec and his men, the six guards casually positioned themselves to protect their patron and his lady on the return to the Dower House.

Dalgliesh nodded at Jed as they reached the house. "If I might see you later," he said. "You can tell me what Wilson said."

"Very good, sir. Anytime."

It was an unpleasant meeting when Dalgliesh met with his men fifteen minutes later in the armory. He'd excused himself from breakfast, pleading work. Understanding the full extent of his obligations, Zelda had graciously sent him off.

Alec was feeling far less gracious. "Someone should be whipped," he growled, taking his seat at the head of the table and glaring at his men. "Miss MacKenzie was almost killed. How the *hell* did it happen!"

"From what I can gather, boss," Jed said, "one of the jockeys who comes here regularly disappeared right quick after the shooting. Since he was vetted, no one thought to question him."

"Who?"

"Cummings, sir."

"Find him. Bring him to me."

"Yes, sir. I'll send up a message when we have 'im."

The earl softly sighed. "We're going to have to increase surveillance on my wife. I thought we had enough men in the city. Apparently not."

"Yes, sir."

"She has to be followed wherever she goes. See that we have paid agents in every house of consequence in the city. I want to know where she goes, who she talks to, what she says. Bring in men from Warwickshire if you have to." Another of Dalgliesh's hunting estates.

"Any men from Crosstrees?"

Alec smiled. "Is Gordon itching for a fight?"

"He always is, sir."

"Do as you like. I suppose he wants his cousins with him."

"I expect so, sir."

"Have Fulton arrange for supplies, weapons, billeting."

"He already has, begging your pardon, sir."

Dalgliesh laughed. "I should have known. But no more mistakes, hear? That was too bloody close for comfort. The lady is going to be my wife." He scanned the men seated around the table. "She's to be protected from Violetta's malice. I'll need a full complement of men to escort her to the Highlands tomorrow. Everyone well armed."

"Consider it done, sir."

Alec grimaced. "I haven't told her yet that I'm sending her back." He softly sighed. "A word of warning. You may have a sulky lady on your hands on the trip north. Treat her delicately. Do anything she wants"—his brows rose—"within reason."

CHAPTER 25

THAT NIGHT, ALEC took special care to indulge Zelda's desires with a professional artistry and an obsessive regard for sensation, and she responded to him as she always did, with unprofessional passion and generosity. And much later as she lay in his arms, sated and blissfully content as intended, he gently broached the subject of her departure.

An unexpected business emergency in London had come up, he said. Another crisis—a minor one, but he had to attend to it. Some politicians needed added inducements to support his cause, some required an additional dose of courage to resist Rhodes, both of which he was to personally dispense. He didn't know how many days the meetings would last, he explained. He knew she didn't care to be seen with him in London, although she was certainly welcome. Unfortunately, he didn't know whether he'd have time to entertain her. Perhaps she might like to go home for a short while. He'd come for her just as soon as he could. A week— two at the most.

Lies, lies, and more lies.

She, in turn, pretended to believe him. He was gracious,

at least, in sending her away. So she smiled and nodded and agreed and said all that was required of a well-behaved lover about to be discarded.

She wondered afterward how she'd managed when his first words had struck her like a punch in the gut. Perhaps facing down bandits in Mongolia or headmen in the jungle had schooled her not to blink or move a muscle or show emotion. Perhaps it was sheer obstinacy that carried her through. She refused to dissolve into tears—not with a man who viewed women as disposable. In any case, she doubted he'd be moved by female tears.

Their good-byes in the morning were exquisitely polite.

His smile perhaps was more practiced than hers, but then he'd had more opportunity to use it in situations like this, she decided. He, on the other hand, didn't know what to think; he'd never felt such a wrenching sense of loss.

The dowager was gracious as ever. As though her son had women in residence at Munro Park on a regular basis.

Chris was consoled by his father's explanation that Miss MacKenzie would return soon. A fiction, Zelda observed, but Dalgliesh knew best how to deal with his son. As for Creiggy, her civility couldn't be faulted; small wonder from the woman who'd taught Alec his manners.

Everyone's conduct was proper enough for a levee at court.

By the time they reached the private rail station at Munro Park, however, Zelda's smile was stiff and brittle, her nerves on edge, her heart near to breaking—only poetically, of course. In reality, it kept obstinately thudding along without regard for her anguish. She fought to keep her tears at bay, her breathing quickening under the strain, only sheer will stemming the tide.

What saved her—quite by chance—was the size of her escort lined up on the platform. She was first shocked, then astonished. "So many men," she said on a small caught breath, her maudlin concerns eclipsed by the staggering number of men-at-arms loosely deployed in rows under the bright morning sun.

"Most of the men are on their way to Crosstrees for the

holidays." Only a partial lie. "The others will see you safely home." Dalgliesh smiled. "And tell me where to find you again. The tracks through the Highlands can be obscure."

She didn't dissemble as well or perhaps found suave urbanity more difficult with the huge lump in her throat. "Thank you"—her voice broke—"for all your kindness."

"The pleasure was mine." Ignoring her stricken look, he held out his hand, his demeanor relaxed. "Come, I'll help you inside."

After entering the parlor of his private car, he introduced her to the waiting staff. He spoke to each retainer with a casual familiarity, made them laugh, dismissed them after a few moments with polished grace. "If you wish for anything," he said, turning to Zelda, "you need but ask. Soames is in charge inside, Jed outside. They have instructions to indulge your every whim," he added with a faint smile.

She had to bite back the comment on the tip of her tongue; she didn't think he was included in her whims. "I can be quite selfish, then," she lightly said in lieu of breaking into a torrent of tears.

"Feel free, darling, to be anything you wish."

"Thank you again, for everything. I had a very nice time." There. She could be dégagé, too, if she put her mind to it.

"I don't suppose there's a telegraph office near your home." He was perhaps not completely dégagé.

She shook her head.

"Or a telephone."

"I'm afraid not."

"Then I'll send a messenger to warn you when I'm coming."

She almost believed him; she very much wanted to believe him. "I'd like that," she said, unable to keep her voice steady at the last.

The helpless pain in her eyes almost made him change his mind and carry her off the train. He could lock her away at Munro Park, strengthen his patrols, keep her safe. He could assemble an army to guard her. But his mother had almost become a casualty within the confines of her own home. He dare not take the risk, no more than he dared kiss Zelda good-bye. If he touched her, he was lost. "You'll see me soon." He found it difficult to keep his breathing even. By conscious will, he summoned a smile, then turned and quickly left.

He stood on the platform as the train pulled away, not noticing the cold wind or how tired he was, touched by a sadness he'd not felt before. Wishing he hadn't had to send her home. Wishing Violetta hadn't forced his hand. Wishing there wasn't always a price to be paid for every joy.

Her face pressed against the window, her eyes brimming with tears, Zelda watched him until his figure diminished to nothingness. Then he was gone. Perhaps forever.

She had no way of knowing.

She also didn't know if she even dared hope for a future with a man like Alec, who was much sought after by women and unrestrained in his amusements. She knew men often said what they didn't mean, that honesty was particularly elusive at the conclusion of an affaire.

Still, hope springs eternal, someone of roseate disposition once said. She sighed. With a profligate like Dalgliesh? Perhaps not. Although, if nothing else, the bonny earl had become the yardstick by which every future lover would be measured. She smiled. Damn though, he was going to be difficult to replace. On the other hand, he'd given her an abundant supply of glorious memories—a veritable encyclopedia of sybaritic delight. Partial recompense at least for her loss.

On the journey north, as promised, everyone was the soul of courtesy. Zelda had but to incidentally mention something she liked and it appeared as if by magic or someone saw to it that the train was stopped and the item fetched for her. Two lady's maids were aboard to serve her, as well as a chef, three footmen, and the redoubtable Soames. Jed Green, who was in charge of the troop, checked in from time to time to see that she lacked nothing. She could have been traveling royalty with the size and charitable intent of her retinue.

But what she liked best during her journey were the times when Jed would talk about Alec. He'd take the whiskey she offered, sit for the time it took to drink it, and answer her questions. He wasn't averse to recounting incidents from Alec's youth. The men had grown up together at Crosstrees and were friends. But when it came to answering questions about Alec's adulthood, Jed was more circumspect. There were always women in Alec's life. He was a man who attracted female attention.

When they disembarked at Inverness, a smaller troop accompanied Zelda on the last leg of her journey, the danger having diminished with the increasing distance from London. Although, aware of what the lady meant to Alec, Jed took no risks. His twenty men were well armed and vigilant.

Zelda's father came hurrying out to greet them as the cavalcade rode into the yard, his eyebrows flying up at the size of her escort. Sir Gavin offered Dalgliesh's men the hospitality of his house, but Jed graciously refused, explaining that the train was waiting for them at Inverness.

"It takes a wee bit o' cash to hold up a train that long," Sir Gavin noted a short time later as he and Zelda entered the baronial manor with its imaginative Renaissance architectural details overlaying the original fifteenth-century castle.

Zelda smiled. "Dalgliesh has more than a wee bit, Da. Are the boys home?"

"Aye. I saw them riding into the stable yard just as you arrived. Come, take your ease and tell us of the doings in the south."

As Sir Gavin ushered Zelda into the large sitting room, with its fine painted ceiling where the family gathered in their leisure, her three brothers turned from the hearth. They were ranged before the huge fireplace that was large enough to roast an ox, their faces ruddy from the outdoors, their hunting plaids damp on their shoulders, their boots muddy from tramping the hills. They each had a horn cup of whiskey in hand.

"You needn't stare," Zelda said, walking into the room decorated with four and a half centuries of weapons. "I had a fine, couthie (agreeable) holiday. I even had a proposal of marriage that Dalgliesh might actually mean. But if he doesn't, I still had a very nice time."

Her oldest brother, Hugh, broke into a smile first. "Don't say ye might a' caught the elusive earl."

"Maybe."

John and Robbie said in unison, grinning, "Dinna his wife mind?"

"You'll have to ask the wee bitch yourself," Zelda silkily replied. "He's getting a divorce. He might actually mean that as well."

The brothers exchanged skeptical glances. Well-favored men, they knew their way around a boudoir. Promises made were part of the game; promises kept were rare.

She smiled. "How polite you are, my darlings, but by the bye, we'll find out whether Dalgliesh means it or not. So, tell me, how's the shooting?"

"Damned fine," her father quickly interposed, putting little stock in proposals of marriage from a faithless married man, preferring the subject be dropped. "And we're right pleased to see ye home, lass, and that's God's truth. Come, take a seat by the fire and I'll call up something from the kitchen. Hugh, pour your sister a grace cup to welcome her home."

MEANWHILE, DALGLIESH WAS cooling his heels in a drawing room at Munro House, his London residence he'd not entered in four years. No matter Munro House was a block long and large enough to accommodate both he and his wife, he preferred his apartment in St. James Place.

Arriving in town shortly after Zelda left, he'd discovered that Violetta was at Lady Mull's country house and wouldn't return until the following afternoon. He'd briefly debated accosting her at Charlotte's but decided against making a public scene.

There'd be publicity enough soon.

He'd left Violetta a message, however, informing her that he wished to speak with her the next day at three. Nevertheless, he'd been kept waiting for—he scowled at the clock on the mantel—twenty-five bloody minutes. He was badly out of humor, insulted, not in the habit of being ignored in his own house. He couldn't even get a servant to reply to the bellpull. Violetta had her own staff. But he paid for them all, damn the bitch. He wondered what they'd do if he fired the lot.

Since he was sober, it was only a passing thought—his sobriety a thankless state for a much aggrieved husband who preferred a drink or two or several when dealing with his wife. But this business demanded a clear head and perhaps a degree of diplomacy, so he paced instead of raising holy hell, silently fumed, and contemplated various forms of future revenge.

After another irritating and lengthy interval, which further fueled Dalgliesh's resentment and eroded any prospect of diplomacy, a footman came to fetch him. Following the man up the main staircase and down familiar corridors, Alec was ushered into Violetta's little bijoux of a sitting room off her boudoir by the young flunkey who, he suspected, was also warming his wife's bed.

Although perhaps the fellow would have to get in line today, Alec noted, his expression deliberately vacant. He recognized the man seated beside Violetta on her blue damask settee.

"You know each other, I presume," Violetta said with a flick of her fingers in Fitzwilliam's direction. "You're usual whiskey, darling?"

He politely said, "No," to her grating familiarity and wondered whether his new counsel could be trusted. Fitzwilliam hadn't wasted any time making himself at home in Violetta's boudoir. The two were very cozily situated side by side, Fitzwilliam lounging at his ease, one arm resting intimately on the settee back inches from Violetta's blond curls.

"The countess and I were discussing the merits of the case," the barrister said as if reading Dalgliesh's mind.

"Do sit, darling," Violetta said, oversweet and smiling. "Join the discussion. I'm sure it's of material interest to you."

Pausing in the doorway, Alec said mildly, "I prefer standing, thank you. I've only come to apprise you of the full extent of my enmity and resolve. Since you've become an unreasonable danger to everyone I love, you no doubt know I've reached—"

"My goodness. Love? You mean your new Miss MacKenzie?" Violetta's brows arched upward in scoffing derision. "How charming, darling. I thought you were only amusing yourself—again . . . as always."

"A decision," he finished as though she hadn't spoken. His voice softened, as if he were saying something unimportant. "I intend to have this divorce. Over your dead body, if necessary. I trust I've made myself clear."

"May I caution you, my lord," Fitzwilliam interposed, his gaze heavy lidded, his lounging pose unaltered. "The lady has certain protections under the law."

"Very limited protections, as I understand, and wholly at the discretion of the judge. Furthermore, those protections, limited or not, won't do her much good if she's dead."

"Come, come, my lord. There's no need for threats. The courts will deal with this matter in a competent manner, I'm sure."

There was a short silence. Then in an unemotional, perhaps cynical voice, Alec said, "You must decide to whom you're committed, Fitzwilliam."

The barrister's expression was equally unexcited. "Please, sir, don't say anything you'll regret."

"My only regret is wasting four years of my life. It's over, Violetta. Do what you will, say what you will, I don't care anymore," he said, his voice dying away at the last. Then he seemed to collect himself and his voice took on a crispness. "Just stay away from me and mine. As for you, Fitzwilliam, you'd better decide whom you're representing." He turned, grasped the door handle, hesitated, then turned back. "Don't be too greedy, Violetta. I'm not in the mood. Perhaps you can help her in that regard, Fitzwilliam. I'm sure you know the usual settlement sums."

After the door slammed on Alec, Violetta feigned a little

shiver of alarm. "You see what I've had to deal with all these years. I've often lived in fear of my life. He just threatened me again. You witnessed it."

"How terrible for you," Fitzwilliam commiserated. "A small, fragile woman against such a monster. I'm not sure I can represent a man like that."

"How sweet you are." Leaning in close, Violetta ran her finger down the fine silk of the barrister's waistcoat. "I'm sure we could come to some agreement over a retainer if you'd be willing to represent *me*. Alec has more money than he needs in ten lifetimes. And he's always been generous. Together we could reach a comfortable settlement, I'm sure. Do you have time?"

The look she gave him was familiar and wanton and left him in no doubt what she meant by *time*. "I'm at your disposal, my lady."

She smiled. "No scheduling conflicts?"

"None I can't ignore."

"How amenable you are."

"With good reason, my lady. You're a beautiful, fascinating woman, and I confess, you've always interested me."

Her brows rose in faint query. "Have we met before?"

"I don't believe so. But you're the most dashing female in the beau monde. I've worshiped you from afar."

She slowly smiled. "Come, darling, you're not the type to worship anyone."

He softly laughed. "Then may I more bluntly say, I've wanted to fuck you for a very long time."

Her silvery trill matched the pleasure in her eyes. "Why wait any longer, my dear Fitzwilliam. You look like the kind of man who knows how to please a lady."

He was. His talents weren't exclusively devoted to the courtroom. Nor were his pleasures, although he loved to win in court, he *lived* to win in court. But he was also handsome, lithe, athletic, well-endowed, and when he rose from Violetta's bed several hours later, he left behind a satisfied woman. And took away with him all the information he'd come for.

After a brief detour home to bathe and change, he had himself driven to Dalgliesh's apartments in St. James. A cool, self-possessed butler of considerable consequence took his name, said, "The earl is waiting for you," and had a footman escort him to a paneled study with a fire on the hearth and Dalgliesh seated before it, drinking.

The earl didn't rise as Fitzwilliam approached. He only looked up and gruffly said, "What the hell were you doing there?"

"I charge more for that tone of voice."

"Charge what you want. Answer my question."

"I'll have a drink first. She worked me like a galley slave."

Dalgliesh stared at him for a fraction of a second and then burst out laughing. "But it wasn't a complete hardship for all that, I'll warrant," he said, still chuckling as he handed over the bottle he held in his hand. "Glasses over there," he said with a wave toward a drinks table. "And more liquor if you don't like whiskey."

"Whiskey will do, thank you," the barrister said, taking the bottle and sinking into a large wingback chair on the other side of the hearth. "Christ, I'm exhausted."

"You deserve a bonus for services rendered. Add whatever you wish to your fees. And I await your pleasure once you've rested and drunk your fill." Coming to his feet, Dalgliesh strolled over to the drinks table and carried back two more bottles. "I've a feeling we have something to celebrate," he said with a grin. Sitting down, he leaned over, placed one bottle by Fitzwilliam's chair, uncorked the other, and lifted it to his mouth. "By the way, what's your Christian name."

"Francis."

"Well, Francis, let's drink to my freedom."

"Your freedom in due time, my lord. Even though your wife incriminated herself rather conclusively this afternoon, the case still needs to be presented to the court. Nothing is guaranteed. An unsympathetic magistrate, a counter suit, some unanticipated technicality. Things can go wrong."

"I understand. But by and large, Violetta's case is indefensible, don't you agree?"

"Particularly should you disclose the more sordid details."

"If I have to, I will. I haven't told you yet of her plot to murder Zelda. We found and interrogated the man she hired. He signed a confession."

"She wants Miss MacKenzie dead, not you?"

"Yes. She wants *me* to live a very long life. For if my cousin inherits, she'd have to survive on her dower stipend." His lashes drifted downward. "That's hardly pin money for Violetta."

"She said you were generous."

"Out of indifference, not kindness. Although, if you plan on seeing her again," Alec said with a faint smile, "I wouldn't recommend going in unarmed. Nor would I eat or drink anything."

"Consider me warned. So tell me about this man she hired. Is he still in your custody?"

Alec nodded. "She's looking for him though. She has men staked out at his apartment."

"Did *she* pay him or did someone else?"

"Her personal footman paid him. You saw him—the large, good-looking fellow. Very young. I imagine he's delighted to be allowed in her bed from time to time—not that a bed's required for Violetta, as you no doubt discovered."

Fitzwilliam's brows rose. "Indeed." He slid down on his spine and exhaled softly. "Forgive me, my lord, but I'm fagged. Ask me what you wish and I'll try to answer. If I fall asleep, shake me awake."

"Finish your drink, then go home and sleep. We can talk tomorrow."

"Thank you, sir."

"It's for me to thank you," the earl graciously replied. "You've apparently not only gained valuable information, you've renewed my faith in humanity. I wasn't quite sure what to make of you when I saw you lounging in Violetta's boudoir."

"I'm very dependable, sir. I pride myself on my loyalty."

"Good. Get me this divorce and I'll make you a very rich man."

"I'm already rich."

"Would you like me to buy you a title, then? I know the chief whip, Akers-Douglas. Not that you have to be a personal friend anymore. The tariff for a peerage is common knowledge."

"Which, of course, makes it less valuable."

"You don't want one?"

"I'm not sure."

"Well, it's yours if you wish. Or anything else you'd like. Let me know." He was prepared to pay handsomely for results.

"If we win, I'll decide."

"I always win."

"As do I."

Dalgliesh smiled. "Well, then, it's just a matter of you deciding if you want to be a peer of the realm or not."

After discussing the details of the case, the men parted on good terms, Fitzwilliam returning home to his solitary bed, Dalgliesh staying up late, drinking and coming to terms with the remarkable changes in his life. With the temporary aberrations and the future ones, with all the curious *startling* changes. With the even more curious obsessions, when all his grown life he'd relied on detachment as his means of survival.

Because all his grown life, he'd understood that he was irredeemably alone. Not that he didn't have a mother who loved him, and Creiggy, of course, and the servants who were like family. But even when young, when they'd finally left the main house and taken up residence in the dower house, he'd found himself the master of the establishment. His mother, never strong, had given up the struggle to save her marriage and had retired to her music and books. Her love for him was unconditional, but when strength was required or special skills to forestall his father's inroads, it had been left to him to face the storm. He was big for his age and capable—thanks in large part to Creiggy's stout training—and he'd managed his difficult, disputative, drunken father more times than he cared to remember.

Ultimately, whether here or in South Africa, whether large or small, his decisions had always been his own. And now, for the first time, the purpose of his life had expanded beyond caretaking and business and estate governance.

He'd found love. Or love had found him. The quiet misery of his life had been forever altered, and he wished to protect this newfound joy at all costs. For a man who'd always guarded his privacy from outside intrusion, he was in awe of the breathtaking intimacy of love.

His greatest strength had always been his ability to stand alone, to influence or militate, to prejudice or persuade, to prevail. To not belong but to lead. And now, because of an extraordinary woman, he was about to share both his privacy and power.

He started to make plans.

Contingency plans.

He didn't know if he could abide the slow grinding wheels of justice required for a divorce. He didn't know if he had the patience. He didn't know if a month of more or less continuous fucking would allow him that freedom of choice.

No, no, and probably not.

Good. He was rather of a mind, anyway, to expedite things.

Rising from his chair, he glanced at the clock. Midnight. Was James still awake? Not that it mattered. He'd wake him.

He had lists on top of lists he needed to dictate.

And first thing tomorrow, he wanted to find Freddy.

Hopefully, not in Violetta's bed.

CHAPTER 26

ALEC WAS DRESSED and breakfasted before six. If Freddy wasn't at Violetta's, who'd been entertaining him rather exclusively of late, he likely was at Brooks's or home in bed. Since he had no intention of making his proposal to Freddy at Violetta's or at Freddy's wife's garish pseudo-chateau on Park Lane, Alec started with Brooks's. Walking the short distance to the club, he entered the quiet foyer, greeted the porter with a smile, handed his coat to a footman, asked for Freddy, and was sent to the gaming rooms, where a few diehard gamblers in various stages of cast-off evening rig were still at play.

He knew everyone; some looked up and waved, others were too far into their cups to notice. Freddy was one of the latter.

Walking up behind him, the earl looked at Freddy's depleted pile of markers and nodded at Jameson, who was the only one who appeared completely sober and, in consequence, was the only one who appeared to be winning. "How much does he owe you?"

"Enough that his wife's going to want his balls," the viscount said.

"How much?"

"Twenty thousand."

"I'll have my man send over a bank draft. Freddy's out. Come, Freddy," Dalgliesh said, plucking the cards from his hand and bodily lifting the marquis from his chair. "I have something you might like to hear."

Freddy's heavy-lidded gaze lifted, and a drunken grin displayed a set of perfect white teeth to go with the perfect face and perfect body that had brought him a rich wife and an unhappy marriage. "Alec, you old dog! Gettin' a divorsh, I hear." He hiccuped, took a moment to regain his train of thought, and muttered, "Wish like hell I could."

Alec smiled. "Is that so?"

Having manhandled the tipsy marquis from the gaming rooms, Alec made for a quiet corner in the reading room, which was empty that time of day, and dropped Freddy into a chair. He ordered him coffee and breakfast, woke up Freddy when it arrived, put a cup of coffee in his hand, and pointed at the plate of eggs and kippers on the table.

"Drink your coffee, then eat something," Alec said. "I want you to hear what I have to say."

"Can hear jes fine."

Dalgliesh made a drinking motion with his hand. "Do it. I just paid your tick with Jameson. You owe me."

"Jeez, for that, I'll drink the whole bloody pot."

"Good, I'll wait while you do that."

Alec sat back in his chair and patiently watched Freddy Chambers, Marquis of Mytton, indeed drink the entire pot of coffee. "Now eat something."

Freddy scowled at him.

"The toast at least. I have a business proposition for you, and I want you semisober so you understand."

"Ain't much for business, Alec." Freddy plucked a nicely buttered, as ordered, toast triangle from his plate and shoved it whole into his mouth. "You know that." The words were slightly muffled through his chewing, then he swallowed.

"The man you should talk to is my father-in-law. Vulgar turd, but he knows how to make money."

Gratified that Freddy was no longer slurring his words and his gaze seemed relatively focused, Alec finally said what he'd come here to say. "If someone were to give you thirty thousand a year to get you out of your marriage, would you?"

Freddy's head came up with a snap. "I'd do it for ten."

"You wouldn't say that if you were sober."

"Damn right, I would. Who's paying?"

"Me."

"Why?"

"I'll tell you."

Afterward, Alec said with a fixity of purpose, "I had to know you'd agree before I went to your father-in-law."

"Christ, he hates me. He'll go cheap."

He didn't as it turned out. A steel magnate who'd risen from the blast furnaces to own the largest steel mill in England knew how to negotiate.

But the rough, burly, red-faced man who lived with his only daughter and despised son-in-law in the house he'd built for them on Park Lane, eventually leaned across his desk, put out his hand that still showed the scars from his early days in the foundry, met the earl's gaze with a calculating one of his own, and said, "You have a deal." Then he dropped back into his chair and smiled thinly. "I don't suppose you want to tell me why you're doing this."

"A private matter."

A droop of his eyelids. "Was this Fitzwilliam's idea?"

"You're well-informed."

"I like to be. I expect you are, too."

"Yes, generally. I know about your daughter's affaire, for instance."

"I'm surprised you paid so much then."

"Let's just say I'm not in the mood to haggle."

"You can afford to be."

"You don't need the money either."

"Maybe I worked harder for mine. She's my only child. And her husband didn't treat her well."

There was no point in arguing who'd worked harder for their money; Alec rather thought that six years of scorching heat, bloodshed, and squalor in the mining camps counted for something. But he said only, "I'm sorry. Freddy's rather selfish, I'm afraid."

The bull of a man lifted his chin. "Can you trust him to do what you want?"

"If it's in his interest. This is."

"Do you mind if we use Fitzwilliam, too?"

"I don't mind. You'll have to ask him though. Personally, I'd prefer buying off the entire Court of Chancery, if it were possible. I'm in a hurry."

"There are two *arbiters of justice*," the older man mockingly emphasized, "for sale. Wives with pretensions, poor sods. But good for people like us. Would you like their names?"

"Yes, thank you." Alec waited while two names were scribbled on a piece of paper and slid across the desk.

"Servants everywhere. One never knows."

"If you pay them enough it helps," Alec said, folding the paper and slipping it into his pocket.

"I'm sure you blue bloods know more about that than me," Freddy's soon-to-be ex-father-in-law sardonically noted. He surveyed the young grandee impeccably dressed by his tailor and valet lounging across from him. Then he smiled. "It was a pleasure doing business with you, Dalgliesh. Best of luck in your private matter."

"Thank you." Alec rose from his chair, offered a smile in return. "Although I'm rather of the opinion that luck is much overrated. I prefer money and power to advance my interests."

"Bloody right." Tom Reeves smiled a real smile this time. "If you ever need a financial partner for any of your ventures"—he dipped his head—"my purse is always open to you. You're a ruthless young thug. I like that in a man."

They agreed; ruthlessness was a prerequisite for victory. "I'll keep your offer in mind." Alec nodded toward the door. "And you might tell whomever was listening they'd be advised to forget what they heard."

"Oh, hell, it's probably my daughter. You needn't worry about her. She's probably in the chapel by now giving thanks to all the angels in heaven. Damned religious like her mother. But then someone has to keep us men on the straight and narrow. Your lordship excepted, of course, the high life being what it is," he finished with an indulgent flick of his fingers.

How to answer when faced with the hard truth. Dalgliesh gracefully said, "I appreciate your understanding." He bowed faintly. "Your servant, sir."

On leaving Tom Reeves' study and stepping into the quiet corridor, he discovered that the angels weren't yet being thanked. A fashionably dressed, slender-to-the-point-of-thinness, ordinary young lady who must be Reeves' daughter was waiting for him in the hall. "You heard?"

"Oh yes, and I'm ever so grateful to you, Lord Dalgliesh," Freddy's wife breathlessly exclaimed, her excitement bringing a glow to her wide, cornflower-blue eyes that were really quite pretty. "I didn't know what to say to Papa. Not at the beginning. Nor ever. He put such store in me being a marchioness, you see."

Her plain face was flushed with pleasure, and Alec couldn't help but be charmed by her joy. He knew the feeling. "I'm pleased to be of service, my lady."

"How did you know about Charlie?" she asked, blushing bright red to the roots of her sparrow brown hair. "We were ever so careful."

He smiled. "Apparently not careful enough. Your father knows, too."

"Papa has spies though."

"So do I."

"My goodness! Does everyone?"

"I'm sure not. Sometimes one must, that's all. Although your Charles talks of you more than he should. I expect he can't help it when he's in love," he said with a smile. Charles Fairchild was a nice young man just starting his career as a solicitor; he'd waxed eloquent to his colleagues about his great passion.

"That's all I think of, too—my darling Charlie. I—that is—we—dearly wish to marry. Must we wait long?"

"That I'm only beginning to understand. I'm afraid I know very little about the process."

A small pout crinkled her lips. "But I don't want to wait."

A cherished only child, an heiress with a doting father. "I'm sure your father can help."

"It's not that I dislike Freddy," she quickly said, as though remembering her manners. "He's the most beautiful man in England, no offense to you, my lord."

"None taken," he said, suppressing a smile.

"We just don't suit. We never have. He's too set in his ways, I suspect, to ever be a good husband."

"I'm sure you're right." On the other hand, Violetta and Freddy would suit admirably, *he* suspected. So long as the magnanimity of his financial support continued.

"I shall include you in my prayers, my lord. You've made me so very, very happy." She smiled. "And I know I can speak for Charlie as well. We shall both pray for your soul."

Her simple devotion touched him. And if anyone's soul needed praying for, it was his. "May I offer you and Charles much joy," Alec said. What he didn't say was that Charles was his next appointment. "Good day, my lady." Walking away, he set his sights on his next interview.

He couldn't afford any loose ends; he needed the full cooperation from everyone involved in order for his plan to work.

Excluding Violetta. She wasn't apt to be cooperative.

But he rather thought the prospect of a marchioness's coronet would win the day with Violetta. She was a vain, pretentious little bitch.

Charles Fairchild was clearly alarmed when Dalgliesh explained that he'd just come from Tom Reeves'. The young man blanched and glanced out the windows of his office in Grey's Inn as if he expected to see a man with a horse whip outside.

"There's no cause for alarm, Mr. Fairchild," Alec sooth-ingly said. He always disliked a show of force unless necessary. "Mr. Reeves is aware of your attachment to his daughter and has chosen not to interfere as far as I know. While—ah . . . I'm afraid I don't know your sweetheart's name."

"Caroline," the solicitor said with a rapt sigh.

"Yes. Well . . . while Caroline is quite pleased that I spoke to her father about a matter that concerns us all. She'll be divorcing her husband as soon as may be with the object, I gather, of marrying you. I only wish to be assured that such is your intent as well."

"Oh heavens, yes! It's my greatest desire!"

His face lit up very much like Caroline's had. "Perfect." Alec came to his feet. "That concludes my business with you then, Mr. Fairchild. I wish you both happy."

"I don't understand how this concerns you?"

"It doesn't anymore. I've known Freddy for a very long time. He needs taking care of. Let's just say I've taken on the job."

"He's been a most disgraceful husband," the solicitor spleenishly said.

"I'm afraid he always will be." Alec smiled faintly. "A difficult childhood, you see. Quite sad," he prevaricated, thinking Freddy was probably no worse than any number of men he knew. "I'm sure you'll be an excellent husband to—ah—Caroline." A nod, another polite smile. "Thank you for your time."

He stood outside on the pavement for a moment afterward, shook the tension from his shoulders, and noticed the sun had come out. An omen—if he believed in omens. But certainly it had been a very satisfying day's work.

Although he felt like a bloody watchmaker who'd spent the last hours systematically assembling all the working parts and arranging them to specifications: a spring here, a screw there, a gear wheel meshing with another, a drop of oil to lubricate the mechanism. And now his intricate little scheme was complete and functioning smoothly, thanks to liberal amounts of money, a deal of persuasion, and the occasional velvet-gloved threat.

Costly simplicity—that's what it was.

But all the pieces were finally in place, squared up and precise.

He'd quickly run his plan by Fitzwilliam, then baring some disastrous news from Knowles, he was off for Scotland in the morning. James had had news late last night that the court case was as good as won. Also, Rhodes hadn't moved any of his militia yet, and even if he did, Knowles had been assured by President Kruger that he wouldn't sanction Alec's properties.

Christ, was it possible that he was about to be released from the punishment of his life?

CHAPTER 27

ALEC AND JAMES were back at Munro Park a cold hour
later, the open automobile damned chilly in December—but
fast. James had been briefed on all that had transpired that
day and given numerous tasks to complete prior to Alec's
departure for Scotland in the morning.

Most importantly, a telegram for Zelda announcing his
arrival.

Two men had been left in Inverness to serve as messen-
gers between the telegraph office and the MacKenzie estate.

Soon after his return, Alec entered his mother's sitting
room, where she and Chris and Creiggy were having tea. It
was finally time to give his mother an account of the con-
spiracy of silence under which they'd all lived.

Creiggy must have sensed what was about to transpire
or perhaps servant's gossip had preceded him. But she found
reason before long to take Chris back to the schoolroom.
Alec offered her a grateful smile as she left.

Alec set down his drink, uncrossed his legs, and leaning
forward, rested his forearms on his knees. "I don't know

how much you've heard from the servants, but I wanted you to know I've fallen in love."

"With Miss MacKenzie. Everyone knows," the dowager countess said with a smile. "Congratulations, darling. I'm so pleased."

"I'll be getting a divorce. One that could turn out to be very nasty."

"I understand, dear. It seems to me most divorces are—or at least all the court proceedings one reads in the papers suggest so."

"Mine might be worse." A cool, bloodless statement.

Her pale brows lifted ever so slightly. "And you're worried about me."

He softly exhaled. "Yes. I want you to know all the sordid details before you read them in the papers. But the possible shock to you concerns me."

Her smile was affectionate. "I survived quite a few years with your father before you were old enough to understand what was happening. You'll find I'm relatively strong."

"So Creiggy tells me. She's been urging me to speak to you for some time."

"As you know, Creiggy's always right." His mother reached across the small distance that separated them and touched her son's hand. "Tell me now. I promise not to faint away."

As he talked about his father and Violetta, little Julia, and the illness that had almost taken her life, the dowager countess said, "Oh my," once and, "My goodness," twice and "Is that so?" in a chill voice he'd never heard before. When he finished, he sat back, ran his fingers through his hair, and softly exhaled. "That's everything," he said, his wary gaze trained on his mother's face.

"That's quite a lot, isn't it?" she softly noted, drawing in a deep breath. "And you've taken on all these grave difficulties to spare me distress." She smiled ruefully. "You've been much too good to me while I've selfishly neglected your happiness. You never should have married. Certainly not because of me."

He would have done more to save her life. "It was my

decision alone," he kindly said. "I wanted Chris as much as you. I still do. Marrying Violetta wasn't that much of a hardship."

"Of course it was," his mother quietly said, understanding what it was to suffer under the yoke of a brutal marriage. "I'm filled with guilt."

Alec smiled. "Don't say that in front of Creiggy. She'll see that you do penance in any number of ways."

"And so she should."

His mother's voice was anguished. "Nonsense. You've been the best of mothers. I couldn't have been more fortunate. Remember, you were the one who urged me to go to India, who wrote to the viceroy, saw to it that I had an appointment to his staff. If not for that, I never would have seen South Africa." He grinned. "So I owe you millions, Mother dear. There's no need for regret."

The dowager countess restlessly twisted a ring on her finger, then looked up and met her son's gaze. "I know you're trying to make me feel better. But, tell me, are you truly happy now?"

"I couldn't be happier. The sun shines for me alone."

She breathed more freely. "I'm so glad, darling." Then she frowned slightly. "Does Miss MacKenzie know what you told me?"

"Some of it—not all. I've avoided the worst of it." Just like he'd avoided enlightening his mother on his day's activities.

"Have you spoken to her of a divorce?"

His smile broke. "Yes. She doesn't believe me."

"Darling, what woman would with your reputation?"

"I agree. Which is why I'm going to Scotland in the morning to convince her of my sincerity. James is busy arranging things as we speak."

"I'm so pleased for you." Leaning over, she took his hand and smiled. "I've heard that love is quite wonderful."

"It is, Maman," he softly said, wishing she hadn't had such a comfortless marriage, wishing she'd felt the same joy. She was still beautiful, pale, and fragile; what would her life have been if she'd not been married off by her family for all the wrong reasons? Then knowing how she loved children, he said to cheer her, "Zelda and I hope to start a family soon. In fact—"

"You'd better see to a swift divorce," she advised with a sparkle in her eyes, releasing his hand and sitting back. "You know how the servants talk. Your avid interest in Miss Mac-Kenzie kept the kitchen all achatter. I believe there's various bets concerning any number of events apropos you and Miss MacKenzie that are keeping the servants entertained."

Alec groaned.

"We all wish you great joy, darling. The staff would walk over fire for you. As for the scandal of the divorce, I know I can speak for everyone—let the papers print what they like."

"You can be sure they will, if they have the chance," Alec muttered. "On the other hand, my counsel, Fitzwilliam, is being paid to keep me out of court. One can but hope."

"It doesn't matter in the end, darling. Nothing matters so long as you're happy. I'm completely indifferent to scandal." She smiled again. "That shouldn't be a surprise."

He laughed. "What was I thinking?"

Her eyes were luminous with delight. "What indeed? And now we must see that little Julia comes to visit, if you don't think John and Lily would mind?"

"They wouldn't in the least. Julia and I are good friends."

"Life takes strange turns, does it not?" the dowager countess said in a musing tone. "But I think we've found a generous foothold on happiness now or contentment or—"

"Love. For me, it's love."

And his newfound love marked him in many ways.

Cheered him like a perennial explosion of spring.

Gave him physical joy that stole his wits and reason and heart and emptied him of despair. He was grateful to his marrow.

CHAPTER 28

EARLY THE NEXT morning, at Munro Park's private rail station, the door on Dalgliesh's stable car had just clanged shut. The skittish horses had nearly escaped and their sweating grooms breathed a sigh of relief now that the earl's pricey bloodstock were finally in their stalls aboard the train.

The conductor was standing on the platform, his watch in hand, generously paid not to notice they were behind schedule thanks to the earl's high-strung thoroughbreds. Dalgliesh, having eventually stepped in to calm his hunters, was now mounting the stairs to his railcar, and the conductor allowed himself his own sigh of relief. Keeping the London and Northwestern Railway waiting for over forty minutes was, of course, the prerogative of extremely wealthy aristocrats like Dalgliesh, but Mathieson also had to accommodate his superiors. Fortunately, the earl's man had handed over enough large bills to placate the rail authorities from here to the ends of the earth. Still, it was with pleasure that he heard the door to the earl's private car shut with a thud. Mathieson nodded to the engineer, who'd had his head hanging out the engine window for the last half hour.

When the red-faced footman in livery came racing down the platform, screaming the earl's name, Mathieson briefly considered putting his boot out, tripping the man, jumping onto the train, and waving the engineer on.

Alas, the plutocracy still ruled the world despite Labor's inroads in the last two elections. With another sigh, Mathieson signaled the engineer to wait.

The footman wasn't in the earl's private car for more than five seconds when Dalgliesh could be seen leaping to the platform and dashing toward his chauffeured car still idling near the station.

James quickly followed his employer, explained to the conductor that the horses had to be unloaded, the private cars detached and shunted onto the siding. He apologized for the inconvenience—giving no reason—then dispensed more large bills.

Five minutes later, Alec strode into the entrance hall at the Dower House and into a highly charged atmosphere. Two uniformed constables were planted squarely in the middle of the hall, stubbornly unmoving even while Fulton, surrounded by numerous staff was as stubbornly refusing them entrance.

"We're here on the court's business and we ain't movin' until we sees the Earl of Dalgliesh."

"I'm Dalgliesh." Alec handed his coat to a servant.

The two policemen spun around at his words, both red-faced and pugnacious.

Alec stared at them coolly. "State your business."

"We're here to deliver a writ for custody of one Christopher Clarke."

"Get out."

"We're here on official business!" One of the constables waved a folded paper he held in his hand. "This here writ says the boy comes with us!"

"Get out or I'll throw you out." Dalgliesh was beside himself with rage. "Now."

"See here, you can't refuse a court order!" the older of the constables sputtered. "I don't care who you are!"

"I know who I am and I'm refusing your writ, and if you don't leave this instant, I'll see that neither of you will continue in your present profession for another day. Is that clear? IS THAT CLEAR?" Alec's voice rattled the chandelier overhead. With a glance at Fulton, he grabbed one of the constables and frog-marched him to the door, the second following behind in Fulton's harsh grip.

Two footmen swept the double doors open and, seconds later, Her Queen's constables were picking themselves up off the drive.

"Lock the fucking door."

A footman sprang to obey Alec's snarl.

"Have my car brought around to the back," Alec ordered to no one in particular in the mass of retainers, then taking Fulton's arm, he led him away.

Ten minutes later, after two cryptic phone calls to avoid the prying ears of the telephone operators—the first to Fitzwilliam, the second to Tom Reeves—Alec turned to Fulton. "Neither said anything to anyone. There's always Freddy, of course, but I don't think he's that stupid. He knows if he alludes to my fostering his marriage proposal to Violetta, he won't get a penny."

"So the bitch did it on her own," Fulton muttered.

"So the bitch did," Alec said, each word reeking with contempt. He glanced at the clock. Eight. Since it wasn't yet noon, Violetta would still be in bed. "Come with me," he said to Fulton. "Armed."

Less than an hour later, Alec and Fulton arrived at Munro House. They swept past the few servants who were up in an establishment unfamiliar with early morning hours, took the stairs at a run, and came to a stop outside Violetta's apartment.

"Guard the door," Alec said. "Shoot anyone who tries to get in."

"Anywhere special you want me to shoot them? Just checking," Fulton said with a faint smile, having stood side by side with Alec in more than one ticklish situation in South Africa.

"Somewhere that doesn't trigger a murder indictment. She's not worth it."

"Keep that in mind yourself," Fulton cautioned. "Tempting as it may be."

Alec nodded, although he was thinking the temptation might be too great after what she'd just tried to do. Chris was terrified of her; Fulton said Creiggy had spirited the boy away the moment word of the constables had reached her.

"Take a breath or two, boss."

Alec's gaze swung to Fulton, and after a pause, he grinned, breathed deeply, and said, "Better?"

"Not really. Just don't shoot her."

In his current mood, another evasive nod was the best he could do. Then, he pressed down on the ornate levered handle, pushed open the door, and entered Violetta's silent sitting room. Crossing the plush carpet, he passed into the bedroom, strode to the windows, threw open the drapes, and moving to the foot of the bed, waited, flint eyed and unsmiling as the occupants bestirred themselves.

When Violetta's drowsy gaze fell on him, she frowned, pushed herself up on the pillows, and indifferent to her nudity, theatrically lifted her brows. "It's damned early, Alec."

Ignoring her nakedness as well as her remark, Alec said in a low, suppressed growl, "What the fuck did you think you were doing?"

"I told her not to do it. I told her you'd come," Freddy quickly interposed. He was aware of Alec's grim reputation for violence after all the stories about his battles with his father and those in South Africa over mining claims that were bloodshed first and bargaining later. Brushing his fair hair from his eyes, sitting up, Freddy held Alec's gaze for a telling moment, offering up his innocence. "She wouldn't listen."

"A shame." Then Alec turned to his wife and regarded her for an unhurried moment. "You've caused me a great deal of trouble, Violetta," he finally said, "but this time you've gone too far." He kept his breathing even and his

voice, although his eyes held a weariness of spirit that always
overcame him at the sight of her. "The boy's only six and
frightened to death of you. You're his mother. You should
care even just a little. But you don't, do you?" he said in an
almost inaudible tone. He looked bleak for a moment, like
a man who'd seen too much cruelty. "So then," he brusquely
said, as if having made the decision he'd been avoiding for
four long years, he could now shed any semblance of equanimity, "If you want war, Violetta, you'll have war. To the
last one standing, to the bitter, bloody end. You might want
Freddy to leave," he went on in that same curt tone. "You
might not want him to hear what I have to say. It might ruin
your fucking image."

"I doubt it's my image that interests him," Violetta coolly
replied.

Alec dipped his head to the right. "Your call, Freddy.
What I'm about to say might keep you up at night."

"Really, darling," the marquis noted. "This little marital
spat is between you and Alec." Sliding from the bed, he
picked up his trousers from the floor. "If you'll excuse me."

"What if I need a knight in shining armor?" Violetta
sportively queried.

Freddy glanced up, one leg thrust in his trousers. "You'd
have to look elsewhere, darling. I've no more chivalry than you."

"That must be why we get along," she purred. "Order
some breakfast for us, will you, dear? I'm sure I'll be hungry
after this little skirmish with Alec."

"Such confidence." Alec was watching Freddy move to
the door, buttoning his trousers as he went. "One has to
admire your brazen belief in yourself. But this isn't some
trivial row, Violetta, where you lie to me until I leave." The
door closed on Freddy, and Alec turned back to Violetta,
menace in his gaze, in the set of his shoulders and the hard
line of his jaw. "Now, listen to me," he said, his voice cold
as ash. "You will not frighten Chris again. You will not
repeat your stupidity over custody. You will *not* oppose me
in this divorce. You will, if it pleases you, continue enjoying
my financial assistance so long as you behave. If you chose

to be foolish, let me point out to you that I'm much too powerful to offend.

"I'll see that no drawing room in London, or indeed anywhere in the civilized world, will receive you. I'll broadcast your story to the farthest reaches of the planet: about Father and Julia; about poisoning Mother; about the man you sent to murder Zelda—I happen to have a signed confession from him. Did I mention Joe Clarke's death? Ah—that one surprises you. You didn't cover your tracks well enough, or rather, I had good detectives and unlimited funds. Now, I know you and Freddy get along famously. You're both selfish to the bone. But consider—if you were reduced to Freddy's company alone—" He shrugged, a quick dismissive lift of his shoulder. "Even you can't fuck all the time."

Her expression hadn't changed from a kind of bland interest in what he was saying. "What do I get if I agree?"

"*Jesus Christ.*" An explosive breath, acid with disgust. "Was this custody writ just another extortion demand?"

"Is."

Her smile was like the one he'd seen on his wedding night when his father had delivered his news; Violetta had been there to revel in her triumph. He felt the same anger and revulsion. "Don't, Violetta," he softly said. "Just don't. I'm tired of this. I should just kill you and be done with it. It would be more economical."

"Pshaw. As if you would. And may I say, I always enjoy watching you in your role as guardian to the weak and suffering on earth. So dutiful and sweet. You certainly didn't learn that from your father."

"The only thing I learned from my father was to strike first. A lesson I've resisted in your case for the sake of others. But you're no longer safe. I told Mother everything. Your leverage is gone. So whether you live or die doesn't matter anymore. No, let me correct myself. I'd prefer you dead," he said flatly.

Even she recognized that tone. Her chameleon face suddenly showed fear. "You're just as brutal as your father," she spat, wanting to draw blood, wanting to wound and hurt.

Alec drew a short breath. "No," he said. Although it had always been his greatest fear. But no, he wasn't that kind of man. He hesitated for a moment, then his face set, he spoke in a voice that didn't travel beyond the bed. "Let me repeat myself. I'm finished with you and your games. I expect your custody suit to be withdrawn. I expect you to comply with the terms of the divorce. I expect to be free of you with all due speed. No obstructions or delays, not so much as a second wasted when your signature is required on some document. Do you understand?" When he received no answer, he thought of all the evil credited to her, of the need to bring it to an end. "Just do it," he said. "I have no more patience."

"I'll be a marchioness, you know," she defiantly proclaimed, looking him in the eye, her chin raised, her smile vaunting.

"Is that so? Freddy, I presume?" They were both capable of performances.

"He's come into an inheritance," she boasted. "A very good one. He's divorcing his wife for me."

"How nice. Congratulations." If satisfaction could be weighed, his would break every scale in the world. "You came out on top again." One could be generous in victory. Then he walked away from the woman who'd ruined so many lives and shut the door on her. Stepping into the sitting room, he nodded at Freddy, who was lounging on Violetta's settee. "I won't be back," he said, moving toward the hallway door.

"It's over then?"

"She saw the error of her ways."

"You *are* persuasive," Freddy said with a grin.

"You're sure you're all right with this now?"

"I know about Joe."

That brought Dalgliesh to a stop. "And even then?"

"You wouldn't understand. You have scruples. Some of us don't. But I thank you for giving me my freedom," the marquis quietly said.

Alec lowered his voice as well. "Come to me if you need

anything. You're not obliged to risk your life by staying with Violetta. We can make other arrangements for your expenses."

"Jesus, Alec, do you fucking walk on water?"

"The mood I'm in right now, I might. Thanks to you."

"So you're in my debt," Freddy said with a grin.

"Don't push your luck," Alec replied with a lift of his brows.

"I *did* take her off your hands."

"And you're not at Park Lane anymore, not that you often were."

"Often enough. Too often." Freddy raised his hands. "I surrender to your logic. We're even."

"I'm poorer."

"But happier."

"You're right. We're even." Alec lifted his hand in a brief wave and a moment later he walked out into the hall.

Fulton pushed away from the wall and kept pace with Alec through the corridors of Munro House, down the stairs, and out the door.

He didn't speak until they were outside. "Should I hire another train?"

Alec shook his head. "I'd prefer the morning express. It's faster. We'll go tomorrow. I think I'll take Chris with me. Just to be safe. We boys can go north hunting," he pleasantly said.

"Among other things."

"Among other things," Alec murmured, a smile forming on his lips. "Oh, Christ, I forgot to send a telegram explaining my delay."

CHAPTER 29

AFTER THEIR RETURN to Munro Park *and* after Alec's mother and Creiggy had been reassured in terms of Chris's custody, Alec excused himself and immediately went to his office to have a telegram sent to Zelda.

So sorry. Family emergency. Will arrive on express train tomorrow.

His messenger delivered the telegram to the MacKenzie porter two hours later. But unfortunately, it arrived too late. Zelda, along with her grooms, had ridden into Inverness very early that morning. Too excited the night before to sleep, she'd risen at dawn and left.

He was coming; he'd said he would and he was! Glory, hallelujah, and smiles for the universe. She was in love—wildly, blissfully in love!

Her best friend Janet Grant was having breakfast in bed when Zelda swept into the room, bursting with patent good cheer and blithe spirits.

Janet smiled back. "Something very good must have happened. What ungodly hour did you leave home?"

"Half past five. I couldn't sleep. He's coming today, really and truly! Can you believe it?" she breathlessly intoned, not expecting an answer. "My, that looks good." Having reached the bed, Zelda contemplated her friend's breakfast tray and helped herself to a plump little pastry. "I forgot to eat."

"I'm hungry." The pretty brunette put her hands over her tray. "Ring for my maid and get your own."

Zelda was already striding toward the bellpull. The women had been friends from childhood.

"I don't suppose I need ask who *he* is?"

"I don't suppose you do, unless you weren't listening last time I was here." Zelda jerked on the embroidered pull and turned around. "We've been apart five whole days." Her smile was one of blinding happiness. "Did I mention he misses me dreadfully?"

"How lovely. For you, for him, for everyone." Bubbling over with breathless wonder, Zelda had already shared news of her new love the day after her return from Munro Park. Janet had never seen Zelda giddy as a schoolgirl—even when a schoolgirl. And they'd always shared the intimate details of their lives. She'd taken great pains that day, however, not to let fall the fact that Dalgliesh's reputation for debauch was well-known in Inverness. He had a hunting lodge in the Highlands, and his hunting hadn't been confined to four-legged prey.

But Zelda was so ecstatic over Dalgliesh's visit that Janet served as benevolent listener all that day while Zelda talked and talked, over breakfast, then lunch, while they played with the children in the nursery later that afternoon. Janet marveled at the incredible change love had wrought in her friend. She was no longer the dégagé woman who turned down suitors with bland politesse. No longer a woman who found her raison d'être in exploring strange, exotic locales around the world. Nor a woman who embraced casual passion but never love. And if the delight of her heart had been anyone but Dalgliesh, Janet would have unreservedly rejoiced at the news. But Dalgliesh was married. He also bedded women with careless charm and total lack of involvement. And he was married.

Janet offered only one friendly warning before Zelda left—suitably couched she hoped in casualness: Enjoy the delicious earl, but don't forget men will be men.

Zelda frowned. "Is Johnny giving you trouble?" In her joyous mood, she was immune to the personal nature of the warning.

"No, no, not that kind of trouble. It's only that he's forever out hunting with his friends." She had to say something.

Zelda knew Johnny Grant; he enjoyed the company of men like so many of his class. Whether hunting, golfing, fishing, or drinking. "You should go with him sometime."

Playing her part, Janet wrinkled her nose. "I prefer the comforts of home."

"As I recall, you also prefer your husband's talents in bed. In fact, I believe you married him for those."

"You're right," Janet said with a grin. "I've no complaints there. He gives me every attention I crave."

"He's faithful?"

"There's no question he is."

"Then you're a silly goose to want every minute of his time."

The topic of faithfulness was too fraught with danger apropos the Earl of Dalgliesh. Janet changed the subject. "You must bring your darling Alec to visit when he's here," she said, sincerely wishing all the best for her friend despite the daunting odds.

"I don't know how long Alec can stay, but if there's time, we'll come. And thank you for listening to me rave on like some lovesick lunatic. You're a dear. And look, the train will be into the station soon. I really must go."

Her heart racing, Zelda took her leave. Soon, soon, she'd have Alec back!

And she had some special news for him.

Very special news.

Too special to even share with her best friend.

Twenty minutes later, with the winter wind whipping their coattails and nipping at their cheeks, she stood beside her groom, Sandy, and watched the train empty without any sign of Alec. Going to the station master, Zelda made enquiries. But he knew nothing about a private railcar or the Earl of Dalgliesh.

She shouldn't have been so quick tempered. Really, it was one of her worst shortcomings—her temper. There must be some reasonable explanation. There better be, damn him!

The head groom had known the laird's eldest daughter from the cradle. One look at her face as she spun away from the window in the station and he was glad Preston was with the horses. The boy wouldn't have known what to do. He, in turn, moved out of reach.

Zelda noticed him moving back two steps and scowled. "Good God, Sandy," she muttered. "Have I ever hit you?"

"No, miss." But he could see her gloved fingers flexing on her quirt stock, and he'd seen her lash out at her brothers often enough to take heed. Not that she hadn't had good reason; the boys had been a wild bunch—still were.

"Damn him to hell!" At her outburst, a few straggling passengers turned to stare but didn't long withstand her chill regard. They quickly looked away, although the men by and large considered the red-haired, tantrumish beauty swathed in velvety black astrakhan damned tempting even with the quirt in her hand. "I should have *known*!" Zelda raged. "What was I *thinking*? That he was going to *change*?" A low seething litany of expletives followed, hissing through the frosty air. After which, she said, bitterly, "There's nothing for it but to go back home."

"Now?"

"Of course now," she snapped, as if the road home wasn't a treacherous track with the winter rains. As if the sun hadn't set an hour ago. As if heavy clouds didn't obscure the moon.

Sandy wasn't concerned for himself, but Sir Gavin would have his hide if anything happened to his bonny daughter. "Are you sure, miss?"

Her frown deepened. "Don't I look sure?"

She looked like she was ready to hit someone. "Yes, miss." But he hoped like hell the horses didn't lose their footing on the quagmire of a trail.

"I have to send a telegram before we go. I'll meet you at the horses."

A clipped, curt, woman-scorned tone of voice to which Sandy knew better than to reply. The servants were au courant with everyone's business, including who was going to get Miss Zelda's scorching telegram.

To whit—a short time later, James walked into Alec's office, interrupting his conversation with Fulton.

Alec looked up, took note of his secretary's face and the telegram he held. "What? Another catastrophe?"

"That's for you to say, sir," James guardedly replied.

Alec took the offered missive and swiftly scanned it.

Long ride for nothing. I'm sure you have a perfect excuse. Don't bother. I hate excuses.

Alec groaned.

"I'm sorry, sir," James said. "Would you like to reply?"

"I'd better. The telegram to Miss MacKenzie went out this morning, right?"

"Shortly after eleven, sir."

"It reached her home?"

"At two, sir." The men had telegraphed on their return to Inverness. On Dalgliesh's particular orders.

"What the hell went wrong?"

"Do you want the men to ride up tonight and find out?"

Alec eyed his secretary. "Do I detect a note of discouragement in your voice?"

"Yes, sir. Jed said the road was almost nonexistent at the end. And in the dark?" The import was clear.

Alec sighed. "Very well. No sense in risking life and limb. I'll make my apologies to Miss MacKenzie when I see her tomorrow."

After James walked out, Fulton offered his employer a broad grin across Alec's desk. "An apology. Now, there's a first for you. I wish I could be there to see it."

"Very amusing. Perhaps you could come along and I'll send you in first to take the initial artillery rounds."

"If only my full attention wasn't required here to see that

your mines aren't blown away by Rhodes' inept militia, should it come to that," Fulton drawled.

Another groan as Alec slid into a disgruntled sprawl. "Jesus, being in love requires some major adjustments."

"You mean you can't just walk away and forget their names?"

"Yes, that's exactly what I mean," the earl said with fastidious malcontent.

A small pause developed. Lengthened.

"On the other hand," Alec grudgingly noted, finally breaking the silence, "the advantages far outweigh the disadvantages." He shoved himself upright in his chair and smiled faintly. "I actually like her name and, more to the point, her. And that's a much more consequential first, my dear Fulton."

"Well then, boss, it seems some bowing and scraping are in order tomorrow."

"Christ, I suppose so." Alec grinned. "How exactly does one do that?"

CHAPTER 30

As it turned out, he had to learn on the fly, for the moment he was announced the following evening and entered Sir Gavin's sitting room, four pairs of male eyes and one female's looked up and glowered at him as if he were the devil incarnate.

Or perhaps it was because of his mud-caked boots and breeches. Not that a coating of mud wasn't a small price to pay for surviving the perilous roads. But whatever the reason for the manifest displeasure, he decided, advancing into the room, it was up to him to dispel it. He smiled his very best smile that had been known to assuage the mistrust of obstinate men, jealous women, and pious martinets—the sadly dull Queen included.

"Allow me to apologize most profoundly for all the trouble I caused yesterday. I have a very good explanation, although, under the circumstances," he added as the frowns remained in place and no one moved in their chairs, "I understand an apology is hardly enough to redeem myself."

"Damn right, it isna enough. She dinna get home until near ten, I'll have ye know," Sir Gavin growled, the drink in his hand sloshing over the rim in his indignation. "It was a bloody dangerous ride."

He didn't need that fact pointed out to him with the state of his clothes, and his horses still nervously curvetting in the yard. "I'm so very sorry. I'm afraid my telegram must have reached you too late. But the emergency I referred to in my telegram had to do with my son, Chris. May I sit down—ah, well, let me explain it to you." *Standing here.* "Just as the train was leaving the station yesterday morning, I received news that two constables were at my door serving custody papers. My—er—soon-to-be ex-wife had sued me for custody of Christopher."

He heard Zelda's sharp intake of breath, felt his suit might be in the way of prospering, and quickly went on. "Naturally, I immediately returned to the house and sent the constables on their way. Without the boy," he added, his nostrils flaring at the memory. After a nearly imperceptible pause, he said in the temperate tone he was exercising before the—newly adjusted—four and a half accusatory stares, "At that point, it was imperative that I go to London." He wasn't going to mention Violetta again. "It took some time to resolve the issue, but in the end, the custody suit was dropped, my son was safe, and I was able to return to Munro Park. But by then, it was too late to resume my travel plans." He finally looked directly at Zelda, who sat in a chair beside her father, looking more pale than he remembered. "I'm so very sorry." He spoke as if only she were in the room, his brows slightly drawn. "If there's any way I can make amends for the distress I caused you, please tell me. That you risked those trails at night alarms me no end. It was my fault entirely," he said to a woman for the first time in his life. "*Everything* was my fault," he added very, very softly, not sure he hadn't lost her forever, thinking too that this must be how it felt standing before a firing squad. But then he went on because he'd learned long ago that it was necessary to take risks. "If I might, I'd like to fetch Chris. He's waiting in the entrance hall. And a six-year-old's not very good at waiting."

Zelda instantly came to her feet and swiftly advanced toward him. "Poor child out there all alone. And after that long ride. Why didn't you say Chris was with you?"

"I wanted to explain first. I didn't want him to hear about the constables having come to take him away. Creiggy had whisked him upstairs as soon as everyone realized what was happening." As Zelda reached him, he debated taking her hand but chose prudence. "Come, say hello to Chris. He's been looking forward to seeing you."

He kept pace with her as they walked from the room, her family following close behind. "I didn't dare leave Chris behind after what Violetta did," he explained, as they traversed the carpeted hallway. "I told him we're going hunting. I hope you don't mind."

She gave him a jaundiced look. "There's things enough I mind, but that's not one of them. You can imagine what I thought when you didn't come."

He had no intention of pursuing that topic. "Whatever it was, you were wrong." He risked a small smile, took note of her response, then took a further risk and grinned. "If you knew what I did to get here, you'd fall on your knees and thank me."

"Is that a fact?"

But she was smiling now and her color had returned. "You might think about it later," he murmured, taking a chance and winking. "The falling on your knees part."

She met his eye and sniffed like women do when they don't mean it. "Libertine."

"Nevertheless, I guarantee you'll like it."

"I have something you might like as well. Some news." She hadn't been going to tell him right away or perhaps at all. She thought she'd first see if he deserved to know. And he'd looked unslept but now she knew why.

At the unmistakable delight in her voice at the word *news*, he grabbed her wrist and dragged her to a stop. "What news?"

"Lord, Alec, I can't tell you now." She shot a look behind her and hissed, *"Move!"*

He moved. But he also slid his fingers downward, took her hand firmly in his, and felt a kind of exaltation reserved for heavenly ascensions and Derby wins. He leaned in close and whispered, "Are you sure?"

"Please, Alec, not now." Another worried glance over her shoulder.

"When then?" It was true. Your heart could skip a beat.

"After dinner. Don't do that," she nervously said as he pulled her close. "Let me go. They might shoot you."

"Then I'd have to shoot back." At her shocked look, he allowed a small distance between them, although he didn't release her hand. "I was only teasing, darling. I'm not armed." He was, of course. He knew the Highland code of honor, and she had four brothers and a father, not to mention the usual Highland home, in which weapons were the decor of choice, the walls awash with swords and targes and firearms. "Chris will go to bed early. Come with me when I tuck him in."

"If they let you stay."

His brows lifted. "Seriously? Am I on probation?"

"Oh, yes. Definitely. You must have seen the militant glares."

"I was mostly concerned with yours."

"You're forgiven. How could I not after your explanation?"

"But it wasn't good enough for your family?" He seemed surprised.

"You're married." She lifted her brows in pointed intent. "I believe that's considered a deterrent to courtship."

"If that's all they're concerned about," he crisply said, "I can address those misgivings. I won't be married for long. For any number of reasons, none of which need concern you, I have Violetta in an agreeable frame of mind. Don't look at me like that. I offered her enough money, that's all. And she's getting married to the Marquis of Mytton, so she'll be advancing in the peerage. A definite plus for Violetta."

"Mytton! He's already married."

"More business for Fitzwilliam. I promised our counselor a peerage, too, if he wants it."

A teasing light shimmered in her eyes. "You've been busy."

"Just a little," he said in vast understatement. "All for you, my darling. Now here comes Chris." Alec bent and held out his hands.

A moment later the fair-haired child charging them, head down, was swung up into Alec's arms, and after a quiet admonition from his father, quickly said, "Thank you for inviting us for a visit, Miss MacKenzie," after which he immediately launched into a high-pitched enthusiastic account of their trip, the gun his father was going to give him for hunting, and the horse he'd been riding instead of a pony.

While Chris rattled on, his voice swooping higher and higher, Zelda gave him her full attention, and Alec contentedly gazed at the woman he loved, inhaled her sweet, heady scent, felt the warmth of her body against his, and didn't care whether he was on probation or not.

He'd managed more difficult situations than this.

No one had threatened to kill him—or at least not yet, he drolly thought, glancing at the four men a short distance away measuring him for his coffin.

Dinner was awkward, although he'd sat through worse. One didn't occasionally make the effort during the Season without having attended a dinner party in which liquor alone served to preserve one from gross incivility.

And he was in good company tonight; the Scots liked their whiskey.

Fortunately, on Zelda's suggestion, Chris had been included in the guest list. Unaware of the charged atmosphere with the reassuring ordinariness of his father's expression and conversation, the young boy kept up a continuous chatter. To which Zelda mostly responded, although Alec easily replied as well when required. He also caught Zelda's admonishing glances from time to time when he held his glass up to be refilled. But a good many drinks aside, he was disturbingly sober.

While the MacKenzie males were clearly unhappy.

He practically leaped from his chair when Zelda said after dessert, "It's getting late, Chris. Your father and I will take you up to the nursery."

"Don't be long," Sir Gavin growled.

Zelda looked up as she took Chris's hand. "For heaven's sake, Da. You'd think I was ten."

"We won't be long, sir," Alec politely replied. Having been seated across from Zelda, he walked around the end of the table and took Chris's other hand. "It's been a long day for a youngster. I expect Chris will go directly to sleep."

"But I'm not tired, Papa!" A common childish protest at bedtime.

"Then you may stay up once you're in bed. I brought some of your books along. If you'll excuse us, gentlemen," Dalgliesh said with a faint dip of his head, and as the trio exited the dining room, Alec spoke quietly for Zelda's ears alone. "They haven't shot me yet."

"You shouldn't have drunk so much. I was beginning to panic."

"No need. I'm sober. Raw nerves."

She cast him a playful look over Chris's head. "You?"

He grinned. "I know. The world must be coming to an end." He blew her a kiss. "We'll have to build a new one for ourselves."

"I'd like that."

"We'll go wherever you want. We'll engineer our own Arcadia. You decide where."

"Are we going somewhere?" Chris interjected, having heard the last comment addressed to Zelda in a normal tone of voice.

"We're thinking about it," Alec said. "Miss MacKenzie's going to decide where."

"May I help decide? May I, may I? Creiggy says I know my atlas better than you did at six."

"You'll have to ask Miss MacKenzie. She's in charge."

Chris's astonishment was unmistakable. His father had always been the ultimate arbiter in every decision; even

Creiggy deferred to him in the end. "Since when?" he guard-edly said, his gaze shifting from one adult to the other.

"Since a month ago." Alec's smile was as bland as his voice, but then epiphanies needn't be all rattle and thunder.

"Really," Zelda said on a small indrawn breath.

"Did I forget to mention that?" His voice was soft as silk.

"Are you going to get all lovey-dovey like Henry and Baptiste's sister? They're forever doing *this*." The little boy pursed his lips in a parody of kissing. "Creiggy says they better get married soon or she'll know the reason why. Are you and Miss MacKenzie getting married, Papa? I hope so."

"We thought we would."

"When, *when*?"

Alec caught Zelda's eye and grinned. "It depends on a few things."

"*What* things?"

"Grown-up things."

"You're not going to tell me," Chris said with a boyish pout.

"You'll be at the wedding, so you'll know when."

"Oh, good. Are we going hunting tomorrow? You prom-ised." A six-year-old's attention span was limited, especially a six-year-old who'd been generously indulged in his whims.

"Yes," Zelda said, understanding the required answer. "You'll have to dress warm."

"Creiggy packed me all warm stuff, didn't she, Papa? She's from here, you know. She knows what to pack."

A half hour later, a six-year-old who insisted he wasn't tired was fast asleep, the long journey north having taken its toll. Leaving Chris with a young maidservant who promised to call them if he woke during the night, Zelda took Alec down a flight to her bedroom. "We can't stay long," she said as Dalgliesh shut the door behind him. She was standing in the middle of the room, smiling at him. "Ask me now."

"When did you know?" He slowly measured her with his gaze, his expression speculative. He pursed his lips. "Are you sure?"

Her eyes were bright in the candlelight, aglow with pleasure. "I knew two weeks ago. I thought you might notice. And I'm sure."

"I should have noticed. I'm sorry."

"You were working day and night. You're forgiven."

He hadn't moved from the door. "Things can go wrong."

"Nothing's going to go wrong." He didn't speak for so long she thought he might be averse to the news. "Would you rather I wasn't having this child?" she asked, not sure she wouldn't shatter in a thousand pieces if he said yes.

"God no. Don't even think it." He moved then, crossing the small distance between them in three long strides, taking her in his arms, holding her close. "I'm pleased beyond words."

She lifted her face and met his gaze. "You don't seem pleased."

"I am."

His voice was without inflection. He seemed uncharacteristically at a loss. "I'm having this baby whether you like it or not," she said, incontrovertible resolve in her words. "I don't care what—"

He stopped her protest with a gentle finger to her mouth. "I *want* you to have our baby. Don't think for a minute that I don't want this child. I just never thought—or hoped, I suppose . . . that something like this could really happen . . . to me." That he would achieve such happiness, that such delight would be his. He wasn't in the habit of being happy. "Now that it's actually happened"—he sucked in a breath— "you'll have to give me some time to get used to it. And you'll always come first in my life, you and this child," he said, his voice strained, his throat jammed, wanting everything to go right, not sure he could bear it if it didn't.

"And Chris," she kindly said.

It felt as though his heart was in his throat. He quickly swallowed. "And Chris," he answered. "Truly, I'm so very happy about all of this, I can't begin to tell you how I feel."

"You can tell me later," Zelda softly said, gazing up at him, her heart in her eyes. "Don't cry or I'll cry."

"I never cry." He never had in memory. Although he

wasn't so sure right now. A child, his and Zelda's child. What had he done to be so extraordinarily rewarded?

A door closed downstairs.

Zelda drew in a quick breath. "We should go before they come up."

He stepped away. "Let me talk to them." Quarrelsome men he could deal with; it wasn't so impossible as this. "I'll make it clear to your family that I won't be repeating my mistakes. That's what they want to hear. And Fitzwilliam is buying off two magistrates. He promised me the speediest divorce in history."

She laughed. "He'd better hurry."

"I'll make sure he knows the schedule has tightened appreciably." He smiled. "By the way, you're not allowed to ride anymore."

"What?"

"You heard me."

"Don't you dare!"

"I'll show you what I dare later. Very gently. Don't worry," he pleasantly said, a seasoned player at this particular game. "You'll be satisfied. I'm very good at consoling you."

Her face lost its petulance. "You do have an engaging manner."

"Practice," he said with a grin and ran for the door.

He heard her shoe hit the door as he escaped into the hall.

CHAPTER 31

ALEC ENTERED THE dining room under the punishing gaze of the MacKenzie men. The table had been cleared, two port decanters resided on the polished mahogany, and on his entrance, each man set down the glass they were holding.

To free their gun hands?

Not that Alec cared to test the truth of his drollery, with the woman he loved waiting for him upstairs. And, of course, the larger issue of his marriage to Zelda required that he mind his manners. Regardful of those constraints, Alec schooled his expression to a bland courtesy, shut the door behind him, and calmly met the brooding scrutiny of his tribunal. He took note of the absence of servants; the men hadn't wanted witnesses. He'd expected no less. Breaking the cool silence, he said, "I have come to present my case. If after hearing me, you have any questions, I'm prepared to answer them." What he refrained from saying was that he'd have Zelda for his wife whether they liked it or not.

His hands folded before him, his gaze steady, he went on in a cool, dry voice. "First, I want you to know that my divorce is before the courts and my barrister promises me swift action. Second, several weeks ago, I asked Zelda to be my wife, she accepted and made me happier than I'd thought possible." He stopped for a moment, his eyes open and unseeing. Then, because he was here for a reason, he blinked and went on, although more slowly. "Happiness is a new sensation for me. All my life I've carried the imprint of my father's cruelty, so the joy I now feel is unthinkably sweet. For that alone I'd marry your daughter and sister. But I also love her for herself. She's a gift I don't deserve. But she's accepted me, and with all due respect," he said with his heart if not tact, "I mean to keep her."

Aware of the continued, uncompromising silence, in an extraordinary act of submission, he went on to reveal what only a handful of people knew. "My marriage was a forced marriage. Not for the usual reasons or only partly for the usual reasons. Zelda knows the circumstances. I've told her. You may ask her if you wish." He couldn't, in the end talk, of Violetta and his father to these strangers. "I've not been private with the Countess of Dalgliesh since our wedding day four years ago." He took a small breath, the memory of his wedding night still capable of making him want to retch. "The countess has been warned off in the strongest possible terms. She'll not trouble Zelda or myself or anyone in my family. I've taken every precaution to assure Zelda's safety and happiness. As for—"

"That's enough my boy," Sir Gavin gruffly said. He'd known Alec's father; a foul, depraved man with a vast fortune and no soul. Sir Gavin's heart when out to Alec for a childhood such as his. "Come. Sit. Hugh, pour Dalgliesh a bumper of port. A damned fine vintage, if I do say so myself. Move over, Robbie. Make way for your sister's betrothed."

"There's one thing more, sir," Alec said, moving toward the chair pulled out for him, not sure he wished to disturb the precious détente. But the news he had to tell them wasn't inconsequential. Nor would it wait. "It has to do with Zelda, with me as well. Us together," he deliberately added.

"No need, my boy," Sir Gavin bluffly asserted. "Everyone

knows about the bairn. Her maid broadcast the news below stairs the first morning Zelda came back." He gave Alec a mindful look as he sat. "I expect ye'll see that she's married in good time."

"God yes. You can be sure of that."

Sir Gavin chuckled. "Aye, ye'll want your heir all right and tight in the peerage."

Alec shook his head, then studied the port in his glass for a moment before looking up. "I never considered having children until I met Zelda. So an heir's not my first consideration. I have other titles and fortune enough so no child of mine would be without resources. Rather, I'm concerned for Zelda. I don't wish to see her viewed with censure by society, and for that I'll move heaven and earth to ensure a prompt marriage."

"You'd best keep your notions about children to yourself, my boy. Zelda's mad for bairns."

Alec smiled. "Too late, I'm afraid. But she knows I'm more than willing to alter my views. You might say she was instrumental in my transformation."

"She's a right powerful lassie, no doubt o' that," her father proudly said. "Not even daunted by Chinese bandits, damn her spunk."

"Keep it in mind, Dalgliesh." Zelda's oldest brother, Hugh, grinned. "Nor does society's censure matter to my sister. She's not in the least conformable."

"He'll find out soon enough," Robbie cheerfully noted. "Ye can't return the merchandise though, laddie."

With a grin, John raised his glass to Alec. "And stay clear of her when she's got a quirt in her hand."

Sir Gavin chuckled. "Now, boys, dinna scare off the bridegroom." Leaning over, he topped off Alec's glass. "Drink up, laddie. We've a wee bit o' celebrating to do."

Forty minutes later, Zelda appeared in the doorway in a heavily quilted, velvet robe of deep hyacinth, her flamboyant hair tumbled on her shoulders, her feet in sheepskin slippers to ward off the drafts. "I'm keeping him, so you mustn't frighten him away." Her gaze was limpid, her smile of good cheer as she surveyed each of the large, flame-haired men in her family. "No shooting, mind."

"Don't worry," Alec said, raising his glass to her. "We're friends."

Her father's smile was teasing. "Aye, an' he says ye're not to ride anymore."

"Is that so?"

"Naturally, it's open to discussion." Alec knew better than to debate the issue here.

"Well, I'm pleased to hear that," she sweetly said. "Now if you'll kindly set down your glass, Dalgliesh, I have need of you. If you stay much longer, you willna be much good to me."

As Alec pushed his chair back and left the table, a drunken chorus of raucous and overly personal exhortations having to do with willful women and henpecked men followed him. All of which he sensibly ignored. Reaching Zelda a few moments later, he smiled. "Forgive me, darling. I've been busy improving my image with your family."

"And doing it very well, it appears," she murmured, drawing him out into the hall and moving toward the stairway. "Now you may turn your pleasing efforts on me. I've been waiting what seems a very long time."

"I'm sorry. Your father has some excellent port."

"I'm so happy to hear it."

He knew that tone of voice in a woman. "I'll make amends, darling, for my discourtesy. I'm at your command. I'm damned sober. And," he said with a lavish smile, "six days necessitous. By the way, they knew about the baby."

She shot him a look as they ascended the stairs. "No!"

"Yes. Before I told them or as I was making a hash of telling them. Your maid apparently spread the news. Your father had the family bible brought in and pointed out the page where the name of our firstborn will be written."

"Oh, Lord, and I suppose he showed you the hair from our first haircuts and our baby teeth. He's impossibly sentimental when he drinks."

"Actually, I found it very nice." In contrast to his father, who spewed hate at his son. "I enjoyed seeing it all. We must get ourselves a bible." He grinned at her shocked stare. "For the baby names. Did you think I was going to have you reading passages from the bible or make you go to church instead of hunt on Sunday?"

"Make me go to church?" she said, having forgotten the reason for her surprise.

"I can make you do things," he softly said.

"Not that."

"Maybe I could. With the right compensation."

A raised brow, a lush smile. "What kind of compensation might that be?"

"As soon as we get to your bedroom and I lock the door, I'll show you."

"Lock the door?"

"Just to be safe."

"From whom?"

"Mostly your family." His smile was wicked. "Were you worried about something else?"

"No, no, of course not."

"Maybe you should be. I haven't seen you in days."

"You said you'd be gentle."

"I will be. I might just be gentle for a very long time."

"How long exactly?" she said in a soft purr that brought his cock to parade-ground attention.

"As long as you can stand it," he said with unimpeachable confidence. He knew what he was doing, he'd known what he was doing for a decade or more and had the reputation to prove it.

When they reached her bedroom and Alec locked the door, the small metallic click sent an edgy little frisson of excitement racing through her senses. She spun around in a shimmer of purple velvet and a flurry of heliotrope scent. "How do you do it?" She held up her trembling hands. "Make me like this?"

"I'm glad I do," he said, pocketing the key, moving closer, and gently taking her hands in his. "You don't know how glad I am." Raising her hands to his mouth, he brushed her knuckles with his lips, then looked up, his gaze slipping over the curve of her fingers. "You're more precious to me than life." He stared at her for a moment in amazement, frightened, too, not quite sure he deserved this quiet happiness. She reminded him of some fairy-tale beauty in her long velvet robe, her hair tumbled on her shoulders, her eyes like midnight orchids. Then, recovering, his smile appeared and his eyes sparkled. "Now if I'm to please you, what would you like first?"

"Surprise me," she said, teasing like him, because she, too, was frightened. She'd never loved anyone like this. She hadn't known love could make your heart ache and fill you with alarm.

"I'm not sure I have much left in my repertoire you haven't seen or felt or"—he grinned—"screamed to." He cast a swift glance around the turret room of the original castle, his gaze flickering over the tapestry-hung stone walls stout enough to withstand cannon. "Not that sound's a problem here. Come," he said, drawing her to the high, carved bed, unquestionably on familiar ground once again. "Wait for me while I stoke the fires. I wouldn't want you to be cold."

Unlike his homes where he'd had central heating and electricity installed, the castle hadn't yet been similarly equipped. A large green tile stove like those seen in the Baltic countries served as the primary source of warmth, although the large fireplace functioned as well to keep off the chill. And lamplight lent a radiant luster rather than a brilliance to the room.

Resting against the bed pillows, Zelda filled her eyes and heart with the sight of the man who'd swept her up in a wave of unbelievable happiness. His dinner coat stripped away, he squatted in shirtsleeves before the open door of the stove, feeding logs into the fire with his broad, strong hands. His physical presence never failed to bewitch and delight her: the unusual height, the powerful shoulders and limbs, the length and bulk of his body, his dark hair carefully trimmed by Jenkins so it curled on his neck, his profile as it was now, limned by golden firelight, a combination of classic beauty and pagan splendor.

When he finished, he shut the stove door, stood, and turned to her. His memorable eyes, bred to calm by his difficult life, heavy lidded, long lashed, were smiling now for her alone. "We are lucky, you and I," he softly said.

Her heart swelled with love. "From this moment on. Promise me," she said with the alarm she couldn't quite suppress.

"I promise," he said, spare and sure. "For now and always." His happiness came from her.

She lifted her arms as he neared the bed, and sitting beside her, he took her hands and kissed them both. Then he set them at her sides and reached for the top button on her robe. "I've missed you. I didn't know I could miss anyone so much," he said thickly. He took a deep breath and slowly exhaled. "Don't worry, though. I know enough not to frighten you. I'll be gentle."

"I don't think you have to be."

His heart was beating rapidly. He'd not been celibate for so long a time since he'd married. He was tense with restraint. "I think I do."

"Perhaps I can change your mind."

He looked up, was silent for a moment. "We'll see," he politely said. And once her robe was discarded and her nightgown set aside, he sat very quietly, disciplining his wolfish lust. "Are you warm enough?" An automatic politesse, a mannered distraction.

"Yes, yes. Undress," she impatiently said, self-restraint bred out of the MacKenzies centuries ago.

"I will in a minute." The heat in her eyes was familiar, seductive. "Let me look at you and the baby first," he said. "Even if there's nothing yet to see."

Her smile was instant and sublime, her eyes dancing with joy. "Here—feel, here." She took his hand and placed it on her stomach.

An unqualified sense of wonder struck him for a moment, and the world grew in splendor. "Will it have red hair or black?" he said with a smile like he had that morning at Crosstrees.

"I don't care." She looked up sharply. "Does it matter to you?"

"Not in the least." He ran his fingers gently over her stomach. "Whatever you give me will be perfect."

"You're sure? Some men want sons who look like them. Some men don't want daughters at all."

"I'm not some men. You can do no wrong, darling, when it comes to this child. Or to anything," he quickly added with a grin. "There, did I catch myself in time?"

"Only just," she said with the dazzling smile that warmed his entire world.

"Then I must be sure to practice more."

"I have something you can practice. As soon as you undress," she said in a small, exacting tone.

"Yes, dear," he waggishly replied. But he immediately rose to his feet and began unbuttoning his waistcoat. As he quickly undressed, he took in the subtle changes in her body that only a lover would recognize. Her breasts were nominally larger, her slender waist and belly a modicum less slender. Her lush sex sent a familiar jolt of lust through his body, the exquisite feel and taste of her etched in his memory. He paused a moment in his undressing before he regained his composure and contemplated the rest of her body—her long, shapely legs and finely formed feet. He smiled. "Your toes are curled."

"I'm desperately curbing my lust."

"Is that my cue to perform?"

"As I recall, you didn't usually need a cue."

"I'm on a very tight leash tonight."

"Don't be silly."

"I'm not taking any chances." The thought of a child was enough to make a fearless man fearful.

"You have to think of me, too," she said, reproachfully.

He softly laughed, pulled his shirt over his head, and kicked off his shoes. "I gather you're tired of waiting."

She restlessly shifted her hips. "It's been way too long."

He knew that feverish tone. "Just a minute," he said, already sliding his underwear and trousers down his hips. He looked up at her small moan and quickly left his last garments on the floor. "Wait!"

She dragged in a ragged breath. "I never knew pregnancy made one so ravenous for sex."

He shot her a narrowed glance as he moved toward her. "You better have behaved."

"Oh dear, I forgot to send away the men from under my bed."

"Very funny," he grumbled as he lithely settled between her legs. "I'm wildly jealous. Just so you know. I shall watch you like a hawk."

"And you're not allowed to talk to other women."

"Perfect. We agree." A shocking testament to love from a man who, some said, had screwed every woman he'd met, since his marriage, at least. Braced lightly above her so his weight only grazed her body, he guided himself to her pulsing sex and smoothly entered her—quickly, as ordered, but with noticeable restraint.

"I won't break," she whispered, wrapping her legs around his waist, her arms around his neck.

"Good," he said, unclasping her legs and placing them back on the bed. "Still. Let me do this my way." And calling on all his willpower and abundant skills, he beguiled and bewitched, stimulated and provoked, and brought her to the swift orgasm she preferred with a minimum of injudicious wildness and a sharp curb on his libido.

"You didn't climax," she gasped when she finally stopped screaming.

"I will." He moved gently inside her. "Next time."

"I love you madly, madly, madly," she breathed, in a blissful, throaty whisper. "You're incredible."

He wasn't unaware of his sexual talents after years of similar praise, but it had never mattered like it mattered now. Now, he only wished to please one woman, give her every pleasure. "You're having my baby. I think you're pretty incredible, too."

Her eyes filled with tears. "Tell me you'll love me forever."

"Longer than that," he softly said. "Don't worry." He kissed her tenderly and shifted into a gentle rhythm, his lower body moving in a masterful cadence, not too far but far enough, not too deep but deep enough, slowly, carefully, the measured pace reasonable, responsible. A new father-to-be on his best behavior, prudently measuring increasing degrees of rapture in Zelda's breathy moans and sighs.

But as the heated glory amplified, a building hysteria engulfed them both. She was panting hard, very near to climax, and when she wrapped her legs around his waist, this time he didn't push them away. He'd never been celibate so long; the woman he loved was impaled on his erection. He was perhaps allowed a small departure from prudence, this man who'd not understood the word in conjunction with sex these many years. And when she cried, "More, more, more," what man with breath in his body could resist?

He gave her more in full measure.

Her wild cry was familiar. He knew that sound.

And he met her climax, pouring into her sleek, glossy cunt, flooding her with days of pent-up semen. A record celibacy for the prodigal Earl of Dalgliesh.

When he found adequate air to breathe once again and his mind yielded to reality, he took note of Zelda's blood-less skin, her arms thrown out in a terrifying lethargy, her shut eyes, the too slight rise and fall of her breasts, and immediately jerked backward onto his haunches. "Oh Christ, I'm sorry." He drew in a ragged breath and gathered her into his arms. Sitting in the middle of the bed, he scrutinized her for graphic evidence of his brutality. "I hurt you, didn't I? Where does it hurt?" He was disgusted with himself that he'd not had more sense. "I'm so sorry. That's it. No more."

"Don't you dare!" Even in the half trance following a staggering orgasm, she was shocked back to her senses at such a terrifying prospect.

"I'm not arguing about this," Alec firmly said, wracked

with guilt. "I refuse to hurt you for something that can perfectly well wait."

"Don't be stupid," she said as firmly, not about to wait just because he was ill informed. "Sex during pregnancy is normal. And you don't understand—you *must* accommodate me. I need you now even more than I did before."

"Jesus. Don't say that." That his cock found merit in her unquenchable lust was immediately apparent.

"See," she said as his erection swelled against her hip. "You want to."

"I never said I didn't. I just don't think it's wise." Lifting her off his lap, he seated her a small distance away.

"If you don't make love to me, I'll cry and cry and cry."

He was reaching for her robe and paused.

"I will," she said to his startled glance. "I'll cry all night long—and tomorrow, too, and my father and brothers will wonder what you did to me."

"Blackmail?" he said in a dangerous voice. He wasn't a man who took kindly to coercion.

"Would you prefer womanly wiles?"

He dropped the robe in his hand and sat back very carefully. "I don't like either one."

But his erection appeared to like something; it was rock hard and enormous. She took a small breath, a covetous look in her eyes. "My cravings are irresistible, you're irresistible. Tell me what I must do to have you make love to me. I'm without pride. Just tell me and I'll do it."

A dilemma he'd never faced before—having to resist. While the woman asking for his help meant the world to him. How do you choose? "I don't suppose there's any way to evade this."

"You won't hurt me. On the contrary," she softly said.

"I'm reluctant." His voice dropped so she had to strain to hear it. "Fearful actually."

"Please don't be. There's no need. None whatsoever." She flung her arms out wide. "Look. I'm perfectly fine."

It took him a moment to answer with her ripe breasts

quivering and the urge to eat her alive beating at his brain.
"I want to make sure you *stay* that way."

"So you're going to become a monk?"

He shrugged.

"I don't care to become a nun," she sullenly said. "What
do you think of that?"

He didn't know what to say. He couldn't say, *You have
to or I'll lock you away.* He didn't want to be thrown out on
his ear. Not when he planned on marrying her.

"Fine. Be difficult," she said with distaste. "I'll have to
find my dildo. You'd be better. A thousand times better—not
that your ego needs bolstering in that regard."

His dark brows settled into a frown. "You've been using
a dildo?"

"Haven't you been listening? I'm ravenous for sex. It's
the pregnancy."

"You could hurt yourself." Dildos weren't very flexible.

She stared him down. "Don't you even *think* of saying
what you're thinking. I'll shoot you where you sit."

There was a silence. "If I agree," he finally said, "nothing
wild. Don't ask for that."

The sun came out even at night. "I won't, I promise. If
you like, we could talk to the midwives in the morning. You
might feel better if you knew more."

"Or you might learn more."

She smiled. "You won't have your way on this, darling.
I've already talked to them. I've been reassured."

"But you asked."

"No. It never crossed my mind. They told me in the
course of their initial tutorial. Apparently women ask. I can't
imagine why."

He looked at her for a moment, then pulled a face. "I
should be grateful, I suppose."

"I'd rather think you might be."

"Perhaps I could make amends somehow for my ignorance," he said, reaching out to pull her close, a familiar
warmth in his eyes. He grinned. "Perhaps we can conjure

up some missionary delights. I'll have to make a few adjustments."

She was already dissolving inside. "Whatever you say, so long as you do it quickly."

So he did; with grace and charm and levels of delight, he took great pains to deliver with both carnal splendor and love. With a degree of caution and reserve as well that required exceptional skill to disguise. And perhaps not exclusively tempered by praise worthy theological precedent in the end.

When he finally stopped, it was for her, not him. She was more fragile now regardless what she said. He noticed her fatigue. Although the state he was in, he very much wanted to go on. He was nowhere near done.

By sheer will, he restrained himself, and when he'd gotten his breathing under control and had subdued his demanding cock, he lay like a shriven monk with his wife-to-be resting in his arms. He was still struggling with his libido, so he didn't hear her at first. Dragging himself to attention, he glanced down at her. "What did you say, dear? I was half dreaming."

"You're tired, aren't you, after your long day?"

He wasn't quite sure what she meant, although in the past he would have, and immediately said no. Tonight, he chose a neutral reply. "I'm not too tired. You were saying?"

"I was just saying how happy I am now that you're here. I was absolutely distraught when you didn't arrive on the train that first time. I thought I'd lost you."

"Why would you think that?" he asked with male naiveté. "You must have seen my telegram when you got home."

"I considered it just another excuse. It's easy to send a telegram."

Not so easy for his men to brave the hazardous roads, but he wasn't about to point that out. "I won't do that to you. Make excuses. Not ever."

"Promise?" Her eyes suddenly welled with tears. "Oh, God, I never would have even thought of anything so stupid before. It's the baby. I'm impossibly weepy and clingy now. It's disgusting."

"I like you clingy. You have my permission to be as clingy

as you wish." He brushed a fingertip over the curve of her breast and smiled. "Preferably without clothes on like this."

She looked up at him, her wet gaze teasing. "And weepy? I'm afraid it's a common mark of pregnancy. What do you think about that?"

He swallowed and manfully said, "Weep away. I'll have Jenkins order more handkerchiefs."

"Cook has ten children. She says you always cry buckets."

His spine went rigid. "You don't want ten children, do you?"

"Don't you?"

He glanced down and studied her face in the lamplight, trying to gauge her sincerity, debating truth versus affection before he answered.

She grinned. "Scared you, didn't I?"

"Perhaps just a little," he said, the muscles in his back relaxing. "I'm not sure I care to share you that much." As an only child, raised in a secluded environment, depending on himself more than others, he didn't know to what extent he could comfortably expand his family circle.

There was something in his tone—evasion, forbearance, shrinking demur. "Surely, you *want* the baby?"

"Yes, yes, above all things." He said it because he loved her and wanted to please her, although truth be told, the actual reality of a baby was still slightly unnerving. "I'm sorry, darling, I've been alone too long."

"And now you have me—and our baby—and you love us both."

She said it with the bold assurance that had captivated him from the first. "I do, and if you should actually want ten children, I suppose we could talk about it," he gently said, wanting to give her the world for what she'd given him.

"We can decide later," she whispered. "We already have Chris and Julia. Three might be enough."

"Whatever you like," he softly said, meaning it without qualification or restrictions. But beneath his largesse and the wonder of the child to come existed a degree of uncertainty and doubt. Could he protect a child from a childhood such as his? Would he be good enough as a parent? Would he fall into unwanted patterns of behavior? Would he let his child down in some unknown way? The fear of all that was too bewildering and new to marshal into reasonableness.

And, of course, the greatest stumbling block would be the need to share the great love of his life. To do it kindly. He didn't know if he was that unselfish.

While he struggled with his trepidation and sensibilities, he watched Zelda's eyelids gradually close, her breathing soften as she drifted off to sleep. Uncertainties and doubts aside, he understood how very lucky he was to have met the magnificent Miss MacKenzie, to love and be loved. To have a ready-made family—and a baby on the way.

His lips curled faintly in a smile.

All in a brief few weeks.

After she was sleeping soundly, he carefully slid her head from his shoulder and eased away. Tucking the quilt around her to keep her warm, he quietly left the bed and found his robe and the satchel of business documents he'd carried up to Scotland. The mines didn't stop working because he was in love, nor parliament close its doors. Also, Fitzwilliam had sent a lengthy telegram to Inverness, cryptically worded, that required concentration to decipher. It looked like one of the magistrates at least was amenable, Fitzwilliam was still dealing with the second, and Violetta had signed some initial papers that were needed. Good. He'd have to ask about Freddy's divorce in his correspondence. The men he'd brought with him were expecting to set out for Inverness at first light with his messages.

It was close to three when Zelda woke up and saw Alec at her desk, writing with the lamp down low. "Come to bed," she drowsily murmured.

"Soon." He added another sheet of quick, clear handwriting to the stack before him.

She pushed herself up on her elbows. "Business?"

"Yes, it never goes away."

"How will you get your telegrams?"

"My men will bring them." Not knowing how lengthy

his visit might be—even a week was too long for his business to go unattended—he'd rented four houses yesterday on his way up to accommodate the relays of men he'd require. Without a telephone or telegraph, he'd need a large complement of riders. Now with the baby, the leases would have to be extended. And James and Jenkins, who'd been left at the last house, could be summoned.

"For how long?"

"As long as you wish to stay."

"You'd do that for me?"

He turned in his chair and smiled. "Of course. I love you and you're having my baby."

"I'm going to feel guilty."

"Why should you? I'm perfectly content." There were lies that mattered and others that didn't, and this one mattered so much he willingly offered it.

"You don't have to do this for me."

"I want to." The world of affairs would have to do without his full attention in the coming months.

"Are you doing this because you don't want me to ride?"

He hesitated before he said, "Perhaps. I don't know."

"My mother rode through all her pregnancies, Da says." *But she's dead.*

When he didn't answer, Zelda said, "Mama died from a putrid throat and a fever. Duncan was five. It had nothing to do with a pregnancy."

"I understand." Alec sighed. "Still, I'm not sure I want to take the risk. You don't know what you mean to me. I couldn't bear it if something happened to you."

"We could ride very slowly, go by short stages. You really can't conduct your business from here. Not for any length of time." She'd seen his office at Munro Park, the number of employees, the bustling activity.

He didn't move or speak. He didn't want to argue.

"It would be better to go now, rather than later."

His head lifted slightly.

"A trip to Inverness would be more dangerous when I'm farther along."

"We could stay here until the birth."

"I want better care than I can get out here in the wilderness."

"Better?" Sudden alarm colored his voice. "Is something wrong with the doctors and midwives here?"

"Good God, Alec, all the best doctors are in"—she almost said Edinburgh which was true—"London," she finished because there were good doctors there as well and Alec would be where he was needed. At Munro Park.

"Are you sure?" He restlessly ran his fingers through his hair. "Christ, I don't know anything about this."

"I'm sure. I'll be sure for both of us. We could leave tomorrow. The sooner the better."

"Jesus, Zelda, when you say things like *the sooner the better*, it scares the hell out of me. Do I have to worry about this pregnancy? Or how much do I have to worry about this pregnancy?"

"No, you don't have to worry. I'd just rather be closer to London."

"That's all?" He scrutinized her.

"Absolutely," she said with alacrity.

"Nothing else?"

"Nothing, truly. I'm extremely healthy."

He softly swore, then rose from his chair and walked toward the bed, the crimson silk of his robe catching the light from the fire, his dark beauty limned by flickering flame, his large, powerful body a masterpiece of nature. Sitting on the edge of the bed, he reached for her hand and absently stroked it, his eyes resting on her face. He let out a breath. "You know I can deal with anything but this. I'm a complete novice and you're too bloody important to me."

"Then let me decide. We can talk to my sister. She's five months pregnant. She's been dealing with this longer than we."

He considered her with guarded interest. "Is your sister nearby?"

"Over the hill."

"We'll go in the morning. I'll carry you."

"Stop, Alec," she quietly said. "You'll drive me mad. I'm not the first woman to have a baby."

"You're the first woman I care about who's having a baby. There's a difference."

"And you always bend the world to your will," she testily said, trying to snatch her hand away.

He smiled at the small heat in her tone, his grip unrelenting. "Usually."

"But not always, damn it. And not now. Will you let go?"

He did because it suited him. As for the rest, he hadn't decided yet.

"I'll walk to Francesca's myself. You can hold my hand if you wish."

He was learning patience. He smiled his most conciliatory smile. "Yes, ma'am."

"That's better. And now that I'm awake, you can make love to me. I'm very amorous now, as you know. And after we talk to Francesca tomorrow, you can have the horses readied. We're going back."

"Just like that?" His voice was mild. Or pleasant-offensive. He knew how to do that, too.

Perhaps she picked up on the small belligerence. "Yes, just like that," she said, with faint irritation. "Unless you care to be celibate for the next eight months."

"Don't."

She made the fatal mistake of looking arch. "Don't what?"

"Play those kind of games."

His voice was so brutally cold she flinched.

"I'm sorry. Now I've frightened you." But his politesse was as hollow and remote as his gaze.

"I was only teasing," Zelda whispered.

As if coming awake at the sound of her voice, he looked at her and said without tone or emphasis, "I'm sorry. Did you say something?"

"I said I was only teasing," she repeated, looking alarmed. "I didn't mean it in the least. You know that. I adore making love to you. I adore everything about you."

He softly exhaled and forcibly suppressed the old ruinous memories. Stifled the mindless anger prompted by Zelda's insolent threat. Locked away the dangerous resentments where they couldn't frighten her. And returned to the matters at hand, to a centuries-old room in a Highland castle, to the woman he loved. "Forgive me again. I didn't mean to frighten you." He ran his hand through his hair and swept it back from his forehead. "I've had four wearying years of game playing. I overreacted and I apologize. It won't happen again, I promise."

"You're forgiven, darling. But I'm not like her," she quietly said.

"God no. Not even remotely." Intent on changing the subject, once again in command of his senses, his smile was boyishly sweet, although his blue gaze was perceptibly worldly and sexual. "Now, I believe you said you were in an amorous mood. I can help you with that. As soon as I stoke up the fires so you won't get cold," he said, coming to his feet and untying his robe. "Then I'll see about doing my husbandly duty by you."

"I like the word husband," she purred.

"Good. Because I'm here to stay." Letting his robe slip to the floor, he turned and moved toward the fireplace first.

"Ummm . . . my own personal stud," Zelda murmured, her gaze on his strong, sleek body, the beautifully trained muscles, and inherent grace.

He glanced back. "Count on it."

"For how long?"

He turned at those familiar, cajoling little words that called on him to please her, and looked at her with his sleepy, bedroom eyes, and smiled his unreasonably beautiful smile that had charmed countless women in the past but was now for her alone. "As long as you can stand it," he whimsically answered, offering himself to her without conceit, offering all his natural talents and acquired skills. Offering his love.

And in the days and weeks and months ahead, beyond the endearing qualities of love and affection that bound them, beyond the sweet friendship Alec had never known with a woman, beyond their attachment to the children in their life, the substantive, immodest, physical bond between the Earl of Dalgliesh and his lady was as it was at the beginning that first hunt weekend in Yorkshire: fiercely passionate; wildly provocative; at times, tender, precious; and always, *always* blissfully gratifying.